Johannes Cabal

THE NECROMANCER

Johannes Cabal

THE NECROMANCER

⚜

Jonathan L. Howard

DOUBLEDAY

NEW YORK   LONDON   TORONTO

SYDNEY   AUCKLAND

DD

DOUBLEDAY

Published in the United States by Doubleday, a division of Random House, Inc., New York.
www.doubleday.com

DOUBLEDAY and the DD colophon are registered trademarks of Random House, Inc.

Reprinted by permission of the publishers and the Trustees of Amherst College from THE POEMS OF EMILY DICKINSON, Thomas H. Johnson, ed., Cambridge, Mass.: The Belknap Press of Harvard University Press, Copyright © 1951, 1955, 1979, 1983 by the President and Fellows of Harvard College.

Illustrations by Snugbat.

LIBRARY OF CONGRESS CATALOGING-IN-PUBLICATION DATA
Howard, Jonathan L.
Johannes Cabal the necromancer / by Jonathan L. Howard.—1st ed.
p. cm.
1. Magic—Fiction. 2. Devil—Fiction 3. Wagers—Fiction. I. Title.
PR6108.O928J64 2008
823'.92—dc22
2008028390

ISBN 978-0-385-52808-5

PRINTED IN THE UNITED STATES OF AMERICA

1 3 5 7 9 10 8 6 4 2

FIRST EDITION

For Noel and Enid Howard

A Clock stopped—

Not the Mantel's —

Geneva's farthest skill

Can't put the puppet bowing —

That just now dangled still —

EMILY DICKINSON

CONTENTS

CONTENTS

Johannes Cabal

THE NECROMANCER

Chapter 1

⊰ IN WHICH A SCIENTIST VISITS HELL AND A
DEAL IS STRUCK

Walpurgisnacht, the Hexennacht. The last night of April. The night of witches, when evil walks abroad.

He stood at a desolate and lonely place where there would be no interruption, no prying eyes. The air smelled metallic with freshly spilt blood; the body of a decapitated virgin kid goat lay nearby. He had no alloyed metal about him but for a thin-bladed sword of fine steel he held in his right hand; that arm was naked, his shirt sleeve rolled up to the biceps. A silver coin wrapped in paper nestled in his waistcoat pocket. Before him burned a fire of white wood.

His name was Johannes Cabal, and he was summoning a demon.

". . . Oarios! Almoazin! Arios! Membrot!" The chanted names faded into the unusually still night air. Only the crackling of the fire accompanied him. "Janna! Etitnamus! Zariatnatmix . . . and so on." He drew a deep breath and sighed, bored with the ritual. "A. E. A. J. A. T. M. O. . . ."

There was hidden meaning in the names he must call, the letters he must chant. That didn't mean he had to approve or even be impressed by them. As he recited the Grand Conjuration, he thought that some magicians might have better served the world by writing crossword puzzles.

Then space distorted, and he was no longer alone.

The demon's name was Lucifuge Rofocale. He stood a little taller than Cabal's six feet, but the bizarre fool's cap he wore—three flopping horns, or perhaps tentacles, ending with arrowheads—made his height vary from moment to moment. In one hand he held a bag containing, at least symbolically, the riches of the world. In the other, a golden hoop. He wore a segmented, studded leather skirt rather like a Roman soldier's. Beneath it, fur-covered legs ended in hooves. He had a fat anteater's tail, and a silly little Hercule Poirot moustache. As is often the case with demons, Lucifuge looked like an anatomical game of Consequences.

"Lo!" cried the demon. "I am here! What dost thou seek of me? Why dost thou disturb my repose? Smite me no more with that dread rod!" He looked at Cabal. "Where's your dread rod?"

"I left it at home," replied Cabal. "Didn't think I really needed it."

"You can't summon me without a dread rod!" said Lucifuge, appalled.

"You're here, aren't you?"

"Well, yes, but under false pretences. You haven't got a goatskin or two vervain crowns or two candles of virgin wax made by a virgin girl and duly blessed. Have you got the stone called *Ematille?*"

"I don't even know what *Ematille* is."

Neither did the demon. He dropped the subject and moved on. "Four nails from the coffin of a dead child?"

"Don't be fatuous."

"Half a bottle of brandy?"

"I don't drink brandy."

"It's not *for* you."

"I have a hip flask," said Cabal, and threw it to him. The demon caught it and took a dram.

"Cheers," said Lucifuge, and threw it back. They regarded each other for a long moment. "This really is a shambles," the demon added finally. "What did you summon me for, anyway?"

*T*he Gates of Hell are an impressive structure. A great adamantine finger of rock a mile in diameter and two miles high punches through the surface of the cracked and baking desert plain of Limbo. On one side of this impenetrable edifice are the Gates themselves: massive iron constructions hundreds of feet wide and a thousand high. Their rough, barely worked surfaces are pocked and pitted with great bolts driven through in ragged lines, huge bands of brass running across in uneven ranks. One could be forgiven for thinking Hell's a popular place to get into.

Perhaps surprisingly, it is.

On the outside, one wonders what happens once you pass through that terrible, cruel portal. Some believe that all Hell is somehow crammed within the rock, a place where dimensions mean nothing. Others say that immediately beyond the Gates, within the hollowed rock, is a great chasm that opens into the pit of Hell, and that those stepping within must surely plunge straight to their eternal dooms. Others believe that the rock conceals the top of a very big escalator. Nobody on the outside knows for sure, but everyone wants to find out, and they want to find out because anything—*anything*—is better than the forms.

Lots of forms. Stacks of forms. An average of nine thousand, seven hundred, and forty-seven of them were required to gain entrance to Hell. The largest form ran to fifteen thousand, four hundred, and ninety-seven questions. The shortest to just five, but five of such subtle phraseology, labyrinthine grammar, and malicious ambiguity that, released into the mortal world, they would certainly have formed the basis of a new religion or, at the least, a management course.

This, then, was the first torment of Hell, as engineered by the soul of a bank clerk.

Nobody *had* to fill in the forms, of course. But, given that the alternative was eternity spent naked in an endless desert that has never known night, most people found themselves sooner or later queuing up at the small porter's door set into one of Hell's Gates. There they would receive a form entitled "Infernal Regions (Local Authority) Hades Admission Application—Provisional (AAAA/342)" and a soft pencil.

Congas of hopeful applicants wound around the gatehouse like a line drawn by somebody wanting to find out how much writing you could get out of a box of ballpoints. The formerly quiet desert hummed to a steady drone of sub-vocalised reading and flipped pages. New arrivals and old hands queued patiently at the porter's door to hand in and receive forms. The quickest route through the paper trail necessitated the completion of two thousand, seven hundred, and eighty-five, but nobody had yet fulfilled the extremely narrow conditions that would permit such a speedy passage. Most could anticipate three or four times as many, not counting forms rejected for mistakes; the hand-picked team of administrative imps that dealt with admissions didn't like errors at all, nor did they issue erasers.

*T*hrough the muttering crowds, stepping over form-fillers and never pausing to apologise, came a pale man. Johannes Cabal was walking to Hell.

Tow-headed, lean, in his late twenties, but with any spirit of that youth long since evaporated, Cabal seemed otherwise unremarkable except for his air of intent, his unwavering advance on the gatehouse, and his clothes.

"Hey, watch it!" barked Al Capone, wrestling with the spelling of "venereal," as Cabal stepped over him. "Why don't you just . . ." The protest died on his lips. "Hey . . . Hey! That guy's dressed! He's got clothes!"

That guy did, indeed, have clothes. A short black frock coat, slouch-brimmed black hat, black trousers, black shoes, a white shirt, and a tidy black cravat. He wore dark-blue tinted glasses with side-baffles, and he carried a black gladstone bag. Unexciting clothes, but clothes nonetheless.

It was the first sensation that the desert had ever experienced. The damned parted before Cabal, who, in his turn, seemed to accept this as his due. Some excitedly speculated that he must be a messenger from the Other Place, that the end times had finally arrived. Others pointed out that nothing in Revelation referred to a man in a black hat and sensible shoes.

Cabal walked directly to the porter's door and slammed his hand on the closed window. While he waited for a reply, he looked about him, and the damned withered beneath his soulless and impassive gaze.

The window snapped open.

"What do ye want?" demanded a weasely man wearing a teller's shade from the other side, a man named Arthur Trubshaw.

Sartre said that Hell was other people. It transpires that one of the other people was Trubshaw. He had lived a life of bureaucratic exactitude as a clerk out in a dusty bank in a dusty town in the dusty Old West. He crossed all the "t"s and dotted all the "i"s. Then he made double entries of his double entries, filed the crossed "t"s, cross-referenced the dotted "i"s in tabulated form against the dotted "j"s, barred any zeroes for reasons of disambiguation, and shaded in the relative frequencies on a pie chart he was maintaining.

Arthur Trubshaw's life of licentious proceduralism was brought to an abrupt end when he was shot to death during a robbery at the bank. He did not die heroically: not unless one considers demanding a receipt from bandits as being in some sense praiseworthy.

. Even in Hell, Trubshaw had continued to demonstrate an unswerving devotion to the penny ante, the nit-picking, the terribly trivial, the very things that had poisoned his soul and condemned him in the first place. Given such a mania for order, a den of chaos like Hell should have been an ideal punishment. Trubshaw, however, just regarded it as a challenge.

At first the demons assigned to torment him laughed diabolically at his aspirations and looked forward greedily to the sweet juices that drip from crushed hopes. Then they discovered that, while they had been laughing, Trubshaw had rationalised their tormenting schedules for maximum tormenting efficiency, organised a time-and-motion study for the imps, and, in passing, tidied the underwear drawers of the demon princes and princesses. Lilith, in particular, was mortified.

Never one to squander such a remarkably irritating talent, Satan put Trubshaw in charge of admissions. Hell had grown a new, unofficial ring.

"I want to see Satan. Now." Cabal's accent was clipped and faintly Teutonic. "I don't have an appointment."

By now Trubshaw had noticed the clothes and was considering possible explanations. "And who might ye be? The Archangel Gabriel?" He started the sentence as a joke but modified his tone halfway through. After all, perhaps it *was*.

"My name is Johannes Cabal. Satan *will* see me."

"So ye're nobody special, then?"

Cabal gave him a hard look. "It is hardly my place to say. Now, open this door."

Clothes or no clothes, Trubshaw decided he was on pretty familiar ground after all. He produced a copy of AAAA/342 and pushed it towards Cabal.

"Ye'll need to fill this in, mister!" he said, and indulged himself in a chuckle, a horrible noise, like a clockwork crow running down. Cabal gave the form a cursory glance and handed it back.

"You misunderstand. I'm not staying. I have business to discuss. Then I'm leaving." There was a muted gasp from the interested onlookers.

Trubshaw narrowed his eyes. "Leaving, ye reckon? Well, I reckon ye're wrong. This is Hell, sonny. Ye just can't come gallivanting in and out like a lady's excuse-me. Ye're dead and ye're staying. That's the way it's always been and that's the way it is now, y'hear?"

Cabal looked at him for a long, long moment. Then he smiled, a cold, horrid rictus that travelled up his face like rising damp. The crowd went very quiet. Cabal leaned close to Trubshaw.

"Listen, you pathetic little man . . . you pathetic little *dead* man. You're making a fundamental error. I'm not dead. Tried it once, didn't like it. Right now—right this instant, as I look into your rheumy little gimlet corpse eyes—I am alive. I have come here at great inconvenience, causing considerable disruption in my work, to talk to your seedy fallen angel of a boss. Now, open the door before you regret it."

Everybody shifted their attention to Trubshaw. This was going to be good.

"No, Mr. Fancy-Pants-Living-Fella, I ain't gonna open the door, and I ain't gonna regret it, neither. Know why? Because, as ye spotted so neatly despite them damn foolish spectacles, I'm dead, and, better yet, I'm on the payroll in these parts. My job's to make sure people fill in the paperwork. *All* the paperwork. Elseways, they don't get in, and right now, right this instant, I'm guessing that means you, too, ye lanky son of a bitch. So—what're ye going to do about that? Eh?"

For his answer, Cabal raised his bag until it was level with the window. Then he carefully opened it and, with a flourish like a stage magician, produced a skull.

Trubshaw shied away momentarily, but curiosity overcame him. "What ye got there, ye freak?"

Cabal's horrible smile deepened.

"It's your skull, Trubshaw." Trubshaw blanched and his eyes widened as he gazed at it. "I . . . 'liberated' it from your old town's cemetery. They still talk about your death there, you know. You've quite passed into local folklore."

"I always did my duty," said Trubshaw, unable to tear his eyes away from the skull.

"Oh, yes. Your name lives on to this day."

"Yeah?"

"Indeed." Cabal waited exactly long enough for pride to start swelling agreeably in Trubshaw's withered excuse for a heart before adding, "It has become a byword for stupidity."

Trubshaw blinked, the spell broken.

"Oh, yes. Well, what do you expect if you get yourself murdered for the sake of a receipt? Children say, 'You're as dumb as Trubshaw,' to their little playmates. When their parents refer to somebody remarkably stupid, they'll say, 'Well, there goes a proper Trubshaw and no mistake.' You can get souvenirs and everything. It's quite the cottage industry."

He smiled, and something like benevolence slipped into his expression for the first time. It was almost certainly a trick of the light.

Trubshaw incandesced with fury.

"How the heck do you reckon you're gonna get by me now, you goddamned Kraut? You really got my goat now, y'know. By jiminy, it'll be a cold day around here afore I let ye through!"

Cabal affected a yawn. "Your reputation is well deserved, Arthur Trubshaw. You think I stole this skull as a keepsake? Do you know who I am?"

"I don't care who ye are, mister! You can take yer bag a' bones and shove it right up ye—"

"I am Johannes Cabal. Necromancer."

It went very quiet indeed on both sides of the door. Word gets about in the shadowed places. Corpses exchange scuttlebutt and gossip, and they know all about the necromancers, the sorcerers who use the dead. They are the Bogeyman's Bogeymen.

"Now, Arthur, your choice is clear. You can open the door and let me in. Or I can go back to the land of the living in a truly abominable mood, raise you up from this place, put your cankerous soul into something that will do as a body, and then make you wish you were dead all over again. Repeatedly."

Cabal pulled down his smoked-glass spectacles far enough to show his hard, humourless eyes—grey flecked with blue that suggested tempered steel and difficult times ahead for any foe—and Trubshaw knew he meant every word. "Which is it to be?"

𝒯he Arch-Demon Ratuth Slabuth had been informed that Hell had been invaded and, being a general of the Infernal Hordes, did he intend to do anything about it? Flying devils were sent to reconnoitre the enemy force, but these quickly returned and—somewhat crestfallen—reported that the invaders consisted of one man with a short temper and sunglasses. Intrigued, the general had decided to take the situation into his own hands, claws, and writhing thorned tentacles.

Ratuth Slabuth, a stack of shifting non-Euclidean angles topped by a horse's skull in a stylised, ancient-Grecian helmet, looked down from a great height upon the insolent human.

"This is Hell," he tried to explain for the third time. "Not a drop-in centre. You can't just turn up and say, 'Oh, I was just in the neighbourhood and thought I'd call by and have a bit of a chinwag with Lord Satan.' It simply isn't done."

"No," said the infuriating mortal. "It hasn't *been* done. There is a difference. May I pass now?"

"No, you may not. Satan's a very busy . . . um, *is* very busy right now. He can't go interrupting his work for every Tom, Dick, and Johannes"— he paused for effect, but the human just looked at him with a faint air of what seemed to be pity—"Harry, that is, who turns up demanding audience."

"Really?" said Cabal. "I had no idea. I thought this would be an uncommon occurrence, unique even, but you seem to imply that it happens all the time. Fair enough."

Ratuth was just thinking how well he'd handled things when, suddenly, Cabal pointed directly at him. "I call you liar!" he spat. "I call you duplicitous, mendacious, and thoroughly amateur at both enterprises."

"What?" shrieked the demon general. "WHAT? You, a mere mortal, dare to call me thus?" The eldritch angles unfolded, the darkness about him deepened as he rose like some dreadful bird of prey. "I shall destroy you! I shall rend the very flesh from your skeleton, hollow your long bones, and play your funeral lament upon them! For I am Ratuth Slabuth! Dark General of the Infernal Hordes! Father of Desolation! Despoiler of Innocence! Look upon me, mortal, and know thy doom!"

Cabal, he noticed through his rage, looked calm. Worryingly so.

" 'Ratuth Slabuth,' eh?" said Cabal. "You wouldn't happen to have started your career as Ragtag Slyboots, Despoiler of Milk and Entangler of Shoelaces, would you?"

The effect was electric. Ratuth Slabuth folded up like an especially large deck of cards in the blink of an eye until he was the same height as Cabal.

"How did you know that?" he asked quickly.

"I'm a necromancer. You'd be surprised at the sources we dig up. Now, then, do I get my audience with Satan or do I spread rumours about a certain diabolic general's personal history? Which is it to be?"

"Johannes Cabal. Johannes Cabal. I'm sure I know that name."

Lord Satan was actually pleased to have something to distract him from the dull day-to-day administration of the Eternally Damned in all their massed homogeneity. He'd simply waved an embarrassed and apologetic Ratuth Slabuth behind his throne and settled down to be amused.

The throne was only a throne by dint of its vast scale; otherwise, it was simply a big stone chair on the end of a rocky peninsula that extended into the centre of a lake of boiling lava. All in all, it was less of an audience and more of a fireside chat.

Satan sat comfortably on the unyielding basalt throne, massive and urbane. All things to all people, he looked exactly as you'd imagine. *Exactly.* He snapped his fingers.

"Oh, of course. The necromancer. Now I recall. You have a contract with me, I think. Yes?" He gestured, and a demonic secretary appeared in his colossal hand. "Nip over to Contracts and pull whatever we've got on Johannes Cabal, please." The demon made a note on a yellow pad before soaring into the sulphurous air and out of sight.

"Yes," replied Cabal. "You have my soul. I'd like it back."

Ratuth Slabuth choked down a laugh. Cabal gave him a milk-curdling look and continued.

"I traded my soul over to you some years ago. That was a mistake—its absence is proving an intolerable burden. Therefore, I should like it back."

Ratuth Slabuth was making idiotic muffled guffawing noises. Satan quelled him with a glance before addressing Cabal.

"Now, you see, Johannes, we have a little bit of a problem there." The secretary landed on Satan's casually opened hand and passed him a roll of parchment before ceasing to exist. Satan unrolled it between his fingers and read it as he spoke. "You see, as a rule of thumb, I don't give souls back. It might set a precedent. These things do. This"—he indicated the parchment with the wave of a finger tipped with a nail the size of a very well-manicured tombstone—"is a perfectly standard contract with the exception of a proviso about you giving up your soul immediately rather than my having to wait until you're dead or after a set period, the Faust clause, that sort of thing. My notes indicate that was your idea."

"I believed my soul was irrelevant to my researches, so I determined to see what empirical differences there were between the soulful and the soulless, which is to say, me. I was wrong to believe in its irrelevancy. The interference caused by its absence, I can no longer countenance."

Ratuth Slabuth leaned forward, interested. "Interference?" he asked. "What sort of interference?"

"Not to be obtuse, your interference," replied Cabal, pointing at Satan.

Satan tapped his chest in surprise. "My interference?"

"Constant interruptions. Stupid games. Interference. You know perfectly well what I mean."

For a moment Satan didn't seem to. Then the great brow cleared and he nodded. "Your soullessness must be attracting avatars of mine. Fancy that."

Cabal, apparently, did not fancy that at all. "Especially an irritating little man with a big beard. But it goes further than that. The spiritual vacuum within me is actually causing freak results in my experiments. I cannot perform the same procedure twice in full confidence that I will see the same results. I've wasted years trying to locate the problem. Now that I have, I'm here to rectify things."

It was the truth, but it wasn't the whole truth.

As a scientist, Cabal preferred to work in scientific absolutes wherever possible. The lack of a soul, however, was a quantifiable hindrance in as much as it lent his researches a variable percentile of veracity and therefore rendered them 100 per cent useless. This was a scientist's cavil, a good rational reason. Johannes Cabal had no trouble accepting it and expressing it.

But there was something else. Something deeper and very, very well hidden. Given Satan's legendary ability to worm out secrets, Cabal could not afford to give him the faintest whiff of this other truth, for he knew Satan would worry at it like a dog with a rag. Cabal didn't intend to let that happen; it was his business, and his alone. So he focussed on the scientific and the quantifiable and did not allow even a tremor of this other, this greater truth into his voice.

Satan was studying the contract. "You sold your soul to gain an insight into necromancy in the first place. If I were to give you your soul back, I would want that in return. That would invalidate the whole scheme, perhaps?"

"I need that knowledge," said Cabal. "That is non-negotiable."

Satan smiled. "That's that, then. You can't eat your cake and have it, too, Johannes. Sorry and all that."

For a long minute Cabal glared at Satan. Satan continued to smile, twiddled his thumbs, and awaited developments. He wasn't disappointed.

"I'll . . ." Cabal paused. It was as if he were dealing with an alien concept. "I'll . . ." He coughed. "I'll make you . . . a . . . wager." He stopped, uncertain if he'd used the right term. "I believe that you have a reputation for accepting . . . wagers. I should like to make one."

Satan waited, but there was no further clarification. Finally, he leaned forward and said, "Fine. Wagers, yes, that's good. I like them. What's your wager?" Cabal was clearly stumped. "Not something you've ever done before, hmm? Never mind, shall I suggest one?"

He allowed Cabal's continued silence to become slightly embarrassing before taking it for assent. "Now, as I've already said, I can't start giving souls back willy-nilly or else I'll never hear the end of it. There'd be a queue from here to Tartarus of ne'er-do-wells whinging and whining and wringing their hands, and I get enough of that at the best of times. So you must appreciate that it can't be anything easy. *Pour décourager les autres.* You follow me so far?"

"I understand."

"Excellent. So what I propose is that you must replace your soul in my little collection . . ."

"You just want another soul?"

". . . a hundred times over."

"A hundred?" The number staggered Cabal. "A hundred? What do you take me for, a mass murderer?"

"You're not listening, Johannes. I want souls, not carcasses. Not dead. Damned. Signed, sealed, and delivered. I'll provide the forms, and the signatures don't even have to be in blood. Although it would be nice if somebody made the effort now and then."

Cabal looked at the floor, thinking deeply. After a minute's consideration, he grudgingly said, "I suppose it may be possible . . ."

"And you've got a year to do it in."

Behind his glasses, Cabal's eyes narrowed. "Are you insane? A year? It can't be done."

"Oh, come, now, Johannes. A bit of that silver tongue of yours and people won't be able to sign up for damnation fast enough. Those flashing social skills that you've spent so long honing to a fine edge—"

"Sarcasm ill becomes you," said Cabal. "I came here in expectation of dealing with a mature individual. Instead, all I get is petty slights and pointless whimsy. Good day."

"I suppose I am rather whimsical these days. I'm sorry, Johannes, I didn't mean to bruise your pride. Really I didn't," said Satan with an expression that indicated that he didn't give a toss for Cabal's pride one way or the other. "I like you. It takes a lot of courage to come down here when you really don't need to. Yet. I don't want you to go away in a huff and think that I didn't give you a fair hearing. In fact, I will even help you get your hundred souls."

It's difficult for a horse's skull to raise an eyebrow, but one of Ratuth Slabuth's gaping eye-sockets may have widened slightly.

"Slabuth," said Satan, "do you still have that jumble box handy?" As the general quickly searched through his intra-dimensional pockets, Satan leaned down and said confidentially, "The general and I were just having a bit of a spring clean. You'd be surprised how much rubbish builds up, and then, before you know it, it has to be sorted out again. No rest for the wicked."

Ratuth Slabuth produced a battered tea chest from somewhere and passed it to his master. Satan went through it, sighing.

"No. No. No. Why did we ever give half of this nonsense room? No." Then he pulled a bundle of files from the box and studied the label on the first. "Dear me, I'd forgotten all about these. One of these would be ideal."

"What are they?" asked Cabal, interested despite himself.

"Do you enjoy going to fairs, Johannes?"

"No."

"Then these *will* be ideal. They're fairs, carnivals, amusement parks, and the like. I've had a hand in quite a few over the years. Absolutely splendid, they are. People looking for a good time drop their guard, you see. Then in you dart and you've got 'em. Splendid. Not so popular these days, unfortunately, but you can't beat them for style." He had opened the first file and was reading the notes inside. "Cougar and Dark's Carnival. Regrettably, no. That one's been wound up." He dropped it back into the box and studied the next. "Brown's Carnival, 'Doctor Brown of World Renown.' Whatever happened to that? Whatever happened to him?" He read a little further. "Oh dear. How unpleasant."

"You're doing a very poor job of engaging my enthusiasm," said Cabal.

Satan wasn't listening; he was already on to the next file. "Dr. Diabolo's Torture Garden." He smiled, evidently proud. "Terrific success. We're franchising that."

This seemed like a positive development to Cabal. "So—will I . . . ?"

"No," said Satan, "you will not. That would be far too easy. This is meant to represent a challenge, Johannes, not a cakewalk." He dropped the file back into the box. This left him with one last set of papers. He took the top sheet and read out loud.

"Pre-production schedule. 'Carnival of Discord' Project." He flicked through some other sheets. "Proposed by Leviathan, seconded by Balberith.

That's a novelty, eh, Slabuth? First time he's ever agreed with anything. Oh, here's why. *Function: to tempt to contentiousness, to blasphemy, argumentation, and murder.* Typical, only Balberith would think that people want to go to the carnival to have a good bicker, spit on a Bible, and then kill each other. No wonder it got shelved. Still, the rest of the proposal has Leviathan's paw prints all over it. Very professional indeed. With the right man at the helm, this could be a regular little soul-stealer." He looked down at Cabal. "What do you think, Johannes? Do you think you could be the right man?"

"I am not notably light-hearted . . ." Cabal started.

"Gosh, really?" said Satan with total innocence.

". . . I have no grasp of what is involved in this 'carnival' business, and I am hardly gregarious. Frankly, I don't think your challenge is entirely fair."

There was silence for a long moment.

Satan's periods of good nature—in common with many managerial types—lasted precisely up until the moment he was challenged. He scowled monstrously, the smile falling from his face like a greased pig off a church roof. Quickly, over a period of seconds, the lava lake cooled. The glowing red rock turned dirty grey and then black. It was getting distinctly colder. Frost started to appear on the stone walls.

" 'Not entirely fair,' " repeated Satan, all trace of jovial hail-fellow-well-met gone. " 'Not entirely fair'?" His voice became that of the inferno: a rushing, booming howl of icy evil that flew around the great cavern, as swift and cold as the Wendigo on skates. "I am Satan, also called Lucifer the Light Bearer . . ."

Cabal winced. What was it about devils that they always had to give you their whole family history?

"I was cast down from the presence of God himself into this dark, sulphurous pit and condemned to spend eternity here—"

"Have you tried saying sorry?" interrupted Cabal.

"No, I haven't! I was sent down for a sin of pride. It rather undermines my position if I say 'sorry'!"

"I have my pride, too. Yet you insist on sending me off on a ridiculous errand posing as some sort of showman. Where's the justice in that?"

Satan leaned back in his throne, and his voice dropped to the low tone of somebody who is about to abort an interview. "Look up 'Satan' in a thesaurus at some point, mortal. You'll find terms like 'elemental evil,' 'wickedness incarnate,' and 'the begetter of sins.' If you find 'nice chap,' 'good bloke,' and 'the embodiment of fairness,' then I would suggest you buy a new one. Do you accept the deal?"

Cabal considered. "One hundred souls?"

"Yes."

"One year? Until the midnight of the next Walpurgisnacht?"

Satan groaned. "Oh, it's not Walpurgisnacht, is it? I knew I'd forgotten something. I'm supposed to be abroad, cavorting with witches." He curled his lip truculently. "I really can't be bothered this year; I'll let the avatars deal with it. So—you were saying? Oh, yes. Next Walpurgisnacht midnight, yes."

"I get the carnival to help me?"

"Just so."

"What if I fail?"

"I don't care very much. I suppose I could"—he looked about for inspiration—"take your life. That seems fair enough. By my standards." Cabal looked dubious. "It's the only deal you're going to get, Johannes Cabal. Take it or leave it."

The frost was gently melting from the frozen lake as it started to warm up again.

Cabal looked around, questing for his decision. If he didn't take the wager, his researches were useless. Worse yet, if by some fluke he did succeed in them despite the lack of a soul, they would be pointless. If he took the wager and failed, then he would end up in this fatuous medieval monk's idea of eternal torment.

He clicked his tongue. No choice at all, then.

He nodded. "I accept your offer."

He had no concept of why people might want to waste their time and money at a carnival when they could be doing something important, but he was sure that as soon as he applied himself he might be able to think down to that level.

"Good. Splendid." Satan tossed the large file at Cabal, who avoided it concussing him only with difficulty. "There's your carnival, there's your budget." He squeezed his hand shut until his nails drove into the flesh. A single drop of black blood fell to the floor and formed into a glistening, gelid sphere about the size of a medicine ball. "And there's your year." He snapped the fingers of his other hand and an hourglass appeared. He turned it and placed it in front of Cabal. "Enjoy it in good health. Now shoo. You bore me."

"Hold on," said Cabal, uncertainty turning to suspicion. He pointed at the sphere. "What do you mean, 'budget'?"

"The Carnival of Discord never became operational. All the materials were allocated, but it was never manned. It's all in the file. That ball of blood is my diabolical influence and power. Every time you call upon it, the ball will diminish. Use it wisely, Johannes Cabal. Now"—he spoke with finality—"this audience is at an end."

He snapped his fingers again and, abruptly, Cabal was elsewhere.

Chapter 2

IN WHICH CABAL PRACTICES HIS MAP-READING
AND MEETS AN OLD ACQUAINTANCE

The Flatlands rolled as far as the eye could see in any direction—remarkably flat, remarkably boring, and not nearly high enough above sea level for comfort. The fields all looked like marshes waiting to happen; in some cases, the wait was over. Dilapidated wooden fences made a poor job of delineating one unhealthy-looking patch of land from the next. Stone walls didn't last here; they sank. In three directions it was hard to see where the grey land merged into the grey sky. In the fourth, a long earthwork ran until it faded into the distance.

A dreary, depressing place, and Cabal was very surprised suddenly to be in the middle of it. He spent an undignified few moments trying to get over the fact that he was no longer in Hell, wheeling on the spot like somebody who has walked into the wrong toilets. When he finally deduced that he had been unceremoniously translocated, he marked the revelation with a filthy curse in a language that had been dead eight thousand years, so managing to be amazingly erudite and amazingly uncouth in the selfsame instant.

Cabal put down his gladstone bag, beat the last few whiffs of sulphurous smoke out of his clothes with his hat, and opened the file. Several sheets down, he found a map of the area that he withdrew before reclosing the file. He took a moment to orientate himself. Without a compass or a visible sun to work with, a map of the Flatlands tended to be like one of those pictures which look like something completely different when you turn them upside down. In this case, it looked really rather similar no matter which way you turned it.

He found a few lanes that ran straight until it seemed that whoever built them had realised there was no point in pretending that anyone was ever going to travel them. These lanes had been hastily finished with odd little curlicues, as if that had been the intention all along. Only the earthwork stood out in that tedious landscape, but, unfortunately, it didn't seem to be on the map. Finally, after some exasperated and faintly histrionic sighing, Cabal noticed a faint dotted line on the map labelled "Route of proposed spur line." The red cross that he assumed was his destination lay on the line, but the line had been so slight, he simply hadn't seen it.

That must be it, he concluded. It was an old map, and the spur line had been built. The earthwork was a raised railway bed. Simple. Pleased with his deduction, he turned to pick up his bag and found that he was no longer alone.

The two men whom he'd caught in a pantomime of stealth were of a disreputable appearance. There was a sense that if you opened an illustrated dictionary and looked up "disreputable" there would be a picture of one or the other of them. Possibly both. After all, if there was some minor detail of reprehensible untrustworthiness that couldn't be found in one of them, it was certain to be present in his partner. One was short and greasy. The other was taller, and looked like his mother had been scared—scared quite badly—by a scabby vulture. They grinned, and Cabal almost sighed with the pathetic predictability of it all. Oh well. Best to get it over with.

"Can I help you gentlemen?" he said with no hint of irony.

"Oh, he called us 'gennlemen,' Dennis, didja 'ear 'im?" said the short one.

"Hur-hur. 'Gennlemen.' Hur," answered the tall one, Dennis, who seemed to be the straight man.

"Tha's very perlite, innit? Very perlite indeed. Ho, yus. Spoke jus' like a gennleman."

" 'Gennleman,' hur-hur. Yus, Denzil. Verr perlite." Dennis nodded and showed the poor state of his dentition.

Cabal was getting irritated. He was on a tight schedule and just wished they'd hurry up and mug him.

"Werl," said Denzil, the brains of the operation, "we wus wondering if you'd paid the toll, see?"

"Of course," said Cabal, who spoke Bare-Faced Liar like a native when the situation called for it. "I paid at the toll gate."

Dennis and Denzil looked nonplussed. They'd spent weeks practising this criminal act; diagrams on blackboards, little dioramas with figures representing them and their potential victim—a tin Sioux Indian, a small bear with a pair of cymbals, and a llama respectively. Somehow this particular eventuality had never been covered.

"There b'aint be no toll gate," muttered Denzil.

"No? Then there can't be any toll," said Cabal with an easy irrationality that ran against the grain of his brutally rational mind. He knew he'd regret it in the morning, but he just wanted to get this whole situation over and done with as quickly as possible.

Dennis was shaking his head slowly as he ran through the contingency plans. They'd never made any, so it didn't take very long. They had considered making some, but, then, they'd also considered getting drunk at the same time. If they had ever actually come up with a contingency plan—and there is no evidence that they did—they had forgotten it again somewhere around the tenth pint. It had been no great loss: they had never needed a Plan B before. Indeed, they had never needed a Plan A before, dependent as it was upon actually finding somebody to rob amongst the dreary and seldom-travelled lanes of the Flatlands. With the unexpected discovery of an actual viable victim, the gaping holes in the scheme were quickly becoming apparent.

Dennis shook his head again, but when his cognitive process half-heartedly kicked in, the sensation of thinking was like worms in a jam jar, and he wished it would stop. Meanwhile, the incisive wit of Denzil had come to the rescue.

"I don't care if there b'aint be no toll. We're robbin' you anyway." He drew a short, rusty blade and elbowed Dennis until he drew his. Now they were on solid ground. They'd killed before and, by some miracle, had got away with it. If this thin streak of piss didn't stump up the cash right this minute, they'd be taking their chances with the gallows again, and the devil could take the consequences. Cabal shrugged.

"I don't have any money," he said truthfully.

Denzil pointed at the bag. "What's in there, then?"

There comes a time when the thin skein of possibilities that suspends us above the unknown stretches and tears in places. For Dennis and Denzil, that moment was now. The skein grew thinner and more transparent as Cabal reached down and picked up his bag.

"Nothing that you could want. I'm a scientist. This contains my equipment."

"A scientiss?" moaned Dennis. He put his hand on Denzil's shoulder. "He woan have no money. C'mon, Denzil. Less go."

The skein thickened and started to knit itself back. Denzil, however, had decided that he really didn't like Cabal. Even if Cabal had nothing that they wanted, Denzil was damn sure that he was going to take it anyway. He angrily shook Dennis's hand from his shoulder.

"No, I want whatever you've got, you milk-faced bugger. Open the bloody bag before I cut ya." The skein grew thin as a bubble, tight as a drumskin. Cabal pursed his lips and opened the bag. The skein tore from side to side. Although Dennis and Denzil hadn't been fully acquainted with the facts yet, they were doomed men.

Cabal reached in and drew out a human skull. Denzil and Dennis took a step back. Cabal wondered for a moment how he was going to explain concisely why he was carrying a bank clerk's skull and decided not to.

"This is a *memento mori*," he said instead. He could see they were going to say it—no, it was a skull—so he quickly added, "A reminder of mortality. That we are all clay. That we all *die*." This last was said point-edly, but the pair of thieves was too busy gawping at the skull to be paying much attention to the nuances. He replaced the skull and took out a small leather folder. He flipped it open to reveal gleaming scalpels and probes. "These are my surgical instruments."

"Yer a doctor, then?" asked Denzil, trying to guess how much the instruments might be worth. Cabal put them away again.

"Not really. These," he continued as he produced a box about the size of a binocular case, padded inside and out, "are phials containing Test Batch 247." He worked the catch with his thumb and opened it to show the heads of several test tubes, each sealed with wax into which the imaginative might have thought they saw a curious symbol worked.

Denzil could see that they weren't going to be retiring after this job. "Wassat worth, then?"

Cabal closed the case and put it away. "If you don't know how to use them, nothing at all. And finally," he said, rummaging deep in the glad-stone. "This is a Webley .577." Cabal drew the biggest handgun either Denzil or Dennis had ever seen in his life. Dennis cheered up.

"Werl, that's gotta be worth something, eh? Eh, Denzil?" He turned around to see Denzil running as fast as his fat little legs could carry him. Somewhere deep in the reptilian part of his brain, Dennis got the feeling that he might be in trouble. The bullet that smashed through his back did nothing to diminish this. Even as Dennis was falling, his minimal amounts of brain activity flickering down to nothing, Cabal was carefully levelling the revolver at Denzil's diminishing form. The first shot threw up stone fragments close by his heels. Cabal raised his aim a little and tried again. Denzil went down like he'd been poleaxed.

It took some time to find a spot where he could climb through the strag-gling and unhealthy hedgerow that grew alongside the earthwork, and another few minutes of climbing through brambles to reach the top. As he'd surmised, this was indeed the "proposed spur line" mentioned on the map. The dilapidated state of the line made him wonder how old the map was: the rails were heavy with undisturbed rust, the sleepers were rotting under moulds and mushrooms, weeds and young trees grew waist-high along the full length of the track as far as he could see. He consulted the map again. From his vantage point he could finally make out a few of what might, locally at least, be called landmarks: ponds, marshes, and forks in the roads. He turned the map through a few angles until he could work out where he was, reorientated himself facing north, and then looked directly along the line where the map carried an enigmatic "X." The vegetation seemed far more mature there, a dense copse of trees that straddled the line and spread down each embankment. That, he hoped, must be it.

He set off towards the trees with determination, but after a few steps he was halted by the sound of something falling heavily on the track behind him. He turned and snapped, "Do keep up! We don't have all day." Denzil blinked slowly at him and then down at Dennis, who was trying to get up, but his foot had caught under a rotten sleeper. It took a moment for Denzil to realise that he might help by kicking Dennis's heel repeatedly until it came loose. He took slow, careful aim, swung his leg with great force, missed, and ended up on his back. He blinked uncomprehendingly at the grey sky. It seemed much more difficult to get things done now that he was dead.

Cabal pulled a little black book from his pocket, drew a pencil from its spine, and made a note. Batch 247 seemed to act quickly, but it certainly didn't help co-ordination in any practical sense. With hindsight, perhaps he should have made some effort to take their souls on a more formal basis as the first donors of the hundred. That he hadn't was partially down to not being quite sure how one actually sets about taking souls on a more formal basis, but mainly because they had peeved him. "I'll be over there." He pointed towards the trees and put his notebook away. "Catch up when you're able." That, he thought ruefully, might be some time.

As Cabal got closer to the trees, he began to see how long the copse was—perhaps a quarter of a mile. Given the stunted state of everything else in sight, that was suspicious in itself. Nothing else seemed likely to produce much more than toothpicks, while these trees were great twisted brutes that stood on the landscape as if painted in black ink. Leafless branches clutched at the sky, and the convulsed bark of the trunks looked, to a fanciful mind, like human faces twisted in torment. "This," he said quietly, "must be the place. It's *so* melodramatic."

In a nearby tree that might have been an elm before being regularly watered with LSD, a carrion crow sat and regarded Cabal keenly. It tilted its head and cawed mockingly at Cabal. Then it saw Dennis and Denzil stumbling along the track a hundred yards behind him and, full of hope and appetite, flew to investigate them.

Cabal passed the tortured elm, stepped over the roots of a lunatic's vision of a witch hazel, and came face to face with the Monster.

Cabal exhaled sharply, and his always pale complexion turned an ugly grey for a second, until he brought himself under control. He didn't move, tried not to breathe, tried not to let the great black Monster know he was alive. Then he took a deep, shuddering breath, stepped forward, and placed his hand upon its face.

He had to step on the cowcatcher to reach, though.

It was the most astounding piece of engineering he thought he'd ever seen, and he'd seen a few. A massive locomotive that even here, dead and neglected, its firebox long cold, demanded and received unthinking respect. It bore some affectations of the Old West—the cowcatcher, the fluted smokestack—but the body seemed more Old World, aggressively squared and not afraid to shunt every carriage ever built from here to Hell. Perhaps it was capable of that. Cabal nodded approvingly: he might not be an engineer by trade, but he knew solid workmanship when he saw it.

Apparently, so did all nearby creatures. Despite any number of tempting perches for local incontinent birds, the only dirt on it was the coating of curious black rust that came off on his fingers like very coarse soot. Cabal sniffed at it cautiously and was instantly put in mind of energetic evenings down in the cellar, sawing up the evidence and putting it in the furnace before the police arrived. He pushed his tinted spectacles up his nose and blinked thoughtfully behind them. What exactly did this thing run on? He hoped it was wood or coal; it would be much more convenient.

A commotion made him turn. The crow had settled on Denzil's head and was trying to get a meal out of him. Specifically, out of his eye socket. The hapless dead man had his head down and his arms outstretched and was running a clumsy circle in an effort to dislodge the bird. It wasn't working; the crow seemed to have stapled itself in place. Dennis wasn't helping things by trying to hit the bird with a sickly sapling he'd torn up. Blows rained down on Denzil's back, not even remotely close to the target, and soil from the roots flew everywhere.

"Stop that!" barked Cabal. Both walking dead and bird stopped that. Dennis tried to hide the tree behind his back. "You there. Crow. Come here." With utmost reluctance, the crow launched itself from Denzil, swooped low until it was almost touching the ground, then swept back up to head height, slalomed nonchalantly through the intervening trees, and landed on Cabal's shoulder. Cabal turned on his heel and started to walk down past the huge locomotive and towards the train of carriages and cars linked up behind it. "You'll be fed shortly, bird, so no further trouble, yes?" The crow blinked. "Oh, by the by, if you ever shit on my shoulder, you'll be in a taxidermist's window so fast as to beggar belief. Understood?"

"Kronk," said the crow, which may have meant, "Yes, master." It could equally well have meant, "You'll have to catch me first, buggerlugs." Either way, it kept its sphincters tight.

Cabal walked slowly along the train. There were a few carriages, several flatcars stacked with once brightly painted boards, and, towards the back, a good number of sealed boxcars. He arrived at the first of them and stopped by the large sliding door that ran for a quarter of its length. He was just considering how to get in when it slid open of its own accord with a hideous shrieking of rusty metal. "Oh," said Cabal, unimpressed. "It's you."

The Little Old Man finished dogging the door open and looked down. "Aye, it's me, young Cabal. You've taken your time."

Cabal placed a foot on a metal rung, gripped the rail by the door edge, and pulled himself up. The crow flapped off his shoulder and landed on a nearby stanchion. It settled down to practise looking at things beadily.

"You're lucky I'm here at all. The map was next to useless," Cabal said as he brushed rust off his hands and shoulder where the doorframe had touched him. He looked at the man. "I was hoping Satan might send something else rather than you, you contrary old bastard."

The man laughed. Actually, he cackled.

"Oh, we go way back, Johannes. His Worshipfulness thought you might like a familiar face."

Cabal was looking around the gloomy car. "Only if I thought blowing a hole in it would make any difference," he replied offhandedly.

The Little Old Man was not, in any real sense, little or a man. He was certainly, however, very old. He was an embodiment of an archetype: the old codger with the flat cap and the grey beard. He cackled, he rolled his own foul-smelling cigarettes, and, when on form, he could be relied on to dribble. He was exactly the sort of person that makes youth fashionable. He was also one of Satan's numerous avatars: fragments of his personalities and random thoughts that had taken form in the mortal realm. They allowed him to maintain a steady background hum of elemental evil in the world while he concentrated on more important things down in Hell. His cribbage game, for example. Until recent events, the Little Old Man had been Cabal's only contact with Satan. This was the entity that he'd sold his soul to years before, and the entity that had invalidated more lines of research with his wilful interference than Cabal cared to remember.

The Little Old Man sat on a crate and watched Cabal investigate the dark corners. "Oh, Johannes. I'm hurt," he said cheerfully. "After all we've been through."

Cabal, his cursory examination of the boxcar completed, walked back to him. " 'All *we've* been through'? All you've put me through, surely? If you hadn't bought my soul and then been such a pervasive nuisance ever since, none of *this*"—he made a gesture that encompassed the whole train—"would have been necessary."

The Little Old Man shrugged. "I was only doing my job. You can't expect altruism from one of Satan's little helpers."

Cabal sighed. "Look, I'd really like to be able to say that I'm delighted that you could make it and it's a real tonic to see you, but I'd be lying."

"I know."

"So do you think we might cut along with a little more alacrity, all the quicker to get you out of my sight? I am, after all, on a rather tight schedule."

"Schedule," said the Little Old Man, holding up a finger. "I'm glad you reminded me. You'll be needing this." He reached into his grubby old coat and produced an hourglass a little over a foot in height. Instead of sand, however, it seemed to be filled with an incredibly fine powder. Tiny motes made their way from the upper chamber into the narrow neck and cascaded downwards. Despite the steady stream, the floor of the bottom chamber barely had a dusting upon it. "This shows you how much time you've got left. You know how one works, don't you?" Cabal gave him a look. " 'Course you do, clever lad like you. Anyway, when all the grains have fallen from top to bottom, time's up. Simple. Oh, one thing to remember. This isn't the actual glass that my better part has down in the hot place. It's a sort of repeater, relay thing. You can do what you like to this one but it doesn't affect the time you've got left. See?" He turned the glass. The motes fell upwards regardless. The Little Old Man held it at different angles, but nothing made any difference. Time was still passing, and the grains carried on falling in a steady, gravity-boggling stream. "Neat, eh? Goes down a bomb at parties, I can tell you."

"Really?" said Cabal as he took the glass. "I'll have to hold a soirée just to impress my friends."

"You haven't got any friends."

"I'm not holding a soirée, either. You have a problem with sarcasm, don't you? Now, do you have anything else fascinating to impart or can I kick your wrinkly little carcass down the embankment, as I so dearly wish?"

The Little Old Man huffed. "You're not nice."

"Your"—Cabal searched for the right word—"*founder* has given me the task of sending one hundred souls to eternal torment. To be quite frank, I don't think my name is ever going to become a byword for popularity."

"You're right there." The Little Old Man searched inside his capaciously shapeless coat and finally found a thin file box as broad and wide as foolscap by an inch deep. He undid the thin black tape ribbon sealing it, took off the lid, and showed the contents to Cabal. It was a pack of forms printed on some sort of faintly yellow parchment. Cabal leaned forward and read the top line.

" 'Voluntary Damnation Form. To be filled in by the damnee. EAGH/1.' " He straightened up. "I see the hand of Arthur Trubshaw at work here."

"You're not wrong," replied the Little Old Man as he tied the package up again. "One hundred forms to be handed in fully completed in a little less than a year's time. Feeling up to it, Johannes?" He passed over the box. Cabal hefted it and looked around.

"I'm not sure. I accepted this challenge on the understanding that I would have the Carnival of Discord on my side. As yet, all I seem to have been given is a rolling junk shop. Tell Satan—no carnival, no deal."

"No carnival? No *carnival*? This is it! Wagons roll! The Greatest Show on Earth! Use your imagination, why don't you?"

"Imagination? I'd have to be hallucinating before I could believe this shambles was the Greatest Show on Earth."

The Little Old Man got up from the crate and walked over to the back wall, shaking his head and muttering about young folk today. Leaning against the wall was a stack of broad wooden boards half covered by a tarpaulin. This he whipped off in possibly the weakest theatrical flourish Cabal had ever seen, to reveal that the boards were signs—battered and peeling, but signs nonetheless.

"Here you go. Here are your sideshows. 'See! From the Mysterious East! The Enigmatic Cleopatra! Three Thousand Years in the Tomb Yet Still the Most Beautiful Woman in the World!' Good, eh? What's this one? 'Marvel at the Bat-Faced Boy! Direct from the Darkest Jungle!' Woooooh! Scary stuff, isn't it?"

"The sheer preponderance of exclamation marks is terrifying in it-self."

"That's just traditional. 'Gasp! At the Log-Headed Girl!' That can't be right." He probed at the flaking paint. "Surely it should say 'Dog-Headed Girl'? Oooh, no. It *does* say 'Log-Headed.' That'll pull the crowds." He nodded confidently at Cabal.

Cabal had lost patience with the Little Old Man's drivel. He stood by the open door watching Dennis and Denzil's painfully slow progress along the trackside with the mildest interest possible.

"Oh, yes," he said over his shoulder. "They'll come from miles around for this. 'Roll up, roll up. See the world's largest collection of antediluvian signage. Gasp at the decrepitude. Be astounded by the grammar. A fascinating show rivalled only by the lint in your navel.' I'll have to fight them off with a stick."

The Little Old Man narrowed his eyes and thought carefully.

"That's sarcasm, isn't it?"

Cabal looked out at the Flatlands again. He really didn't care anymore. This whole thing was another of Satan's dim-witted jokes. He had no idea why he bothered.

"Yes," he replied. "That's sarcasm." He turned and walked over to the stack of signs. "This is a pointless enterprise without personnel. I don't have any."

A sound made them turn to the door. Dennis had reached it and was just contemplating how best to climb up when Denzil—who'd got the rhythm of walking worked out to his satisfaction but hadn't yet appreciated the myriad complications involved with stopping—walked into him. They both fell out of sight. After a moment, there was the sound of a slow and considered fight.

"Well, none worth speaking of," Cabal corrected himself. "If I'm not even to be provided with people to try to make something of this mess, then you might as well have these forms back now."

The Little Old Man cackled.

"How can you say that, Johannes? Don't you like a challenge? Where's your sense of adventure?"

"Easily outweighed by my sense of being made a fool of."

"But you *have* been provided with people. Sort of. Look around you."

Cabal looked around him. He was still alone in a grimy dump of a boxcar with only the dubious company of the Little Old Man. "I *am* looking. All I am *seeing*, however, are candidates for landfill. What are you getting at?"

The Little Old Man went to the centre of the car and swept his arms around to encompass all that was lying about the place. As a dramatic gesture, it might have been at home in musical comedy. Light musical comedy. "Here are your people, all around you." He reached into a box and pulled out a bone that Cabal immediately recognised as a human femur. "Here are your riggers"—he dropped it and plucked a ball of hair from a sack—"your barkers"—he put his hand on what Cabal had assumed were rolls of cloth leaning in the corner. "Your concession-stand holders. Your whole carnival is here. Just use a little"—he tapped his temple—"*imagination.*"

Cabal walked over to inspect a roll. "What do you mean?" He looked closely at the material and belatedly realised what it was. "This," he said dryly, "is human skin." There was no reply. He looked around, but the Little Old Man had vanished.

Marvellous, Cabal thought. I don't even get an instruction book.

He took a small black object from his pocket and squeezed a button on its casing. A wicked-looking blade flicked out. He unrolled some of the "cloth" from the dark roll and cut a long strip from it. Then he got a small ball of hair from the sack, a rag from a barrel, and finally the femur. He carefully tied the hair to the bone, using the piece of cloth. "A rag, a bone, a hank of hair," he intoned quietly as he wrapped the whole thing in the strip of skin. He regarded the finished object with a scornful shake of the head. "I hate this sort of thing." He looked for some clear floor. " 'I invoke thee.' " So saying, he lobbed the untidy mess into the clearing.

Down in Hell, a black ball of blood diminished very slightly in size.

The mess came apart long before it reached the floor with more violence than might be regarded as natural. The bone hit the floor first and stopped abruptly, standing neatly vertical. The skin struck it and wrapped tightly about it, so tightly that after a moment it was impossible to tell where its edges were. The bone lurched as more bones budded and flowed from it, but as quickly as the new bone appeared it was submerged in the flowing skin. The small ball of hair landed on top of the growing stack of organic material, teetered, and fell off. It tried repeatedly to regain a perch but seemed doomed to failure. The rag whirled around and around the structure, too fast for Cabal's eye to follow closely but he got the distinct impression that it was changing colour. The stack of bones was producing a spinal column with a painful clicking pop as each vertebra grew out of the one beneath it. As it completed the thoracic section, ribs sprang out like the opening of a clothless umbrella. The skin flowed upwards like the rising level of a liquid within a glass, almost concealing the bubbling formation of organs within the torso. Arms suddenly burst out as swiftly as the blade of a flick-knife, reminding Cabal to put his away. The circling rag swept in and flew a complex weaving pattern over the surface of the body, and where it flew, clothing appeared. Like ghastly toast, the skull popped up from the neck and grinned maniacally in the way that skulls do. Even when the skin wrapped over it, it continued to grin at Cabal with immodest glee. The skin rolled over the ivory vault of the brainpan like a rising tide over a boulder on the beach, met at the top, and sealed.

Standing before Cabal was a man who hadn't existed a minute before: slightly shorter than he, black, painfully thin, and dressed in black trousers, white shoes with black spats, a white shirt, and a gleaming waistcoat of black and white vertical stripes. In his hand was a straw boater with a yellow band about it. The man clapped it on his head just in time to prevent the hank of hair settling on his entirely bald skull. A few hairs made a dive for his forehead and knitted quickly into eyebrows, but the rest balanced on top of the boater forlornly for a moment before dropping lifeless to the floor. The man watched it go with dawning dismay, quickly lifting his hat and checking his skull. He was disappointed to find that he was as bald as a cue ball.

"Oh," he moaned, "oh, man," and finally, with an air of exasperation, "oh, shit!" He looked down his body, examined his wrists, looked at Cabal as if the roof had just fallen in, and ran around. "A mirror, man! There's gotta be a mirror around here!" Cabal watched him run. The man found a large grimy piece of silvered glass that may have once been part of a mirror and held it up to his face. He couldn't quite believe what he was seeing and scrubbed at the surface. It didn't improve things.

"Look at me," he wailed. "Look at me. You've made me the skinniest guy in the whole world!"

"I did nothing of the sort," said Cabal testily. Everybody was *such* a critic. "I summoned you. That's just the way you turned up. Don't presume to blame me for any physical shortcomings you might display."

"But, but . . ." The man put down the mirror and approached Cabal, emphasising every syllable with his hands. "But you were the one sortin' out the components, man. Where's my fat?"

"Fat?" Cabal realised he may have made a small oversight. "Rag, bone, hair. That's traditionally it. Nobody ever said anything about fat."

The painfully thin man waved his hands in disbelief. He looked quickly around the car and ran for the corner in long, angular strides. He grasped a crate and pulled it out into the open. Stencilled on the side was a single word: "Lard."

"Just a little dollop, that's all, man. That's all I needed! I could've been a fine-lookin' man, guy. Instead of which, I'm nothin' but a bag of *bones*." He looked beseechingly at Cabal. Cabal looked back at him with a profound lack of sympathy.

"Well, *Bones*, what do you expect me to do about it? An intravenous drip of melted butter, perhaps?"

"D'ya think that would work?" asked Bones with piteous hope.

"Not for a second. Look, in a little less than a year, all this"—he indicated the immediate environs—"goes, and you, my vain friend, return to the components whence I raised you. So—you must try to understand one simple thing. In one year's time, there won't be enough of you left to amuse a dog. Thus, I don't care what you look like, and neither should you. Our immediate concern should be getting this show on the road. Now, are you going to help, or am I going to have to dispose of you as an unsuccessful experiment and try again?"

Bones put his hands on his hips and allowed himself to slouch into a sassy pose not unlike a crane-fly with attitude. "You am de boss, baaaahss. Dis dumb-ass boy sure am yours to comman', an' ain't *dat* de trufe?"

"Excellent," replied Cabal, unperturbed. "Now, come over here."

"I was bein' sarcastic," said Bones in his normal voice—a cadenced tone in a largely American accent with perhaps a hint of French growling through the long vowels—as he walked to where Cabal crouched by the stack of signs.

"You were being tiresome. Look at these."

"Freaks, derring-do, eighth wonders of the world. Looks pretty standard sideshow stuff to me."

"So which ones are exciting? Which ones will people come from near and wide to see? I need to know."

Bones looked at him questioningly. "Why you askin' me, boss? You the man with the plan, aren't you?" He looked closely at Cabal. Cabal continued to go through the boards, trying to find the secret. "You *have* got a plan?"

Cabal stood up and stepped away. He glared at the signs. "I don't understand. Why would anybody want to waste their time looking at this sort of nonsense? It's just rubbish! Bogus exhibits, deleterious mutations, lies! None of this is real! None of it's lasting! They're just . . ." He sagged. He hadn't felt so useless in years. "Dreams. I don't understand it."

Bones was having a few problems as well. "But you volunteered for this, didn'tcha? Him downstairs wouldn't just sock you with this gig unless you knew what you were doing, would he?"

"It's . . . a wager."

"A bet?" If Bones had lived a generation for every one of the five minutes he had so far drawn breath, he still couldn't have been more surprised. "You got a bet on with the Man himself? You're crazy! Nobody ever wins against the Man! He's . . ." Bones tried to think of a convincing metaphor. He failed. "He's the MAN, man!"

Behind the dark spectacles, fire returned to Cabal's eyes. "He's not going to win this one."

"You're kiddin' yourself!" muttered Bones with evident disdain. "Only folks in stories get the drop on His Satanic Luciferiness. Sorry to be the one to break the news an' all, but you're screwed, Jack."

Cabal ignored him. He was looking at the signs again.

"I have to work to a budget, so I can't just start everything. I have to make some management decisions about what to go with and what to leave. Some of these sideshows will be useful; others will just waste my resources. I need advice. Mr. Bones, which sideshows shall I invest in?"

Bones shook his head regretfully. "I can't help you, boss. End of the day, I'm just walkin' dust. You're the only real person round here. Your call."

"I can't," replied Cabal conclusively. "I don't understand people, either. I'll have to get my advice from somewhere else." He looked into the distance for a long moment. Then he took a deep breath. "I think I know just the person." He walked to the exit and jumped down onto the track. Denzil and Dennis were sitting by the train, throwing stones at the crow. None were going even remotely close, but it watched the proceedings with keen interest all the same. "You two," he spoke sharply. "Obey Mr. Bones's instructions until I return."

They looked up as Bones stuck his head out and looked down on them from immediately above. He grinned. "Howdy!" They smiled dozily and waved back.

"Crow! Here!" Cabal ordered. The crow flew to him without hesitation and landed upon his shoulder. "You're coming with me, so I know you're not up to mischief."

"Kronk!" said the crow smugly.

Bones leaned on the doorjamb. "So what do you want me and the corpse boys to be doin' while you're gone, chief?"

Cabal pointed towards the engine. "I'm not sure how long I'll be gone. It might be a few days. In the meantime, clean out the locomotive and get together some fuel. Do you know what it burns?"

"Just about anythin'."

"Good. Load up the fuel car with wood, and fill the boiler with water. There are lots of ponds and streams around here. That shouldn't be a problem. Then see if you can get the line clear back to the junction. We'll need to be under way as soon as the carnival's put together."

Bones glanced at the trees and pursed his lips. This didn't look like a small task. "Is *that* all? Nothin' else?" Cabal thought hard. Bones sighed. Him and his big mouth.

"Yes, if you've got any time left, I want the name of the carnival painted on the first broad-sided car, both sides. Can you sign-paint?"

"Sure, I can sign-paint, I can do most stuff if I put my mind to it. What do you want to call it, boss?"

Cabal told him.

Bones whistled appreciatively. "Man, you're just *full* of surprises."

Chapter 3

Burial: it's a personal choice. There are, of course, those who don't care to be buried at all but prefer to be burnt or left in the open for vultures to pick at or something else equally unhygienic.

They are of no concern here.

Those who do want their bodies interred have different visions of how they'd prefer the environs, as if it would make a difference to them at this juncture. Some imagine a green churchyard on a spring day, the sound of bells calling the faithful to worship, the immaculate grass verges, the white pebbled paths. Some—usually the ones who wear a lot of black and think that Byron must have been mad, bad, and *fabulous* to know—dream of tenebrous graveyards in the shades of monstrous Gothic churches, beneath a dark, lowering sky that threatens thunder and lightning any second. Being near a mountainous sea wouldn't hurt, either. Others would like a tree to be planted over their otherwise un-marked graves, so that their bodies might nourish the roots of a mighty oak or sycamore.

All these desires can be understood and to a greater or lesser extent sympathised with. It is, however, impossible to have the faintest idea what was going through the minds of the people who bought plots in the Grimpen Burial Ground. Perhaps they hated their relatives and wanted to drag them into one of the ugliest and most depressing places on Earth, if only for the funeral.

The Grimpen Burial Ground stood—if that is the right word, and "lay" if it is not—in the heart of the last marsh in the land that, until recently, contained malaria. No effort had been necessary to wipe out the last of the disease-carrying anopheles mosquitoes; they simply seemed to give up the will to live.

The burial ground itself had been cunningly placed on the head of a peninsula that could be safely reached only by traversing a long and serpentine isthmus surrounded on all sides by a sucking bog of the sort that makes frequent appearances in adventure stories. None could guess how many arch-criminals, diabolical Gypsies, and Things Man Was Not Meant to Know had breathed their last, frantic, gasping breaths before vanishing beneath the clinging filth. It was likely to be a fair few.

Then onwards, along the winding, desperate path, until one reached the burial ground's rusting gates. Predictably, one hung from a single hinge and screeched eerily, given the excuse of the faintest breeze. And in the Grimpen Burial Ground, breezes never got stronger than faint, for anything stronger might perhaps have made headway in shifting the mists. That would never do. People talk about the London pea-soupers, but although those legendary fogs may have been yellow, unhealthy, and thick enough to bottle, they had absolutely no class. The Grimpen mists, in contrast, had style to spare. They drifted slowly and enigmatically, eldritch and eerie, ever encroaching, enveloping all. They had the air of watching and waiting. People hated attending burials there; the mists, the infamous mists, seemed to be watching the living. And waiting for them to die.

Yet the burial ground was closed because it was full. Full of the dead that people *wanted* to forget. The malevolent fathers and the bastard sons, the insane mothers and the diseased daughters. They came, one and all, in their coffins of bare pine or fashioned teak, to be interred in this distant place and conveniently allowed to slip the memories of the people who stood, dry-eyed, by their yawning graves. Some of the last resting places were marked with ornate gravestones of exotic marble or hard granite brought from far away. Others, less wealthy or less hypocritical, marked the sites of the less-than-dearly departed with local slate, cheap limestone, or even wood. Loathed magnate and embarrassing heir by the second under-stairs maid lay side by side, their gravestones sagging in the moist soil, united by the simple fact that no living human heart had any place for them.

For all that, however, the burial ground wasn't *quite* filled. In the rear of the burial ground, overlooking the bogland at the farthest point from the gates, there was one place that lay only partially occupied. It was the one and only family crypt to be found there, and its story is an extraordinary one.

*T*he Druin family could follow its line back to the Norman invasion; their name was presumed to be a corruption of "de Rouen," although there was no evidence that they originally came from that place. Their ancestor's role in the invasion is open to interpretation. The family claimed that he rode at William the Conqueror's side because he was a trusted aide and confidant. In light of their more recent and documented history, it has been mooted that William was simply keen to keep an eye on him. Whatever the truth of it, it is fact that the family was granted a plot of land for perpetuity, a plot that included the bogland that the burial ground now stood upon.

The family muddled through the centuries, frequently backing the wrong horse in a multitude of conflicts yet always managing to get onto the winning side at the last through some dazzling act of treachery. Richard III is rumoured to have known he was doomed when the Druin's defection to the House of Lancaster actually during the battle was reported to him. He made some comment about rats and sinking ships before going off to look for his horse.

From the Plantagenet years onwards, the Druins were said to be capable of swapping from Protestant to Roman Catholic and back again within the period of a single church service. Indeed, a secret library discovered during renovations of Druin Manor contained a copy of the catechism; the Bible in Greek, Latin, and English; a treatise on Calvinism; the Koran; the Tripitaka; and an Arabic book bound in curious leather that was later stolen by a gang consisting of an antiquarian, a mobster, and a woman with a lisp.

The family managed to maintain a place in court throughout many changes until the Industrial Revolution happened along and they discovered that they could make more money the nouveau-riche way. Mills and railways were heavily invested in, children sent down mines, the word "philanthropy" carefully crossed out in the family dictionary; the Druins became richer and richer and richer.

It was about then that the effects of great wealth and a small gene pool started to spell their doom. Inbreeding, largely imposed upon them by a world that put too much store in bad reputations, started to strip the gears of their collective sanity. They became madder and madder and madder, and they never did so cheaply.

Beatrice built the Museum of the Legume, housing the world's largest collection of peas. Horace excavated an inversion of the Palace of Westminster, a huge jelly mould of the Mother of Parliaments. Jeremy formed a hunt of foxes with which he used to go beagle-hunting before moving up a level and storming people's houses with a troop of crack badgers.

The atmosphere of mutual loathing and unilateral insanity became almost palpable. Aunt Sophia, the only one to maintain a marble count in double figures, went abroad in a determined attempt to find some curative Measure.

Apparently, she failed. Yet she came back, after years of travel, curiously calmed and tolerant, perhaps even a little smug.

Her first action on her return was to create the Grimpen Burial Ground and have the Druin family crypt built in its most inaccessible corner. Every surviving member of the family had a place allocated, with the sole exception of Sophia herself. Asked why, she replied with grim satisfaction that if she had learned anything in her travels, it was that the family could never hope to lose the taint of madness and was doomed to extinction. As to why she had no place reserved in the crypt, it was because she would survive them all.

The rest of the family looked at one another significantly. Mad or not, they needed no weatherman to tell them how the wind blew.

Sophia's luck suddenly seemed to leave her. She suffered a series of accidents, all of them fatal. Several times she was declared dead, as misfortune—sometimes embodied as a plummeting sack of concrete, sometimes as some other heavy, fast item that had coincidentally happened to cross her path at head height—dogged her every step.

By a striking happenstance, the rest of the family was always some distance away when misfortune struck—heavily—and always had cast-iron alibis, sometimes typed up days in advance. Yet Sophia would inevitably sit up on the mortuary slab, stretch, and ask what time tea was.

Ultimately, however, she was overtaken by a particularly unfortunate accident that brought together a steamroller, Sophia, and almost four tons of gelignite at the same time and the same place. This time there was no possibility of any requests for elevenses during the post-mortem. Aunt Sophia was taken down from the trees, scraped off the road, and plucked from the surface of the duck pond with shrimping nets, placed with all due ceremony in her favourite hip bath along with her favoured bathtime accoutrements, and interred in the darkest corner of the family crypt. And that was that. For very nearly two months.

Then, one morning, the surviving family woke up and found themselves one short for breakfast. They discovered Beatrice tied by her ankles to the chandelier. Her expression was one of purest horror, and she was quite dead. There were a lot of peas in the room. The post-mortem discovered another five pounds of them forced down her throat, jamming her oesophagus shut and clogging her airways. A month later, Jeremy's head appeared on a plaque in the trophy room. A fortnight after that, Horace's shattered body was found at the peak of the inverse Westminster Tower, some three hundred feet below the surrounding ground.

One by one they died, apparently at the hands of somebody who knew all their little foibles very well indeed. Felix died beneath a menhir. Daphne drowned in aspic. Given Julian's favourite pastime, it's perhaps just as well that they never found the lower half of his body. Quickly the Druin crypt filled.

If only somebody had thought to check Aunt Sophia in her hip bath. If only somebody had cared to investigate where she'd been during her years abroad. If only somebody had made enquiries into the sudden outbreak of childhood anaemia in the area. Ah, the mysterious "Grimpen Plague." No child died from the disease, and any that moved away for their health quickly improved. The doctors were baffled.

If they had compared notes more carefully, they might have been intrigued by another curious trait that all the child victims shared. All had suffered the same nightmare the night the sickness had taken hold. All had dreamt of a dark, grimy room, like a cellar or a gaol, with deep recesses in the wall. All had found themselves compelled to walk to a corner where the room turned into a dingy alcove. In that forsaken place they had been surprised to find an old-fashioned hip bath. Then, before their terror-stricken gaze, they realised that there was somebody sitting there, a pale old woman with cruel, hypnotic eyes and an expression of such bottomless hunger that they whined and keened at the memory of it. They hadn't been able to move, or to run, as the woman rose from the bath and advanced on them, slowly and surely, with horrible inevitability, like some great albino spider. "The Loofah Lady! The Loofah Lady!" they screamed.

Even after the last of the Druin family had vanished into the crypt, the anaemia outbreak continued. For years it was assumed that the bogland was unhealthy, and those parents who could afford it sent their children away until they were old enough to "resist" the "disease." Meanwhile, the burial ground slowly filled with the discarded dead that nobody wanted. When it became full, it was curtly abandoned. Time began to crumble the place back into the ground.

Nobody would visit that place unless he absolutely had to. Even the most cynical and laudanum-crazed poet could think of a lot of things that he'd rather do than sit on one of the burial ground's tombs and compose a sonnet. Even a haiku would require more time than felt comfortable.

So the ugly and forsaken place was forgotten, and the "anaemic plague" continued.

Until, that is, about eight years ago.

Johannes Cabal stepped past the ruined gates and looked around speculatively. The burial ground had deteriorated quite visibly in the eight years since he'd last been here. Nor were there any signs that the place had been visited in the interim. This didn't surprise him in the slightest. The gravestones leaned a little more crazily, the moss had encroached a little farther across the stonework, and it would take time with a wire brush and oblique lighting to read the inscriptions on anything. Of signs of any human interference, however, there were none at all. Good, he thought. That would remove further variables from what already stood to be a tricky business. He hefted the carpetbag he held in his left hand and moved on. The crow bobbed around on his shoulder, its gaze flicking this way and that. An air of wariness hung about it; it didn't like this place at all.

Cabal wended his way through the stones and the high tufts of grass, proceeding as directly as he could to the Druin family vault. As he walked, he remembered his early studies on the nature of life, of death, and of something in between. Studies that had brought him to this place and finished with him, if not running, certainly walking quickly back down the causeway.

Distracted by his memories, he tripped over something lost in the long grass and staggered briefly—the crow flapping fantastically—before recovering his balance. Turning back, he opened the shutter on his dark lantern to find what had tripped him. An inexpressive man by nature, he still raised an eyebrow and mouthed a quiet "Oh."

It was an old army-surplus field-telephone box, its wooden box in an advanced state of decay, and he did not care to touch it. The Bakelite handset lay discarded by it, and the telephone wire itself led, Cabal discovered after a moment's investigation, down into a tomb whose lid had been slightly moved. Cabal distantly remembered seeing this box on his last visit. He pursed his lips and straightened up. The abandoned field telephone doubtless had some weird tale associated with it, but he really didn't have the time or the inclination to find out what. He had come here with a mission and could countenance no distraction. He turned once more towards the Druin vault and walked on.

The vault was mainly underground, sealed against the high-water table by superior craftsmanship and a lot of lead. Above the surface, the entrance was a small, utilitarian structure not unlike a coal shed with Gothic pretensions. Its only features of note were the name DRUIN in large roman capitals over the door, and the door itself, an impressive feature of stone plates held together with anodised iron straps. Cabal was more concerned with the lock. The door's own internal lock had been destroyed in the past by an amateurish attempt to pick it. It had originally been backed up with a huge padlock running through hasps anchored firmly to the surface, but this lock lay partially concealed by the unwholesome scrub grass that grew in clumps around the area. Cabal didn't need to look at it to know it had been laboriously cut through with a hacksaw. In its place was a gleaming padlock of stainless steel. He hefted it with one hand and slid back the sliding keyhole cover with his thumb. It moved easily: the whole lock seemed in pristine condition, despite its years in such damp conditions. There were no signs of tampering. Cabal took a key ring from his pocket with his free hand and selected a small key. He placed it in the keyhole and slowly turned it. He was aware of every sliding piece of metal within the padlock's case as the key turned slowly and with no impediment through a full circle. The click of the lock releasing was barely perceptible. Cabal was quietly pleased with it as he gently disengaged it from the hasp and put it into his pocket. It pays to invest in quality, he thought.

The door opened with a low whining growl to reveal a stone stairway, barely wide enough for a coffin and bearers to descend. A pale, preternatural glow faintly illuminated the steps, apparently generated by a phosphorescent lichen. It seemed to cover everything in a thin patina, disconcertingly producing a light so dim that his eyes couldn't be sure it was there at all. Like an afterimage seen on the inside of the eyelid, he could make out the edges of the steps, the stones stained with ghost light, and something at the bottom of the stairway that might have been shattered pieces of wood.

Out of sight, around the corner, something moved across the floor, across fragments of coffin that shifted and scraped.

The steady sound of the crickets and the whippoorwills and frogs croaking out in the bog ponds stopped abruptly. The crow launched itself from his shoulder and headed for the gate, emitting a solitary worried "Kronk!" as it did so. Cabal looked around peevishly.

"So. It's like that, is it?" he said quietly. Lifting the dark lantern up, he opened the shutter fully and threw the light of the bright acetylene flame down into the depths. Whatever was moving stopped immediately. Cabal cleared his throat in the ensuing silence.

"I've come back," he said. Down in the crypt he heard a sharp exhalation, almost a hiss. It sounded very nearly human. "I have a proposition to make," continued Cabal. Nothing. Cabal leaned forward, placing his hand on the doorframe. "D'you hear me? A proposition." Still nothing. Cabal's finger started tapping on the frame. "I know damned well that you can hear me. We can talk like grown-ups, or I can just lock you up again, throw the key in the handiest bog, and forget all about you. It can't be much fun down there. Imagine it for decades. Centuries." He heard movement again, but it stopped almost instantly. "Right," said Cabal. "That's fine. If that's your attitude, then I hope it keeps you good company. You're going to need it. Goodbye." He made as if to close the door.

Down below, the thing moved again. Out into the circle of light it came, creeping slowly on four thin limbs like a great spider. Dishevelled and ill defined, it crept or crawled through the wooden fragments until it was at the bottom of the stairs. Cabal reduced the light from the torch a little. He found he had trouble looking at that awful thing.

"There," he said with a confidence he didn't feel. "That's better." The thing in the crypt brought its head up sharply at the sound of his voice, and Cabal recoiled slightly under the withering gaze: a gaze that swept up towards him from faintly luminescent eyes alight with a hatred of chilling intensity. Cabal became aware that, despite the coolness of the night, he was sweating. This was much harder than he'd thought it could possibly be. The thing coughed gutturally, as if making its throat work for the first time in years.

"You bastard," it said. Its voice was gravelly with disuse. "You utter, utter bastard."

Cabal blinked. He hadn't expected quite this amplitude of enmity. "How's Sophia?" he asked, working for time. The thing never looked away.

"Dust. Like you should be." It lowered its gaze. "Like I should be."

"You got her, then? I knew you would."

The thing made a noise that could have been a cough or a laugh.

"Oh, yes. I got her. Too late to do me any good."

"Were any of the others . . . ?"

"No. Why should they be? She never killed anyone *that* way. Always those idiotic murders. Ironic, they were meant to be. Ironic. The children, she didn't want to harm them permanently. The others down here were just corpses. Or at least they didn't squeal when I ate them." A pause. "I got hungry."

Cabal heard the note of unconscious apology in the voice. Good, there was still some humanity left there. Perhaps this could be resolved after all.

"As I said," he continued, "I have a proposal to make to you."

"A proposal." The thing made the noise like a cough or a laugh again. "I always expected you to come back. I always *hoped* you'd come back. To release me, rescue me. Now you turn up with a *proposal*. You haven't changed at all." The glowing eyes focussed on Cabal's face again. "Why did you abandon me? I thought your nerve had gone, but now you make me wonder. Perhaps you just left me salted away down here for some time in the future when you might need me. Was that it?"

Cabal thought of the way his guts had wrenched when he'd heard the scream from below all those years ago. He remembered how the stone-and-iron door had felt under his hand, how it had sounded as he slammed it shut, closed the hasp, and locked it with the padlock they'd brought with them for emergencies. He remembered running in an ecstasy of fear, falling over the stones and leaping back to his feet in single paroxysms of panic. He remembered running until his lungs had burned inside his chest like a furnace, falling in the long grass, and sobbing until the sun rose again. Most of all, he remembered the voice calling behind him, muffled by first the door and then the increasing distance, until the ends of words became indistinguishable. He still knew what they were. "Johannes! Help me! Help me!" He breathed deeply until he was sure that he could speak without his voice trembling.

"Something like that," he lied evenly. "But what happened, it was never planned."

"The sun went down a full hour earlier than we'd planned for. You were the one with the almanac. How could you make a mistake like that?"

"The clocks had gone forward. I hadn't reset my watch. It was a simple oversight."

"*You* don't make mistakes like that," hissed the thing with palpable loathing. "You never made mistakes like that."

"I made one this time," replied Cabal sharply, distraction making him snap. "I'm only human."

The coughing laugh again. "How nice for one of us." The pause grew until it became embarrassing.

"My proposal. I've—"

"I'm hungry," the thing interrupted. "How long have I been down here?"

Cabal did the calculation in the time that it took to blink. "Eight years. A little over."

"How 'little over'?"

"Thirty-seven days."

"Eight years and thirty-seven days." The thing thought for a moment. "I'm *very* hungry."

"I'll find somebody for you," said Cabal impatiently. "Can we get on now?"

"You'll find somebody for me?" The laugh was losing the coughing element, but only to replace it with a hard cynicism that Cabal found far more threatening. "Have you any idea how cheap that makes you sound? From amateur necrothologist to pimp. You *have* gone up in the world."

"Necromancer," corrected Cabal without thinking, and immediately regretted it.

"Don't give yourself airs. We discussed that, remember? To get that sort of knowledge you'd have to . . . Oh, Johannes. You *didn't*?" The thing gasped with disbelieving joy. "You did! You idiot!" The thing started to laugh, a full-throated laugh that made it double up with glee. "You mo-ron! *Nothing's* worth that." The thing rolled around in hysterical laughter, too hysterical for comfort.

Cabal's lips had drawn into a thin line. "It was necessary."

"For what?" The thing was on its back, the laughter slowly ebbing. "For what? You've no idea why you do this anymore, have you?"

"The same reason as ever," said Cabal quietly. The last dregs of laugh-ter died abruptly.

"It's been over eight years, Johannes," said the thing disbelievingly. "You've even made the sacrifice. I thought you must have failed."

"I haven't tried yet. I have to be sure I can succeed. There's no sec-ond chance. It might . . ." Cabal faltered. "It might already be too late."

"I can't help you. It's already too late for me. You might as well lock me up again and walk away."

"No," said Cabal firmly. "I need your help."

"The last time I helped you, I ended up with an extended tenancy in somebody else's crypt. Y'know, I don't feel really very motivated to help again."

"I think you should."

"What? Help you or feel motivated?"

"Both. I think I might be able to reverse what happened to you."

"You *think* you *might*. Boy, positivism like that has just got me fizzing with enthusiasm. How?"

"The . . . disease . . . that you were infected with contaminates the soul. I've had a lot of experience with that area recently, including the au-thorities that deal with them. I might be able to get you a cure."

"There's that 'might' word again." The thing sighed. "All right, what do you want me to do?"

"I've . . ." Cabal looked for the best way to phrase it, but they all sounded ridiculous. "I've recently come into the ownership—temporary ownership—of a carnival."

The thing looked at him with open disbelief. "You? *You?* A carnival? They haven't changed the definition while I've been away, have they? A carnival is still a place where people go to have fun, isn't it?"

"I believe that's their purpose."

"With all the best will in the world, Johannes, you're as much fun as a leper at an orgy."

"Why are all your similes sexual? That always irritated me."

"You've answered your own question. A carnival? What possessed you to buy a carnival?"

"I didn't buy it. I've just borrowed it. For a year—less now. It's part of a wager."

"A wager. Will wonders never cease?" The thing shook its head. "You don't bet, you're no fun. This doesn't make any sense."

"The wager is—"

"No, don't tell me. Let me work it out. I've had little enough to amuse me all this time. The highlight was the spider races. I used to eat the losers. Then I'd eat the winner so he wouldn't get cocky. Anyway, let me see if my brain still works." It paused, deep in thought. "You'd never have made a wager unless it was for something that you wanted incredibly badly from somebody who would never willingly part from it. So whoever this other party is must be the one who can't turn down a pleasing bet. They must have made the terms—you'd never have suggested something involving a carnival. That suggests somebody with a sense of irony—that word again—or at least a sense of petty sadism. Who does that remind me of?"

It didn't need to think for long.

"Oh, Johannes," it moaned in exasperation. "You utter idiot. This is to get your soul back, isn't it? Don't you know anything? You can't beat him. He only bets on certainties."

"So people keep telling me," replied Cabal, growing exasperated himself. "Well, I say 'people,' but that's a fairly loose term. I need my soul back. That's not open to negotiation. I took the only deal he would offer. Take it or leave it. I took it. Perhaps he can't be beaten. I don't know, nor shall I until I give this the best I can. And if I fail, it won't be through lack of will or defeatism setting in. I'll be able to look Satan in the eye and say, 'I did my best, and it came pretty close. And while you just sat down here on your fat, sulphuric arse, I stretched for the impossible, so don't imagine for a moment that this is your victory, you smug, infernal bastard.' " He stopped, breathing heavily.

"Well," said the thing, "I'm glad you've got your gracious loser's speech all worked out in advance, because you're going to need it. What exactly are you supposed to be doing with a carnival anyway?"

"It's one of the diabolical carnivals, like the Dark Carnival or the Carnival of Demons."

"Does this one start with 'D,' too?"

"The Carnival of Discord. It was mothballed, apparently for reasons of internal politics. Can you believe it? One would have thought immortal beings would have better things to do."

"Pointless and time-consuming. Seems perfect for passing the millennia. Carry on."

"The wager is to garner a hundred souls in a year."

"A hundred." Cabal noticed something unfathomable in the thing's voice. "A hundred souls."

"I know. It's a tall order."

Cabal thought he heard the thing sigh.

"So why are you here? Why aren't you tearing up and down the highways and byways relieving the great unwashed of their souls for, I assume, the usual beads and mirrors?" it said.

"I . . . don't actually *have* a working carnival, per se. I've got a lot of equipment in a fairly poor state of repair, and the wherewithal to fix it up and provide staff."

"Sounds lovely. Don't forget to send me a Kewpie doll."

"A what?"

"A Kewpie doll. A cheap doll that you can give away on the concessions as a prize."

"Concessions to what?"

The thing shook its head slowly. "You're going to have to rewrite your loser's speech, Johannes. Get rid of the bit about coming pretty close. You haven't the faintest idea what you're doing."

"I know," Cabal accepted. "That's why I need you. You know what goes on in places like that. I don't. I need your expertise."

"Expertise? I never worked on anything like that."

"But you visited some. I remember that you visited some."

The thing heard the note of desperation in Cabal's voice. Somewhere deep within itself, something human softened just a little. "Well, yes, I went to carnivals whenever I could. Used to hang around them. Even considered joining one. Perhaps I should've. I wouldn't be here now."

Cabal shrugged. "For all the good it does, I'm sorry I left you. I thought you were dead. Or worse."

"Right on both counts," said the thing bitterly. "I still don't see why you've come to me, though. So I visited a carnival or two. It hardly makes me an expert. There must be people who can be hired to do this, who actually have some real experience?"

"I don't think that degree of knowledge will be necessary. In many respects the carnival will run itself. It has few overheads—no wages, and the prizes, food, and drinks are provided. We don't even have to worry about taxes, as the place will cease to exist before the end of the next tax year, and—despite their reputation for tenacity—I doubt even tax collectors will descend into the Infernal Pit just to collect the revenue. What I really need is somebody who understands people. What they want when they come to a carnival. Besides, finding somebody with a better curriculum vitae might well founder on the vexed 'Incidentally, the carnival's sponsored by Satan, and we're far more interested in stealing a hundred souls than in making money' issue."

The thing grunted in amusement. "I take your point." It crouched in silence for some moments, before raising its head to look Cabal in the eye. "Do you really think you can undo"—it gestured hopelessly at itself—"this?"

Cabal found he couldn't lie. Not this time. "I don't know. But you have my solemn word I'll try. I think I have an insight into your *condition* that has only recently been vouchsafed to me. I'll try. I'm sorry. That's all I can promise."

The thing looked closely at him and, after a very long moment, smiled. A rapacious smile to be sure, but one Cabal knew was honest. Even so, the sight of those yellow-white teeth and the thought of what flesh they'd torn made him uncomfortable.

"That's about the only thing I ever admired about you, Johannes. You're a man of your word. Or at least you used to be. I'll take the risk that you still are, soul or no. Very well, I'll run your carnival for you. Decide what's fun, lose what's not. That's what you want, yes?"

"Yes, exactly." Cabal couldn't keep the relief out of his voice. "I need somebody to attend to the day-to-day . . ." The thing looked hard at him. "I'm speaking figuratively, of course. The diurnal?—nocturnal?— nocturnal running of the carnival. While I attend to the winning of this ludicrous wager. Are you agreeable?"

"Not as a rule, but, yes, you know me, anything for a laugh."

"Excellent. There just remains one thing. The matter of my personal safety."

The thing's eyebrows raised in all innocence. "Why, Johannes. Do you really think I'd hurt you?"

"Yes," replied Cabal levelly. "Sitting down there in the darkness for eight years . . ."

"And thirty-seven days."

". . . may have made you feel uncharitable towards me. You may have thought I was somehow responsible for what happened. To you."

"Oh, heaven forfend that I have such unpleasant thoughts. Just because I was out here in the first place at your insistent request, went down here in the lead because I was 'more sure-footed,' was attacked by something thoroughly unpleasant thanks to your incompetence at keeping up with whether the clocks had gone forward or not, and then, in my moment of need, was abandoned. Just because of all this, you think I might have some sort of grudge against you? Dear me. How unkind. I'm quite hurt."

"Spare me your mordancy. I need your assurance. Otherwise, I'll just close this door and find another partner. What do you say?"

The thing looked at him with an air of quiet amusement that Cabal didn't like at all. "What do I say? Let me put it this way."

The thing blurred. Cabal had a momentary impression of something dark shifting through the light beam far too fast for his eye to register, and suddenly he was on his back with the thing on top of him, his arms pinned to the ground. It had travelled up the twenty feet of steep steps in the pause between exhalation and inhalation. Cabal gulped. He had an awful feeling that might be the last time he might ever gulp, so he did it again in an attempt to calm himself.

"That," said the thing, nose to nose with him, "is what I say. I could have killed you at any moment since you opened the door. I could have torn your head off and sucked your kicking corpse dry.

"But, despite everything, I'm a reasonable man. I waited to hear why you'd come back after such a long time, when anybody else, even if they were as terrified as you obviously were, would at least have come back at daybreak, when they knew they'd be safe. Would have at least made the effort, even if they knew it was probably hopeless.

"Well, I've listened to your deal. A deal. You arrogant little shit. If you had any way of reversing this, you should have come back here to offer it to me with no strings attached. There's only one thing preventing me from killing you right now, and next time it won't. Believe me." It leapt easily to its feet and stepped away. "You have your deal. But that's all you've got. I run this carnival for you, you reverse what happened to me, I walk away."

Cabal climbed to his feet more slowly. "I thought your clothes would probably be in poor condition by now," he said, studiously pretending that nothing had happened. "Here are some new ones." He opened the carpetbag and unrolled a suit and shirt from it. The thing took them, looked critically at the cut, sighed, and started to get dressed. "I've also got some toiletries. A comb and brush and some shaving kit." A thought occurred to him. "You do cast a reflection, don't you?"

The thing, now beginning to look more human, glanced at him with disgust. "How should I know? Give that here." He examined himself in the mirror. "Seems to work perfectly well. Another old legend bites the dust. Good grief, I've hardly aged. Handsome dog. Still look terrible, though. Ill." He looked meaningfully at Cabal. "I need feeding."

Cabal backed away. "You said you wouldn't hurt me."

The thing looked at him and smiled slightly. "I said I wouldn't kill you. You're not going to die."

"If you infect me, I won't be able to help you!" said Cabal urgently.

"It doesn't work like that. None of the children changed, remember? It has to be a reciprocal thing. It's the blood mingling that spreads the infection. I just wish I'd thought of that before I tried eating Sophia." Cabal was looking for the lichgate and was obviously planning to run. The thing stopped following him and spread his hands. "Look, what's bothering you? It's the homoerotic aspect, isn't it?"

Cabal was running. "Well, don't flatter yourself," shouted the thing after him. He had been heterosexual before his unfortunate change in circumstances, and now he had doubts that he was even that. "It's just a transfusion, for crying out loud." Cabal had almost reached the gates. "You always were such a nuisance," said the thing to himself, and blurred into motion.

It took slightly longer to get back to the train than it had to get to the Grimpen Burial Ground, as they'd only been able to travel at night. Eventually, the low hills gave way to the marshlands, and soon they were close to the disused rail spur. Even at a distance, they could see the long ridge rising above the surrounding land, and the flare of work lights in the middle of the obviously thinned copse of trees. As they got closer still, Cabal pointed out the train itself, its dark bulk looming ominously along the length of the earthwork.

As he spoke, he absent-mindedly placed his hand on the twin puncture wounds over his jugular vein. He had been relieved to discover that he was still able to go around in the sun with only his hat and dark glasses for protection, rather than the coffin lined with the soil of his homeland that he had feared. Even the detail of the coffin had turned out to be an old wives' tale; Cabal's travelling companion had been happy to sleep anywhere during the day, just so long as no ray of sunlight had been able to touch him.

As they got closer still, they started to make out more details. The trees blocking the train's access to the main line had been chopped down and the stumps torn up. Many of the other trees in the copse had also been felled. The woodpile on the train looked impressively high. The logs would be green and damp, but at least they would fuel the train until it could get better supplied. Great naphtha torches had been thrust into the chippings of the rail bed, flaring into the night sky. Here and there, figures worked diligently and without pause. Bones had created some extra personnel of his own volition. Cabal wasn't sure if that was good or bad at first, but, given the scale of the work, it couldn't possibly have been done in time if Bones had only had the dubious services of Denzil and Dennis to call upon. Bones had done the right thing, he concluded.

"My God," he heard his companion sigh when he saw the locomotive close up, and he was secretly pleased. Bones and his workers had done a magnificent job. The demoniacal locomotive had been carefully cleaned and repainted. The black was so intense that it was hard to say where the train stopped and the night sky started. A thin red line, the colour of venous blood, ran along the side of the boiler and detailed the cowcatcher and smokestack, the only concessions to colour. But it was the first car after the fuel tender that caught the eye. Painted in reds and yellows against a blue-and-black background, the name of the carnival curved and twisted in extravagant fairground curlicues, ornate yet instantly readable. His companion stopped and laughed.

"You were very confident, Johannes," he said.

"I knew if I couldn't get your help it was a hopeless case. Alternatively, you'd kill me. Either way, it couldn't do any harm to anticipate."

Bones spotted them and stepped down to the edge of the track. "Hi, boss! How do you like her?" He gestured up at the board. " 'The World Renowned Cabal Bros. Carnival,' just like you asked."

"Excellent work, Mr. Bones. I knew I could rely on you. Incidentally, I'd like to introduce . . ."

His companion stepped forward, smiling, and held out his hand to Bones. "Horst Cabal. Delighted to meet you."

Chapter 4

 IN WHICH CABAL APPLIES HIMSELF
WITH MIXED RESULTS

Johannes Cabal sat at his desk and watched his blotter rock. Across from
him, a large clothes chest lay in the angle of the wall. It was long and exactly the sort of furniture that makes avuncular uncles—the worst kind—
point and say, laughing, "Ey up! Have you got a body in there?"

Of course he did. Inside lay the body of his brother, Horst, on a layer
of blankets, cold as clay but irritatingly handsome with it. Horst's effort-
less charisma had always galled Cabal deeply, and the discovery that he
even made a fetching cadaver once he'd had a chance to clean himself up
a bit was almost an insult.

Cabal widened his eyes, blinked a little, coldly exterminated an infant
yawn at the back of his throat. The sun was almost down, he realised.
Standing, he went to the window. The countryside slid by, glowing red beneath a clouded sky. They were leaving the flat marshlands and starting
to climb into the low hills to the north. He watched the sunset for a
minute longer, searching for what he'd once found beautiful in them.
Then, turning, he returned to the desk. Halfway there, he paused to listen to the locomotive's whistle.

The black train surged into a darkening horizon. Now and then, its steam whistle screamed, a lost and lonely sound with an undertone of shuddering horror and menace like Grendel calling for his mother. Up front, on the cavernous footplate of the locomotive, Dennis and Denzil took turns pulling on the whistle cord. They had been equipped with overalls and nice Casey Jones hats and looked the best they had ever looked. Now Denzil watched with an authoritarian eye as Dennis picked up logs and lobbed them into the firebox. It was going well, Denzil thought in the detached way of the fairly dead. It was pretty close to the way he'd thought before Cabal had murdered him, so the adjustment had been easy. He was secretly glad that he didn't have to eat human brains. Steak and kidney pudding made him queasy enough. Admittedly, he liked his meat cooked fairly rare now, but that was probably more the effect of the exalted circles he was moving in. Eventually, he was sure, he'd be on steak tartare, which was pretty damned sophisticated and no mistake. He sniffed the air. Despite the occasional strand of wood smoke from the green logs, the air was pure and cool. Yet he could distinctly smell cooking. It was probably all this thought of food. Then he noticed that he was leaning directly against the side of the firebox and his left forearm was probably closer to "well done" than was normal for a forearm. If it had been a steak, he would have been inclined to send it back to the chef with some harsh comments. As it was, Denzil said his first word since his change of lifestyle. It wasn't a nice word.

Behind the locomotive were carriages and boxcars full of equipment, flats, things that would pass for people in a bad light, and things of more reliable description. Horst had worked indefatigably through the nights of the last eight days, studying what they had, throwing bits of it away, creating anew, drawing up plans, rotas, schedules. During the days, Cabal had implemented them. Sometimes he might make changes to the commission of a task, but never to its purpose. He had to trust Horst implicitly. At first, mindful of squandering away the ball of Satan's blood resting down in Hell, he'd asked why some decisions had been made the way they had. Why that form of sideshow barker, why this kind of concession, why that sideshow over this? "Well, look at them," Horst had said, lifting up two signs, one from the "accepted" pile and the other from the "firewood" stack. Cabal looked. One was for *Marko the Moulting Man*, the other for *Layla the Latex Lady*.

"They both sound ridiculous beyond words. No, I have no idea why anybody would want to see either."

"You're dead right about one of them. Marko here"—Horst had hefted the sign—"is a man with hair that falls out. It doesn't fall out to order, or leave interesting patterns, or grow back on command. Marko's only abilities are to bung up plug holes and make himself unpopular in furniture showrooms." The sign was thrown back in with the firewood. "Layla, on the other hand, is . . . well . . ." He had looked closely at his brother and decided he was wasting his time. "People just like that sort of thing. Trust me."

And Cabal had to. Horst knew what people liked, he always had. He had cut a swathe through the social circuses of school, then university, and then adult life. Men admired him, women adored him, and his younger brother had loathed him. Loathed him for his easy manner, for his extended circle of friends and the utterly, utterly loathsome way that the world behaved as if it really did owe Horst Cabal a living. He changed jobs, even careers, frequently, and it always worked out. His parents made a lot of Horst, who never had to fear that their new son would supplant him in their affections. No chance of that, thought Cabal bitterly. He'd had to work hard for their attention.

"Penny for your thoughts," said a voice behind him. Cabal turned to find Horst sitting up in his box. The sun had gone down while he had been thinking.

"I was just remembering how much I used to hate you," he said, and walked back to the desk.

"Honesty. I like that. Usually. I knew you resented me, but hated? Oh, come on, Johannes. That's strong."

"Water under the bridge, I believe. May we attend to the matter in hand?" He unfolded a map and indicated a town on it. "Merton

Pembersley New Town, our first port of call. We reach there just before dawn. I need to be sure that we can deploy effectively."

Horst yawned, displaying exaggerated eye-teeth.

"We've been through this a thousand times before."

"Twelve."

"Whatever. Yes, we can set up in six hours and be ready for sundown easily." He grinned broadly. "The poor rubes won't know what hit them."

On the shelf, the hourglass dribbled sand into the lower bulb. The rolling motion of the train never perturbed the flow so much as an iota.

*T*he stationmaster looked hard at the train and then harder at Cabal.

"You can't park that there," he said finally, and started to walk back to his office. Cabal walked quickly after him.

"Well, we have to stop somewhere. We've got a carnival to set up," he said, and smiled. The stationmaster stopped, saw his expression, and shied away.

"Look, mate, you have to have permissions. You can't just bung your train up somebody else's siding and expect to get away with it."

"Why not? Nobody else is using it."

"Aaaah, but they *might*."

Cabal knew then that he was dealing with the kind of official that he always lost his temper with. He lost his temper.

"Don't be ridiculous. The grass on that spur is hip-deep. It hasn't seen a train in years. If you want some sort of, I don't know, berthing fee or something, say so, but kindly stop being so damnably obtuse."

"Berthing fees? Are you trying to bribe me?" cried the stationmaster in a manner just a little too melodramatic to be insincere. "I've worked for the company man and boy for nigh on thirty years. If you think you can buy off that sort of loyalty for some dirty little bribe, you've got another thing coming!" He stormed into his office. Cabal followed him.

"How about a dirty *big* bribe, then?" he asked experimentally.

"I, sir, am a loyal employee of the company. Take your offensive offers of baksheesh and get out of here! And take that bloody train with you!"

Cabal could tell that subtle diplomacy wasn't working. The two men glared at each other for a moment, until the stationmaster decided he could do his in comfort and sank into his big leather swivel chair. As he did so, his eyes flickered to a drawer he'd left open in his desk. Cabal saw his expression become momentarily stricken as he quickly slammed the drawer shut. Not quite quickly enough to stop Cabal getting an idea what was in there, though. He drew his smoked-glass spectacles down far enough to let the stationmaster know that he was looking narrowly at him, slid them back into place, turned, and left.

Back at the train, Bones sat waiting on the caboose step.

"Is that guy goin' be the kind of trouble he looks, chief?" he asked as Cabal approached, stepping easily over the disused railway tracks concealed in the long grass. "You want me and some of the boys maybe pay him a visit, if you know what I mean?"

Cabal looked back at the station over his shoulder as he pulled out his black kid gloves and drew them on. "I really don't think that will be necessary, Mr. Bones. I'm sure we can come to some sort of arrangement. The stationmaster has some . . . *interesting* magazines in his desk. I think he has an itch that he can't really scratch."

Bones rested a bony elbow on a bony knee and placed his bony chin in the bony palm. He hated it when the boss thought he was being clever. "What kind of magazines? *Dermatology Today* or somethin'?" he asked blandly.

"Not that kind of itch. Get Layla and send her over. And make sure she's wearing an overcoat."

"Layla? Rubber girl Layla? For why, boss?"

"She's going to make him an offer he really can't refuse," replied Cabal with a smile so malevolent that Bones was glad he had no hair to stand on end. "Meanwhile," Cabal continued, "start to unload. We'll use that meadow over there to set up on."

"You got permission?"

"I don't need permission." Again, the smile. "If anybody complains, send them to me."

Somebody did complain: a florid farmer in his fifties who stormed up the steps and into Cabal's office with some boringly incoherent speech about agriculture and laws of the land. Cabal listened to him attentively, or, more accurately, he *watched* him attentively; the farmer had an interesting supra-orbital ridge of a type that wasn't common in humans. Quite unconsciously, Cabal started making a sketch of it while the farmer stormed. When the farmer saw the pencil moving, his fury went up a notch, and he demanded to know what Cabal was scribbling.

"The percentage deal for allowing us to use your land," said Cabal. "I was thinking of twenty-five per cent."

"Gross or net?" asked the farmer suspiciously.

"Net."

"Thirty per cent."

"Let's skip the finagling. Twenty-seven."

"Thirty," said the farmer, growing enthusiastic.

"But this is fallow land, you said so yourself. You're not even using it." The farmer creased his eyes and looked firm. Cabal shrugged in good-natured defeat. "I can see I'm not going to be able to shift you on this. Very well, thirty per cent it is." He leaned over the table and shook hands with the farmer, who settled himself down into the chair with complacent smugness. Cabal unlocked a drawer in his desk and drew out a densely written contract. "I'm afraid I'll need your signature. It's all right," he said, seeing the farmer's expression. "The tax man will never know about our little arrangement. The form's just for my own records and head office." The farmer took the piece of parchment and examined it. Cabal affected disinterest but was glad that Arthur Trubshaw had discovered the illegible delights of four-point bold italic copperplate.

He himself had been over the contracts with a jeweller's loupe and was satisfied that the signatory did not need to know precisely what he was signing to make it binding. This had led him to consider more . . . *direct* methods of getting the forms signed, but he had discarded such schemes as both inelegant and dangerous. The last thing he needed was to spend this vital, unrepeatable year being pursued from pillar to post by the forces of justice and order and perhaps even the police. No, he would play Satan's game by the rules, although he wouldn't be above bending them slightly if the situation, as now, allowed.

"What's this bit, 'To be filled in by the damnee'?" The farmer looked suspiciously at Cabal again. "Damnee? What's one of them, eh?"

"Just some anachronistic legal term. Probably left over from medieval common law. Drink?" He stepped towards the tantalus.

"Aye, whisky and water. Don't drown it," said the farmer as he signed. Cabal handed over the drink, took the form, and locked it safely away in the desk again.

One down, ninety-nine to go, he thought.

The carnival limbered up rapidly; without the human need for frequent tea and smoke breaks, things went quickly. Tents and temporary wooden buildings grew across the meadow like giant mushrooms—the type that come with guide ropes and gaudy billboards designed to excite and entice.

Through the feverish activity walked Cabal with Bones at his elbow. None of it made much sense to him, but, nevertheless, he had slavishly followed the ground plan drawn up by Horst, who seemed pretty sure he knew the way to go. "It's a first site. We'll make mistakes. We'll learn from them." Horst was full of galling truisms, thought Cabal.

They arrived at the steam calliope. It was a huge and ornate piece of machinery that had a car all to itself when they were travelling. Great organ pipes thrust out of the top like Baroque mortars rising from the curling confusion of brightly painted wood. Across the front was a representation of a bandstand filled with gaudy automata holding almost accurate little model instruments. At the front stood a bandmaster with a baton. He was more heavily articulated than the band members and was currently caught in the midst of a cheerful wink to the audience. At least, guessed Cabal, it might have been intended as a cheerful wink, but it looked more like a knowing leer to him. A small mob of riggers were around the back, arguing.

"What seems to be the problem?" asked Cabal. "Sunset's in less than an hour. This thing must be running by then."

One of the riggers came to him, wringing his cloth cap. "We can't get the music loaded up," he admitted, shamefaced. "It just don't want to seem to go. And even if we manage to, *they* still won't let us draw steam from the engine."

"Who won't?" asked Cabal. The rigger pointed at the great locomotive. Dennis and Denzil were leaning out of the cab and grinning maniacally, as if it were their job to be nuisances. Denzil waved cheerfully, and Cabal noticed that bits of his left forearm were coming off. He'd have to do something about that, or else the fool would scare the customers. *Rubes*, he corrected himself.

Cabal walked over and looked up at them with crossed arms. "What do you two think you're playing at?" Denzil stopped waving and grinning. Dennis didn't until he was elbowed with enough force to break a rib. Possibly two. He toppled out of sight, and there was the sound of a head hitting iron sheeting with a loud crack. Dennis said *his* first word since dying. This wasn't a nice one, either. Cabal pointed at Denzil's char-grilled arm. "You're a disgrace. Look at the state you're in." Denzil hid the offending limb behind his back and looked misty, his lower lip wobbling. Cabal went very, very pale. "Don't you dare get emotional with me! Get down here this instant."

Denzil climbed down and stood before him, his head hanging. Cabal snapped his fingers: a nasty, perfunctory sound through the leather of his gloves. "Show me." Denzil slowly lifted his arm. Cabal studied it closely, doffing a glove and replacing it with a surgical one. Bones watched the swap with unconcealed disbelief.

"Why're you carryin' rubber gloves, boss?"

Cabal looked levelly at him. Then he thrust his finger into Denzil's forearm up to the second joint. The flesh squelched out of the way like unset blancmange. Denzil made a horrible, shrill, shrieking intake of breath that Cabal ignored. "That's why." He drew the glove off with a snap that sent beads of liquescent meat flying off in most directions except over Cabal. He threw it to a rigger, who caught it without thinking. "Get rid of that, there's a good chap." Cabal turned back to Denzil.

"I should have left you face-down on the road, you blubbering fool. You were a waste of protein when you were alive, and now you're dead you're denying some tree sustenance." He slapped the offending arm with the back of his hand and suddenly remembered he'd just that minute removed his rubber glove. He wiped the muck off on Denzil's overalls. "This damage is irreparable. D'you understand that? There's nothing I can do about it. It's either going to have to come off or . . . or . . ." He considered carefully. "I can render it down, seal the stump, and attempt to animate the bones. Interesting problem. Report to my office at nine-thirty tomorrow. That's all." He noticed the riggers and recalled why he'd come over there in the first place. "And give the riggers every assistance in connecting the steam calliope with the engine's boiler. Understand?"

A caw made Cabal look up. The crow had landed on the tallest organ pipe of the calliope and was looking down on him with an unwarranted air of superiority. "And you," said Cabal, pointing at it. "If you do anything down one of those pipes, I will personally wring your neck. Understand?"

The crow moved its head in a very human "Oh, heck, you never let me have any fun" sort of way and flew down to settle on a tent peg.

Cabal had turned on his heel to walk away when he heard a sound that made him turn back. A bloodied tatterdemalion of a figure was leaning out of the train's cab. With clumsy fingers it tried to get its scalp to stay in place, but this kept flopping forward like the brim of a particularly unappealing novelty hat. It looked at Cabal and held its hands out, dark with congealing blood. It groaned shudderingly. With the exception of Cabal, everybody took a step back.

"All right, that's enough overacting," snapped Cabal. "You turn up at ten."

*T*he music roll still needed installing. Cabal turned his logical eye upon the mechanism. Moving quickly, he reached in, pulled a lever back that brought a cross-arm with it, flipped up two side guards, took the music roll from one of the fascinated riggers, studied the arrows printed on it for a moment, flipped it over, drew off some loose sheet, thrust it into an unimportant-looking slot, aligned sprocket holes with teeth, slapped the bulk of the roll into a recess, held it in place while he closed the guards with his free hand, and finally pushed the lever home.

"I fail to see the difficulty. I trust you memorised all that."

The rigger smiled uncertainly. Cabal stood up and worked a cramp out of his shoulder. "Do we have steam pressure yet?" Bones rapped a dial with one knuckle, squinted at the flickering needle, and gave the thumbs-up. Cabal opened a valve and engaged the clutch.

For a moment the calliope did nothing but make unsettled huffing and clicking noises as the steam ran throughout its plumbing. A governor started to rotate slowly as the paper music was drawn with painful slowness into the reader. The punched holes started to process by, and a moment later a pipe gave a doleful hoot. The bass drum thumped. Some other pipes blew in ragged succession, to be punctuated by the bass drum again, a strike of a triangle, and the most dolorous paradiddle on the snare drum. The wooden bandleader finished winking with the utmost difficulty and twisted back to face the automaton band in a strange movement that suggested he was an avant-garde dancer with a spinal injury.

"Look and learn," said Cabal to the riggers. "Open the valve first." He pointed. "Wait till that gets up to speed"—he pointed at the governor—"and *then* engage the clutch." He tapped the lever. "This slow start-up sounds dreadful."

The balls on the tips of the governor arms were barely visible now as the assembly spun faster and faster, a glittering band of ghostly brass. Slowly, the ring widened and rose as the governor reached its operating speed. Then a thin wisp of steam started to expel from the collar, and Cabal turned his attention to the music.

He didn't know much about music, but he knew what he liked. The clear corollary was that he also knew what he didn't like, but this, it turned out, was untrue. The music was a curious piece in waltz time, full of odd cadences and deliberate discords. Cabal watched the bandmaster automaton wave its baton in approximate time and leer over its shoulder once every twenty-one and a bit bars while he tried to make up his mind. He picked up the tube in which the paper roll had been stored and read the label. *"Manège"* par J. Lasry. He put it down again, his mind still uncertain.

A sticky-fingered tugging at his coat broke him out of the reverie. He looked down to see two small boys, perhaps eight or nine years old. "What do you want?" he asked curtly.

"When do the rides an' stuff start goin', mister?" asked the snottier of the two, wiping his nose on his sleeve for punctuation.

Cabal looked over towards the gate. The fences had been up for hours. He looked back down at the boys.

"How did you get in?"

The less snotty produced a seriously crumpled piece of card and showed it to him. "We got commmply-mennary tickets."

"I doubt that," replied Cabal, taking the card between finger and thumb. He straightened it out a little and read, "Cabal Bros. Carnival of Wonders! Complimentary Ticket. Admit One. Valid One Night Only."

"I got one, too," said the nasal boy, and offered Cabal a ticket that not only was crumpled but also appeared to be seeping.

"That's all right," said Cabal, returning the other boy's ticket. "Might I ask who gave you these?"

" 'E did," said Snotty, and pointed past Cabal.

Cabal turned slowly. "Good evening, Horst. I didn't realise that it was time for you to get up." He eyed Horst's clothes. "Where did you get those?"

"Oh, just something I asked the haberdashery to run up for me. Do you like it?" It was an extraordinary suit in imperial purples that scintillated slightly under the electric lights. The frock coat was cut long over a delicately embroidered waistcoat in silver, red, and black. Horst tipped the dark-purple top hat for effect, tucking a silver-headed cane under his free arm.

"Oh, yes," said Cabal without enthusiasm. "You certainly look the part."

"Get along, boys," said Horst to the children. "Sundown's when it all starts with *this* carnival." He favoured Cabal with a sidelong glance as he said it. The boys ran off to the main body of the fairground, where rides were beginning to come to life and barkers were beginning to attract small straggly crowds in front of the exhibit tents. Horst watched them go with a smile before looking at Cabal.

"You certainly *don't* look the part. Accountant, yes. Carnival proprietor and showman, no. I'd see the haberdashery tomorrow if I were you."

"You're not me," said Cabal. "You run things up front, I run them from behind the scenes. That was the deal."

"Yes," admitted Horst. "That was the deal." He smiled a smile that Cabal had seen make spiders run for cover.

"Oh, no. Oh, no. Let me pre-empt any amusing little surprise you might have for me with the words 'No, not in a thousand years.' "

"We miscalculated the number of sideshows we've created."

"How so?"

"We seem to have a sideshow/barker disparity that needs addressing."

"Barkers. The ones who stand in front of the shows and shout about how wonderful they are, yes?"

Horst nodded, smiling quietly. "Yes."

Cabal didn't like the way this was going. "Too many barkers?" he ventured, with rare optimism.

Horst's smile broadened. Cabal's frown deepened.

"No. No. No. If you have trouble with any of these terms, you can consult with me in my office."

"You don't want to get your soul back, then?" asked Horst with an appearance of innocence that might have been applied by grease gun.

Cabal bit his lip. "It's only one sideshow."

"But it might be *the* one. You never know. We don't have that many, after all."

Cabal made a show of thinking it over, but he knew Horst was right. There really was no choice. "Very well. For tonight only."

" 'For tonight only.' " Horst held his hands up to an imaginary sign. " 'Thrown out of the best universities, excommunicated from all the most popular religions and many of the obscure ones, fresh from his recent engagement in Hell, we present Johannes Cabal, Necromancer!' Toot toot toot!" He mimed blowing trumpets.

"You're a constant font of hilarity, aren't you?" said Cabal, unsmiling. "And I'll have you know that I was never, ever thrown out of any of my universities. I always left of my own accord."

"And always in the early hours of the morning," added Horst. "Look, Johannes. Despite everything, I've always sort of liked you. Back in the days before you abdicated from the human race, your heart was usually more or less in the right place. This will be a doddle. The House of Medical Monstrosity has been set aside for you. You know about the human body—how it works, how it doesn't work, how, if it isn't working, you can get it sort of ticking over again. Sort of." He laughed, and Cabal knew he was thinking of Dennis and Denzil. Cabal bridled: that damn test batch was going down the plug hole the instant he managed to develop something better. "Anyway, it's something you have an enthusiasm for. Believe me, talking about something that excites you will excite others. It communicates."

"It communicates?" echoed Cabal. He didn't believe that for a second. Far too many boring people had cornered him in his youth who were fascinated by things very boring indeed. Their enthusiasm had not "communicated" in the slightest.

Horst's expression of uncertainty showed he wasn't so sure of the principle when it involved his brother. "I'll draw up some notes for you," he said in a conciliatory tone.

"𝔄hem. 'Roll up, roll up. Prepare to be shuddered to the very core of your being. Prepare to witness the most horrible tricks Mother Nature has played upon humanity. Prepare to enter the House of Medical Monstrosity.' " Cabal paused from his notes and looked up. He had an audience of precisely one, a small girl who was sticking her tongue out so hard at him it might actually be hurting slightly. Cabal could only hope. He drew a deep breath and continued.

" 'Within the walls of horror behind me lie the most terrible mutations, the most grotesque freaks, the most fearful occupational injuries. See.' " He belatedly realised he'd been missing the exclamation marks. " 'See! The man with the exposed intestine. See! Alicia and Zenia, the two-headed girl. See!' " He couldn't understand why he had to keep repeating "See!" He couldn't imagine the average rube wanting to touch, smell, or taste the show's stars. Not the *average* rube, anyway. " 'See! Mr. Bones, the Living Skeleton.' " It had been very good of Bones to make up the numbers. In fact, he had leapt at the chance to lounge around in a thong all evening.

Cabal looked up. There was still only the small girl. She was still sticking her tongue out. Her mother bustled over.

"There you are! I've been looking all over! And what have I told you about pulling faces? Your face will stick like that if the wind changes."

"Certain surgical techniques would do the trick, too," observed Cabal.

The woman looked up at him with an habitual animosity. "And what do you do?" she asked. "You look like a funeral director."

Despite his black clothes, Cabal knew he looked nothing like a funeral director. He could never have managed the sanctimonious expression if he'd had a month to practice. "Madam," he said. "Or may I call you 'florid termagant'?"

"Ooo la!" she said, delightfully outraged. She patted her resinous perm. "I'm a married woman."

"Forgive me. May I say, he's a very lucky man," lied Cabal. His face moved into something that, by strict dictionary definition, was a smile. The girl whimpered and tried to hide in her mother's skirts. "Madam, the exhibition behind me is the House of Medical Monstrosity. See!" He found his place in his notes, drew breath, and let it out again. He put the notes away.

"Madam," he started again, "behind me is a freakshow. An exhibit of the unfortunate, the despised, and the outcast. An exhibit where all such are drawn together to give you, a normal member of the general public, a chance to jeer and laugh at those less fortunate than you. Imagine! You may be unhappy about the shape of your nose, the line of your jaw, the way your eyes stick out. But all this fades into insignificance when you see a man whose spine grows out of the top of his head. Unsightly facial hair? We have a bearded woman! Weight problem? We have from one end of the spectrum to the other: a living skeleton, and somebody so astoundingly, grotesquely fat that we haven't actually been able to discern his or her sex. If you have any feelings of inadequacy whatsoever, then here is the place to come, to point and say, 'There, but for the grace of God, go I!' "

A crowd was growing. A young woman nervously held up her hand. "I . . . I . . . I have freckles."

Cabal gestured fiercely over his shoulder with his thumb. "We have the Dalmatian Boy. Next?"

A man called, "I have a bit of an overbite."

"Then gaze in delighted wonder upon the Human Shark. Next!"

"My nose is a little too pert," said an almost stereotypical blond woman on the arm of a wealthy man.

"It can't be as pert as Simone Sans-Nez the Noseless Girl's. Next!"

"I'm ginger," called a teenage boy.

"So you are. Yes, my friends! The House of Medical Monstrosity! Slake your thirst for abomination and abnormality! Feast your eyes on the people who really are worse off than yourselves! Draw self-esteem from their abasement!" There were a lot of people in front of him now, but nobody wanted to be the first to buy a ticket. He needed a sheep to lead the flock. He flicked his gaze quickly over the rapturous, vacant faces until he saw one whose gaze was locked on one of the lurid paintings that decorated the front of the sideshow. Cabal glanced quickly at them, following the man's line of sight. Then, with quiet confidence, he looked back out into the crowd in no particular direction. It was a complete coincidence that his eyes met the man's as he said, "And, for the first person to buy a ticket, the chance to have your photograph taken with Layla, the luscious, lissom, lithely Latex Lady."

"I'll buy a ticket!" shouted the man unnecessarily loudly, the sweat showing on his lip. "Me!"

Cabal was beginning to realise that this year could well turn out to be an interesting experiment into behavioural psychology. He doubted Marko the Moulting Man would have turned the trick.

"You, sir! You're a very lucky man! Here you go! Ticket number one!" The spiel was beginning to come along as well. You just had to give the poor fools the impression that you were doing them a favour and they ate from your hand. The money was handed over, and the small piece of pasteboard exchanged. The man was almost feverish with excitement. Cabal wondered what he would give in exchange for something more than a photograph. He began to think that he'd let the stationmaster off very lightly indeed. He addressed the crowd.

"But don't be disappointed! Throughout the evening, we'll be offering other spot prizes based on your ticket number, so . . . so . . ." There was only one thing left to say. "Roll up! Roll up! Come one! Come all! Tell your friends that you were brave enough, that you were bold enough, to enter the House of Medical Monstrosity!"

And so, its welcoming smile widening until the fangs showed, the carnival began its first night.

Chapter 5

IN WHICH CABAL PLAYS WITH DOLLS AND
HORST BROADENS HIS VOCABULARY

Fairs and carnivals are not, by nature, profound experiences. They are there to amuse and distract, to draw the citizens from their grey workaday lives into something that has a flavour of the extraordinary. The lights dazzle, the sideshows amaze, the rides excite, the stalls frustrate, but all pleasantly. It is a jolly pickpocket and a charismatic confidence trickster. The rubes . . . the suckers . . . the *customers* know full well that their wallets and purses are slowly deflating every second that they walk upon the fairground, but the customers . . . the suckers . . . the *rubes* would have it no other way. They do not mind being taken for a ride, as long as the ride is fun. This is the nature of fairs and carnivals.

The Cabal Bros. Carnival was something special, though. Something unusual. Something different. Whereas a normal carnival is a shallow, ephemeral experience intended to take average persons out of the mundane world and fool them—for as long as they are prepared to be fooled—into believing that fun really does travel the highways and byways as a bolus of giggles and glee, the Cabal Carnival wore that belief as a mask. It was, however, merely a facsimile of a façade. Behind the wide, welcoming smile was a mantrap baited with desires and delight, pleasures and popcorn, hedonism and hot dogs of dubious content. Satan, who was after all something of an authority in matters of temptation, was quite right when he had said that the carnival lowered the defences of those who walked through its gate. Everybody comes to the fair to have a good time in the full expectation of being ripped off at some point. All that was different here was the scale of the loss.

But all this is theory. Examples are more salutary.

"**W**e're here to have fun." It was said in a tone that indicated that the alternative was a split lip.

Rachel hoped it wouldn't come to that; the last one had only just healed. "I *am* having fun," she said, and smiled. It wasn't a very convincing smile, but it showed sufficient compliance for Ted to uncurl the fist that had unconsciously formed at his side. His hands spent a lot of their time balled.

He looked around. Before them spread the carnival, a whirling chaos of sound and light and smells that promised so much. Calliope, neon, and the scent of fresh popcorn created a new world: a place of wonders and excitement and fun. Yes, its true function was to tempt to contentiousness, to blasphemy, argumentation, and murder, but you could also win coconuts.

Ted regarded it all with the sour expression of a man who expects disappointment, and usually deals with it by putting the source in the hospital. He held out his hand towards Rachel, and she took it quickly, allowing herself to be drawn through the gates and onto the fairground proper. As they walked through, they passed the farmer on whose land the carnival was set up.

He stood, thumbs hooked into his waistcoat pockets, looking very pleased with himself, smiling and nodding at everybody who paused at the gate to buy tickets as if he owned the carnival, too. In truth, he was keeping a headcount, partially to make sure that he wasn't cheated out of his rent, but mainly for the sheer pleasure of running the steadily increasing number through some simple mental arithmetic and revelling in the hefty sum that popped out starboard of the equals sign. He would doubtless have been less happy if he had known what was waiting for him in the shrouded future, at a time shortly after he left his deathbed. If he'd been under the impression that the Ministry of Agriculture was addicted to unnecessary paperwork, first contact with Arthur Trubshaw would set things in perspective.

In the wide paths that led between attractions, Ted and Rachel walked. Had a curious bystander watched them for a few minutes, he would have observed that it was not immediately obvious why the couple had come at all.

Rachel seemed to be walking through a partial version of a carnival. Most of the time she seemed guarded and anxious, and though occasionally she would suddenly react pleasurably to something that caught her eye, it would quickly fade from her face, driven out by a shadow of conditioned ambiguity. She had long since learned not to have opinions, and if she couldn't help but have one, she was careful not to express it around Ted. After all, he might disagree. The ambiguity extended to her appearance, a gallant but hopeless attempt to be pretty for Ted, and nondescript for all other men. She simply ended up being a smudge of a woman, in nice but dull clothes, in nice but dull colours. She wore too much make-up—eye-shadow and concealer—that concealed her natural prettiness, and something else, too.

Ted was also a figure of uncertain purpose. He was at a funfair, but he was not having fun. He had a girlfriend, but she was not his friend. He did not walk with her, but instead herded her like a grudging sheepdog, alert for any possible threat to his ownership. He was caught in the conflict between showing her off and the real possibility that some man might actually look. If the curious bystander had continued to watch for a moment too long, he would certainly have found himself with Ted, wide-eyed and mouth-breathing, Sunday-clothed and poorly hair-cut, standing toe-to-toe and demanding to know what the curious bystander found so fascinating about his girlfriend.

They washed between stalls, he fraught with suspicion, she with shifting apprehensions, unaware that they were objects of attention for a curious bystander.

Horst Cabal, invisible to all but the most perspicacious of cats or suspicious of dogs, watched them go by. Rendering himself imperceptible by men and animals was one of the little tricks that came with being less alive than most, along with his speed, strength, and—when need be—mesmerism. His perceptive eye and sympathetic heart, however, were all his own. He watched and he listened to their stilted conversation—his all statements, hers all prevarication—and he drew his conclusions.

He waited until they were out of sight before allowing himself to seep back into visibility, and stood quietly, an expression of speculative contemplation on his face. Then he blurred and the place was empty again.

𝔍ohannes Cabal was just finishing his first session as a sideshow barker when Horst found him. Horst sprang into being in full sight of several customers, who all performed simultaneous shocked jumps and squeals.

"My brother," Cabal explained to them. He smiled with all the warmth of a dollhouse oven. "Rather a gifted magician." He waited for the subdued and not entirely convinced crowd to dissipate before turning angrily to Horst. "What are you trying to do? It doesn't take much to scare these sheep off."

Horst passed him a bottle he had picked up in his rapid trip from there to here. Remarkably, its contents had survived the transit. "Drink this," he said, unmoved by Cabal's anger. "You need to save your voice for your next session."

Cabal took the bottle testily and swigged from it. There was a moment's pause, just long enough for Cabal's expression to change from testy to horrified revulsion. He spat the liquid violently onto the grass like a man who has got absent-minded with the concentrated nitric acid and a mouth pipette. He glared at Horst as he took off his spectacles and wiped his suddenly weeping eyes. "Disinfectant? You give me disinfectant to drink?"

Horst's surprise was replaced with mild amusement. "It's root beer, Johannes. Have you never had root beer?"

Cabal looked suspiciously at him, then at the bottle. "People drink this?"

"Yes."

"For non-medicinal reasons?"

"That's right."

Cabal shook his head in open disbelief. "They must be insane." He carefully put the bottle down, but continued to watch it from the corner of his eye, as if fearing it might force itself upon him. "So—what have you been doing?"

"Watching."

He said no more, waited for the silence to have its effect and for his brother to start almost visibly fuming, and then continued. "I think you may be in luck tonight."

Cabal's face showed a sudden light of hope that troubled Horst, but it was quickly replaced by suspicion. "I thought you didn't approve."

"I don't. I didn't say I was going to do anything to move things on. Just that you may be in luck tonight."

Cabal considered. "And . . ."

Abruptly, he was alone. He let his breath out in a deep sigh. It hardly seemed worth becoming irritated, especially as he knew that was exactly why Horst had left in such a fashion. Johannes Cabal regarded the bottle of root beer and decided he would rather be somewhere else, too. If there was a chance that the carnival would claim its first real victim tonight, he was anxious to see it happen. If necessary, he would make it happen, and, given the agency by which he had come into temporary management of the carnival, this seemed a likely necessity. First, however, he would need somebody to take over the barking for the House of Medical Monstrosity.

"You." He snapped his fingers and pointed peremptorily.

A passing ten-year-old boy with a Dr. Terwilliker beanie cap, a red-and-white-striped T-shirt, and a paper bag full of freshly roasted peanuts gawped at Cabal. Uncertain, he tapped his chest. "Me, sir?"

"Yes, you. Here. Come here. Up here, behind this podium. No, perhaps not—nobody will see you there. To the side. Take that ridiculous hat off. Now put this ridiculous hat on. There. Now publicise this sideshow until I get back."

Cabal left the boy panic-stricken in an overlarge straw boater. "How do I do that?" the boy called after him, but he received no answer.

In truth, however, Cabal was equally unsure of his next actions. Despite a careful search, the carnival had failed to produce anything as basic as a user's manual.

Cabal wandered among the chattering common folk—who were both very chatty and very common—and sought inspiration. It shouldn't be difficult, he reasoned. The whole carnival was an excrescence of Hell, an outpost, a departure lounge for the pre-damned. The whole place should hunger for the souls of the unwary. Therefore, he theorised, it should only require a light prodding to do what came naturally. He paused, a dark rock in a flow of humanity. He wasn't quite sure as to how one should set about lightly prodding a carnival. Perhaps he was, abominable as the thought was, over-intellectualising the problem. Perhaps he should trust his instinct. This would be difficult, he knew—his first instinct was always to use rational thought—but perhaps, just this once, he should listen to his intuition.

He tried to clear his mind, tried to silence the thousand buzzing thoughts that made up his consciousness, tried to ignore the sound of the crowd. He concentrated and focussed until there was nothing.

Nothing at all.

Certainly nothing helpful. He made an exasperated noise and let his mind, resentful of even those few moments of inactivity, whirr back up to speed.

Prickly at the failed experiment, Johannes Cabal looked straight ahead and saw the carnival's penny arcade. He'd expressed surprise when Horst had insisted on it being added to the complement of attractions, but—as always—his brother had known what people liked. While it was unlikely that it would ever play much of a role in gathering souls, it did seem to be doing an excellent job in gathering spare change from those who could afford it and redistributing it to those who were running short. The idea was that the sideshows were where the real chances lay; in the dark corners and shadowed booths, these were where the deals of dubious theological probity would be debated and decided. In contrast, the penny arcade was largely intended as a wealth-redistribution centre, it being notoriously difficult to lead folk into temptation if they can't get past the ticket barrier. Mr. Bones had explained all this to Cabal while the arcade was being built by two of Horst's more fanciful constructs, Messrs Lintel and Scree. They loped around like stilt walkers on overly long, overly thin legs, their equally long thin arms waving around. They wore black suits and dark glasses and had hair of an uncomfortable shade of yellow, and the thickness of darning wool. As he watched them totter back and forth barking at each other in an incomprehensible language of their own, Cabal had been confident that they were intended as gross parodies of himself, but refused to rise to the insult by saying as much. Still, they certainly knew their business, throwing together wood and metal, glass, paint, and varnish in a whirl of apparent chaos that spat out penny cascades, mechanical horse races, and bagatelles of precision engineering and pristine form. Cabal liked things to be precise and pristine, and so had warmed to Lintel and Scree, although, again, he wouldn't say as much. This kind feeling came to him now as he looked at the penny arcade, the result of their labours. He would try his luck here.

The arcade was busy. At the one-armed bandits, a man was consistently losing while his less well-off neighbour was on a lucky streak, both unaware of the arcade's Marxist tendencies. Elsewhere, tin monkeys shinned up tin palm trees, ghosts appeared at the windows of a haunted house only to be met by a fusillade of shots on a shooting gallery,* and a mechanical Gypsy told fortunes from the security of a glass-fronted case.

The Gypsy was—according to the legend painted across a board at the top of the case in swirling orange, yellow, and black—one Madame Destiny, and she took the form of a young woman with a headscarf, loop earrings, and a vertiginous cleavage. She sat, hands raised motionless about her crystal ball, silently waiting for the gang of teenaged boys gathered in front of her case to stop trying to peer down her top, making ribald and obvious comments as they did so. Finally, one of them, spurred

---

* "That makes no sense at all," Cabal had said. "You can't exorcise ghosts with a rifle. I have some practical experience in the area, and that simply isn't going to work." Mr. Lintel had thought about it for a moment. Then he said, "Tink." Mr. Scree said, "Dakuoof," or something very like it, and they had returned to their work.

on by the others, fumbled a coin into the slot. Madame Destiny immediately whirred into life and obligingly looked into her crystal ball. Deep within it, strange colours flickered and swirled. The boys grew quieter, and an air of discomfort developed around them as they watched the mechanical Gypsy's hands move in a very realistic manner for wood or plaster, her fingers bending where no hinges were evident.

Abruptly she juddered to a halt, the light died within the crystal ball, and the boys recovered their bravado a little. Then, with a percussive twang of spring-loaded machinery that sang through the machine's case for long seconds, a piece of card dropped into a tray set into the base beneath the glass. Grinning at the comments of his friends, the boy took the card and read it.

It seemed to take a long time to read those few lines, but after the first words his eyes widened a little, and the smile slowly faded from his face as if massaged away by invisible fingers. He went back and began to read the words again, then onwards to the end. Then, ashen-faced, he turned and staggered out of the arcade, his suddenly concerned friends asking him what was wrong.

Cabal watched them go grimly. He walked over to Madame Destiny, made a show of finding a coin in his pocket, and leaned down to put it in the slot. As his face grew close to Destiny's on the other side of the glass, he whispered, "Very amusing for you, no doubt, but hardly in line with what we're trying to do here. The intention is to tempt them in, not scare them off like rabbits." Unseen by any but Cabal, Madame Destiny raised a finely painted eyebrow. With another reverberant twang, a new card dropped into the tray, despite no coin being inserted. He read it where it lay.

MADAME DESTINY KNOWS ALL AND SEES ALL.

VERY AMUSING INDEED.

I HAVE TO HAVE A LITTLE FUN.

MADAME DESTINY'S ADVICE:

THERE ARE RICHER PICKINGS TO BE HAD.

Despite the insubordinate tone, there was good news here, and Cabal was cheered a little by the knowledge that Madame Destiny seemed to know of at least one alternative prospect. "Richer pickings . . . Where precisely?"

Madame Destiny's eyes rolled in their sockets until she was looking directly at him. She held his gaze for a second, then looked back down into the crystal. The strange light bloomed within, and with a whirr of gears she gently fluttered her fingers across the surface of the ball, never once touching it. A click, a twang, and a new card fell into the tray, covering the one already there. Cabal took them both, dropped the older in his pocket, and examined the new one. It read:

MADAME DESTINY KNOWS ALL AND SEES ALL.

MADAME DESTINY'S ADVICE:

BEHIND YOU.

Cabal turned. He was now facing the arcade's entrance. Beyond it was a surging torrent of humanity, washing from here to there and back again. No single face stood out, no one figure drew his attention. Cabal scowled. "This is no use," he said in an undertone that he knew Destiny could still hear. "I need some better indication of whom I am looking for than . . ." His eyes darted down to reread the card, and he stopped. For now the card read:

MADAME DESTINY KNOWS ALL AND SEES ALL.

MADAME DESTINY'S ADVICE:

AHEAD OF YOU.

Experimentally, he tried turning the card through ninety degrees. Madame Destiny's advice underwent a metamorphopsychotic* transition and now read, "TO YOUR LEFT."

Cabal nodded slightly, impressed. Considering she was essentially half a mannequin, a small cabinet, and just enough cogs and gears to make a tolerably accurate mantel clock, she certainly had her uses. Cradling the fortune like a cardboard lodestone, Cabal set off in search of his prey.

He walked headlong into the crowd and, inured by nature and habit against the complaints of those upon whose feet he trod and whose peanuts he spilt, he proceeded to close upon his mark. First, he used a rough triangulation to give him a very approximate range and bearing. Then he put his head down and ploughed a path through the mass, leaving a wake of disgruntlement. AHEAD OF YOU, said the card. AHEAD OF YOU.

Abruptly Cabal's headlong pursuit foundered upon an immoveable rock, all wrapped in a Sunday suit. He looked up, and a brow beneath a bad haircut beetled down upon him. Cabal quickly checked the card again. MADAME DESTINY'S ADVICE now read, THAT'S HIM. APOLOGISE. QUICK.

Cabal tucked the fortune teller's card away into his breast pocket and touched the brim of his hat. "Good evening, sir," he said to the large man, "I'm terribly sorry I ran into you like that. My most humble apologies." The man glared at him, his hands rapidly curled into fists, and he went pale. Cabal knew more than enough about the intricacies of the endocrine system to appreciate that a man who goes pale with anger is a great deal more likely to strike out than one who goes red. Unbidden, Cabal's free hand moved across to his cane, took the silver skull at its head firmly in his grip, and twisted it slowly until the catch disengaged. He knew Horst would probably regard running a rube through with a sword cane as poor public relations, but in Cabal's book, "The customer is always right" became academic the instant the customer drew back his fist.

---

* Metamorphopsychosis—a stage illusion that allows objects and persons to transform while in full sight of the audience, a variation of the more famous Pepper's Ghost so obscure that even most magicians haven't heard of it. Try mentioning it to any that you may encounter. It baffles them.

"Please, no, Ted!" A woman appeared around the windward side of the mountainous man. She was as pale as the man—Ted—but for different reasons. Her dark make-up showed livid against the white skin. "Please! He's not worth it!"

Cabal—who at one time or another had been pursued by village mobs, town mobs, the police, the army, two Inquisitions, and sundry other concerned citizens—was entirely positive that he was worth it. The phrase on her lips, however, had the air of a formula worn by use into a ready invocation, a cantrip against the extremities of Ted. Under such circumstances, Cabal was prepared to forgive her presumption. For Ted, on the other hand, he had conceived a strong dislike, and those for whom Cabal developed a strong dislike rarely prospered.

"Please, allow me to introduce myself," said Cabal, releasing the head of the cane and using that hand to tap his chest as he spoke. The gesture also confirmed the presence of one of Trubshaw's contracts, folded and ready in the inside pocket of Cabal's coat. "I am Johannes Cabal, joint proprietor of this carnival."

Ted seemed to calm down with remarkable rapidity, Cabal noted. Obviously cowed by authority. His dislike for Ted deepened.

"Allow me to apologise once again for my earlier clumsiness. Please, I'd like to make it up to you in some way. Is there some attraction or sideshow for which I can offer you a complimentary ticket? An exhibit?" Ted's eyes scanned back and forth, apparently considering his choices. His expression gave no assurances that he would come to a conclusion soon. "A stall, perhaps?"

"You like to shoot," suggested the woman in a small, cautious voice.

Ted thought about this, then nodded.

"He likes to shoot things," the woman said to Cabal.

"I shot her dog," added Ted.

It took an effort, but Cabal didn't show even the flicker of a reaction.

"If you'd come this way, please, sir," he said in neutral tones, indicating the way to the shooting gallery.

The shooting gallery was, in common with all the carnival's stalls, a carefully judged amalgam of every fairground shooting gallery that had ever been or ever would be, an archetype, a functional mean. It offered the opportunity to shoot at tin silhouettes of little men standing to attention, tin silhouettes of caricature ducks, and tin silhouettes of clay pipes, which processed and spun across a pellet-peppered backdrop. The weapons it offered were break-barrel .22 air-rifles—Cabal had been mildly amused to discover that they were age-ing Webleys, of the same manufacture as the .577 Boxer revolver currently ly-ing in his desk drawer—their sights all artistically crocked so as to be worse than useless. In return for the feat of striking down moving targets with ill-maintained rifles, the stall offered the chance to take home desperately ill goldfish, disconcerting Kewpie dolls, decorative knick-knacks of dubious quality and taste, and ill-proportioned baboons stuffed with kapok.

Cabal arrived with Ted, the latter carving a channel through the crowd much like a surly ice-breaker. In their wake, Ted's girlfriend, Rachel, walked quickly, head down, giving apologies to anybody who looked like they were owed one. Cabal quietly explained to the stallholder that Ted was to be allowed five free games, and to be awarded any prize that he might win just as if he had paid. Bowing a little too stiffly to be truly unctuous, Cabal withdrew to a safe distance and observed.

Ted turned out to be an effective marksman, inaccurate sights or not. He cracked open the rifle as if it had insulted him, thumbed in a slug, snapped it shut, raised it to his shoulder, and fired with barely a pause un-til all five slugs were gone and two unhappy little tin ducks, two tin men, and a tin pipe had been laid low. The stallholder showed him the utter tat that was his for the asking, but Ted waved such very minor temptations aside. He intended to accrue five tokens from his five gratis games and go home with an altogether classier piece of tat from the top shelf of prizes.

Cabal watched, discomfited. He had been banking on the nefarious true purpose of the carnival making itself known in certain stealthy, subtle ways only evident to the watchful and educated observer, if for no other reason than that that was its nature. Instead, he was looking at an oaf doing quite well for himself in an egotistical show of physical superiority. He might as well have been watching professional sports. In short, unless the carnival was being so stealthy and subtle about its soul-stealing that even Cabal couldn't see it happening, then he could only conclude that he would have to move matters along himself.

Everything at the carnival was ultimately dedicated to taking the souls of the unwary. That was a given. Therefore, unlikely as it seemed, even the shooting gallery must be capable of this. Cabal didn't know how, but surely the stallholder did? As proprietor, it was merely Cabal's role to make the decision, to give the signal, and then stand back and watch the carnival draw the snare tight around the prey. Well, he had made the decision, so it would seem that he should give the signal. Cabal caught the stallholder's eye while Ted was mowing down more hapless tin casualties, and gestured in a way he hoped would imply that the stallholder should get on with securing Ted's soul.

The stallholder stared blankly at Cabal.

Cabal tried again, but the stallholder just cocked his head on one side and looked at him with an expression of deep bewilderment. Cabal tried a different soul-stealing gesture, and then another.

With a sudden mild breeze, Horst was standing beside him. Horst took a look at Ted. "Oh, you found him, then. Well done."

Cabal ignored his brother and carried on trying to semaphore his intentions to the shooting gallery.

"Johannes," said Horst after some moments of watching him, "what are you doing?"

"Gesturing," said Cabal, continuing to gesture.

"Gesturing, is it?" This apparently impressed Horst. "It's very good."

Cabal ignored him. Horst followed the line of gesticulation to the shooting gallery, where the stallholder was just handing out the next fistful of .22 slugs to Ted while keeping one curious eye on Cabal.

"What exactly is it that you're trying to communicate with this . . . ummm . . ."

"Gesturing."

"Quite. This gesturing?"

Cabal ceased gesturing, partially because it didn't seem to be working and partially because he was developing cramp.

"I'm trying to get that idiot on the shooting gallery to do something diabolical so I can get a contract signed. It doesn't seem to work."

"No manual, I take it?"

"None."

"Actually, brother mine, that was along the lines of a snipe at your lack of comprehension and imagination." As Cabal turned his attention from Ted to glare at Horst, so Horst turned his own attention from his brother and to Ted. "He's a very good shot, isn't he? I think he's going to get one of the top prizes. Wait here a mo'."

Another breeze, and Cabal was alone. Another breeze, and Horst was back, with company. In his hand he held one of the top prizes, a doll of a precocious young woman with a disproportionately large head that, in comparison, made her disproportionately large bust and bottom look properly to scale with the rest of the body. The doll, its head made from celluloid and its body from cloth, had a coquettish expression on its face. Horst angled the whole doll back and forth, and Cabal noticed one eye winked. The overall effect was of a repulsive intimacy. He was very unwilling to take it when Horst proffered it to him.

"What do you expect me to do with this?" said Cabal, as he finally took it, carefully, between forefinger and thumb.

In answer, Horst waggled his fingers at it and adopted a significant expression.

"Are you gesturing?" demanded Cabal.

Horst sighed. "You've still got a good quantity of diabolical influence to call on, haven't you?" He nodded at the doll. "Stick a jigger in there."

"Stick a . . . ? Have you lost your senses? Look at him!" He nodded at Ted. "The man must shave with a lawnmower!"

Horst looked at the proposed victim. "He certainly has his hair cut by one," he conceded.

"What possible use is a doll, demoniacally influenced or otherwise, when you're dealing with a man like that?"

"Have you any interest in psychology?" asked Horst.

"Certainly not," replied Cabal. "I'm a scientist."

"Oh, so dismissive. Put the 'fluence on Trixie here and then allow me to demonstrate."

"Trixie?" said Cabal, not sure he'd heard correctly.

Horst grunted with impatience. "Just do it, will you? He's almost got his five tokens!"

Cabal saw it was true, and also saw that he had no better ideas himself. He held the doll at arm's length and muttered, "I invoke thee," under his breath. He felt the vague sense of evil being directed through him—a sensation somewhere between grief and toothache, with which he had grown familiar during the carnival's creation but never even faintly inured to—and then it was done. He quickly handed the doll back to Horst before it grew fangs and attacked him, but it did nothing at all.

"Good" was all Horst said, and then he blurred into not-thereness.

Cabal saw him suddenly snap back into visibility at the side of the shooting gallery. He no longer had the doll; it had been returned to the middle of the top row of shelves.

Horst's timing was perfect—Ted had just won his fifth token. He looked along the prizes, but his gaze did not linger on the doll.

"The doll's pretty," said Rachel. Ted slid her a look of corrosive disdain.

"It's my prize," he said. "I choose."

"That's lucky," said Horst, who had suddenly appeared farther along the gallery's counter. "I quite fancy getting that doll, and it seems to be the only one they have."

Ted turned to look past Rachel at Horst. "It's a girl's doll," he said in a tone that implied that he had made deductions as to Horst's sexual preferences, that he found them contemptible and disgusting, and that by association, he found Horst contemptible and disgusting, too.

"Quite," said Horst, paying for five games. "It's for my girl. What's the point of doing well on something like this if you can't have bragging rights?" He loaded his rifle. "I win that doll, give it to her, tell her how difficult it was to win, how good I am." He aimed. "Then she's all mine." He fired. A tin man took the slug square between the eyes and flipped backwards. He lowered the rifle and grinned at Ted. "That's psychology."

Ted didn't care about psychology, not even when it so obviously lacked logic. He cared a lot about ownership, though.

"I'll have the doll," he said to the stallholder.

"Oh!" said Horst in convincing disappointment, as Ted received the doll and then thrust it into Rachel's arms with scarcely a glance. He walked off, Rachel clutching the doll to her chest.

Horst was watching them vanish into the crowd as Cabal joined him. "And that's psychology?" said Cabal.

"Yes. Not what I told him, but certainly what I did to him." He looked sideways at his brother. "You do know what went on there?"

"I'm not a complete dolt. I know spitefulness when I see it. There is something I don't understand, however."

"Oh?"

"Why exactly are you helping me in such an overt manner? You made no bones about how little you like what is going on here, and insisted you wanted no direct involvement in the carnival's . . . core business, shall we say? Why the change in heart?"

Horst looked thoughtful. "Well, Johannes, it's . . ."

When the silence drew out, Cabal turned to ask for the rest of the sentence. Horst had gone. Cabal swore, an ancient expletive involving sexual congress between an extinct tribe and an extinct species.

Now what? His inclination was to shadow Ted and his miserable girlfriend; he couldn't help but admit that he was very curious to know how the doll was supposed to make a man sell his soul away. With great reluctance, however, he decided trailing them around would probably be counterproductive. Horst and he had taken a direct interest, they had burnt up a little more of Satan's blood; if they needed to get more involved still, then that would do for next time, and Ted could be considered a failed experiment.

Cabal went back to the House of Medical Monstrosity to recover his straw boater from a small boy.

Rachel was outwardly as happy as she could be while associated with Ted, but inside she was wrought with conflicting thoughts. On the one hand, it was very kind of Ted to have won the doll for her, even if she had a suspicion that he had done so purely to spite that nice-looking man at

the shooting gallery. The fact that it was only a suspicion and not a definite fact in her mind was evidence of the filter of delusion she had woven
about her.

In her honest opinion, Ted was a nice, decent man. Yes, he had his
little foibles—the uninhibited way his fists tended to travel about, his perfectly reasonable desire to get drunk four times a week, his manly ten-
dency to see insults and slights all about, at which point his fists would
again become uninhibited—indeed, positively libertine—in their desire
to conjoin with chins and eye-sockets—but what man didn't?

Most of them, as it happened, but it was too late. For now Ted was
her metric for men, and she had, therefore, an instinctive knowledge of
the truth of her belief, a gut feeling. She had faith that this was about as
good as it got: not perfect, but she was sure that, by the power of her love,
she could change him for the better.

But this is no longer faith; this is desperation. It is no accident that
the same women who say, "You have to love a bastard," with a twinkle
in their eye, are the same women who—later, when it transpires that the
bastards that they loved and let into their lives are, indeed, utter bastards—then complain, "All men are bastards." Given the skewed sample
of their survey, it's hardly a surprising or reliable conclusion.

Weighing against this uncritical appreciation of any small kindness
he might show her—such as not hitting her, not spitting on her, or not
groping her best friend while in her sight—was the distinct sense that
there was something not right about the doll itself. It had seemed fine
while it was on the shelf at the shooting gallery, even though, now that
she thought back, she couldn't remember why it had seemed so appealing that she had asked for it. Now, however, the only thing that was preventing her from foisting it onto some passing child or even dumping it
in a bin was the sure knowledge of Ted's wrath. The doll felt wrong in her
hand, actually felt "undoll-like" in an ill-defined, equivocal manner
whose very vagueness was upsetting in itself.

Suddenly Rachel made a tight, frightened little cry and dropped the
doll. It fell on its bottom and sat there on the trammelled grass of the carnival field as neatly as if it had been posed. Ted whirled—he had been

three steps ahead, of course—and glared at her, then at the doll. "What's the matter with you?" he demanded, snatching the doll up.

"It . . ." She paused, realising how stupid it would seem if she said what she thought. "There's something sharp in it," she said instead. "It stuck into me." She looked at her finger. A small crescent of red dots was coalescing into a single drop of blood. She sucked her finger and looked warily at the doll dangling in Ted's hand. She was sure it hadn't been smiling like that before. Smiling, yes, but not like that. Not showing its teeth.

Ted scowled at Rachel as if it was just typical of her to be injured by a toy. He looked at the doll. It was of a shapely young woman, with black hair in spit curls, wearing a short red dress. He guessed it was a cartoon or comic-strip character, but he didn't recognise her. Something sharp in it, was there? It would be because it was just some cheap tawdry tat, made in a sweatshop somewhere, he was certain. He squeezed the doll, almost wishing that the sharp bit of metal that was surely in it somewhere would prod out and stab him, maybe even draw blood. He hoped so. That would give him the excuse to go back to the shooting gallery and hit the stallholder.

He squeezed, but nothing stuck into his hand. Quite the opposite; the doll seemed soft and pliant in his fist, satisfyingly so. He squeezed it again, firmly, not violently. The doll, lolling in his grip, winked lazily at him. He gazed at it, and it seemed to gaze back, the moment drawing out like wire. Rachel watched him, nervous at first that he would suddenly be hurt and blame her, then more nervous still when he wasn't. He just stood there, staring at the doll.

The doll felt warm in his hand. He could feel the curves of its body, of her body, beneath the red dress. She felt good. Like a woman should feel. Soft and warm and curved.

Rachel quailed as he looked up and shot her a hostile glance that was somehow different from the hostile glances she had grown accustomed to. He looked down again, studying the doll. She could see his thick, powerful fingers slowly working around it, and she felt both an unexpected jealousy and an unfamiliar flavour of fear.

Ted wished he had come to the carnival by himself. Now he had to put up with Rachel following him around like a sheet of misery. He never had any fun. If he had a girl like the doll, things would be different. She looked good, she dressed good, she felt good. He could almost imagine finding a woman like that, here, at the carnival. He would chat her up, make small talk, ask her what her name was.

I'm Trixie.

Trixie, he thought, *that's a pretty name.*

Thank you. What's your name, hun?

"Ted," said Ted.

"What?" asked Rachel.

He shot her another dirty look, turned on his heel, and walked on. Rachel waited for a moment, unsure if she had done anything wrong or not. Then she followed.

Ted strode onwards, the crowd opening and closing around him, flowing. He barely knew where he was going. He barely cared.

She doesn't love you.

He had always known that. Of course, he had always known that. He couldn't imagine why anyone would want to love anyone. Loyalty, that was one thing, but love . . .

She doesn't even like you.

It hadn't really occurred to him that Rachel might have opinions. He paused in the shadow of the Helter-Skelter, the delighted screams of children rolling over him as they swept around and down the slide. He had a half-formed impression of the screams carrying on beneath ground level, and seeming much less delighted. The night air was cool, but he was sweating, feverish. In his hand, something writhed.

I like you, Ted.

He was looking at the bright light bulbs running down the side of the Helter-Skelter, the light flowing in primary torrents. He could barely hear himself think over the music and the chatter and the laughter and the screaming. He certainly didn't hear himself say, "I like you, too, Trixie."

With time, maybe I could even love you.

Loyalty, that was one thing, but love . . .

"Ted? Are you all right?" He whirled drunkenly. Some woman with too much make-up was looking at him. "You look terrible! You look ill,

Ted!" He didn't look terrible. She looked terrible. Her head was too small. She wasn't wearing a red dress. "You've got to get home, you're coming down with something!"

He said something that was supposed to be "Get away from me," but the syllables just fell out of his mouth like rotting potatoes. Frustrated and too dizzy to find his anger, he turned his back on the woman and stormed away. The crowd, full of faces with wide eyes and wide smiles, looked through him, but parted like loud ghosts.

The woman was right about one thing, thought Ted: he had to get home. He had to get home with Trixie. He clutched the doll to his chest and half walked, half ran to find the exit.

Beyond the archway, the air would be cool. He would be able to think again. He would be happy. He would be loved. Trixie felt good against his chest, as good as a real woman, better than a real woman. That woman (Did he know her? Rachel? That sounded familiar) was a real woman, but there was so much wrong with her. She would never be right. She had life and wants, and now it turned out she even had opinions. He remembered how Trixie had felt when he had first squeezed her, when he had been expecting some wire to stab him. Now he imagined squeezing Rachel, squeezing any "real woman" like that, imagined all the sharp wires of their lives and history, of their desires and thoughts, unwanted, unnecessary, stabbing into his hands as he squeezed, the blood coming from his wounds, staining their dresses red. All that pain, and all that frustration; he would never be happy.

He could feel Trixie against him, held tight. Love and happiness. He passed under the archway.

And it all went away.

He stopped dead in his tracks, a grown man clutching a doll. He took her in both hands and looked at her, shock and a terrible longing growing in him for something he hadn't even known he had wanted until a few minutes ago. He squeezed her, he squeezed it, but it was just a doll. He shook it, but that only made her winking eye clatter spastically open and shut *tikatikatika.*

He turned and looked up at the archway. Walking through it had been like flicking a switch. Inside/outside: Trixie/doll. He made to re-enter, but the turnstile wouldn't move. He shoved ineffectually against the steel arms, until he noticed the man in the booth smiling darkly and tapping a sign that read *No Re-Admittance on Cancelled Tickets*.

Ted thrust his hand into his trouser pocket and threw all his change onto the small metal counter. He didn't know how much he'd given, nor did he care. Neither did the man in the booth. Without even checking how much was there, he worked the machine, and a ticket, as red as ripe pomegranate seeds, clacked from the slot in the counter. Ted took it like a drowning man clutching at a straw and threw himself against the turnstile again. The man in the shadowed booth let him beat against it for a full five seconds until, still smiling darkly, he released it, and Ted staggered back into the carnival ground.

Instantly, Trixie was Trixie. He stood clutching her, ecstatic yet terrified by the knowledge that, when the carnival moved on, so would his happiness. Perhaps he could hide here, somewhere behind the scenes, make the few days last, hide in a dark corner, holding Trixie. He ran blindly in an agony of fear at the uncertain future, for longer than he knew.

When he paused, he found himself away from the carnival proper, down near the railway, near the train. There was a man standing there. Ted recognised the man who had blundered into him, the man who had given him the free games at the shooting gallery. Like a dream, the man seemed to be expecting him; and, like a dream, this seemed perfectly rational and proper to Ted.

Ted walked forward, taking his hat off and crushing it in his free hand. The other held Trixie, tender and close, in its crook. "Mister," he stumbled out, "sir . . ."

"The Cabal Brothers Carnival thanks you for your interest," said the man, speaking with a faint German accent, "but we have no vacancies at this time."

"But . . ." Ted realised that the man had known even before he had that he had wanted a job there. It was perfect. If he insisted, perhaps? If he begged . . .

"No . . . vacancies at this time." The blond man pushed his straw boater up at the front. It was an odd choice of headwear, considering he was otherwise dressed much like an undertaker. He nodded at Trixie. "You like the doll?"

Ted hugged her protectively. The man shook his head with restrained incredulity. "Agalmatophilia. Wonders will never cease. I owe my brother an apology."

The man reached into his inside pocket and produced a folded piece of paper. As he flicked the paper open with an easy snap of his wrist, he took a pen from the same pocket. "I believe we can come to an arrangement."

Ted didn't listen to what the man had to say. He just felt Trixie squirming against him, heard her voice in his mind, and he reached for the pen.

Later, Horst found Cabal in his office aboard the train, examining the signed form with every expression of satisfaction. "I never expected it to be this easy," he said, holding up the paper so Horst could see Ted's untidy signature.

Horst sat down on the other side of the desk and leaned back into the leather chair. "Neither did I," he replied a little grimly. "Perhaps Satan didn't, either. We should be careful."

"Given my profession, being careful is what separates the successes from the failures."

"Ha! What makes you think you're such a success, Johannes?"

"Because I'm not tied to a post, up to my knees in bonfire." He frowned; Horst was spoiling his little victory. Cabal decided to make some effort to jolly him along. "You were right, though. I couldn't see what possible use a toy filled with the diabolical spirit could be in bringing us an adult male, but it did. He virtually begged to sign this. There are, however, a few things that I don't understand about this evening's business."

Horst looked wearily over the desk at him. "Do you need to understand everything?"

"Of course," said Cabal, dismissing such a silly comment. "Firstly, what precisely happened there? Did the doll come to life, or did it somehow create a paraphilia in"—he looked at the signature—"Edward . . . somebody. Terrible handwriting."

"A para-*what*? Paraphilia? Where do you get these words? What's a paraphilia?"

"A fetish. What exactly did Satan's blood do to the doll? Possess it or curse it? I'm interested to know."

"I have no idea. A little of both, maybe. Perhaps. Does it matter?"

"It may, at some point. Something else I would like a definite answer to, though." He waited until Horst looked at him before continuing. "I would like you to answer the question I posed you earlier."

Horst sagged back into the chair, and looked at the ceiling. "I don't remember it," he said, though he obviously did.

"I asked," said Cabal with cryogenic patience, "why you had decided to help me, after making it quite plain that you would not directly help me get these"—he waved the contract—"signed. Then, at very nearly the first opportunity, you do. I would very much like a clear and honest answer, without you wafting out of here like a manifesto promise the day after an election. Well?"

Horst looked like he wouldn't speak at all for several seconds. Then he drew breath and said, "Well. He was going to Hell anyway, so why not get it on an official basis right now and save him the embarrassment of being snubbed by Saint Peter. Can you imagine, all those nuns and things in the queue behind you, and Saint Peter telling you you're not on the list and you can't come in?"

"I'm not sure it works like that—although, having seen one postmortem bureaucracy, perhaps it does. I do know, however, that you're being evasive. There must have been any number of likely candidates for damnation in here tonight, yet you settled upon that one person like . . . well, like yourself on any moderately attractive girl at a party."

Horst raised his eyebrows. "Good God, you're not still bitter about that time at Conrad's party, are you? I've apologised for that a dozen times over. It was a *joke*."

"It was a calculated humiliation, but I won't let you distract me. Why him?"

Horst settled back into his chair. "His girlfriend."

"What? That mousy woman? Not your usual type at all. Far too much make-up, too."

"That make-up," said Horst slowly, "was to hide her black eye."

Cabal sat up. "Black eye? You mean . . . that man? Edward . . . whatever his name is?"

"I could smell the violence on him, even through his cheap aftershave. I know his sort. One day, he would do something a great deal worse. I decided he needed to be stopped."

"You decided, did you, Horst?" Cabal glared at his brother.

"I decided. I really do know his sort, Johannes. I've seen it time and again. His girlfriend was nothing more than a toy he plays with now and then. And he's the kind who breaks his toys. Well, I decided he deserved a toy that would play with him for a change." He paused, his gaze distant. "Maybe it will break him," he added coldly.

There was a silence. Finally, Cabal said, "Being dead has made you rather less liberal than I remember."

Horst shrugged. "My motto always used to be 'Live and let live.' Under the circumstances, I need a new one."

Cabal looked at the contract. "Now you've told me your motives for helping me get this signed, it's taken the shine off it somewhat. We're supposed to be doing the devil's work and you've gone and contaminated it all with the whiff of virtue. I really don't think you've quite got the hang of being an agent of evil."

"Early days yet, Johannes." Horst stood up and stretched. "Practice makes perfect."

Pertaining to Satan's blood, a brief quantitative and qualitative analysis of its use in the creation and running of the Carnival of Discord, also known as the Cabal Bros. Carnival

The diameter of the ball of Satan's blood as originally provided as the carnival's "budget" was exactly 356mm. The ball, initially gelatinous and therefore variform to a degree, rapidly settled into a perfect sphere of a smoothness greater than the surface of a neutron star, previously believed to be the most perfect sphere possible.

By the equation $V = \frac{4}{3} \pi r^3$ where r is the radius and V the volume, we discover that the sphere's volume is—rounding up—23,624 cubic centimetres (also millilitres) of diabolical blood, or 23.624 litres. Or, as near as damn it, 5.2 British gallons.

Costs incurred against the "budget" are defined in cubic centimetres (cc). Examples are as follows. Note that no two entities created thus had exactly the same cost, even if functionally identical. This is probably due to the inherently chaotic nature of Hell.

Animates
- Low-grade: e.g., riggers   20cc
- Medium-grade: e.g., barkers   25cc
- High-grade: e.g., Bobbins   35cc
- Character-grade: e.g., Bones, Layla   50cc

Structures
- Concession   30cc
- Sideshow   50cc
- Ride   80cc

Wishes Granted

(This is impossible to quantify effectively, given the wildly differing scale of the wishes asked for. Some were major undertakings consuming upwards of 200cc, while others were rendered without resort to the ball of blood, using either the carnival's plentiful profits or already existing entities. As an aside, none were granted exactly as the recipient intended. This is a point of principle in such transactions.)

Chapter 6

⊰ IN WHICH CABAL MAKES AN UNPLANNED STOP
AND TALKS ABOUT THE WAR

So the carnival moved on and moved on, and it left a thin line of misery and discord behind it at town after town.

Cabal lifted the unsigned contracts from their box, placed the signed ones at the bottom, and replaced the blanks on top of them. Then he put the lid back on, placed the box in the top right-hand drawer of his desk, and locked it. One day, and it had better be some day within a year after he'd started on this whole ridiculous wager, the topmost form would be signed as well, and he would have won. Then he could have his soul back.

And, a small, still voice said within him, you can spit in Satan's eye, because that's really what this is all about now, isn't it, Johannes? It might have started with your soul, but it's all about your pride now.

But Johannes Cabal didn't have a great deal of time for small, still voices. He ignored it, and in that small, deliberate inattention, he summed himself up.

Cabal arched his fingers and rested his chin on their tips while he carried out a rapid mental calculation. Providing they stayed on schedule, and providing the other communities they visited were as base and venal as Merton Pembersley New Town, Carnforth Green, and Solipsis Supermare had proved to be, then the target would be reached comfortably within the time limit.

At which point, the train shuddered to a halt.

Cabal jumped down onto the track and looked around. This couldn't be right; the track was in only slightly better condition than the line on which he'd originally found the train. They were in a long cutting that ran through the countryside, and Cabal couldn't see an end to it in either direction. The embankments were overgrown with straggling bushes and well-established trees whose branches loomed almost into the train's path. To one side, Cabal could see a family of rabbits sunning themselves while they watched the carnival with mild interest. This definitely couldn't be right. This was supposed to be a main line they were on. Cabal made his way to the locomotive but was met by Bones coming the other way. The unnaturally thin man was carrying a rolled-up map.

"Bad news, boss. We are on the wrong line."

"Really?" said Cabal, looking at the healthy growth of weeds along the track bed. "You do surprise me."

"It's true," replied Bones, long inured to Cabal's easy resort to sarcasm. "It's a definite done deal."

"How did it happen?"

"Dunno. Those smart folk on the footplate didn't notice anything was wrong for an age, far as I can figure. I'm guessin' some kids tripped the points and we just"—he planed his hand through the air—"whoosh into the middle of nowheres."

"How do we get back?"

"Depends on where we are. Look." Bones unfurled the map on the gravel and weighted its corners down with stones. "We could be on this spur here, or that one there. See? Now, if we're on that one"—he pointed at a thin line that branched off a thicker one—"well, that's cool. We just go on till we reach the main line again, there, and we don't hardly lose no time. If we're on *that* one, though, there ain't nothin' but buffers in a hillside. We *got* to go back if we're on that."

"And there's no way of knowing which one we *are* on?"

"Not without some sort of landmark, no."

Cabal pursed his lips. Kids tripping the points? He doubted it. Far more likely it was the handiwork of one of Satan's avatars. Anything to make things difficult. Without a word, he went back to the train and hoisted himself up onto an external ladder.

"Where you goin', boss?" asked Bones, shielding his eyes against the cold sun.

"Looking for a landmark. Pass me the chart, would you?"

From the top of the car, Cabal still couldn't see very far. The sides of the cutting were simply too high. Discarding the options of jumping up and down or standing on tiptoes as both pointless and damaging to his dignity, he looked up and down the length of the track instead. Ahead he could see nothing beyond the long, gentle curve. Looking back, however, he could just make out the roof of a building that must lie beside the track. Checking against the chart proved fruitless; both potential lines had assorted unidentified buildings along their lengths. Still, perhaps he could get a clue there. He dropped the chart back to Bones and climbed quickly down.

"There's a house or something back there," he said, pointing. "I'll go and make enquiries."

Bones looked along the track without enthusiasm. "You want me to come with you?"

Cabal was already walking along the sleepers. "Unnecessary. I'll be back shortly."

As the impatient huffing of escaping steam grew quieter behind him, Cabal began to feel oddly alone. He had spent the vast majority of his life alone, of course; both his temperament and profession had made that a given. This, however, was different. Every step he took away from the train made him feel more isolated from all humanity, and the sensation, combined with its very unfamiliarity, was becoming more than disconcerting. He stopped and was alarmed, as well as slightly disgusted, to feel a shiver travel through him. Then, worse still, the hairs on the nape of his neck rose.

Unusual, he thought. *I think I'm frightened.* Fear wasn't entirely a stranger, true, but on those previous occasions he had always had something to be frightened of. Things of his creation that had got out of the laboratory or the oubliettes or, once, out of the furnace, and had hung around the house in the shadows waiting for an opportunity to jump on him and kill him. That had worried him. That night at the Druin crypt. Yes, he might have felt a little discomfited then. On those occasions, however, there had been a very real threat to his life and work. Here there was . . . nothing. He looked back at the train and seriously considered returning, reporting that there had been nothing of interest at the building, and carrying on until they either reached the main line again or were forced to back up.

"Pull yourself together," he said quietly to himself. "There's no time for this childishness." He mentally shook himself by the shoulders, drew himself up, and marched down the line.

The fear grew still worse. Now, however, an uncompromising mixture of determination and pride outmatched it. The feeling deepened into an impression of impending doom mixed, oddly, with loss. The burden of a sudden nameless longing made Cabal gasp with unfamiliar emotion. No. No, it wasn't unfamiliar at all, just suppressed, and the sudden whirl of remembrance made his eyes prickle. He gulped, then sucked in a breath and kept walking. With agonising slowness, the building revealed itself around the bend as he walked purposefully on, and he belatedly realised that it was a station. This was good news; although it had clearly been abandoned years ago, there must still be a sign or something to say which station it was, information enough to deduce which line it stood on. He willed the clue to be somewhere obvious: the pain in him was so intense now, he just wanted to sag to his knees. The feeling of loss was like a spear through his heart. Keep walking, he kept telling himself. If you succumb, you're lost. Just get the information and then walk back to the train, mission accomplished. Don't run. Don't falter. Control it.

The station had clearly once been very well run indeed. By the platform were flower beds in which nasturtiums and poppies fought gamely for soil against weeds. The stones that surrounded the beds still showed signs of having been assiduously whitewashed a long time ago. The paint was peeling, posters hung from their frames, and the windows were grimy. Yet there was a sense of order gently giving way to entropy. The fact that the windows were all intact was interesting; Cabal had learned a lot about human nature over the past few weeks and knew full well that where there were boys and unattended glass, there was also likely to be some property damage in the near future. Cabal had already had several run-ins with wilful young lads who seemed to believe that their age and sex gave them some sort of dispensation to commit petty acts of vandalism. One such had particularly infuriated him and was now a permanent fixture in the House of Medical Monstrosity. They'd moved smartly out the next day before the local constabulary got involved.

That the station windows were still in place argued that the station was rarely if ever visited, which, in turn, raised the question "Why build a station in the middle of nowhere, where nobody is ever likely to use it?" It was a question that turned the balance in Cabal's mind. Up to now, he would have been content to learn the station's name and go back to the train. Now, however, there was a mystery, and Cabal hated mysteries. The strange emotional turmoil he was in still frightened him, and because it frightened him, it also angered him. It felt so . . . imposed.

And, of course, it was. He felt foolish for imagining that its root had been within him at all. It was from outside. It was from . . . He looked up at the station. It was coming from here. The vague feelings that had so disturbed him were replaced with cold logic as he put them in their place. It was some form of empathy, he knew now, almost certainly supernatural. He still felt the fear and the loneliness and the dreadful sense of loss, but now it no more touched him than being warm or tired could emotionally touch him. It was simply a sensation, something that his body had detected and that he'd stupidly assumed to be part of him. He climbed up off the line, walked to the waiting-room door, in passing checked the station's name—Welstone Halt—and entered.

If he was expecting an immediate solution to the mystery, he was disappointed. The waiting room obviously hadn't been used for many years. There were a few tables, and a bar with a large tea urn on it, and glass displays that must have once been temporary home to sandwiches and cakes. The strange feeling was very strong here, Cabal noted. Sometimes a spasm of tension travelled down his back, making his head twitch involuntarily. He noted that, too. There were yellowed newspapers lying on one of the tables. He picked one up and studied its front page. There were a couple of advertisements for cigarettes that consisted of the name of the brand reprinted several times in a column—cutting-edge marketing for the time—and the headlines "BIG PUSH EXPECTED" and "ALL OVER BY CHRISTMAS." Cabal shook his head. It had been no such thing. Why did people always expect wars to be over by Christmas, as if a kindly fate wanted all the families to be back together and all that unpleasantness over and done with? As a man who dealt with life out of death, he was perhaps more appalled by war than most. He had been chased out of towns by any number of solid citizens, all of whom obviously considered themselves morally superior to him, although they would cheerfully send their sons to die in conflicts that could and should have been resolved diplomatically. Cabal, on the other hand, rarely killed unless absolutely necessary. In the cases of Dennis and Denzil, it had admittedly been a question of eugenics as well as self-defence. It was the gene pool or them. But war? Cabal threw the newspaper back on the table with contempt.

The otherworldly feel had been with him for so long now that he had begun to acclimatise to it, like getting used to a cold: he knew it was there, but it wasn't the be-all and end-all. He walked to the grimy window and looked out into the bright world beyond. This wasn't getting him anywhere; he should just return to the train with the name of the station, see where they were, and leave. But . . . he knew he couldn't. Not until he knew why this place stank psychically to high heaven and why it had been left to fall into stately disrepair for so many years. Cabal didn't just call himself a scientist; he had those vital necessities that so many scientists lack—an enquiring mind and almost painful curiosity.

"I'll just stay for a few minutes," he said aloud. "Then I really must go."

Silence was the only answer. "I'm a necromancer. I understand your concerns. I may be able to help you." He thought of the box of contracts and added, "We may be able to help one another." He continued to look out of the window as he drew a slim cigar from an inside pocket. He didn't smoke as a rule, but he liked the novelty of having at least one vice that he couldn't be hanged for. As he unwrapped the cellophane from the cigar, crinkling it pleasantly between his fingers, he felt the ambience shift in the room. The fear and loneliness were leaving him, leaving the air. He had enough experience of such things to know the source of these feelings beginning to coalesce somewhere nearby. No matter, it would present itself when it was ready. Pocketing the cellophane, he put the cigar in his mouth, took his father's silver matchbox from his waistcoat, and struck a match.

"Spare a light, sir?" said a voice that was near him yet as distant as the grave.

Cabal paused for the briefest moment. Then he lit his cigar. There wasn't a tremor in the flame. He turned slowly and held the still-burning match out. "There you are," he said evenly to the soldier.

Cabal watched him with dispassionate calm as the soldier leaned forward and lit a roll-up. He was dressed in a khaki uniform contemporary with the old newspapers; a cheap peaked cap, gaiters, a corporal's stripes, and buttons polished to a high sheen, despite which they didn't catch the light. It was as if Cabal were looking at him through a light mist. The soldier drew appreciatively on his cigarette, held the smoke for a long second, and released it through his nose in languorous streams. "God bless, sir. It seems like a month of Sundays since I last had a gasper. My mate Bill borrowed me matches off me and never gave 'em back, which is Bill all over. I've been waiting for the tea counter 'ere to open so I can buy some, but I ain't sure it's going to. Rationing, I suppose."

"Not rationing, I'm afraid," said Cabal, making his way to one of the tables and seating himself there. "The buffet is closed permanently. Please, join me." He gestured to the chair opposite him. The soldier smiled brightly and came over. The smile wavered slightly when he saw that the chair Cabal had indicated was drawn under the table. The chair beside it was largely out, and he sat on that one instead.

"Closed permanent? But there's loads of people use it. The works are just over the ridge."

"Really? I must admit, it doesn't seem like a humming hub of commerce here. When was the last time you saw somebody in here?"

"Oh, not long. It can only be a couple of hours since I got off the train. It was odd, though. The place was empty. The stationmaster'll get in trouble over it, I don't doubt."

"A couple of hours," echoed Cabal without comment. "What have you been doing since then?"

"I . . ." The soldier touched his forehead as if trying to recall. "I . . . fell asleep, I s'pose."

"And what did you dream?"

The soldier looked at him oddly. "Who wants to know?"

"You look rather wan," replied Cabal with masterly understatement. "I think your dreams must have been very disturbing. Sometimes they have meaning."

"And you know what they mean?"

"I might. If you don't tell me, I won't be able to tell you."

The soldier took off his cap and laid it on the table. He ran his fingers through sandy hair as he tried to concentrate. "But what if I don't want to know?"

"Then that's your concern. But don't you think you've spent long enough not wanting to know?"

The soldier didn't answer immediately. He slipped Cabal a hard glance, then clasped his hands and laid them against the table edge. He looked intently at them for almost a minute. Speaking quietly, he said, "I dreamt I was on a train. I sat alone in a carriage. I'd been given leave. From the army." He looked up and said, like a well-worn mantra, "Do you think the War will be over by Christmas?"

Cabal knocked the ash off his cigar into an ashtray decorated with the arms of a railway company that had gone into receivership before he was born. "No, it wasn't. Carry on."

"I'd had to tell the guard to stop here when I'd got on. Can you imagine that? A busy little station like this. I had to tell him to stop here." He took a long drag from his cigarette and crushed it out. "I waited for ages. For me dad and me little sister to come. And Katy." He smiled in desperate reminiscence. "She's my lass. We've been courting since school. We're going to get married in the new year, when the War's over and I get demobbed.

"Then I s'pose I fell asleep."

Cabal was watching the smoke curl from his cigar. "And what did you dream?"

"I had a dream about my commanding officer. Captain Trenchard. He was telling me something over and over again, and I just wasn't getting it. It must have been a dream, because the captain's an 'ard man and he don't like repeating himself and he'd have you on jankers like a shot if he thought you were taking the rise, like. He puts the wind up me, and I know I'm not the only one. Anyway, he was saying the same thing over and over, and I wasn't getting it, but he wasn't getting angry, and I wasn't scared of 'im, I was just sort of laughing like I couldn't get my breath back. He'd say something and I'd miss it, and he'd be all patient and say it again. That's how I know it was a dream. The captain don't have a bit of patience in his whole body. It couldn't have been real."

"You have no idea what he was trying to tell you?"

"No. 'Course not. It was only a dream, see? It wasn't real."

"This dream, do you remember what happened when you woke up?"

"I don't know if I do. I think I sort of half woke up, and then had another dream."

"You were back here."

"Yes. I was standing over there." He pointed toward the window. "And I saw this bunch of lads standing out on the track. I don't know what their parents are thinking of, letting them run around on a busy line. I was about to go out and tell them to stop playing silly beggars when one came in. He took one look at me, screamed like a little girl, and ran off with the others behind him." The soldier tapped his stripes. "Authority, see? They just saw a uniform and scarpered."

Cabal examined his cigar, decided it wasn't worth continuing with, and stubbed it out. "I'd agree if it weren't for a small but important detail that you're having trouble coming to terms with." He got up and walked over to the window. He stopped just short of it and looked at the floor, scraping away dust with his foot. Quickly crouching, he scratched at the floorboards with his fingernail and examined it minutely, angling his head to get the strongest light. Satisfied, he straightened up and walked over to the end wall. As he examined it, he absent-mindedly scraped the dirt from beneath his nail with a small file before using the file to probe at a damaged spot in the panelling.

The soldier watched uncomprehendingly. "What're you doing?"

"Have you read any of the Sherlock Holmes stories?" answered Cabal.

"No. I've heard of them, though. Who hasn't?"

"That's a shame. When I was young and still read fiction, I read the whole canon. I liked the application of the scientific method to resolving the chaos that crime generates." Cabal stepped to the window where he'd been standing when the soldier had first spoken to him, looked over his shoulder, turned, and took a long step.

"This," he said, "is where you were standing when you asked me for a light, yes?"

"I think so. Why's it important?"

"You should know. It's also where you were standing when you saw the children on the track, isn't it?"

"I don't know. Why do you ask?"

"Apart from the Holmes stories, Arthur Conan Doyle also wrote tales of horror and the bizarre." Cabal looked at the soldier. "Some ghost stories, too. Would you like me to tell you a ghost story?"

"I don't believe in ghosts," said the soldier, but he said it like a poor liar.

"You should. I do. But, then, I've seen them. Let me tell you about the three types I've come across." The soldier said nothing, but his discomfort was obvious. Cabal came over and sat down.

"Firstly," said Cabal, "there are the ghosts that aren't ghosts at all. Just recordings of dramatic, usually traumatic events. The murder on the staircase, the garret suicide, vicious battles fought out over and over again on bleak moors to terrify the shepherds. That sort of thing. People don't like dying as a rule. All that fear and anxiety, hatred and passion burns their last acts into"—he waved his hands to encompass the air about them—"the ether, for want of a better word. But those aren't real ghosts any more than a photograph of a dead man is.

"The second type isn't really a ghost, either, but at least it has pretensions. I'm talking about how a particularly powerful personality can distort things around the place of its death, or even just where it spent most of its life. These are the kind of ghosts who give the ghost-hunters employment, because, more often than not, they're created by aberrant personalities. That means aberrant effects after death: blood running down walls, screaming skulls, the living being given helpful shoves out of windows. All the sort of things the yellow press gets excited about. But the ghost isn't an entity. It's more like a series of practical jokes left behind by a wilful man or woman. It may give the impression of intelligence, but you can't reason with it. It has no reason." Cabal rubbed ruminatively at his shoulder blade and remembered a provincial theatre that gossip held to be haunted. He'd been lucky to get away with only a fractured scapula.

"And that leaves us with the third type, and the only type that I really think of as a true ghost. The lost soul who doesn't know that it's dead yet. Not common, not common at all. In fact, I've only ever met one." He put his elbows on the tabletop, interlaced his fingers, steepled his index fingers, rested his upper lip on their tips, and looked directly at the soldier.

"Who?" asked the soldier cautiously. Cabal's face darkened.

"The sheer obtuseness of the dead never fails to stagger me. You'd think I'd be used to it by now." He slapped his hands on the tabletop. The slight breeze stirred the cigar ash in the ashtray. The cigarette ash remained entirely still. Cabal rose quickly and walked in impatient strides to the spot where he'd first seen the soldier standing. He stood with his back to the soldier and pointed at the floor to his left.

"Bloodstains, long spray pattern running from there to there. Over on the far wall"—he pointed—"there's a pockmark in the wood. It's a bullet hole. The slug has long since been extracted, but I'd make an educated guess that it was a revolver round, probably a thirty-eight. I notice you're right-handed, so I assume you were looking out of the window at the time. Heaven knows there's nothing very interesting within the body of the room, so that would seem to make sense."

"No," whispered the soldier, "please."

"Don't 'No, please' me," barked Cabal over his shoulder. "I was under the impression that non-commissioned officers weren't issued with sidearms. Bring it back from the trenches, did you? Given the slaughter, you can't have been short of dead officers to loot a revolver from, hmm?"

"I don't know what you're talking about. You're mad," said the soldier, but his words were only meant to soothe himself.

"Mad, is it?" Cabal looked out of the window. "You said you were given leave. Compassionate leave, I assume. You came back here to a station that wasn't used anymore, made them stop the train, came in here." Cabal put his right index and middle fingers to his right temple. "Bang! Blew your brains out." He turned. The soldier looked at him in shrinking horror.

Cabal pointed at the stained floor and said gently, "That's your blood, isn't it? And that hole in the wall is where the bullet came to a stop after it had gone clear through your head." He walked back to the table and sat down. The soldier had buried his face in his hands and was breathing in sobs.

"You've always known it, of course. It's just been a problem accepting it," Cabal said. "The children didn't run from your uniform. They ran from the ghost at the haunted station. And they didn't feel they were in danger on the track because that line hasn't been used as anything but a siding in many years. I'm sorry. You're a lost soul. That's all there is to it." He watched the sobs wracking the corporal's shoulders for a few moments. "The only thing left to you now is to be freed."

"The captain, the captain kept trying to say what had happened," cried the soldier, sounding very young. "He kept saying it, and I couldn't take it in. I sort of got a bit of it and thought it was a joke. I was laughing at him while he told me they were all dead. My family. Just gone. And Katy. And Katy." He looked up at Cabal with eyes red-rimmed with misery. "She was my lass. We'd been courting since school. We were going to get married in the new year when the War was over and I got demobbed."

"I know. I know," said Cabal quietly. All dead simultaneously, he thought. Odd. "You must have loved her very much."

"She was . . . Katy. There was no life without her. I just . . . just couldn't go on. You can't imagine what it's like."

Cabal coughed. "You might be surprised. Do you want to leave here?" The soldier looked at Cabal blankly. "I can free you. I've had some experience with life after death. Do you want to leave here?"

"I keep falling asleep. Every time I wake up, I can just remember another screaming face in my dreams. I don't think I can stand it much longer."

"Then, if you just fill in this form, I can get you on your way."

The soldier looked at him, dazed. "A form? I have to fill in a form?"

"Just a technicality. A signature is all that's needed." He was checking his inside pockets without success. Belatedly he remembered that he'd used the last form he'd taken from the box just before leaving Solipsis Supermare. "Ah. I don't appear to have one on me. If you can bear with me for ten minutes while I get one from—"

"Will Katy be there?"

There was a hope in the young man's eyes that made Cabal suddenly feel very old. He thought of the expanses outside Hell, and the toiling masses trying to come to grips with the notorious question one thousand and twelve of Form KEFU/56. Then he thought of what eternal damnation really means.

If I don't release him, staying here is a sort of damnation anyway, he thought. What difference does it make if he serves it out in Hell or a rural station? He looked at the soldier's eyes again and knew what the difference was. In the sheer cliff over the Gates of Hell, defying modernisation and innovation, was still carved *Abandon All Hope, Ye Who Enter Here.*

"You and I have something in common," he said finally. "You don't have to fill in the form."

Cabal got up and walked to the door, opened it wide, and stepped over the threshold. He took a piece of white chalk from his cigar case and carefully drew a line from the lower edge of one side of the doorframe, across the threshold, and a little way up the opposite jamb. He stepped back into the room, squatted by the line, and wrote a series of peculiar characters alongside it, mumbling under his breath in a discordant chthonic tongue as he did so. Satisfied with his work, he straightened up, put the chalk away, and looked at the soldier. The corporal had stood and moved closer to see what Cabal was doing. Cabal noticed that he was standing in exactly the same spot where he'd taken his own life. Cabal walked to his side and pointed at the open doorway.

"There. Walk through. It's as simple as that."

The soldier bit his lower lip. "I'm not sure I can. I've sort of tried in the past. I couldn't leave here."

"That was before I opened the way for you. See those signs? Those are P'tithian sigils, the single most powerful and dangerous way of forming a portal known to humanity and, guessing from the evidence, four other intelligent species. Believe me, you can leave."

"And Katy?"

"There I can't make promises. But I think the chances of meeting her again are excellent. Now, will you please go? My train is waiting."

The soldier walked hesitantly towards the open door. The sun had moved low, above the top of the cutting opposite, and he was silhouetted. Cabal was unsurprised to see he was faintly translucent around the edges. He stopped right at the threshold.

"Go on," said Cabal. "There's nothing to hold you here. Get moving before I change my mind about the form."

The soldier looked back, and he might have smiled as he stepped forward. Cabal had the vague impression of something dispersing with unbelievable rapidity, and then the doorway was empty. Outside, there was nothing to see. Cabal walked out and looked up and down the track before looking up into the cold blue sky. "Good luck," he said almost to himself. "Give my regards to Katy."

Eventually, he went back to the doorway and looked down at the strange symbols. *I knew learning P'tithian would come in useful one day*, he thought. The P'tithians had been a particularly useless tribe who'd managed to wipe themselves out almost three thousand years before. Cabal had discovered and painstakingly translated a series of tablets he'd liberated from a small museum that he believed hadn't realised their significance. The translation showed that they probably had, after all. The P'tithians seemed to have managed to poison themselves with bread made from rye infected with a particularly virulent form of ergot. In an hallucinogenic haze, they had first assured themselves that they were great sorcerers and then demonstrated their extraordinary abilities by levitating, en masse, from a high place. Perhaps they should have chosen a low place to start with. Cabal rubbed out the phonetic characters with the toe of his shoe as he enunciated them, " 'Eenie. Meenie. Minie. Mo.' There, all gone." Satisfied, he left the station for the last time.

$\mathfrak{B}$ack at the train, it took less than a minute to find Welstone Halt on the map and discover that they were therefore on the right track. Dennis and Denzil gave the engine its head, and soon they were barely behind schedule.

At the junction with the main line, they had to get the signalman to change the points for them. Cabal went over himself, climbed the wooden steps up to the signal box, and delivered the customary bribe.

"No trouble at all, sir," said the signalman. "I'll have to call ahead so that you're expected. It'll take a few minutes for confirmation. Care for a cuppa while you wait?" Cabal took a look at the large tin mugs that hung from pegs behind the sink, thick with accumulated tannin, and declined with passable politeness. Instead, he amused himself by looking at the signal board and found his eye wandering onto "Welstone Halt (Disused)."

"Welstone Halt, sir," said the signalman when Cabal drew his attention to it. "That's been closed since the War. Nothing there, that's why. Not no more."

"I understand it was once a thriving place."

"Oh, it was. I went over there years ago, when I was a kid. On a dare, see? It's meant to be haunted."

"The station?"

"Oh, yeah. But the town, too. Not much of Welstone itself left now. The station's the only bit that looks in any sort of fair nick. It was a terrible thing that happened to the town. Well, I call it a town, but it was really not that big. Really a big village with a market. That's what made it busy."

The telegraph chattered. The signalman read the tape with interest. "There you go, there's your clearance. You'd best get a move on or you'll lose your slot."

On the steps Cabal asked, "Welstone. I need to know. What happened to it?"

"It were wartime, right? These lines were full of soldiers and equipment for the effort. Well, down the far end of the line you just came down, a munitions train ran into trouble. Caught fire. The best thing to have done would have been to take it halfway up and then abandon it. It would have taken the line with it when it blew, but at least the cutting would have forced the blast up, where it couldn't do no harm. But the driver was new on this line. Thought he could save the tracks by taking her down the spur that goes behind the station. He jumped out, did the points himself, and took her there. You can imagine what he thought when he came around on th' spur and found it overlooked Welstone. You could see every house from where that munitions train stood. You'll have to imagine what he thought, 'cause he didn't live to tell anybody. She blew up, then and there. There's a ridge between where the spur was and the station, so the blast was sort of reflected straight out over the town. There was hardly two bricks left standing on top of one another when the smoke cleared. Most of the people living there died in the instant, of course. The irony of it was that the station wasn't touched at all, but without a village to serve, they closed it down anyway. Anyway, you'd best get a move on, sir. Bon voyage."

In his office, Cabal found Horst awake and in his chair. "Well, brother," said Horst without looking up from his book. "What acts of petty despicability have you wrought this day?"

Cabal smiled, and, just for once, it wouldn't have frightened children and old people. "You might be surprised" was all he would say.

MEMORANDUM FROM THE DESK OF DR. OST,
DIRECTOR OF BRICHESTER ASYLUM

Dear all:

As you probably know by now, we have had a little security breach
here at Brichester. Now, this is all very unfortunate, and I have no doubt
that there will be some repercussions, but I don't want this to turn into
some sort of scapegoating exercise. Yes, we have lost almost three dozen
individuals into the community somewhat earlier than planned. Yes,
some, possibly most of them have unfortunate records involving some
entirely forgiveable dabbling in the dark arts. In fairness, however, they
paid for their curiosity by becoming rationally challenged, which is how
they came to be under our care and stewardship.

Although I did say earlier that I didn't want to descend into
apportioning blame for the recent mass breakout, I feel I cannot let the
behaviour of one of our clients go unmentioned. Rufus Maleficarus has
sorely disappointed me personally. I thought he was making quite a good
recovery from what the previous director had unhelpfully referred to as "a
soul-searing, sanity-dissolving, profoundly malevolent appetite for power
and revenge." As it happens, I think the finger-painting lessons were
going very well, at least up until Rufus used the paint to create a
summoning circle, and then rode out of here on the back of an obliging
Hound of Tindalos, taking the rest of his section with him. I'm sure
he had his reasons. I just wish he'd talked through them in one of our
sessions.

Be supportive of one another in this difficult time. Anybody talking
to the press will be fired immediately.

Chapter 7

IN WHICH CABAL DISCOVERS THAT HELL COMES
IN DIFFERENT FLAVOURS AND THAT ONE
SHOULD ALWAYS MAKE TIME

Horst castled and looked out of the window. "How much longer is that signal going to keep us here?"

Johannes Cabal ran a fingertip along his eyebrow while he ruminated, shifted a bishop, and said, "Your game is coming to pieces. Checkmate in three." He stood, stretched, and looked out along the track. "Over half an hour thus far. It's an outrage. I'm going to find out what's going on." He took his long coat down from the hook. "Care for a walk?"

Horst checked his watch. "A little over half an hour until dawn; that should be more than enough time. Very well."

Swathed in coats and mufflers, they climbed down onto the track and made their way towards Murslaugh Station, only two hundred yards away but unattainable by train until the signal changed. "A points failure?" hazarded Horst.

"Hardly. There's been furious activity on the line ever since we got here. Something's afoot, and the churlish scum have failed to tell us what."

"You're in a good mood."

"No."

They arrived at the end of platform two and climbed up. The scene was indeed one of furious activity. A locomotive that seemed to have been pulled out of a museum was making a head of steam while civilians, frantic with anxiety, fought for places in the antiquated carriages. The concept of "women and children first" seemed to have escaped a few people there.

"It's an evacuation," said Horst, aghast. "What's caused it? What's going on? Hi! You there!" He strode forward to argue with a man who'd just pulled two children out of a carriage to give himself space.

Cabal hadn't time for social justice. All he could see were potential souls skipping town. Looking around, he saw a harassed railway official surrounded by a huddle of desperate people. It seemed as good a place to start as anywhere. He made his way through the group, cracking skulls with his death's-head cane and hacking shins with his feet. After the first few cries of pain, a path magically opened. Cabal touched the brim of his hat and said, "I am Johannes Cabal, theatrical entrepreneur. What is happening here?"

"I'm afraid I haven't got time to tell you, sir. The town's in a state of emergency. You'll need to get out as quickly as possible."

Behind him, Cabal was passingly aware of a serious argument breaking out. He recognised one voice as his brother's. To the official he said, "I don't think so. We've only just arrived. I am joint proprietor of the Cabal Brothers Carnival. I am Johannes Cabal."

"Yes, sir, you already said," replied the railway official testily.

Behind Cabal, the argument stopped abruptly with a solid *thud*. The man who had pulled the children off the train flew past at head height. After a moment, Horst joined Cabal. "I shouldn't have done that, but he was just *so* infuriating. I hope I haven't hurt him."

"You'll have to ask him when he lands. This," said Cabal to the official, "is my brother, Horst." The official's testiness evaporated. A strong sense of self-preservation can do that.

"And how can I help you, gentlemen?"

"What's going on?"

"The most dreadful calamity, sirs. We just heard but two hours ago, and the town's been in an uproar ever since. I haven't ever seen anything like it."

"That's as may be, but we've been stuck just spitting distance from the station for the last half-hour or so. Didn't it cross anybody's mind to at least inform us as to what's amiss?"

"What *is* amiss, anyway?" added Horst. "Nobody's being very clear on that."

"What?" said a small, greasy man, rubbing a death's-head-shaped bump on his forehead. "You came here by train?"

"No," said Cabal. "We've got an entire carnival in our pockets."

But a muttering had started. "They've got a train . . . They've got a train." The appearance of a new escape route from Murslaugh was causing a sensation.

"It's not a passenger train, so don't get your hopes up," said Cabal wearily, but it was too late. A small group of men, to whom the phrases "Act in haste, repent at leisure" and "Why a mouse when it spins?"* were equally cloaked in incomprehensible mystery, had rapidly coagulated into a mob and were already climbing off the end of the platform before rushing off into the darkness with the intention of taking control of the train.

"Oh, sir!" cried the railway official. "You have to stop them! They're likely to do anything!"

"You're familiar with the theory of evolution?" asked Cabal.

"Sir?"

"They're about to find out why intelligence is a survival trait. Now, what's all the panic about?"

"There's an army heading this way, sir! An army!"

Horst and Cabal exchanged glances. "We weren't aware that anybody had declared a war," said Horst.

"Oh, no, it isn't that kind of army, sirs. It's an army of lunatics!" In the distance, the bullish "Huzzah!"-ing of the men who'd gone to take the carnival train stopped abruptly.

---

* The classical example of a sentence that is grammatically correct yet semantically meaningless. I'm sure you knew that.

"An army of lunatics. Fancy. There's a football match on, then?"

"No, sir! It's . . . the Maleficarian Army!"

If the official had been expecting a spectacular reaction, he was to be disappointed. Cabal rolled his eyes and Horst said, "Who?"

"Rufus Maleficarus," said Cabal. "Who let him out?"

"I think he broke out, sir. With most of the inmates."

In the darkness beyond the end of platform two, the screaming began. The official started, white-faced. "Nothing to worry about," said Horst reassuringly. "Just those men meeting our security personnel. Johannes, who is this Rufus . . . thingy?"

"Maleficarus. Self-styled warlock and Great Beast. Actually, rather a—what's the term?—wanker. Stole some esoteric tome from one of the great universities, after a lot of work managed to read it, after a lot more work managed to comprehend it. Which is, of course, the last thing you want to do. All that knowledge needed lots of space inside his head, so it heaved his sanity out of his ears. Casting himself as some sort of manifestation of pure evil on Earth, he made unwholesome sacrifices to his dark gods and demanded great power in return."

Horst touched his forehead and feigned dizziness. "Ooh, déjà vu." Cabal ignored him.

"His dark gods obviously have their standards; they gave him a few party tricks and cut him loose."

"Dark gods?" said the official, dismayed by such wickedness.

"Extra-cosmic entities with names that sound like they were typed up by a drunken Egyptologist. Anyway, being able to pull a squid out of a top hat didn't keep him ahead of the authorities. The last I heard, they'd banged him up in a spherical cell at Brichester Asylum. So he's loose again? How nice." The thinness of his lips implied that it was anything but.

"What are you going to do, Johannes?"

"I'm going to deal with it. I've encountered Mr. Maleficarus once before. Not what you'd call a meeting of minds. I'll have a word with him, tell him to take his army of the touched elsewhere."

"He'll listen to you, then?"

"I doubt it, but I ought to give him the option before killing him. In the meantime, we need to do something to stop our potential customers leaving town."

"That's my department," said Horst, and, almost too quickly for the eye to see, he ascended a stack of trunks.

"Ladies and gentlemen, might I have your attention?" he said in a loud, clear voice. There wasn't a shred of interest from the churning crowd. It seemed that the ladies and gentlemen had grown resistant to calls for calm. People continued to fight for room on the train.

The incredibly loud report of a gun followed by the tinkle of glass from the platform roof focussed their attention wonderfully. Even the train seemed to be stunned. Cabal blew the smoke from the barrel of his Webley revolver and replaced it in his gladstone bag.

"My brother has something to say," he said simply in the profound silence.

"Thank you. Ladies and gentlemen, I am Horst Cabal of the Cabal Brothers Carnival. The man with the gun and the will to use it is my brother, Johannes. It is our intention to deliver you from the approaching menace of the Maleficarian Army *and* provide you with the best in travelling entertainment. All that we ask is your patience while the former is dealt with and your attendance when the latter is prepared. Thank you again, and bless you all." He jumped down.

"Bless you all?" hissed Cabal.

"They're going to need it," replied Horst.

*T*he sun was half an hour up by the time Cabal encountered Rufus Maleficarus and his army of the mad. Directed by many grateful citizens, he had made his way through the town lauded on all sides as some sort of hero, which was something of a turnabout, given the way he was usually treated by mobs. Flowers and kisses were a novel change from burning torches and lynch ropes. Not that he liked them much, either.

Then up he walked, out of the town, and onto the broad moor that lowered there like a huge expanse of earth, covered with grass, sheep, and drystone walling. Rufus and his cohort were just marching towards the town when Cabal arrived and stopped and watched and waited. As they got closer, he realised that they were singing. From the tune, their choice of song seemed inappropriate until they got close enough for him to make out the lyric.

> Big Squidhead lies a-sleeping at the bottom of the sea,
> And one day, when the stars are right, he'll wake up presently,
> And then may wipe us all out, which sounds worrying to me,
> While the Tcho-Tcho sing this song . . .

The Maleficarian Army sang with the vigour of scouts fresh out of camp. They could probably keep this drivel up for hours on end. "All together now!" boomed the leader. Even at this range, Cabal could recognise Rufus by his hideously deformed dress sense.

> Aïe! Ftagn! Ftagn! Cthulhu!
> Cosmic horror coming to you,
> The Old Ones are back now with a view to
> Sucking out your brains.

> Big Squidhead lies a-sleeping, although, in a way, he's dead.
> There are dreams that change reality a-running round his head.
> He lies in dread R'lyeh, which is on the ocean bed.
> But pops up and down for fun.

"And the Tcho-Tcho sing . . . ?" demanded Rufus in the tone whose subtext ran, "Anybody not having fun will be smashed in the face with a skillet."

> Aïe! Ftagn! Ftagn! Yog-Sothoth!
> The streets will be chockablock with shoggoth,
> How sweetly their cries "Tekeli-li!" doth
> Improve the slimy hour.

Cabal dimly recalled that the musical genius who'd decided to put on *Necronomicon: The Musical* had got everything he deserved: money, fame, and torn to pieces by an invisible monster.

Rufus had finally spotted him and, throwing up his hand in a gesture suitable for halting a column of war-elephants, advanced alone. He stopped some ten yards from Cabal and eyed him contemptuously. Cabal put down his bag and held his cane in the crook of his arm while he wiped his nose. Behind Rufus, the insane, the deranged, and the eccentric but poor formed up into a herd thirty or forty strong. Rufus was a big man with a fine beard and a romantic mane of hair that got him halfway to being a poet without so much as having to dip a nib. Both beard and mane were, inevitably, red. He wore an Inverness cape, plus fours, and stout shoes. Inexplicably, he also wore a tea cosy on his head, into which the symbol of an eye in a pyramid had been stitched. "Well, well, well," he roared. This was his only volume. "If it isn't Johannes Cabal"—the army jeered and hissed—"the necromancer." The army went very quiet and tried to hide behind Rufus.

Cabal put away his handkerchief. "Hello, Rufus," said Cabal flatly. "Turn around and go away. Thank you." He picked up his bag and started to go.

"Go away?" roared Rufus (*vide supra*). "GO AWAY? Do you know who I am?"

Cabal turned. Even behind his blue-tinted spectacles, you just knew that his eyes had narrowed. "I called you 'Rufus,' Rufus. Perhaps I made a hash of the pronunciation? Let's see, that's 'Rufus,' pronounced 'egotistical, megalomaniac, half-arsed, half-witted, half-baked, swivel-eyed, bubble-brained, slack-jawed, slope-browed, prattling, porcine, dimwit *Scheißkopf*.' There, was that better?"

"You shouldn't have said that," whispered Rufus in a knuckle-whitening fury. If one imagines a tyrannosaurus appearing in light opera and delivering a line *sotto voce*, that was the effect. "Don't make me angry. You wouldn't like me when I'm angry."

"I don't like you anyway, so it makes few odds. I don't like you happy, sad, beamish, or maudlin. The only way that I *will* like you is if you take yourself and your friends there away to where you came from."

"I should have dealt with you years ago, Cabal, when we first met. You never understood the powers that I was acquiring, never understood the cosmic influences that ran through this mortal frame. I have magic that you cannot begin to comprehend."

"You're talking about the one where somebody signs a playing card, you burn it, and then it reappears whole, rolled up in the middle of an orange, yes? You're right, that one's always baffled me."

Some of the Maleficarian Army sniggered. Rufus was too angry to notice. "You've had your warning, Cabal. Now, prepare to face the terrible arcane wrath of Maleficarus!" Somewhere, a sheep bleated and quite ruined the effect. Maleficarus tilted his head forward and glowered at Cabal through bushy eyebrows. Placing his index and middle fingers on each temple, he started to mutter diabolical incantations.

Cabal blew his nose again. "You haven't got anything that works on colds, have you? I think I may be coming down with one." Rufus doubled the intensity of his mumblings. Seconds passed. Cabal checked his watch. "Could you speed this up, please? I'm a busy man." Rufus redoubled. Cabal waited. The only effect he could feel was that his damn nose was itching. *Perhaps he intends me to sneeze myself to death,* he wondered. He clapped his handkerchief to his face as another sneeze came, and so missed Rufus's magical incantation working.

After a momentary sense of falling, Cabal hit the ground going backwards, trailing heels striking the grass first. Belatedly, he realised that something had bodily picked him up and thrown him. He lay on the wet grass for a moment, marshalling his thoughts. He felt all right, although he knew that didn't necessarily mean anything. Still, he could feel his toes, the dampness soaking through his clothes, the fine rain falling on his upturned face. He was just starting to formulate some really unpleasant things that he was going to do to Rufus and his troop when he thought, *But it wasn't raining a moment ago.*

Suddenly somebody was standing over him, a sad, grey man with thin, grey hair plastered to his skull and eyes like failed experiments in egg poaching. "Hello," said the man. "Would you like some tea?"

Cabal sat up. He was most definitely no longer on the moor. Instead, he seemed to have landed in a garden—the sort of large, carefully designed garden that stately homes have resting in several acres. He couldn't see any stately home, though. Just an expanse of slightly undisciplined lawn pocked with bushes and the rotting remains of summerhouses and gazebos. They were in the middle of a large shallow bowl of land that hid the true horizon, the false one itself being obscured by copses of trees that ran in a broad circle about him. Here and there, he could see people sitting in the little buildings or walking, slowly, between them. Nearby, three men and a woman played a very sedate game of croquet. Cabal knew enough about croquet to know that it is a game with undercurrents: calculating, ruthless, and with a cold-blooded desire to destroy the opposition. Not here, though. Here they were just puttering around, shunting balls through hoops. Very odd.

"Would you like a cup of tea?" asked the man again. Cabal looked at him and then at the bone-china cup and saucer he was proffering. The rain had filled the cup to the brim and made it overflow into the already flooded saucer. The only evidence of tea was a faint sepia tinge in the rainwater.

"No, thank you," said Cabal. "I would like to know where I am, however."

"Oh," said the man. "Oh." He had to think for a moment and then added, "Oh. You're in the garden."

"And where precisely is that?"

The man gestured with the teacup, spilling some. "Why, it's here. Where we are."

Cabal had a sinking feeling that he might have been abducted by Dadaists. He tried again. "No, I mean what's beyond the garden?"

The man smiled gently, and Cabal had a sudden urge to punch him. "The garden," said the man.

"More garden."

"No. The garden."

"How big is this garden?"

"It goes from the trees"—the man pointed in a random direction—"to the trees." He pointed in the opposite direction.

"And what lies beyond the trees?"

"The garden."

Cabal succumbed to his urge. He left the man sitting on the grass nursing his bloody nose and set off for the tree line. Nobody raised the slightest objection, nobody even seemed to notice. He walked in long, rangy strides—all the better to be out of this place of the dull—past a decaying bandstand, overgrown statuary, and the croquet players. He noticed in passing that one was crying. Great shuddering sobs made his shoulders quake with misery as he leaned on his mallet for support. The other players were apparently waiting for him to finish his breakdown and get on with the game. They watched him with long, grey faces without a flicker of animation, and Cabal realised that such incidents were common here. No matter. He had a carnival to get back to.

"Fun, fun, fun," he said to himself as he climbed the shallow slope to the trees. When he had reached them, he stopped and looked back. It was slightly odd that there was no pond or lake in the middle of the depression. It must have remarkably good drainage. He shook his head and entered the trees. The copse was dense and dark, and great drops of water never stopped percolating their way down from the dismal sky. He actually seemed to be getting wetter as the stuff managed to get past his hat and scarf and inside his long coat. This couldn't be doing his cold any good. Actually, his cold seemed to have vanished. He paused and wiggled his nose experimentally. There was no itch, no impending sneeze. This was odd, too: Cabal didn't often get colds, but when he did, they stayed. He was starting to have a very bad feeling about his whole situation. He shoved his way through the trees with renewed vigour.

When he finally burst out into the open again, he was disappointed not to be surprised. There, before him, lay the garden, exactly as he'd seen it just before going into the trees. He sighed, found a new entry point into the copse, and tried again. He wasn't optimistic; he knew his course might have deviated some way from a straight line while he was negotiating his way between the trunks, but there was no possibility that he'd performed a complete about-face without being aware of it. Still, he owed it to himself and the scientific method to try again. Several minutes later, he was again rewarded with a vista of grass, garden furniture, and very depressed people playing croquet the way it isn't supposed to be played.

Of course, he'd heard of pocket universes, but he'd always imagined them as rather larger than this. More interesting, too. Rufus seemed to have spent his institutional time on something other than macramé potholders. It didn't look like the sort of place he'd have created as a dump for his enemies; Rufus liked his tortures to involve spikes and straps. Some long-dead sorcerer or thaumaturgist might well have crafted this garden originally as a place for contemplation. Rufus then found it lurking somewhere between the planes and hijacked it. Yes, thought Cabal, that would seem to fit the facts. Well, there had to be a way out. Its original creator must have designed an exit of some description after all. Stifling his displeasure down to a downward cast of his mouth, he made his way back to the heart of the garden.

The man with the cup of tea was waiting. Not especially for Cabal, but just standing around with the cup and saucer in his hand. "You punched me," he said without rancour.

"I broke your nose," said Cabal in a tone of mild disbelief. The man's nose was looking very unbroken. He tapped experimentally at it. Either the nose had healed itself at incredible speed, or the man was taking stoicism to extreme lengths.

"Oh. I suppose you did. I don't think it was meant to be at that angle."

"How quickly did it heal?"

"How quickly?" asked the man with wide-eyed incomprehension.

"How long?"

"My nose?"

"No," said Cabal with an implausible impersonation of patience. "I can see how long your nose is. How long did it take your nose to heal?"

"How long?"

"Yes."

"My nose?"

"Yes."

The man placed his thumb beneath his nose, where it joined the upper lip, and the index finger upon the tip. He carefully preserved the distance between the fingertips as he showed it to Cabal. "About an inch."

For the second time in a short while, Cabal felt he had no choice but to repeat an experiment. The man, cup, and saucer went flying in disparate directions. He lay on his back for a few moments, blinking. "You punched me again," he said, bemused at such strange behaviour.

"Yes, I did," said Cabal. He watched the freshly broken nose with interest as he fished his watch out of his pocket and made a mental note of the time.

The blood stopped flowing almost immediately, after a few seconds the ugly contusion that had started to form was already in abeyance, and then, astonishingly, the nose straightened itself with no external help at all until it snapped back in place with a slight *pop*. The whole process had taken—Cabal consulted his watch—no time. He shook the watch and checked it again. Its hands stayed defiantly still. His first thought was that he had forgotten to wind it, but, thinking back, he'd definitely done so earlier, back on the train, while he'd been waiting for Horst to make a move in their chess match. Then he wondered if water had got into it, but, no, it had been bone-dry when he'd produced it from his pocket, and he'd sheltered it in his hand while he watched the man's nose repair itself. "Have you got the time?" he asked the man as he helped him back to his feet.

"Time?" said the man. "Oh, no." He held out his hand to show Cabal his wristwatch. Its hands were still. "Nobody has any time here. No time at all."

𝔑ever had relativity seemed more pertinent. Cabal could count up to sixty if he liked, but that didn't really prove anything. It seemed like a minute, but that was all. "Seemed" didn't seem to butter many parsnips in the garden, and he said as much to one of the croquet players. "No," agreed the woman, "it's not a vegetable garden." Nor could anybody tell him how long they'd been there. Before long, Cabal realised that everything was "before long." He made the rounds of the twenty or so other inmates, asking them questions to which they had no answers. Objectively, there was no possible way he could have conducted that number of interviews in that depth in less than a couple of hours. Yet, subjectively, it still felt as if he'd been there only a couple of minutes, and this was beginning to do unpleasant things to his psyche. The temptation was to withdraw, perhaps indulge in repetitive behaviour so that it didn't matter when you'd done something—you'd done it lots of times before. Trying to smooth out reality by making each passing moment a tree in a forest of identical trees.

"Would you like a cup of tea?" asked the man. Cabal looked at him, appalled. He suddenly felt like a condemned man seeing a body swinging in the gibbet.

"No, I don't want a cup of tea." He gripped the man by his upper arms. "Listen. This is an artificial pocket universe. Do you understand what that means?" He went on, regardless of the man's silence. "Somebody created it. That means they must have put in an exit, an escape route, so they could get out. Do you understand that? Somewhere here, there must be a way of getting out."

For the first time, a gleam of intelligence entered the man's eyes. "Oh!" he quavered. "Oh, yes! An escape route! The way out! Oh, yes! Oh, yes! How I wish, how I wish, how I wish!"

"Good. I'm glad I've engaged your enthusiasm. Now, I'm going to talk to the others, but you have to do something for me. You're going to have to remember how important it is to find the exit and keep remembering it. Is that clear?"

"Oh, how I wish, how I wish, how I wish!"

"Good, keep it up."

Cabal had taken perhaps two steps when the man continued, "How I wish I'd remembered to put the exit in!"

Cabal stopped for a long, subjective moment. He turned slowly to address the man. "I beg your pardon?" he said with awful calmness.

The man paused to take a sip of rainwater. "Oh, how I wish, how I wish, wish, wish . . . Oh!"

Cabal had grabbed him by the lapels. "How you wish you'd remembered to put an exit in? Is that what you said? *Is that what you said?*" He realised that he was shouting, shaking the man, that he'd badly lost his temper. He pushed the man away. "Who are you, anyway? Why did you create this place?" The man blinked at him. "How could you forget to put an exit in, you damned fool?" Cabal spat venomously.

"Just . . . forgot," said the man, his voice breaking in despair.

" 'Just forgot,' " hissed Cabal, and walked quickly away, before he lost his temper again.

*C*abal didn't know how long it took him to calm down: it felt like half an hour, but that didn't mean anything, either. He sat in some sort of faux-Oriental gazebo and watched the croquet match. After a while, they got through all the hoops, but instead of going for the home stake, they just set course for the first hoop again. It was a game that could never end, and that seemed to sum the garden up all too well.

I can't believe it will end this way, thought Cabal. *I can't believe that I will be trapped here for eternity in the garden. There has to be a way out. The stupid bastard was too absent-minded to put in an exit; he must have made other errors in this place, exploitable errors. If only I could see them.* He looked at the sky. *If only it would stop raining.* The light behind the low clouds never changed, the drizzle never altered in intensity.

The gazebo was shared with a young man in spectacles who was sitting on a wicker chair, playing with brass discs on a wooden board shaped like an arched window. Straight lines had been burnt across it. The young man held out one of the discs to Cabal. "Shove ha'penny?" he asked. Cabal told him to shove something else entirely and walked out.

He found himself in the middle of the endless croquet game. The players had ground to a halt, confronted by the ugly apparition of making a tactical decision. One of them had unaccountably won a roquet and was unsure how to proceed. He placed his foot on his ball, took it off again, made as if to replace it, wavered. This was an unusual situation, and the variation in routine was forcing them to think.

"Allow me," said Cabal, taking the mallet from the vacillating man when the sound of grinding thought processes became too much to bear. The man seemed grateful to have been released from the spectre of the roquet, although having strangers abruptly take his mallet away was also disturbingly new. He looked at Cabal, blinking foolishly. "Tricky shot," said Cabal cheerfully. He eyed the ball, carefully placed his foot on it, and then smashed the vacillating man's brains out with a single powerful blow to the side of the skull.

The other players were stunned for a moment. Then they applauded uncertainly, no longer able to recall whether or not this was actually in the rules. "Well played, sir," said one.

Cabal ignored them. He was already on one knee by the body and checking its pulse. None; the blow had killed him outright, which was just as it should be. But he waited. His own heart sank as the corpse's stuttered back into life, fibrillated, and stabilised. The rapid reconstruction of the broken skull and presumed re-formation of the liquidised brain within predictably followed. By the time the former dead man's eyes had flickered open and he'd said, "Ouch," Cabal had already lost interest. So—there was no death here, either.

He walked slowly in the rain, collar up and hat brim down. He mustn't despair. With despair came acceptance, and with acceptance came the inevitable dulling of his faculties. The vacillating man was already back at his game of croquet, his recent brush with death—less of a brush and more a full-on head-butt—having changed nothing. Cabal couldn't, mustn't allow the same to happen to him. So lost in deep concentration was he that he almost walked into the sundial.

The sheer incongruity of it made him smile bitterly. A sundial in a place where the sun never shone. Ridiculous. Beads of rain stood on the engraved bronze disc or ran down the gnomon. At its edge he noticed some writing. He wiped the drops away with his fingertip and read "TEMPUS." That was all. After it, the metal seemed disturbed in faintly familiar patterns, almost as if another word was trying to force its way through. In slow distraction, he drew his watch again and looked at the face. The hands still hadn't moved even so much as a second. Time, he thought. Time's the key somehow. An idea started to crystallise in the melt of his imagination. It might not work, of course, and there was always the possibility that he might have to upset or hurt a few of these excuses for people. So it wasn't all bad news.

"Would you like a cup of tea?" said a familiar voice.

"Thank you," said Cabal, accepting the cold china. He gave the saucer back, poured the contents of the cup on the ground, and put it in his pocket. "Thank you very much."

He walked away, leaving the garden's architect and first inmate looking at the saucer, the slightly damper part of grass where the liquid had fallen, and Cabal's receding back. "You've got my cup," said the architect plaintively.

The vacillating man was still lining up for his roquet. His ball was now slightly submerged in the turf, having been tentatively stood on so many times. "Allow me," said Cabal cheerfully, and took his mallet. The man immediately shied away, protecting his head. Cabal reached down and drew a croquet hoop from the ground. "You weren't using these, were you?" he said, and walked off.

En route for the faux-Oriental gazebo, he snagged and pulled down a length of vine from a statue of a man in a toga looking thoughtful. At the gazebo, he reached over the young man's fitful game of shove ha'penny and took one of the brass discs. On closer inspection, he realised that they were indeed meant to be halfpennies but looked unfinished. Somehow rushed. On the way out, he passed the architect.

"You've got my cup," he protested. An edge that might have been returning intelligence glimmered in his voice. He was sounding dimly peeved.

"You've got a poor eye for detail," replied Cabal, showing him the disc. "And here"—he showed the architect one of the ivy leaves—"no veins. Very poor, could do better."

"It's not easy, you know. Remembering all these details."

"I didn't say it was. But if a job's worth doing—"

"You pompous prick." The architect threw the saucer down and glared at Cabal.

"It's worth doing well," grated Cabal. "Look around you. We're all here because you made the simplest and most ridiculous mistake. No exit. I believe you made another simple and ridiculous error. I need your cup to prove my hypothesis and, incidentally, get us all out of here. Now, are you going to help or just stand there insulting me?"

"Help? Help how?" the architect asked. His curiosity was outrunning his rancour. Currently, he was curious as to why Cabal was lashing the teacup to the end of the croquet mallet's handle with the ivy.

"Mainly by staying out of my way," said Cabal. He finished tying the cup in place and then started trying to balance the mallet on the edge of his hand. After a few adjustments, he had it seesawing sedately in place. "Look like the centre of gravity to you? It does to me." Marking the place with his thumb, he started to hack at the wood with the edge of the disc. To his dismay, the wood started to re-form slowly. Apparently, it wasn't only the animate that had immortality here. "Nothing for it. I don't need this to function long; I'll cut a new notch just before I need it."

Cabal stepped outside the gazebo and looked up into the sky. The rain showed no sign of changing in intensity. "Perfect," he said out loud. He placed the croquet hoop against a vertical strut at head height and was about to hammer it home with the mallet when he realised that it had the teacup at the other end. "Damnation!" he swore. "I should have done that penultimately. Getting difficult to plan ahead. You!" He pointed at one of the croquet players. "Give me your mallet!"

The woman looked at him uncomprehendingly. "You've already got his," she said, indicating the vacillating man.

In a few long strides, Cabal was standing before her. He tore the mallet from her grasp. "And now I've got yours."

He was gathering a small crowd as he hammered the hoop into the gazebo's doorframe. He relocated the mallet, ivy, and cup assembly's balancing point and feverishly started to hack a notch into the handle there.

His ability to forward-plan was being eroded as his sense of time evaporated, he could feel it. He also had an unpleasant feeling that if this experiment failed, the jig would be up with him. He could look forward to an eternity of repetitive actions, just like everybody else here. In fact, he could forget about the luxury of being able to look forward at all.

The notch was cut. Its ragged edges were already starting to smooth as he settled it onto the wire of the loop. The strange construction wavered gently and settled. "I want my mallet," said the vacillating man, and stepped forward to take it. The architect pushed him away.

"Idiot!" he barked. "Can't you see what it is?" He glared at the vacant faces. "God's teeth, it's a water clock! Don't you see?" He looked cautiously in the china teacup, anxious not to disturb it. The trickling run-off draining from the gazebo roof was quickly filling it. "Time," he spoke reverentially. "We have time."

As the cup filled, the arm of the mallet bearing it dipped slowly, but gathered speed as the centre of gravity moved over the fulcrum. Abruptly it dipped low, and the contents of the cup spilled out. "One Cabal Chronal Unit," intoned Cabal. The cup swung up again and started to refill.

Somewhere in the causal clockwork of the little universe, a pendulum—long still—began swinging.

"Do you think it will work?" asked the architect.

"It already is," replied Cabal. It was true: the light was beginning to change as the clouds scurried across the sky. "You know, I think we may be in for some fine weather."

"The sun!" exclaimed the architect, laughing. "The sun!"

They walked to the sundial. The rain had turned to a fine drizzle illuminated by shafts of sunshine breaking through the clouds. They waited until the dial was caught in light.

The architect leaned low and examined the plate where the gnomon's shadow fell. "It's about three o'clock," he said. Then to Cabal he said, smiling, "Just about time for tea."

Cabal said nothing but smoothed the raindrops from the writing on the edge of the plate. The disturbed metal had resolved itself, inevitably, into the word "FUGIT."

"Time will be . . ." the architect started to say, but Cabal stopped him. "Time is . . ." he corrected.

"*T*ime was when people thought they could stand against us!" roared Rufus.

"Hurrah!" exulted the Maleficarian Army, who were nothing if not uncritical.

"That time has passed! See how our enemies are consigned to oblivion!" He gestured to Cabal's gladstone bag, still lying where he had put it down to blow his nose. Of Cabal himself there was no sign. The army had been very impressed when Rufus had made Cabal vanish like that. "See how resistance crumbles before us! This very day, that town down there will be ours!"

"Huzzah!" This was great. A popcorn vendor could have made a fortune.

"And soon this country! This continent! The wor—"

"Oooooh!" chorused the army, looking straight past him at Cabal's bag. Some of the more proactive pointed. Rufus cast a cursory glance over his shoulder and committed a gross double take that made his plus fours flap in disbelief. Cabal was back. Oddly, in the thirty seconds he'd been gone he seemed to have been caught in a shower, although there wasn't a rain cloud in the sky. He brushed himself down, took his hat off, combed his fingers through his hair, and replaced the hat.

"Hello, Rufus. You're probably surprised to see me."

"But . . . but I . . . I consigned you . . ."

"To oblivion. Yes, well, I didn't have time for it. Although, in a sense, yes, I did." And he smiled one of his smiles. Several of the more nervous Maleficarian soldiers whinnied with trepidation. "All of which is by the by. As I was saying, that town belongs to me, Rufus. Continue at your peril."

"You have tasted the least of my power once, Cabal! Prepare to suffer its full fury!" Once more Rufus tilted his head, placed his fingers on his temples, and started to chant under his breath.

"I must admit, that translocation caught me unawares. You're not a very impressive warlock, but you have your moments. Thus"—Cabal picked up his gladstone bag and opened it—"I'm not prepared to take any more risks with you."

Rufus ignored him, muttering in the lost tongue of a pre-human civilisation that had worked great sorcerous happenings yet had never invented the vowel. Cabal continued talking as he fished around in his bag.

"Your problem, Rufus Maleficarus, is that you never understood why magic was superseded by science. If you listen to the sad old wizards up in their keeps and the witches in the dales, you might believe it had something to do with the passing of the Seelie and the Unseelie from our world. Or the dust-sheet of cynicism settling on our hearts and driving out the wonder. Or children refusing to say that they believe in fairies. Poppycock. I'll tell you why. Convenience. I only practise necromantics because there's no other way of doing it. But when it comes to applied sciences, technologies, any spotty Herbert with a degree and a lab coat can perform greater wonders than Merlin."

Rufus was working himself into a frenzy. The summation of his hexing could only be seconds away. Still Cabal seemed unconcerned.

"You've wasted your mind and your life. Do you understand that? Science can do it all so much cheaper, easier, and, indeed . . ." Will-o'-the-wisps were dancing around Rufus's head as arcane powers peaked. Cabal sighed. Nobody ever listened. "And, indeed," he continued, "faster." He drew his revolver from the bag and fired rapidly three times. Rufus was a big man, but he'd just become host to enough lead to build a platoon of toy soldiers. His chanting stopped on the first impact, and he only grunted when the others caught him. He looked at Cabal with rising horror as he realised that he was dying. He blinked, unable to believe that his life was now measured in seconds. He made a strange beseeching gesture to Cabal, his upper arms against his chest and his hands reaching out as if he thought Cabal could somehow reverse the damage, somehow save him. Then his body betrayed him, and he fell forward heavily in a way no living person can. The will-o'-the-wisps danced over the carcass for the moments it took for them to fade away.

"Now," said Cabal, "what am I going to do with you lot?"

The Maleficarian Army shifted en masse from foot to foot. They weren't sure, either. A cry went up: "Our new leader!" It was quickly taken up and expanded upon.

"Our new leader, Cabal! Cabal! Our new leader, Cabal!"

Cabal put away his gun. "Very well," he said dryly. "You can work for my carnival. Follow me." The army formed up behind him as he set off. "One thing, though," he called over his shoulder. "There are some forms that will need filling in."

Big Squidhead lies a-scheming at the bottom of the sea,
He is counting out the aeons that make up eternity,
And when he's done, it's curtains for the vast majority,
While the Tcho-Tcho get on down.

Aïe! Ftagn! Ftagn! Shub-Niggurath!
We're on the winning side to see the aftermath,
Put on your marching boots because we're on the path,
To the end times, here we come!
To the end times, here we come!
To the end times! Here! We! Cooooooooome!

"And stop that!"

Chapter 8

The good people of Murslaugh responded well to their saviour and showed their appreciation by visiting his carnival in droves. In his school exercise book with the squared paper pages that he thought his brother, Horst, knew nothing about (he was wrong, and Horst found it vastly amusing), Johannes Cabal kept a graph. On the x-axis was a one-year time scale; on the vertical y-axis a scale marked from 0 at the origin to 100 at his topmost point. This was Cabal's "soul chart," and it was looking quite healthy. With the edge of his wooden ruler, he could estimate the best-fit line, and it took him over the hundred-souls mark about two weeks before the deadline. It was a safety margin, but not much of one; it wouldn't take much to make him lose the wager. Not much at all. There was a knock at the door. It was Mr. Bones.

"Say, boss, it's the boss," he said.

Cabal put his exercise book away and leaned back in his chair. "You are making precisely no sense," he said.

"You know? The town boss guy."

Cabal sat up abruptly. "You mean the *mayor*? Well, show him in."

Cabal had little time for politicians at any level in the normal run of his scientific career. Well, perhaps the level marked "live experimental subjects," but that was all. If he had learned anything in the previous weeks, however, it was that local politicians have limited powers but enormous egos. A snub, real or illusory, was all it took to make them apply those limited powers with great vigour and imagination.

Two months previously, a disgruntled alderman had almost managed to close them down for health and safety infractions. Cabal hadn't felt like pointing out that the carnival's governing body—Hell—only has the sort of health and safety regulations that make sure both are seriously threatened. He had accurately doubted it would have done their case any good. It had taken the carrot of a large brown envelope stuffed with used bank notes, and the stick of a midnight visit from Phobos the Nightmare Man (who was pathetically grateful to have been seconded from Tartarus: "It's good to get out, meet the punters. Gets you back in touch, you know?") to clear things up. All because the alderman in question took exception to Cabal mentioning in passing that the last time he'd seen any body as bloated as that of the alderman's wife, it had maggots crawling out of it. The fact that the observation was true was neither here nor there.

The Mayor of Murslaugh was a jolly, ebullient man of the sort who, in a well-ordered world, would be called Fezziwig. That his name was Brown was a powerful indictment on the sorry state of things.

"Lord Mayor," Cabal said, "what a delight to meet you. I'm sorry I haven't had time to call on you."

"Not at all, not at all, a business entrepreneur like you, busy all hours, not at all." He smiled, apparently expecting an answer.

Cabal gave up trying to find a verb in that sentence. "Well, how can I help you? I am, of course, at the service of you and your delightful town."

"Ah, well, yes, marvellous, you see? Maleficarus! Poom! Yes, blink! Of an eye! Marvellous!" Inexplicably, he mimed swiping at a ball with a cricket bat, then watching the ball vanish into the distance. "Exemplary!"

"Oh! I understand. This is about me clearing up that little bit of unpleasantness with Rufus Maleficarus? Really, it was nothing. A pleasure," he added truthfully.

"Nothing? No! Jings, quite substantially not inconsiderable. Taking all points. *All* points, mind! Great thing, great thing." He shook his head at the sheer drama of it all. "Local hero." He looked dolefully at the floor for a moment, drew a great breath, the huge smile reappearing, said, "Busy man! Off now!" and left.

Cabal looked at the door for several moments after the mayor had shut it behind him. "Yes," he said finally. "Well, if I ever suffer brain damage, I know there's always a career waiting for me in local politics."

*T*he ugly man and the fat, ugly man eyed the stall. "What are y' s'posed to do?" asked the fat, ugly man.

"All you have to do is throw a Ping-Pong ball into one of the goldfish bowls," said Bobbins brightly.

"An' I win a prize?" said the fat, ugly man.

"And you win a prize," said Bobbins. Brightly. Bobbins had been the result of some of Cabal's tinkering with the basic "a rag, a bone, a hank of hair (and a quantity of lard)" formula—in this case, by the addition of a tin of Brasso metal polish. As a result, everything that Bobbins did, he did brightly.

"Okay," said the fat, ugly man, faintly echoed by the plain ugly man. "S'pose I'll 'ave a go."

Coins and Ping-Pong balls exchanged hands. The fat, ugly man lobbed a ball in the general direction of the goldfish bowls without taking any time to aim at all. The ball hit one bowl's rim, bounced high, and landed neatly in another.

"Well done, sir!" said Bobbins, brightly. "You win!"

The fat, ugly man and his companion looked unaccountably put out. "Bugger me, Anders," he said to the ugly man. "I've only gorn an' won, 'aven't I?"

Anders looked miserable. "Bugger me, Croal. So you 'ave. Now what?"

"You win a goldfish!" butted in Bobbins, brightly.

Croal ignored him. "Just carry on as usual, s'pose. Okay?" he said to Anders.

"Okay," said Anders. Then, in a theatrical shout, "Blimey! What a con! This 'ere stall's a diddle!"

"Yeah!" joined Croal. "It's a diddle! Cheat! Cheat!"

"But . . . you won?" said Bobbins, slightly less brightly.

As if by magic, a group of perhaps eight large men with pickaxe handles appeared out of the gathering crowd. "It's a set-up!" they chorused. "It's a con job! Smash it up!"

"Oh dear," said Bobbins, his brightness almost undetectable as the men started to destroy his stall.

Cabal was at the steam calliope, loading up an unlabelled piece of music, when news of the disturbance reached him. En route, he stopped by the Tunnel of Love. There he found Horst flattering an attractive young woman to the sticking point.

"Horst! There's trouble. I'd appreciate your presence."

Horst looked like he might argue, but a goldfish bowl arching over the top of the tunnel and landing with a hollow *plop* in the water distracted him.

"Yes, it might be as well," he admitted. Then, to the young lady, "I'm sorry, my dear, but I am required elsewhere. Stay right here. I'll be back soon." As he stepped away, Cabal noticed that her line of sight continued through the space where Horst had been standing a moment ago.

"You can't go leaving mesmerised women littering up the place," he snapped. "It's, I don't know, unhygienic."

"It's a funfair. People are used to seeing odd things," replied Horst. "Besides, I'm famished. It's been days. She's the most edible thing I've seen tonight, and I'm not having her running away. Now, come on." He disappeared into the darkness between the rides.

Cabal looked around, saw Mr. Bones, and clicked his fingers to gain his attention. "Bones! Do something about that woman!"

Bones looked enquiringly at the still form. "Like what, boss?"

"Oh, I don't know. Put a blanket over her or something," he snapped, and followed his brother at a trot.

By the time they got there, it had turned into a free-for-all. The destruction of the stall had sparked fights that had spread to other stalls.

Horst picked up a man who was trying to set fire to a coconut shy by the scruff of the neck, told him he was bad, and threw him into the next field, which happened to be on the other side of the river. The man's despairing scream diminishing into the night sky did a lot to calm matters. Cabal went around and did some further calming with his stick. After a few minutes of applied physical diplomacy, the fight had turned into a lot of people, mainly men, standing around battered, bruised, and sullen. Cabal looked at them with palpable loathing.

"Who started this?" he said, and everybody there past school age had sudden, unpleasant flashbacks to when they weren't. No answers came. He paced up and down in front of them, his hands clasped behind his back. "All I want is the truth. Nobody will be punished," he said, fooling nobody.

"They've gone," said a faint voice from the wreckage of a stall. Faint, pained, but still eager to please. In a word, bright.

"Help him out of there, someone," said Cabal, and immediately several men with scuffed knuckles and nosebleeds went to it, eager to show that they were good people who wouldn't get involved in a common brawl—oh, no.

Bobbins was brought before Cabal like a spoil of victory and dumped at his feet. "What do you mean, they've gone?"

Bobbins painfully picked himself up and looked around. "There were two blokes. One was sort of ugly, and the other was sort of fat and ugly. They had a go on the bowls and won. That's when they went bananas and started saying that they'd been cheated."

"But they'd won?"

"Yes. I was trying to give them their prize when all these other blokes just popped up and smashed everything. I tried to stop them," he implored brightly. "There were just too many."

Horst was kicking around the wreckage. He knelt and picked out a dangerous-looking piece of wood. He showed it to Cabal. "It's a pickaxe handle. Not the sort of thing people tend to carry around for self-defence."

Cabal took it from him and hefted it. "You're saying this was premeditated? Why? And by whom?"

"One of them was called Croal!" interrupted Bobbins, his brightness rekindling by the second. "That's what the other one called him. He was called Andy. Or Anders. Or something."

"But who are they? And why did they do it? And what are you grinning about?"

Horst was looking unpalatably smug. "You don't know much about carny and travelling-fair folk, do you?"

"You know I . . ." Cabal noticed that the chastised brawlers were still standing around, showing a polite interest in the conversation. "Go on! Clear off! The show's over!" Slowly they dispersed. Cabal turned back to Horst. "You know I don't. So go on, have your moment of glory, and astound me with esoterica."

"There's nothing mysterious about it. What's the primary function of a carnival? Not this carnival, obviously. I mean normal ones."

"To let people have . . . fun," replied Cabal as if he'd soiled his mouth with the word.

"Oddly enough, no. That's how it fulfils its primary function. Try again."

Cabal hated being patronised and was starting to seethe. "To make money. I'm not a fool. But we're not interested in the money. I fail to see . . ." The truth of the matter slapped him in the face like a dead cod. "I *am* a fool. It's so obvious."

"Business competitors. *They* don't know we're not in it for the money. That's between you, me, and the big 'S.' " With some satisfaction, he watched Cabal shake his head in disgusted disbelief.

"I suppose this means we'll have to kill them," said Cabal finally.

"Think of the fuss. No, they're businessmen. We'll do a deal. Believe me, they'll listen to reason."

𝕴t didn't take very much detective work to discover that there was a travelling fair in the next town: Butler's Travelling Amusements. Cabal gave them a visit the next mid-morning to sort things out, taking along a thick wad of currency for if they wanted to be reasonable, and Joey Granite—"His Head's Made of Stone!"—if they didn't.

The fair site was quiet when they arrived. Over the entrance, a large, badly painted sign shouted, *Billy Butler's Travelling Amusements! The Best Rides! The Best Sideshows!*

"It looks quite, quite appalling," said Joey.

"Quite so," replied Cabal. "Incidentally, Mr. Granite, I'd appreciate it if you could let me do the talking."

"By all means, *kemosabe.*"

"I mean *all* the talking."

"Certainly. You are, after all, the boss. Might one, however, enquire why?"

"To be quite frank, I've brought you along as muscle. People have some sort of psychological problem with believing a man can be quite mind-bogglingly strong *and* intelligent. It has to be one thing or the other."

"Like pretty women and brains. I take your point. You don't wish me to undermine my threatening aspect by being unexpectedly rather acute. Very well, mum's the word."

Having, he hoped, capped Joey's notorious loquacity for the time being, Cabal led the way to the largest and least tasteful caravan. He rapped on the door and waited.

Eventually, it opened to reveal a short, dishevelled man in his underwear wearing an ostentatious red smoking jacket over the top. Remarkably, and despite every sign that he had just got out of bed, his synthetically black hair lay perfectly, as if varnished in place.

"Wot d'ya want?" he croaked, blinking in the daylight.

"You are the proprietor? William Butler?"

The man screwed up his eyes and considered Cabal. Then he considered Joey. Then he went back to considering Cabal, because it didn't put such a crick in his neck. "Oo wants t'know?"

"My name is Johannes Cabal. I see you recognise it." The man's scrunched-up face had dilated a little. "I've come to return some of your property." He nodded to Joey, who produced the pickaxe handle from within his coat and waggled it at the man between forefinger and thumb, like a blunt toothpick.

"Y'can't prove a thing," said the man. "I never seen that before in my life. I swear on me muvver's grave, I din't."

Cabal was shaking his head. "Slow down, Mr. Butler. The transparent denials come later. Firstly, you *are*, are you not, Mr. William Butler of Butler's Travelling Amusements, yes?" The man straightened himself up a little, and Cabal had a warning flash that this wasn't going to go quite the way he'd planned.

"Only me muvver ever called me 'William.' Billy Butler, tha's me. Showman and entra-pren-ooor. An' you can't come rahnd 'ere 'cuesing decen', law-'bidin' folk like me ov smashin' up your carny wivout evidence, see?"

"You misunderstand me, Mr. Butler. I see no reason to accuse you of anything when we both know you're as guilty as the day is long. No, please, spare me the melodramatics." Butler's red face was speeding towards a beetroot intensity. "If need be, Mr. Granite here would cheerfully tear your operation to pieces until he found Mr. Croal and his provocative friend. I'm sure they would only be too eager to admit their rôle in last night's violence and your part as the instigator, faced with this evidence." He tapped the pickaxe.

"Or I'll make them eat it. Hurr-hurr-hurr!" grated Joey, showing an unexpected and unwelcome bent towards amateur dramatics. Cabal shot him a glance and he shut up.

"I'd like t'see ya try," said Butler unwisely.

𝕬 little over seven minutes passed before Cabal pointed to Butler and said, "Is this the man who sent you to cause trouble at my carnival?" Croal and Anders could only nod in agreement. Talking was proving difficult with half a shattered pickaxe handle shoved in their respective mouths. The two men dangled from Joey's great hands and wished they were somewhere else.

"Bloody grasses," growled Butler.

"None of this is necessary, Mr. Butler. I just want us to come to an understanding. You and your people stay away from my carnival, and I, for my part, will not have every man jack of you murdered and your souls sent express to the lowest pit in Hell."

"Ya couldn't if ya tried," muttered Butler unwisely.

Cabal barely prevented Joey from smashing Croal and Anders together to make something with too many limbs and not enough heads.

"Look, do you take some sort of pleasure in being contrary? Try to understand. This is out of your hands. You do as you're told or things will go so badly wrong for you as to beggar belief. Stay away from my carnival." Cabal turned to Joey. "Put those down and come with me." Joey dropped Croal and Anders in a heap and followed Cabal back towards the road.

When they were out of earshot of Butler and his gang of glowering riggers, Cabal said, " 'Or I'll make them eat it. Hurrr-hurrr-hurrr!' "

"I was merely extemporising on the part you'd given me," replied Joey, unapologetically. "Strong and silent is *so* passé."

"And 'strong and stupid' is at the thespian cutting edge? Oh, never mind. It sort of worked, if not the way I'd intended. And we saved ourselves this large sum of money." He slapped the pocket containing the unused bribe. "Although, frankly, we've got more of the stuff than we know what to do with."

Horst was not happy when the morning's events were recounted to him. "You don't understand these people. You haven't put him in his place, you've just made him look stupid in front of his people. We haven't heard the last of Billy Butler."

Cabal was roused from his bunk just as dawn's rosy fingers were smudging the clouds like the finger-painting of a hyperactive child. He saw the gaudy colours of light through the sleeping car's window and groped for his dark glasses. The colours were too gaudy for comfort. "What . . ." He found his glasses and pulled them on. "What's happening?"

"It's bad, bossman," said Bones. "Fire."

Cabal dragged on his long coat and ran out into chaos. Everybody and everything was running around in a frenzy of indecision. Even the Things from the Ghost Train were out and about, running up to people and shrieking in their faces. "You! Things!" he roared. "Get back under cover before the sun comes up." They dithered. "Immediately!" They went. Horst appeared at his elbow.

"Sorry, Johannes. I'm going to have to go, too. This couldn't have happened at a worse time."

Cabal spun on his heel to glare at his brother. "Meaning what? That I'm incapable of dealing with this on my own?"

Horst, despite almost perfect poise, was taken aback. "No, not at all. I thought . . ." He looked towards the horizon. The sun could only be seconds away. "Look, I don't have time to argue this. I've got to go." There was a disturbance in the air and Cabal was alone.

The sun came up to find a scene of raging natural processes being fought to a standstill by unhesitating rationality and bullish common sense. The riggers and barkers had been formed into bucket lines, and finally a use had been found for Horatio the Human Hosepipe.

"Yo! Baby!" he crooned as he was wielded by Layla. "C'mon, light *my* fire!"

"Don't get him excited or we'll never put the bloody thing out," barked Cabal, sooty and furious.

𝔄fter an hour, there was nothing left of the fire. Nor of three sideshows, four concessions, and an "I Lie Diplomatically About Your Weight" machine. Cabal walked around and around the wreckage, hissing angrily if anybody tried to talk to him, around and around like a vulture over a zombie clambake. A Neanderthal sat naked in a large puddle of water, beside which was a charred sign reading *The Ice Man! Entombed in the Siberian Ice for Ten Million Years!* "What's happenin', man?" he asked anybody who came near him.

Abruptly Cabal stopped, sniffed the air, and turned over a piece of board with the toe of his ruined handmade shoes. Exposed was a small pool of liquid that rolled and glistered in a way that spoke of ultrahydrous viscosity. He knelt by it, ruining his trousers into the bargain, and inhaled the air above it. Bones came over and sniffed cautiously at it, too. Cabal stood up, his face an ugly pallor beneath the fire-fighter's smudges. "Accelerant," he said quietly.

"Yeah?" Bones tried another sniff. "Smells like gasoline to me."

"Arson."

"Well, make your mind up."

𝕭illy Butler realised he had a visitor by the knock at his door. Actually, it was more the way the door was knocked down, torn out, and lobbed into the next county that was the clue.

"You again," he said, lip curled, as Cabal walked in. Outside, there was a swatting sound as Joey dissuaded any of Butler's riggers from coming to his assistance.

"I thought," said Cabal, slowly and carefully, "that we had a deal, Butler."

"I don't rememer makin' no—"

"I thought," continued Cabal, "that we had an understanding. You stay away from my carnival and I let you live."

"I've been in this business man an' boy for comin' on—"

"Yes, that's the point, Mr. Butler. Mr. 'I've *been* in this business man and boy since the dawn of time' Butler. Past tense. You see? It is all over now, and all because you couldn't leave well enough alone."

Butler tried another tack. "This 'ere's private property. If yew don't—"

"Ach! I don't believe it! I'm talking about your imminent death and you're talking about civil action for trespass."

Butler paused. Something seemed to be getting through. "Wot? You're goin' ta *kill* me?"

"Yes. Probably." Never discuss murder plans with the victim, he reminded himself. It takes all the spontaneity out of it.

"Why?"

"Why? You tried to burn down my carnival!"

Butler crossed his arms and smiled smugly. "Prove it."

"Butler, try to under— You don't mind if I sit down, do you? Try to understand, I'm not the police. I don't need evidence, real or fabricated. All I need is reasonable suspicion, and you, Butler, are very suspicious. If, at this very moment, they were testing a suspiciometer in the Antipodes, they would be saying, 'Good heavens, what is this very suspicious object that we have detected? Why, it looks just like Billy Butler, the world-renowned arsonist and bad liar.' "

Butler considered Cabal's words and found them reasonable. "Orl right," he said. "What's this deal, then?"

"History. You had your chance and you let it go by." He gazed out of the flyspecked caravan window. "Look, I don't really want to have your blood on my hands. It would be terribly inconvenient. Why don't we try one more time, eh?"

$\mathcal{T}$wenty-four hours later, Cabal and Joey Granite were back. Thin wisps of smoke could still be seen to rise from Cabal's cuffs and collar, and there was soot on his face. He seemed unhappy about something.

$\mathcal{T}$he previous day's fire had been galling quite apart from the physical damage it had caused. When Cabal had woken from a troubled sleep to find that person or persons unknown had not only poured petrol along the length of the track beneath the train, including the office in which he slept, but also padlocked his door shut, it seemed to be verging upon an insult. He had just been considering which window to break when there had been a splintering, wrenching sound and Horst had opened the door.

"Did you know that somebody'd locked this door?" he had asked with an air of concerned enquiry.

Cabal pushed past him and jumped down onto the gravel by the track. "You two!" he shouted at the cab. "Move the train! Quickly, damn you!"

Dennis and Denzil had looked at each other. They'd half suspected something was amiss when the train had been engulfed with flames but hadn't wanted to cause a fuss by drawing attention to it. Denzil had been about to tell Dennis to get a head of steam up when he'd noticed Dennis's hair was on fire. That had been good for a laugh, or at least the grisly hooting noises that Denzil used instead these days, ever since his lungs had dried out. Dennis had frowned, scratched his head, and set fire to his hand. Denzil had hooted some more.

They'd still have been there if the great engine hadn't decided that enough was enough, and started to move with a monstrous roar of outraged engineering. Cabal and Horst had watched in surprise as the locomotive backed slowly down the track. Where it passed, the fire was sucked back in under the locomotive's belly and vanished in the glimmer of upward motion. Within a minute, there had been no flames left at all except inside the engine's firebox, a firebox that had been damped down and cold but ten minutes before. Now it raged like a furnace. The brothers Cabal had looked at each other: there were still a good few things they didn't know or understand about this carnival of theirs.

*T*hat was then. Now Johannes Cabal and Joey Granite stood before Billy Butler and said nothing. The smell of smoke said it all for them.

Butler smiled nastily. "Oh. It's—" As famous last words go, they lacked a certain something.

"Uppercut, Joey," said Cabal. Joey Granite delivered an uppercut of surpassing science and pugilistic artistry. It was a thing of beauty and kinetic poetry that might be long admired among people who enjoy watching other people beat the living daylights out of one another. It was also powerful enough to lift a small building off its foundations. Anything up to a branch library would have tottered and fallen. Billy Butler, despite a bit of a gut, simply wasn't in the same league weight-wise. By some miracle, his head stayed on his body, but there was little doubt that the police would be making enquiries long before he hit the ground again. "Let us leave, Joey," said Cabal as Butler vanished through the cloud base.

They walked quickly back through the Butler fairground, Butler's men shouting abuse but staying comfortably out of danger, the women running around in predictable hysteria. They pointedly ignored the cat-calls and screaming and were soon back on the road to Murslaugh.

Half a mile on, Cabal stopped.

Something was bothering him. It was the idea of predictable hysteria. Hysteria verging on the rehearsed.

Thinking back, he could have sworn several of the women were screaming "Rhubarb! Rhubarb!" And the abuse the men had shouted— there'd been a lot of fist shaking going on, but what had they actually said? Something like "Raffeln-huffeln-ranty-raa!," was it? "Grrulveln gnash raffer"?

"You're cogitating, old bean," said Joey, mildly curious. "What's amiss?"

"I'm going back," said Cabal determinedly.

"Oh? Why?"

"There's something wrong here. Something fishy about that fair."

"You mean apart from their proprietor being in low Earth orbit?"

"Yes, apart from that. I have a sixth sense that tells me when I'm being made a fool of."

"Oh, I've heard of that. 'Clinical paranoia,' I think it's called."

"I have a sixth sense," said Cabal as he gave Joey the look of a man who knows where to lay hands on a pneumatic drill and isn't afraid to use it, "and it's telling me somebody somewhere is trying to play me for a fool." He turned on his heel and marched back towards the Butler fairground.

It wasn't there. There was barely a sign it ever had been. "I knew it!" Cabal strode across the abandoned site. "I knew it!"

"Well, fancy," said Joey, his great hands on his hips as he looked around with open-faced astonishment. "That's quite a trick."

Cabal stopped and looked at Joey. The ogreish man was very convincing in his surprise, but when all was said and all was done, he was still a product of Hell, created from the very blood of Satan. How far could he be trusted? Even Bones, his major-domo, sprang from the same wellhead. Perhaps Horst was the only one he could really trust. Blood was thicker than water, after all. He had its relative density written down somewhere to prove it.

Joey's hand descended gently on his shoulder and drew him to one side. Half a second later, Billy Butler hit the ground where he'd been standing and made a crater four feet deep. "Thank you, Joey," said Cabal.

They looked into the hole at the mangled corpse. "At least we won't have to bury him," commented Joey. "I'll just kick some earth in there on him, shall I?"

"No," said Cabal dryly.

"Not deep enough? I'll find a spade."

"Not deep enough. Not by a very long way." He crossed his arms and looked down on the body with cold disdain. "How deep is Hell, anyway?"

There was a long pause. Then Butler's head creaked round a hundred and eighty degrees. "How did you guess?" he croaked through his twisted and broken windpipe.

"A little too theatrical to be convincing. That *is* you, isn't it, Ragtag?"

"Ratuth," said the corpse peevishly. The head twisted around again, popping and snapping as it went. Then it extended awkwardly, the vertebrae tearing a slot at the back of the jacket collar.

Joey took a surprised step back. "Oh! I say . . ."

The tear was soon joined by more and more as the thing that had once been Billy Butler erupted into a mess of hands, claws, and writhing thorned tentacles. Non-Euclidean angles sprang up vertically like the scaffolding for the Tower of Babel. At their head, a horse's skull topped with a stylised Greek helmet was squeezed out from the gaps between realities. "General Slabuth to *you*, Johannes Cabal," finished the demon, jaw clattering.

"Whose brilliant idea was this?" asked Cabal.

"I beg your pardon?"

"This half-witted attempt to make me lose the wager. Whose idea was it?"

" 'Half-witted' is a *little* harsh, I think."

"Whose," repeated Cabal, firmly enunciating, "idea?"

"Ah, sort of a committee thing, actually. You see—"

"Yours, then."

They looked at each other in silence for a moment. "Yes," said Ratuth Slabuth finally.

"And what does your master think of this?"

"What? Cheating? He thinks it's a frightfully good wheeze as a rule."

"Well, tell him it won't do. No more interference or the whole deal's off."

"Ah, you can't back out as easily as all that."

"Why not? We didn't sign anything. We didn't even shake hands."

Slabuth managed to purse his lips despite not having any. "It's not in the *spirit* of the thing."

Cabal laughed derisively. "No more interference, understand? Come along, Mr. Granite." He turned on his heel and walked off in the direction of the Cabal Carnival.

Joey paused long enough to say, "Nice to meet you. Sorry, must rush," and rushed.

Ratuth Slabuth watched them go. Then he ignored the earth beneath his feet and plunged into the fiery pit of Hell.

He found Satan on his throne in the cavern of lava, reading a large-print edition of Wheatley's *The Satanist*.

"It's a rum way to warn people off from worshipping me," Satan commented, indicating the book. "It seems to be lots of fun, according to this. Still, I bet they all die horribly at the end. Oh well. Who wants to live forever?"

"Most of them," said General Slabuth.

Satan slammed the book shut and it vanished. "So—how was it? Being human?"

"Cramped. I'd really rather it were later than sooner before I do that again."

"And Cabal?"

"Surprisingly slow to catch on. Still, I managed to wreck about a fifth of his carnival before the penny dropped."

"A fifth? Well done."

"He'll recover, unfortunately. Especially with the help of that brother of his."

"Yes. Horst Cabal's involvement was unexpected. Not to worry, it's done what I wanted. We shan't interfere further. At least, not for the time being."

There was a pause, during which Slabuth hovered awkwardly. Finally, he said, "Lord Satan. May I ask a question?"

"Yes?"

"This whole business has troubled me from the start. While I can see the potential gains to be made by letting Cabal run around doing his best to gather souls, I still don't understand why you gave him the carnival to help him. From our past experiences, we know them to be powerful corruptors within fairly broad parameters. Giving one to Cabal is tantamount to conceding the wager from the beginning."

"And your question is?"

"Might I ask what all this was in aid of?"

Satan smiled sweetly. "No. You may not. Tactics are your concern, Ratuth Slabuth. The grand strategy is mine. You may go."

Slabuth started to say something, but thought better of it. Trying hard to avoid feeling menial, he went.

Satan waited until he was alone. He glanced around briefly. If it were possible for the embodiment of sin to look guilty rather than pleased about it, he could definitely have been described as slightly ashamed. Satisfied that there was nobody about to observe his actions, Satan clicked his fingers. A dog-eared old school exercise book, the sort with squared paper, materialised in his hand. He opened it to a graph entitled, in his neat hand, "Cabal's Performance." The zigzagging line crossed the hundred-souls mark about a fortnight before the deadline. Satan weighed up the setbacks Cabal had suffered over the last few days, smiled, and erased the latter part of the line. Carefully, he put in a revised estimate: now it indicated a hundred souls with barely a day to spare.

"There, Johannes," said Satan. "That should put a little more excitement into your life."

Police Bulletin (issued 22/12/1——):
Laidstone Prison Escapees

Here follows a list of the escapees from Laidstone's "E" Wing, the maximum-security section. All the escaped convicts were incarcerated for the most serious crimes, and all are to be approached with caution. Appendix A contains photographs and physical descriptions.

- *Aleister Gage Baker—"The Beast of Barnwick." Believed largely harmless without his Beast costume, which remains in evidence.*
- *Talbot Saint John Barnaby—"The Pub Poisoner." Former landlord. All officers should avoid gratis refreshment at public houses until Barnaby is back in custody.*
- *Leslie Coleridge—"The Part-Time Children's Entertainer of Death." Approach with caution. If Coleridge offers to make a sausage dog out of balloons, call for immediate assistance.*
- *Thomas Nashton Cream—"The Incompetent Killer." Attempted murders, one. Actual deaths, twenty-seven, all unintentional. Intended victim escaped unscathed.*
- *Frederick Gallagher—"The Brides in the Inflammable Electrified Acid Bath Murderer." Limited threat. Kills only for insurance money. Is prone to overplanning.*
- *Henry George Hetherbridge—"The Cotton-Reel Killer." Murdered his wife, uncle, solicitor, and grocer before questions were raised about the likelihood of four cotton-reel-related accidental deaths in a six-week period.*
- *Gideon Gabriel Lucas—"The Bible Basher." Only dangerous to individuals with the surname Bible.*
- *Palmer Mallows—"The Soft-Shoe Strangler." Officers are warned to beware any impromptu dancing.*
- *Joseph Grant Osborne—"The Unnecessarily Rude Poisoner." Of limited threat, but officers should take nothing he says personally.*
- *Alvin Simpson—File missing. Assumed dangerous, probably.*

- *Daniel Smike—"The Crying Death." Officers should not refrain from using their truncheons while subduing Smike, no matter how tearful he becomes.*
- *Oliver Tiller—"The Rhyming Killer." Ex–army munitions officer with expertise in booby traps. While pursuing Tiller, officers should beware rakes by lakes, toads on roads, and hairs on the stairs. Esplanades are to be avoided entirely.*

Chapter 9

Wat I did at the weakend

by Timothy Chambers esq. VC and bar, bane of the treens.

On saterday my mum and me went to the carnyval. It is caled the CABLE CARNYVAL as it is ownd by two men wat is both caled CABLE. This is becos they are brothers like Victor and me but unlike Victor and me they do not mind being seen togetha. Their was a big gate to stop you getting in unless you have payed but my mate Tony got in on thursday under the fense and he sa "I am like commando with the cat like stelth and can get into carnyvals, radar basis and submarine pens withowt nobody nowing." Wich is a laff as he has the cat like stelth of a dead pig on rolla skates with a polise siren on its hed. Then he jumps arownd, going "Hut! Hut! Hut!" wich is not mi idea of qwiet either.

So we go throo the big gate and my mum sa, "Now now timothy you must stay close to yore darling mama and not rush off chiz chiz chiz where have you gone?" For it is true, deer reader, I have cast off the shakles of maternal luv (uuurgh, pas the sik bag, matron) and flown off like a free bird. (Ha ha like a big fat gopping vulture ha ha, sa my brother victor who hav just red this over my shouldier. Like he would kno, he run skreaming from the interesting natural history progs on the telly, AND NOW WE SEE MOTHER NATURE RED IN TOOF AND CLAW nash, snarl, blood eveeriwhere, the dulcit tones of Victor sobbing in FEER in the kitchen. But I digres.)

Last seene I was running through the carnyval, ta ran ta rah, mi inocent young brane being corrupted by side shows of feersome depravitty. FABULOSO! I see the GOST TRANE and run up to the skinnie bloke in front. "Hello mr can I go on yore gost trane pliss oh pliss oh pliss oh pliss" for I am not above the begging.

"Well, ain't you the enthusiastic one, huh, junior?" said Mr. Bones, looking down on the young boy jumping up and down in front of him. "Where's your mom?"

The boy looked abashed. "Over there," he said eventually, and pointed at half the county.

"Oh," said Bones. "Right. Well, so long's she know where you are, young fella, that's fine. You want to go on the Ghost Train, hmm?"

The boy nodded hard and fast enough to pull muscles in an older man.

"Okay, but you got to understand, this is one spooky mother of a ride, y'hear? We get kids—oh, heck—twice your age goin' in here, comin' out like ooooooold men." He illustrated "ooooooold" by going bowlegged and waggling his hands. "Why, I went in there with a fine head of hair. Now look!" He whipped off his brown derby to show a perfectly smooth skull. The boy laughed delightedly. "Oh, you can laugh now, but look what this ride gone and done to me. I'm only fifteen!"

I think he is being ECONOMIKLE with the troof but no matter for the GOST TRANE do bekkon (mettaforikaly). Aktually, not that mettaforikaly for it hav a normous SKELLINGTON on top wich do the bekkonin wiv a big hand. Also a big grilla with a rock. But, no, quelle horruers, mes petites. For I have no MONI.

"No cash, huh?" said Bones. "Weeeell . . ." He looked around with great drama and then ducked close to whisper, "I s'pose I could push the rules and let you in, yeah? But it's our secret, right? No tellin' your friends, 'cos I'll have to say no to 'em. Okay?"

The boy nodded, excited by the conspiracy.

"H'okay, then," said Bones. He stepped into the ticket booth and slapped out a piece of pasteboard. "Here y'go. One complimentary ticket, courtesy of the management." The boy took it reverentially. Bones stepped sideways out of the booth and said sternly, "You got a ticket? I see you have." He plucked it from the boy's fingers, tore it neatly in two, and returned the stub. Then, brightening, he said, "All aboard the Ghost Train!" and waved him onto the first car.

The driver were a SKELLINGTON too!!! The skinnie blok sa "This heres my frend, driver, so you must be show him a good time." And the driver put downe his racing paper and sa, "OK Bones" wich is a bit ionic rilly. Then the skinnie blok go awa and the GOST TRANE starts up. The TRANE is a propa one with the smoke and steam and not like that rubish one at Butlers Fair wich was driven by a yoof spotier than my bro wich is saying somthing and no mistaik. He just sat there 4 ages talking to GURLS who ar less fussy than can be beleeved. This driver tho was a proper GOST TRANE driver cos he was DED and not just DED UGLI.

So the TRANE pull awa from the platform and enter the TUNEL OF FEER! Wich i no cos it sa so over the topp.

The train accelerated hard and shot into the tunnel like a ferret down a hole, smashing open the doors that kept the interior in gloom. Timothy had a momentary impression of the hideous grinning face painted across the doors changing its expression to one of worried anticipation just before impact, and could have sworn that he heard the doors say "Ouch" in concert amidst the loud buffet as they bounced off their end stops.

"Ha-ha," said the driver laconically to himself. The train swept around a corner and down a small hill that must surely take them lower than ground level, slowed to take a hard jink to the left, and then started to pick up speed. Timothy hadn't been on many ghost trains in his short life, but this one was surely different. Even the way the train ran—heading off into doors to the right of the façade and therefore offering a widdershins ride as distinct from the common clockwise path—seemed calculated to unsettle. For several long seconds, nothing occurred. Then he became aware of a small grey area that, for a curious moment, he felt sure was a window. No, it was too irregular. Suddenly he realised that it was a large toy rabbit, perhaps four feet tall. It had definitely seen better days: one ear was lopsided halfway up its length, the fur was balding down to a hessian quality in places, and one of its button eyes dangled on its cheek by a loose thread.

"THAT'S NOT SKARY AT ALL!" I said, unintimmidatted by the big bunny. "It is not terifying. It is a swiz and a cheat. I wuld ask for my monie back had I pade any. Wich I have not."

"I am the embodymunt of childhood feers, if you must kno," sa the bunny. "I can see Im a bit early in yore case. Just give it 20 years and I will skare you something badd, laddy."

"I do not see how that is possible, my fine thredbear frend," sa I "For I have never had a bunny as a toy and therfour cannot project my Froydian traumas onto one. So yar, floppy ears."

It is then that I notise a tabel in the gloome behind him at wich sit other big toys. They are plaing CARDS and drinkking BEER. They call things like, "Betcha had a teddy bear though or a big toothy monkie called Mr. Nana or a comical squid . . ."

A little voice from the shados sa, ". . . or Cromatty the Frendly Piebald Rat." And all the other toys thro there glasses at it.

"Shut up, Cromatty," they sa, "Nobody ever hav a frendly piebald rat in the HISTORY OF THE WORLD. Shut up befor we biff you up agane."

The horor bunny heave a big sigh and sa, "I hav had just aboute enuff of this. I want some fresh air. Here," he sa waving at the trane driver. "Stopp. I want a ride." So we stopp and the horor bunny, whoose name is Yan, clime in and then we are off agane.

Jan the Horror Bunny took delicate hold of the thread running from beside the site of his dangling eye and pulled gently, drawing the eye back into its correct place. "That's better," he said to Timothy. "It plays absolute hell with your stereoscopic vision having one eye wandering around like that. So, Master . . . ?"

"Timothy," said Timothy in a small voice, although not as small as one might expect under the circumstances.

"Master Timothy, are you enjoying the fair so far?"

"It's a bit . . . funny."

"Oh, yes," said Jan, leaning forward in his seat to peer into the darkness, "it's a funny fair all right."

Suddenly thin figures, apparently made from outsize black pipe cleaners with broken spoons for heads, leapt out of nowhere and danced around, making gobbling noises. Timothy jumped a little. "Garn!" shouted Jan. "Get it out of it, you *beatniks!*" The figures capered out of sight, still gobbling. Jan turned to Timothy. "I mean, what are they meant to be? They're just a mess. We've been on the go for months now, and we've never met anybody who had a morbid fear of surrealism. Dislike?" He seesawed a paw. "Maybe. Fear? Nah."

They trundled on in silence for a few more moments. Something indescribably phobic shuffled out and sat by the track, smoking a woodbine. "I am the thing that lives under your bed. Goorah, goorah." This last delivered as the sort of noise a monster might make if it could get up a bit of enthusiasm.

"No, you ar not," sa I. "For I sleep on the upper bunk and so wot live under *mi* bed is mi brother Victor. And you ar not neerly horribel enuff."

"Oh," said the something. "Bollocks." It shuffled back into the shadows until only the glowing tip of its cigarette was visible.

"You're a tough nut to crack, Master Timothy," said Jan. A wardrobe loomed up, and the door began to open, slowly, menacingly. Jan leaned out of the train and kicked it shut. "Don't waste your time," he called at the wardrobe as it was lost in the gloom behind them. Muffled swearing seemed to be coming from it. "He's only a kid." Jan turned to Timothy and studied him with an appraising eye. A tug of the thread allowed him to study Timothy with two appraising eyes. "We should have a few vampires and zombies and that sort of thing in, shouldn't we? All this psychological stuff is entirely wasted on you."

With another battering of bat-wing doors, they were back out into the open air. "Hey, kid," said Jan as the train drew to a halt and the driver returned to studying the racing papers, "want to see some stuff?"

"Wot sort of stuff?" I sa.

"The stuff of NITEMARE!" he sa back.

"Okey-dokey," I sa.

Timothy and Jan wandered the carnival, drawing surprisingly little comment except a few disparaging ones about the condition of that little man's costume. "Where are we going?" asked Timothy.

"Dunno yet," said Jan. He paused and looked slowly around, as if his ears were radar antennae. "Let's try the Hall of Mirrors."

"Ah, pooh!" said Timothy with gusto. "Halls of Mirrors are boring. All there is, is a lot of mirrors, an' one makes you look fat an' another makes you look thin an' one makes you look wiggly. That's boring."

"You're too young to be worldly-wise, Master Timothy," said Jan. "C'mon, get educated." They went around the back of the sideshow and slipped in through a service door.

"We won't get in trouble, will we?" asked Timothy a little tremulously, for he was basically a responsible lad and respected the privacy of individuals and institutions. Besides which, he hated getting shouted at.

Jan paused to think about it, erecting his floppy ear and flopping his erected one while he did so. "Trouble? Nah, I shouldn't think so. The Hall of Mirrors is much more fun from this side."

They were in a darkened room, the only illumination coming from tall, thin oblongs of subdued light. The oblongs seemed at first to be pictures of a dull room, until Timothy belatedly realised that they were on the other side of the mirrors, looking into the hall itself. From this side, the images were completely undistorted, as if the mirrors were plain glass, and no sooner had he made that realisation than people started coming in. He watched as people trooped past, pausing, laughing, doing knee bends, sticking out tongues, dragging their friends in front of the panes, moving on, all in total silence. "What's so good about this?" asked Timothy.

"Come over here," said Jan, beckoning. Timothy joined him by a mirror that was in a little cul-de-sac off the main room. The light was bad, but there was a woman standing on the other side looking at herself in the looking glass. She wasn't smiling. Timothy squinted; she looked familiar somehow, but this mirror, unlike all the others, didn't give a clear image. It was like looking through a film of oil, or at a body at the bottom of a shallow pond. "Know what she's seeing?" asked Jan in an unnecessary whisper. "She's seeing herself as she wishes she was. Probably a bit younger, probably a bit more shapely, probably not looking quite so much like somebody travelling steerage in the ship of life. Sad, ain't it?"

"Why's she want to be younger? I can't wait to grow up."

"You don't have to wish to grow up, it happens all the same. You can't stop it. Not without the *proper* assistance, anyway."

"She looks all right to me," said Timothy, to whom all adults were much of a muchness.

"Yeah, but you ain't seeing what she's seeing. If you were looking in that mirror, know what you'd see? You'd see yourself in a few years' time."

"As a space pilot?"

"If that's what you want to be. I don't suppose *she* wants to be Daniella Dare, though. Whoa, she's gonna be off in a minute if the boss doesn't shake a leg." The woman shook her head unhappily and turned to go. As if on cue, a tall blond man in slightly archaic clothes stepped up beside her. They started talking. The man gestured towards the mirror, and the woman, despite herself, couldn't help but look. "That's the boss," said Jan, "Johannes Cabal himself." Cabal stood beside the woman, talking quietly, as she looked at her reflection that wasn't really her reflection.

"Jus' a minute," said Timothy, frowning profoundly. "He won't be seeing what she's seeing, will he? He'll be seeing what he wants to be. What's that, then?" Unless Cabal wanted to be a space pilot, too, Timothy couldn't conceive of anything *he'd* rather be than the owner of a carnival. You could go on the rides as much as you liked and eat candy floss for dinner. If he'd looked a little closer, perhaps he might have seen that Cabal wasn't looking in the mirror at all, only at the woman. In fact, he seemed to be making some effort to avoid the sight of his reflection.

"Dunno," said Jan, shrugging. "Oh, here we go."

Cabal was leading the woman away. She kept stealing glances over her shoulder. She looked hopeful. "Sign on the dotted line, get your heart's desire and all at the footling cost of . . ."

Jan looked sideways at Timothy. "Are you *sure* you want to be a space pilot?"

"Oh, yes!"

"More than anything else?"

"Yes!"

Mi nu frend Yan the Rabit of TEROR took me owt of the HALL OF MIRORS and arownd the outside of the fare until we arrive at a big thing. At first I think it is only the gurly Helty-Skelty. But no! It is a MOONROCKET! On the front it have a big sine saing, "ROCKET TO THE MOON! VISIT MOONBASE OMEGA! FIGHT THE SELENITES! EXPEERINCE ZERO G!"

"I own miself impressed, my floppy bunny frend," sa I.

Rocket Ship Erebus swept low over the Sea of Tranquillity. Transmissions from Moonbase Omega had ceased twelve standard space hours earlier, and Space Control had dispatched the nearest rocket ship to investigate. "It's probably the Selenites," gruff Colonel Crommarty had warned them. "They've been quiet just recently. *Too* quiet. Be careful, m'boy."

Now, at the responsive controls of his trusty ship, Captain Timothy Chambers, space VC and bar, coolly appraised the approaching base. "No signs of life, old man. I don't like the look of this. Not one little bit."

His co-pilot, Space Rabbit First Class Jan, nodded thoughtfully. "The

Selenites have never forgiven you for the last time you gave them a bloody nose, guv. It's no secret this is your patrol area. We'd best be on the lookout. It could just be a trap."

The Erebus performed a perfect landing by the base's ground-vehicle bays. "What's the scheme, guv?" asked Jan. "We're nowhere near the main airlocks."

Captain Chambers finished checking his Toblotron Maxi-Multiblaster ray pistol and holstered it on his space suit. "We're going in through the vehicle doors. They won't be expecting us to come from that direction."

"Oh, crumbs," said Jan unhappily. "A moonwalk. They always give me the collywobbles."

Minutes later, the two doughty space heroes were on the concrete apron and heading for the airlock leading into the vehicle bays, Chambers moving in a smooth, rhythmic stride, Jan in cautious hops that carried him twenty feet. Halfway there and caught in no cover, they heard a familiar voice filtering into their helmets, a harsh voice with an underlying counterpoint of clickings and whirrings. "Ah, Captain Chambers. If there is one thing predictable about you, it is your pathetic attempts at unpredictability."

"T'shardikara," said Chambers, halting, crouching, and signalling Jan to do the same. "The last I saw of you, you were being pursued through the Venusian swamps by the local fauna. It would seem that even a predosaurus rex has its standards."

"Make your little jokes, human. I'm not the one trapped out in the open with the guns of twenty Selenite warriors trained upon me."

"Well, there's no accounting for taste," said Chambers evenly, but he was worried. T'shardikara, the atavistic freak with unusually high intelligence that had turned the formerly peaceful Selenites against the benign patronship of Earth, was not to be dismissed lightly. Even now, in his moment of victory, if he said that there were twenty warriors, then there were sure to be at least twice that number. "Jan, old man, I've heard say that Pogo Sticks are fashionable again." He drew his gun and released the "recoilless" toggle.

Jan understood immediately. "Oh, lumme, they're not, are they?" he said with dismay. He hated this.

T'shardikara had many negative traits, but inattention wasn't one of them. "They're up to something," he clicked and whirred at his troops in their native tongue. "Kill them!"

Three dozen Mutron space carbines opened fire simultaneously, but it was already too late. Chambers, space hero to a generation, had fired at the ground beneath him at full power! The pistol, with its inertial compensators deactivated, produced a monstrous kick. In the Moon's weak gravity—one-sixth of Earth's—he was thrown high above the surface. Tumbling head over heels, he reactivated the compensators and started snap-shooting with deadly effect on the snipers. Jan's enormously powerful hind legs had propelled him into the dark lunar sky without the need for assistance, and he fired in valiant and enthusiastic support. Selenite warriors shattered and exploded under the lethal rain, their return fire confused and ineffective. In seconds, one had thrown down its carbine and was running for the safety of the nearby tunnel—certainly the method by which they had taken the base by surprise. Like a trickle forming into a deluge, the others quickly decided that they couldn't face up to Captain Tim Chambers, and they, too, ran, a rout rather than a retreat.

"Re-form, you fools! Regroup and attack!" raged T'shardikara. Suddenly he realised he was alone. Discretion being the better part of valour, he ran, too. "The next time, Captain, you will be sorry for this. Oh, yes!" he grated before throwing himself headlong into the tunnel. Chambers's and Jan's combined fire brought it crashing down on his heels.

Ten minutes later, they were inside Moonbase Omega untying the prisoners. "Great guns, sir!" cried the base commandant, slapping Chambers on the shoulder. "I thought the jig was up there for a little while. Then, when that Selenite who was leading them—"

"T'shardikara."

"They've got names? Fancy that. Anyway, when the leader said it was all a trap to take you in, I thought right then, didn't I think right then, Valerie?"

Valerie, the commandant's beautiful daughter, looked at Chambers with unabashed adoration. "Oh, yes!" she said. Something about her attention made Chambers feel a bit funny and awkward.

I meen, she's a GURL, uech, yak, spu. She wil want to kiss and talk about ponys. Stil, faithfull reeder, I am oddly affkted by her presens. The ol kommadant is stil talking. "I thort rite then, they hav bitten off more than they can chew."

Then Yan the bunny sa

"Think you could do this for a living? Being a hero and everything?"

Timothy was still looking around the room with wide eyes. Light bulbs flickered random patterns in plywood consoles, a painted moonscape was visible through a plastic window, Layla and some giant stuffed toys stood around in tatty uniforms of silver lamé. Layla had an expression of unabashed adoration that wasn't altering by a twitch. "This is great," he breathed.

"Well," continued Jan, "all you have to do is fill in a form and all this can be yours."

"A form?" said Timothy dubiously. "Forms" were the only things about growing up that filled him with fear. They looked complicated, and he knew his parents hated them.

"Oh, don't say it like that. It's your entry to the Space Corps. Your name's all that's needed. Right here." He produced a form from his stuffing.

Timothy looked at it for the best part of three seconds before saying, "Okay."

"That's great," said Jan, flicking pieces of kapok off the parchment. "You won't regret this." In an undertone he added, "At least, not immediately." He passed Timothy a pen.

Then 3 things hapen all at once almost. 1st there is a big smash as if ½ the wall have been knokked down behind us. 2nd the pen just vanish out of mi hand. 3rd Yan the RABIT OF FEER is dangling off the floor. A man who look a bit like the man in the HALL OF MIRORS have him by the throte and is shakking him and being v angry. "I tole you NO CHILDREN!" he showt. Eeep! Now I kno I am in trubble. This place must be for grone-ups onli.

"Mister Cable sa we do whatever is nesesary," sa Yan.

"Then I am cowntermanding it," sa the angry man. "No children! Not now. Not ever. You tell Mister Cable that if he don't like it, he can take it up with ME!" He thro Yan at the wall like he is just a big stuffed toy wich I supose is fare enouf. Then the man turn on the other toys and the shiny lady and sa, "And you all owrt to be ashamed of yoreselves," but the way he sa it, I don't think that he think they wil be. Then he take mi hand and say, "Yore coming with me, young man."

He take me owtside and take me to the gate were mi mum is wating and I kno I'm *rilly* inn trubble. But she just blub and call me Timmy and keep kissing me and half the skool is walking past and going "Yah boo! Little darling Timmy!" Chiz chiz chiz is not fare. But the man, he sa "Do not be hard on Tim. Children get xcited and forget abowt everything else. He did not mean to upset you, I am sure." Wich is true as I did not rilly. I just forgot. So mi mum sa "Thank you, Mister Cable" and take me home and we are halfway there when mi rapeir-like intellijence realise that this is the other CABLE BRO as in CABLE BROS. I hav a piece of toast for supper and a glas of milk and go to bed.

This is wat I had done at the weakend.

Miss Raine, Timothy's teacher, finished reading the report and tapped her lower incisors with the butt of her pen. This made worrying reading; *very* worrying reading. Something really ought to be done. She took the exercise book, walked out of the marking room through the staffroom, and down the corridor to the headmaster's study. She knocked and entered at his invitation.

"Good afternoon, Miss Raine," he said as he finished pencilling in some numbers on the budget figures he was compiling. Miss Raine was notorious for making a big hoo-hah over nothing. He had no doubt that this was going to be more of the same. "And how can I help you?"

"It's Timothy Chambers, Mr. Tanner. I'm a little concerned about his state of mind."

"Tim Chambers? Really? He's always struck me as perhaps a little overimaginative, but nothing that a few years of secondary school won't knock out of him. What exactly is the problem?"

"He handed in a report today about what he did at the weekend." She threw it on the desk. "It's bordering on the psychotic."

As Tanner leaned forward to pick up the report, he noticed that Miss Raine's skirt stopped just shy of her knees. This was a new development. He frowned inwardly; there is such a thing as mutton dressing as lamb. On the other hand, they *were* unexpectedly appealing knees. Very appealing indeed. He flicked through the report but wasn't really paying much attention. How was it that he'd never noticed what a handsome woman Miss Raine was? Very handsome, most attractive. Perhaps she had changed her hair? She was saying something about calling in the district school psychiatrist, and he nodded absently. A possible threat to the other children? Why, that would be most unpleasant. They must do everything in their power, in his power, to make sure that didn't come to pass.

In the space of ten minutes, Timothy Chambers stopped being a nice, decent sort of lad, if a little prone to fancies, and had become a potential serial killer, arsonist, and cannibal. Psychiatric reports were a probability, observational internment a possibility, and removal from the school a certainty.

Tanner watched a pleased Miss Raine leave his study, and he wasn't looking at her back. She turned at the door and added, "After all, I should know. I was at the carnival myself last night. I had a *wonderful* time."

From the journal of the Reverend M——, vicar of Saint Keyna's, Jessop Leazes. April 25th, 1——

The rivalry of Mrs. J—— and Mrs. B—— has reached quite incendiary proportions. This week Mrs. B—— was charged with creating the floral arrangements for the church, a task she relishes. Indeed, she has always created quite most competent displays.

This morning, however, I was called to the church by the sexton, who told me, and I use his exact words, "The darrft ol' biddy's really done it this time, arr." At the time I believed he meant that she had excelled herself in a positive sense. I discovered my mistake the instant that I entered the church.

The stench was appalling, breathtakingly so, like a poorly run pig farm. The source of the smell was immediately obvious. Where I would have expected to see examples of Mrs. B——'s work, there were instead the most extraordinarily repulsive piles of rotting vegetable matter.

I was in the process of discussing with the sexton how we should dispose of the mess, when Mrs. B—— herself entered. I could swear that there was an expression of pride upon her face, but it was wiped away so quickly by the smell, I cannot be sure. She was devastated. Yes, she admitted that she had supplied the floral arrangements as agreed, but could cast no light upon how it was that they had rotted in so short a time. She kept saying how beautiful they had been, how exotic.

I helped carry out the grotesquely wilted remains to the sexton's wheelbarrow, which he had brought around for the purpose. An unenjoyable process: the flowers were wet and dripped some sort of ichor. The sexton was going to dump the mess on the composting heap in the corner of the churchyard, but I told him that I did not care to have such matter upon consecrated ground, to take it away entirely and burn it. This comment elicited a remarkable reaction from Mrs. B——. She put her hand to her mouth, and I heard her say, "Consecrated!" to herself, as if coming to a horrible realisation.

She was just hurrying off when Mrs. J—— arrived. She had her husband pushing along their own wheelbarrow, upon which were several floral pieces. Word travels quickly around the Green, but I was still astonished at the alacrity with which Mrs. J—— had leapt into the breach. Mr. J—— wheeled them through the gate, and again Mrs. B—— reacted unexpectedly, gasping as the barrow made its way through the churchyard.

There followed a harshly whispered conversation between the two women that seemed very unfriendly. From what little I could make out, it appears that they had both attended the funfair the previous evening. Mrs. B—— had purchased a quantity of exotic plants, the acquisition of which had required her to sell some personal item. These plants she had used in her arrangements, although why they had survived all the evening yet rotted so quickly when in the church defeated me. Mrs. J—— had also bought something there, presumably a book on flower arranging, for her work—though it uses only common, simple flowers— was the best I've ever seen.

Mrs. B—— left in a hurry, presumably after the fairground people to demand her money back, although they have already moved on in the night, and nobody seems to know where. I wish her well, but I fear this is most certainly a case of caveat emptor.

1. ~~Merton Pembersley New Town — Mai~~
2. ~~Carnforth Green — Juni~~
3. ~~Solipsis Supermare — Juni~~
4. ~~West Bentley — Juli~~
5. ~~Stilgoe — Juli~~
6. ~~Pogleton — August~~
7. ~~Little Caring — August~~
8. ~~Candlewick — August~~
9. ~~Witidge — September~~
10. ~~Lindisfry — September~~
11. ~~Cottleham — Oktober~~
12. ~~Murslaugh — Oktober/November~~
13. ~~Temple Dorrit — Dezember~~
14. ~~Yallop — Dezember~~
15. ~~Pondesbury — Januar~~
16. ~~Kneasbridge — März~~
17. ~~Montfrey — März~~
18. ~~Bank Top — April~~
19. ~~Jessop Leazes — April~~
20. Penlow on Thurse—April 29

Chapter 10

Francis Barrow folded the last bit of fried bread with his knife and fork, speared it, and used it to mop up the remains of the cooked yolk that had escaped from his poached egg. Placing his cutlery on the greasy plate, he picked up his tea and took an appreciative look out of his dining-room window. It was a horribly unhealthy meal, of course, and one his daughter only allowed him to have once a fortnight. A luxury's only a luxury if you don't get it often, he thought, and picked up the local paper.

Leonie came in as he read the front page. "Anything exciting?" she asked as she cleared up the table.

He sniffed and flicked rapidly through the pages. "No, not really. They're repainting the crossing in front of St. Cuthbert's Primary, there's a Beetle Drive at the parish hall on Friday, and we're playing Millsby at the weekend, of course."

His daughter laughed. " 'We're playing Millsby'?" she said. "When was the last time you wore flannels?"

"Aye, well," he said, and put the paper down. "Showing moral support, then."

"It'll be you and your cronies on the boundary, sitting there in deck-chairs with a relay of local lads running between you and the beer tent. You're incorrigible."

"It's what cricket's all about," he said. He looked at her and could see his wife so strongly in the line of her chin and her nose. The tawny blond hair was all her own, but the way she set her face sometimes . . . Leonie had just turned twenty-five: the same age her mother had been when they'd married. All those years ago. His smile became sad.

There was a slightly frantic knock at the door. "I'll get it," said Leonie, and went out of the room and down the hall. Barrow could hear her speaking to Joe Carlton, who seemed busting to tell her something. After a moment, Joe himself came in, the most excited he'd been since he'd al-most become mayor six years ago.

"Frank!" said Joe. "You've got to see this! Come on!" He did some-thing that looked a little too much for comfort like capering.

"Calm down, you'll do yourself a mischief," said Frank. Joe tried, but he just went pinker. "Now, what's all the fuss?"

"It's the railway station!" One of Joe's legs looked like it might in-volve him in another caper any second.

"What about the railway station?"

"It's come back!"

It was a beautiful morning by anybody's standards. The air was crisp and clear, with birds singing so high in the sky they were little more than dots. The fields were a shocking green beneath the blue vault of the sky, and it was so near perfect it took a little effort to remember that he was going to see something astounding. Carlton had run out of words very quickly, and he now lived for the look he was sure was going to appear on Barrow's face when they arrived. Barrow was notoriously difficult to sur-prise, and Carlton was wishing that he hadn't blurted out what had oc-curred. Still, he hoped the actual sight was going to be astounding enough. They walked down a cobble path that had long been disused, turned a corner by a bridge that stood over nothing, and there it was.

"Well," said Barrow. He took out his tobacco pouch and started to fill his pipe. "I'll be buggered." The station was indeed back.

The station had been built comfortably over a century before, before there was even photography to record its newly built appearance. It couldn't possibly have looked so well as it did now. Beautifully painted drainpipes ran down from the eaves of a roof whose slate tiling surpassed mere human precision; a team of twenty master roofers with obsessive-compulsive disorders and micrometer screw gauges could have toiled a year and not even come close to its perfection. Windows so clear that they seemed to actively repulse grease and grime stood exactly and totally framed in a way that no other panes of glass had ever been framed before. A fire bucket depended from a hook by the waiting-room door; never has a bucket been so red, never has the sand within it seemed so pure and just that the act of stubbing a cigarette in it would reduce any man to tears.

And yet.

And yet, as Frank Barrow looked at the supernaturally beautiful station, he didn't like it. Not at all. It seemed somehow sleek and smug and very, very pleased with itself. Even the illustration of five boys on the chocolate machine seemed somehow unpleasant and unnerving. Then again, it always did. Barrow was still trying to work out how this thing had happened when the door to the stationmaster's office opened and, awfully enough, the stationmaster came out.

He saw Barrow and Carlton and strode over, a natural ebullience and easy manner showing in every step. "Frank!" he called when he was still ten feet away. He walked over and clapped him on the shoulder. "Have you seen? Isn't it wonderful?" He waved his hand at the station and the bridge they'd just come over. Barrow looked back at it and noticed for the first time the tracks that lay there. They were made of some black, dull metal and lay upon sleepers of what seemed to be, at first sight, mahogany. Barrow turned back to the stationmaster.

"Morning, Wilf. And how are you?"

"How am I?" He laughed heartily. "How d'you think? Isn't it a marvel? The old station back? No, no, *better* than the old station. And look,

look." He stuck his thumbs in his waistcoat pockets and struck a pose. "New uniform! Flash, eh?" Barrow couldn't ever remember seeing such a striking cloth. It seemed black with just the faintest hint of grey, like a back-combed mole.

"Very flash. Nice to see you happy, Wilf."

"Nice to be happy again, let me tell you. Back in harness, eh?" He laughed as happily as a child. "Marvellous!"

"Yes," said Barrow evenly. He glanced at Carlton, but he was looking at the stationmaster with an odd expression, like a man who's cracked an egg and found inside a favourite toy soldier that he'd lost when he was five. "Yes, it broke your heart when they closed down this line and tore up the rails."

Wilf's brow clouded. "Yes. Yes, it was a terrible day."

"It's terrible to see a friend go into decline like that. We all rallied round. You know we did."

"Aye, everybody was very kind."

"Yes. We were all very upset when you hanged yourself from the bridge."

"Aye," said Wilf ruminatively. Then he brightened up. "Anyway, I've got work to do. We've got a train coming in this evening. Mustn't show up the station for our visitors. Morning, Frank, Joe. Drop around when things aren't so busy. Have a cuppa." He turned and walked back down the platform, pausing to wave to them as he went back into his office.

"Oh, God," said Carlton quietly. "Oh God, oh God, oh God."

"No call for blasphemy. Besides, I doubt very much God's got anything to do with this."

"But, but"—Carlton pointed at the closed office door—"he's *dead*."

"I know. Looking remarkably healthy on it, I must say."

"We cut him down," said Carlton. Barrow took him by the elbow and started to steer him away. "We buried him. You were there, too." He looked for something to put over the finality of death as he'd been led to understand it to date. "There were *flowers*." He started to mumble.

"I was there, aye. We all were. Everybody liked Wilf. I don't suppose he knows a tramp accidentally burned the station down ten years ago." He stopped by the timetable board. It was empty but for a colourful flyer:

Arriving Tonight! The Cabal Bros. Travelling Carnival! Be There! Be Astounded!

"I already am," said Barrow darkly, and led the muttering Carlton back to his house and a cup of strong tea.

𝒯he hooting started at dusk. A dismal, unhappy sound that echoed from the hills and sent shivers down the spine. It was a faintly pleasant sensation. With no telephone calls or knocks at doors, the town gravitated en masse to the station that hadn't been there as anything more than charred beams and blackened piles of bricks even twenty-four hours before. In huddled groups, the citizens waited. The hooting came closer, joined by a gargantuan, rhythmic snorting and a mechanical clanging of metal on metal. Somebody saw the smoke first and pointed, speechless. The huffing plume grew closer and closer, and the people there didn't know whether to run or to wait. They waited because it was less effort.

And then it appeared: a great, monstrous beast of steel and fire. Sparks flew from its smokestack as they once did from the pyres of martyrs and witches, swirling into the darkening sky like fiery gems on deep-blue brocade. The train's whistle blew, the triumphant shriek of a great predator that has found the prey. And the hooting grew louder and clarified into a horrid, disjointed tune played upon the steam calliope in the fifth car, a death dance for skeletons to spin and stagger to.

The train drew into the station and spat steam across the platform, making everybody skitter away. The engine made a noise that, to Barrow's ear, sounded like a contemptuous "Hah!"

And then nothing. The calliope played its tune, the engine panted slowly to itself, and that was it. A few of the braver souls took a couple of steps closer to the cab. Abruptly, a scarecrow lurched out of the shadows and waved at them, grinning crazily. The brave souls traded in their proximity to it for a little more distance and a mental note to change their underwear at the first opportunity. The scarecrow was clearly designed to scare more than birds; it was wearing a singed and filthy pair of overalls and a Casey Jones hat that had seen better days. The hat had a large stain on it that might have been long-dried blood. Its face was a parody of a man, clownish white make-up fixed in place with what seemed to be several coats of varnish. The crowd was just getting the hang of looking at it without fearing for their stomach contents when another one popped up and waved, too. This one was obviously meant to be fatter, but the weight distribution was all wrong. It looked like somebody had stuffed its coveralls with balled-up newspaper to pad it out. It had the same insincere and crazed grin on its face, the same sheen of shellac. Worse yet, the hand it was waving with—the left hand—was gloved, but ivory bone was clearly visible between the glove and cuff.

Nearby Barrow, a young boy asked his mother, "Mum, can I go to the fair?" in the same way he might have asked if he had to go to the dentist.

His mother's eyes never faltered from the occupants of the engine's cab, nor did the hard, thin line of her lips soften for a second. "Certainly not."

"Oh, Mum," said the boy in a hitherto unknown tone of relieved complaint.

Suddenly everybody's attention was drawn to one of the rear cars. Two smartly dressed men descended to the platform and walked towards them, deep in conversation. As they got closer, scraps of the conversation could be made out.

". . . morally corrupt . . ."

". . . don't lecture me . . ."

". . . treatment worse than the disease . . ."

". . . two more days . . ."

Johannes Cabal stopped and glared at his brother. "All I'm asking is for you to keep your moral outrage under control for two more days. Is that really too much to ask?"

"I have no idea why I agreed to this anymore. I thought nothing could be as bad as eight years with the Druins, but this last year . . . ? If our parents were still alive—"

"Well, they're not, and I didn't see anything in the will that gifted you with the privilege of gainsaying my every decision."

He waited for a witty comeback but was disappointed, as Horst had just noticed their audience. "Johannes. We are not alone."

Cabal twitched with surprise and looked at the townsfolk. He smiled wanly. Somewhere, a churn of milk went sour.

"Not to worry. Dennis and Denzil have been keeping them amused," said Horst, and laughed.

Cabal scowled. His attempts at preserving Dennis and Denzil had become more desperate over recent months. Usage of the mortician's arts had been slowly replaced by those of the taxidermist and finally the carpenter. It was a fraught night when first he had called for varnish and fuse wire. His attempts at cosmetic repairs had been risible, and his next scheme, of making them "look like clowns, people like that sort of thing, don't they?" had been a grotesque disaster at every level, from the technical to the aesthetic. Although he wouldn't admit it to himself, they even scared him a little.

"You two," he barked when they reached the car, "stop gurning like a pair of fools and get back in there." It was unfair to accuse them of pulling faces when these were now the only expressions of which they were capable, but Cabal was long past the point of being fair. Dennis and Denzil withdrew into the shadows of the footplate, grins fixed. Cabal took a deep breath and prepared to patch up the damage to public relations they had doubtless caused. Things had been getting hard recently. If he'd known a year ago that he would need only two souls to reach his target and had two working nights in which to gather them, he would have considered it grounds for optimism. Now, however, he wasn't so sure. Horst had been becoming quite withdrawn and argumentative over the past few weeks. Cabal doubted his brother would actually sabotage his efforts, but there was always the possibility that he might cause problems by withdrawing his assistance at an awkward moment. Worse, though, he had a feeling that Satan wasn't about to let him win his bet just like that. He would have to be on his guard for some dirty tricks being played this late in the game.

He turned to the crowd. They were looking anything from neutral to hostile. This wasn't going to be easy. He gave Horst a sidelong glance to see if he'd speak to the crowd; he was so much better at it. Horst returned his glance, crossed his arms, and looked off into the middle distance. Fine, thought Cabal, I'll do this myself.

"Ladies and gentlemen," he said in a clear, resonant voice, "I am Johannes Cabal of the Cabal Brothers Travelling Carnival. This"—he indicated his brother, who couldn't resist bowing very slightly—"is my brother, Horst. We have come here, to your pleasant town of Penlow on Thurse, to—"

"Why *have* you come here?" asked a middle-aged man. He caught Cabal's eye, and Cabal had an uncomfortable feeling of imminent trouble.

"To bring you the best in wonder, excitement, and family entertainment," Cabal continued. "We have stalls to test the keenness of your eye and the sharpness of your reflexes, sideshows to educate and astound."

"You've already done enough to astound this town," said the man. There was a mutter of agreement.

Cabal looked hard at him. The man wore a dark-grey trilby that was not new, but clearly well looked after. His overcoat showed the same signs of attention, his trousers sported a sharp crease, and his shoes were polished. His dark hair was greying at the temples, and he had a very sensible moustache, carefully maintained. Cabal would have guessed that he was ex-military—he certainly had the air of authority of a commissioned officer, a company or field rank like captain or major. There was a watchfulness in his eyes, though, that was not the product of a life of honest soldiering. Cabal's misgivings deepened. "And whom do I have the pleasure of addressing?" he asked with politeness, but not enough warmth to thaw a crystal of helium.

"My name's Frank Barrow."

"Well, Frank—"

"You can call me Mr. Barrow."

Cabal imagined Barrow upside down in a rendering vat and controlled his temper. "Well, Mr. Barrow, I'm glad to know that our little carnival has made something of a sensation here already." The two men looked at each other, looks that were on the very borderlands of glares. "How precisely did we do that?"

"This place," said Barrow, and jerked his thumb at the station.

"And a fine station it is, too," replied Cabal. He wasn't quite sure

where this was going, but it never hurt to flatter the yokels as to how marvellous the lean-to cattlesheds they called their town were. That said, he
was quietly surprised by how spick-and-span the station looked. It was as
if it had only been built today.

"That's as may be. The point is, it wasn't here yesterday." There were
a lot of agreeing noises and nodding. Cabal fondly hoped he'd misheard.

"I beg your pardon?"

"I said this time yesterday this place was a pile of burnt-out rubble,
this line hadn't seen sleepers or rails in donkey's years, and he"—Barrow
pointed at the stationmaster, who smiled and waved—"was long dead
and buried. Now, what I want to know, and I would guess all these people here would like to know, is how that can be." They all looked at Cabal
expectantly.

Cabal smiled absently, his brain whirring. This was none of his doing, but why would they believe that? No line? How could their arrival
have been planned, in that case? Penlow on Thurse was clearly marked
on the map as an operational station. His smile never wavered as the seconds drew out. He could feel his teeth beginning to dry. There was a
cough among his audience to remind him that they were waiting. Eyes
on him. He couldn't think. Penlow was their last possible stop, their time
was almost gone. He had to find two souls here, and now the whole place
was set against him. A bead of sweat was forming on his right temple; he
could feel it quite distinctly. He needed to think of a reason for the odd
goings-on. Now. Right now. Right this instant . . . *now.* The instant fled by
and he still couldn't think of anything. He knew damn well who was behind this. Look out for dirty tricks? The dirty deed had been done before
they ever got here. He wondered if he could save the box of contracts if it
became necessary to leave hastily, pursued by a torch-bearing mob.

"Torch-bearing mobs move surprisingly quickly," he said out loud.
They looked at him oddly. *Marvellous,* he thought. *Why not put ideas in
their heads?*

"What my brother means is that, only a few months ago, we made a
serious enemy." Horst's measured, reassuring tones immediately started
to weave their own brand of magic. People always wanted to hear what he

had to say. "It would seem that he has reached here before us and intends us to be besmirched by the same necromantic brush as himself, the cur. This, I think, would be the epitome of ironic revenge to his corrupt and diabolical soul."

There was some confused murmuring from the crowd. "What are you talking about, son?" asked Barrow.

"Ladies and gentlemen, may I present to you my brother, Johannes Cabal—Vanquisher." There was a definite capital "V" there. "Vanquisher of the foul wizard Rufus Maleficarus!" There was a gratifying intake of breath. Rufus had long been a darling of the tattier newspapers.

Even Barrow seemed to have heard of him. "Just a minute," said Barrow. "I thought Maleficarus was dead?"

"Slain by my brother's own hand in a deadly duel."

"So how's he doing all this business here if he's dead?"

A reasonable question, but Horst had always got by in life on 1 per cent perspiration, 99 inspiration. "My dear sir, what barrier is death to a necromancer?" The gratifying intake of breath was now released as a hateful hiss. Suddenly Cabal feared Horst was going to expose him. He'd been so distant recently.

"Rufus Maleficarus was an evil man. Now it would appear that his malign influence extends from beyond the grave. When we leave here, we shall postpone the rest of our busy schedule to go back to where he hangs from a gibbet and burn his corpse, as we should have done in the first place. Not even a necromancer can survive the purifying flame." There were sage nods from the sort of people in the crowd who always nod sagely when somebody else says something clever.

Barrow had an eyebrow cocked as he appraised this intelligence. He wasn't about to fall into the trap that Horst had set. That was left to another. "Why didn't you burn him while you had the chance, eh?" asked Joe Carlton, who could always be relied on to ask the obvious.

Horst spread his hands in supplication. "We had the torches lit when along came Maleficarus' mother." He adopted a reedy, aged voice. "'Please don't burn my boy,' she said. 'He's been very wicked, I know, but he's my own flesh and blood. I . . . I don't think I could bear it if you burnt him.' Well, I was all ready to burn the evil sod anyway when Johannes, my brother, held back my arm and said, 'No, Horst. He may have been a necromancer, a murderer, and a thrice-dyed villain, but he was *still* this woman's son. She's suffered enough. *More* than enough. Leave him for the crows and let us be on our way.' " Cabal looked at his feet with pure, disbelieving embarrassment. Luckily, it was close enough to humility to pass. "So we left poor old Mrs. Maleficarus sobbing by the feet of her own little Rufus," continued Horst.

"Please stop," whispered Cabal. "This is killing me with humiliation."

"You think I should skip the bit where you run back and press the whole month's takings on her? If you insist," whispered Horst. Then, louder, "So, if our crime is that my brother could not bring himself to break the heart of a poor widow any more than her evil son had done, then we plead guilty." He took off his hat and hung his head penitently. There was a pause. Then the crowd went mad.

Cabal was bundled up to shoulder height and paraded up and down the platform several times by jubilant supporters. From a harbinger of doom he had become a conquering hero with a heart of gold, in the space of a few mendacious sentences. Such, he mused, is the fickleness of the mob. Horst should run a newspaper.

After he had worked up a hand full of cramp signing autographs, Cabal happened to notice Barrow standing to one side, arms crossed. Watching him. It seemed that at least one person had proved resistant to Horst's public-relations exercise.

"You don't seem impressed," said Cabal. "Why should that be? Didn't you hear my brother? I'm a hero."

"I don't know what you are," said Barrow. "Hero? I wouldn't know. *Did* you kill Maleficarus?"

"Yes," said Cabal. He looked around to make sure nobody was eavesdropping. "Yes, I killed him. I shot him three times."

"Why?"

"Why did I shoot him, or why did I shoot him three times? I shot him three times to make sure he died. I killed him because he was in the way."

"In *your* way."

"If you like."

"And what did you do with the others?"

"Others?"

"That poor mob of fools he had following him around, the others who escaped from the asylum."

Cabal smiled. "Have you ever heard of 'care in the community'? You're entirely right; they're harmless. They just needed some direction in life."

"They're in your carnival?"

"As staff, I assure you. My freaks are all volunteers." The smile slid away into nothing. "By and large."

Barrow snorted. "I understand you."

"No. No, you don't. You read between the lines, but what's written there defeats you. Might I make a suggestion, Mr. Barrow?"

"You can make it."

"In two days, we will be gone from your lives. You can let us do our jobs and bring a little excitement into the lives of the people here, and everybody will be happy. No unpleasantness, no ill-feeling."

Barrow pursed his lips. "If I could really believe that, I'd be delighted to agree."

"But you can't."

"But I can't. I don't believe this story about a dead man climbing down from his gibbet just to make a balls of your public relations. Not for one single, solitary second. What kind of idiot do you take me for?"

Cabal tilted his head at the excited townsfolk, who were washing up and down the length of the carnival train. "That kind of idiot," he said. "It's unfortunate for both of us that I'm wrong." Riggers were beginning to unload the flats from the train. Cabal and Barrow watched them. "I have a long night ahead of me, Mr. Barrow. You'll forgive me if I take my leave of you, I'm sure."

After Cabal had taken a few steps down the platform, Barrow called after him, "I'd be happier if you took leave of my town."

Cabal stopped and looked back at him. "*Your* town? You're not your brother's keeper. Remember that."

"Is that it? No threats?"

"Threats, Mr. Barrow, are the preserve of blowhards and cowards. I am neither." He walked back to Barrow until they were toe to toe. "I don't even give warnings." He turned on his heel and walked away.

"By and large," said Barrow, too quietly for Cabal to hear. Then he turned, too, and walked back towards town.

As the two walked away from each other, they were both thinking exactly the same thing: "That man is going to be trouble."

Chapter 11

IN WHICH CABAL PREYS UPON MISFORTUNE
AND THERE IS UNPLEASANTNESS

It was an utter impossibility that the carnival be up and running the night it arrived. Yet, with less fuss and much less time than putting out a picnic table, a full-fledged carnival featuring thirty sideshows, stands, rides, and exhibits was lit up and functional. Nobody could explain how it had been done; by coincidence, the crowd of two hundred and fifty citizens at the station were all facing the other direction at the time. They all jumped in unison as the steam calliope started up behind them, all turned, and said minor variations of "Oooooh!," one less "o" here, one more exclamation mark there.

"A first-night special offer!" cried the tall, dark-haired pale man with the charisma, while his brother, the tallish, blond pale man who only ever seemed to deploy a smile as an offensive weapon, stood behind him, arms crossed. "Entry free!"

The good folk of Penlow on Thurse had been brought up to believe that it was rude to refuse a gift, so they politely filed in under the archway of gleaming painted woodwork and light bulbs. Barrow walked until he stood beneath the arch and looked up. For a second, it seemed to say

Abandon All Hope, Ye Who Enter Here, but after a moment it definitely proclaimed how the crowned heads of here, there, and everywhere regarded the carnival as ideal entertainment for those of inherited money and limited gene pool, this being regarded as a fine advertisement in some quarters. Barrow decided that he had been mistaken but that his subconscious was trying to tell him something. Forewarned and forearmed, he entered.

Johannes Cabal, necromancer and unwilling carny-huckster, watched the crowd and fretted. This was their penultimate night, and things just weren't . . . right. He couldn't put his finger on it. The crowd seemed to hang together, moving like an extended family from tent to ride to sideshow. Beneath the constant calliope music and the cheerful banter of the barkers lay near silence. People just stopped and looked and moved on. There was a small sensation when somebody bought a toffee apple from a concession stand. "What's wrong with them? I thought I was supposed to be a hero now. Why are they still so suspicious?"

Horst appeared at his elbow, where he most definitely hadn't been a second before. "They're nervous. I may have given them an explanation for the station, but that doesn't mean that they have to like it. This place reminds them that something weird has happened, something inexplicable and out of the ordinary. Face it, Johannes, I doubt anything out of the ordinary has happened in this place since some passing peasant thought it was a clever place to start a town in year dot. Did you see that fuss over a toffee apple? They couldn't have been more astounded if we were selling lark tongues in aspic. This place may be a washout."

"It can't be a washout. It's the last port of call. Two souls. I have to get two souls or this whole thing has been a waste of time."

"And ninety-eight souls."

"Ninety-nine. My life is forfeit."

Horst looked at him sharply. "What? You never said anything about that!"

"Strangely, it wasn't the sort of thing that I like to dwell on. What does it matter? If I don't get my soul back, then I can't continue my researches."

"You just leave a trail of metaphysical disaster behind you, don't you? You made a mess of your life, my life, however many people you doomed in the eight years and thirty-seven days I was stuck in the cemetery, and now you want to spread the good word to another hundred. And for what?"

"You know damn well."

Exasperated, Horst shook his head. "No, no, I don't." He wagged his finger in his brother's face. "I *used* to know. I even sympathised, idiot that I am, and look what it got me. But for what now? I don't know. I don't think you do. I think you just carry on this way because if you stopped and asked yourself, 'Gosh, Johannes, why am I such a total shit to every-body?' I don't think you'd be able to give yourself an honest answer."

Cabal flared. He slapped Horst's hand to the side. "I don't care what you think. I am supremely unconcerned by what you think."

Horst shrugged. "Great. So long as we understand each other."

"No, no, we don't understand each other. Or at least you don't un-derstand me. You never concentrated on anything in your life. You don't understand what it is to be dedicated. You don't understand what it means to go to sleep and wake up with the same thought and for that thought to always be there."

"That's not dedication."

"No?"

"No, that's obsession."

"And this is your big effort to understand me, is it? A label. I shouldn't have expected anything but."

"It's not a label. Look at yourself. Ye gods, Johannes, you were going to be a doctor! You wanted to help people."

"Doctors. Frauds and quacks. Just trying to hold back the dark and full of pat excuses when they fail. Too stupid or too scared to bring back the light. Not me. Not me! I'll be the modern Prometheus no matter what I have to do, no matter how dark I have to make it before I can find the secret."

"And what if there is no secret to find? What if it's beyond mortals? What then? What about you?"

"There has to be," said Cabal, but he seemed very old and very tired as he said it. "There has to be."

Horst took his younger brother by the shoulders. "Listen to me. We've got twenty-four hours—less, allowing for the sunlight—but we've got time. We can think of a way out of this." Cabal just blinked uncomprehendingly. "These contracts always have a hole in them somewhere. I think it must be traditional. We burn the contracts, get you out of this wager, and then find a hole in the contract you signed when you sold your soul."

"There's no hole in my contract," said Cabal. "I signed my soul over in return for the tenets of necromancy."

"And that's all?"

"I don't know. 'The secret of life after death,' the usual stuff."

"That's what you asked for?"

"Something like that."

"Then that's easy! Don't you understand? You wanted the secret of life after death. All you've got is a few formulae that allow you to bring people back as parodies of what they were. *And* you're the one who's had to do most of the work to get that far. They failed to deliver their side of the bargain!"

"That's just quibbling with definitions."

"Oh, come on! You think Satan would miss an opportunity like that if the situation were reversed?"

"What would I want with Satan's soul?"

"Not what I meant. We've got him. It's a philosophical minefield!"

Cabal had a brief mental image of Aristotle walking halfway across an open field before unexpectedly disappearing in a fireball. Descartes and Nietzsche looked on appalled. He pulled himself together. "But I was given the power to invoke the formulae. That was the real boon."

"It's got you nowhere. Give it up. Start again."

"I . . . I don't know." He tried to work out how much research it would require to recoup mundanely the ground that he had lost to the diabolic. It seemed a very great deal.

"Johannes. Do it. It's redemption."

To Horst Cabal, his brother, Johannes, looked like he had when he was six and his dog died. The same numb inability to understand what had happened. Johannes Cabal looked at the floor and the night sky and, finally, at his brother. He seemed very lost. "I don't know," he whispered.

Horst opened his arms. He hadn't held his little brother since he was a child. They had never been close, and Cabal's admission that he'd hated Horst had explained a lot. But even now and even here, blood was still thicker than water.

"Hey! Boss!" Bones came out of nowhere. In the moment that Horst's gaze flicked from Johannes Cabal to Mr. Bones and back again, his brother had vanished and been replaced by Cabal the necromancer.

"What?" snapped Cabal.

"I think we got a live one," Bones said, grinning widely. Horst sighed. The moment had gone. Up until now, he'd quite liked Bones, with his easy smile and bonhomie. Up until now, it had been very easy to forget that he was nothing more than a tiny bit of Hell that had been brought to Earth and put in a boater. That smile had changed everything. They were talking about taking somebody's soul, and it was a cause for delight.

"Where?"

"The penny arcade. She's just wallowin' around and lookin' pretty damn miserable. We gotta have somethin' she wants."

"The arcade? About time that place earned its keep." Cabal strode off with Bones at his heel.

Horst blurred and was there before them.

The penny arcade had consistently proved a good attraction to people wanting to get rid of spare change but had performed badly in the soul-reaping stakes. Now, as always, it was packed with children and teenagers playing the bagatelle boards and one-armed bandits, testing their strength against a brass arm, and watching the macabre events of the penny tableaux. Horst looked around frantically. They would arrive soon, and he would have lost his chance to get the prospective victim out of here. Impeded by bodies, he was unable to move at high speed and was forced to push politely through the throng. He couldn't see anybody who fitted the bill until, finally, a mob of pubescents gave up trying to win fluffy toys from the crane machine and moved away. She was young, probably not even twenty, and Horst had rarely seen such an expression of ingrained misery. Here she was surrounded but untouched by people, her unhappiness a tangible thing that must have seemed to her almost deliberately ignored by others. Horst moved firmly through the mass.

"Excuse me, madam." He was at her elbow. She looked up. Too many nights without sleep. Too many nights crying. He looked towards the entrance. He could see his brother and Bones approaching. He didn't have enough time for subtlety or even just to mesmerise and steer her out of there. "You seem unhappy. May I be of assistance?" She just smiled wanly, uncertain. "I am Horst Cabal, one of the proprietors. It pains me to see one of . . ." Cabal and Bones were almost at the entrance. "Look, what's wrong? Can it be fixed with money? We've got more money than we know what to do with. I can give you as much as you need." Her smile faded, and she just looked confused. He had no more time. He leaned forward and whispered in her ear. "Whatever you do, do *not* give in to temptation. Promise me!" He leaned back to find her looking at him uncomprehendingly. "Don't give in," he hissed, and moved away.

Cabal looked around the arcade. There were any number of women who might have been either miserable or just fashionably inexpressive. Any knack for spotting misery that he may have once possessed had long since atrophied through lack of use. "Who?" he asked Bones.

"*That* one, boss. She's got a face longer than a wet day."

Cabal studied her. She looked a little baffled to him, frankly. "So what does she want?"

Bones shrugged ineloquently. "*I* don't know."

Cabal sighed with exasperation and tried to remember how the arcade worked. The sideshows were so much easier. There you could just ask. He looked around for somebody to ask here, and his eye fell upon the mechanical fortune-teller. Inside her glass case, Madame Destiny promised to tell the gullible punters their fortune, printed on a small piece of card, and all for a single penny of the realm. She'd proved useful in the past, he recalled. Perhaps again?

Cabal walked over to it and surreptitiously struck the case with the base of his fist by the coin slot. Nothing happened. "Stump up, Destiny, or it's a rendezvous with a hacksaw for you," he whispered harshly.

The mannequin in the case immediately whirred into life, obligingly looked into her crystal ball, and stopped. A moment later, a card fell into the tray. Cabal took it and read:

MADAME DESTINY KNOWS ALL AND SEES ALL.

YOU WILL MEET A WOMAN WHO HAS WHAT SHE DOES NOT WANT.

GIVE HER A SOLUTION AND SHE WILL BE GENEROUS.

MADAME DESTINY'S ADVICE:

MANNERS MAKETH THE MAN.

Cabal read it through twice before crumpling it up. He leaned close to the front of the cabinet, as if putting a coin in. "That is precisely no help to me," he whispered. "What does she have that she doesn't want? A disease? Lice? A distinctive and irritating laugh? Give me specifics and save the meaningless generalities for the rubes." To the imaginative, the mannequin might have seemed to purse its lips. Certainly it ran through its little fortune-telling dumb show at an undignified gallop. The card spat into the tray with so much venom that Cabal had to stop it before it fell to the ground. This one read:

OKAY, OKAY.

MADAME DESTINY ETC.

THAT WOMAN HAS A BABY WHO'S DRIVING HER CRAZY.

WON'T STOP HOWLING. NO HUSBAND.

HER MOTHER'S LOOKING AFTER IT TONIGHT.

GIVE HER AN OUT AND SHE'LL GIVE YOU HER SOUL. EASY.

MADAME DESTINY'S ADVICE:

TRY SAYING "PLEASE" IN FUTURE, YOU ARSEHOLE.

With the exception of the advice, it was exactly the kind of news Cabal had been hoping for. "Bones, I want this arcade evacuated, with the exception of that woman."

"Sure thing," said Bones, and moved quietly and surreptitiously around, handing out free ride tickets to all and sundry. Within five minutes, the arcade contained only Cabal and the woman, who was slowly feeding coins into a fruit machine called Fun Time. Or so it seemed to Johannes Cabal, unaware of a figure in the corner who had forced himself into near transparency. Horst Cabal watched and hoped.

In the row of penny tableaux was one covered with a tarpaulin and an *Out of Order* sign on the front. In truth, the Cabal brothers had run out of ideas by the time they'd got to that one, so it was actually empty. Now Johannes approached it, concentrated, mouthed, "I invoke thee," and pulled the tarpaulin away. Inside the cabinet was a tableau of a room. Within it was a tiny automaton that looked strikingly like the young unhappy woman. The room was a tiny squalid bed-sit with laundry hanging from lines strung over a bath visible through an ajar door. The automaton stood by a cradle in which a tiny doll of a baby lay. Small it may have been, but, somehow, there was enough detail to make it clear that this was a child it would be hard for anybody to love. The tableau was entitled "The Mother's Escape." Folding the tarpaulin over his arm, Cabal walked to the far side of the arcade and pretended to be in conversation with the old man in the change booth. In reality, he watched the woman. Nor was he the only one.

The young woman was disappointed when Fun Time started to hand lemons out with harsh regularity. Soon she was short of coins, and the reversal of fortune had depressed her. She left the machine and walked the ranks of its comrades. She would have to be heading for home before long, she knew, and wanted some small piece of pleasure to bide her through the night. She saw the row of penny tableaux and inspected them one by one. They were all horrible: tales of murder and execution, hauntings, and harsh justice. Nothing that she wanted to know. She was about to leave them when her eye fell upon the last in the row. Whether it was the title, or the striking resemblance the automaton bore to her, or the tableau to her own bed-sit, neither Cabal could tell, but it drew her inexorably.

She stopped by the case and looked into it. It was strange, dreamlike. It was as if somebody had taken her life, re-created it in wood, wire, and paint, and put it here, on public display. On slips of paper—aged and yellow despite in truth being less than ten minutes old—were written "The Unhappy Mother" and "The Troublesome Baby," pinned to the tableau's floor in front of their respective subjects. Her eyes prickled. She wasn't alone after all. Somebody else must have suffered as she suffered for the story to be retold here. As she fumbled for one of her few remaining coins, another pair of eyes nearby prickled, grew moist, and silently wept.

She had to know, she had to see how this other person had fared. The tableau was after all "The Mother's Escape." How? How had she escaped? She needed to know with a strange urgency. She put the coin to the slot and dropped it inside.

With a whirr, the tableau came to life. The baby's arms rose and fell with mechanical rhythm as the head rolled from side to side. Crying. Demanding. Never shutting up. In time to the baby, the mother put her hands to her ears and shook her head. She was at the end of her tether. Not a day went by when she didn't consider suicide. The woman rested her forehead against the cool glass and bit her lip.

There was a distinct *click*, and the floor rotated by one-third of a revolution anti-clockwise, changing scenes. Now the mother stood in the bathroom. Using the washstand as a table, she was mixing something. Powders and liquids from the cabinet. It was a strange thing, but, although the largest bottle she handled was the length of a thumbnail, the labels were clearly legible. A jigger of this, a pinch of that went into a mortar and were thoroughly mixed. When she had finished, the tiny mechanical mother poured the solution into a baby's bottle. The implication was all too clear. As she read the label for the scene, "A Solution Presents Itself," the amazing dexterity of the automaton never struck her as remarkable. She was living the little drama herself. She almost moaned aloud as, *click*, the scene rotated again to its final third. Here was retribution, be it earthly or divine; she had seen too many of these machines in her life to doubt a moral outcome. But . . . no. The final scene was of a graveyard. In her funereal weeds, the mother looked radiant as the mourners lowered a tiny coffin into the dark grave. And behind her handkerchief, was that a suspicion of a smile? The automaton looked out of the case, straight into her eyes, and she saw her own face there. Happy. The label affixed to a convenient tomb read, inevitably, "The Mother's Escape."

The machine made another *click* and returned to the hateful first scene. Barely had the whirring stopped before she was feeding it another coin. This time, when the second scene arrived, her lips moved as she memorised the ingredients of the baby's bottle.

*T*he police arrived an hour before dawn. Cabal was perfectly polite with them as they busied around and asked a lot of obvious questions. He was less happy to see that Barrow was in attendance. "I wasn't aware that you were a member of the police force, Mr. Barrow," he said, stifling a yawn.

"I'm not. Just a concerned party," replied Barrow.

"Well, then," Cabal said to the sergeant in charge, "I believe I'm within my rights to ask Mr. Barrow to leave?"

"No, you're not," said the sergeant. "Ex–Detective Inspector Barrow is here at my request and is acting as a consultant in this case."

"'Ex–Detective Inspector'?" said Cabal, impressed. "My, you are a man of many parts. 'Case.' What case is this?"

"There has been a murder. A particularly horrible one. The suspect claims that this carnival was involved."

"A murder?" said Cabal, shocked and innocent.

"An infanticide, to be exact," said Barrow. "A mother killed her own child. Claims that you have some machine in your arcade that tells you how to make poison."

"Good heavens! Really?"

"You mean to say you didn't realise that your arcade featured such a machine?"

"Oh, no, not for a second. We have no such machine. I was just surprised that anybody could concoct such a bizarre story. And that anybody would believe it."

The sergeant bridled. "We have to follow up every lead, sir."

"Of course you do. I understand entirely. Well, what else can I help you with? You have my word, there is emphatically no machine like the one you describe within this carnival. I've never even heard of such a thing."

"The poison she made was a very cruel one, sir. The baby died in agonies."

"Terrible."

"She seems to have been under the impression that it would be undetectable," said Barrow. "She's only a simple girl. I think she's telling the truth in most respects."

"Meaning what?"

"She came to this carnival last night. The very same night she concocts a poison and uses it. I don't think she could have become Lucrezia Borgia at such short notice without professional help."

"What are you insinuating?"

The sergeant coughed. "The arcade, sir, if you would. We would like to look at the machines."

"Very well, but you're wasting your time." Cabal led the way for the little entourage of three police officers and Barrow to the arcade. He unlocked the big padlock that sealed the entrance and stepped aside. "Be my guests." The party entered and stood in a huddle near the door while Cabal went around and opened the shutters.

Barrow's eye lit upon the penny tableaux and he went to investigate, followed by the policemen. Cabal leaned against the wall and affected nonchalance. Barrow studied the row, reading the titles as he moved along it. " 'The House of Bluebeard,' 'The Pit and the Pendulum,' 'The Court of Ivan the Terrible,' 'The Haunted Bedroom,' 'Tyburn Tree.' Very *Grand Guignol*, Mr. Cabal," he said disapprovingly.

"It's what people like," replied Cabal, "Mr. Barrow."

Barrow had arrived at the end of the row, a machine covered with a tarpaulin and with a sign fixed to it. "Out of order? What's wrong with it?"

"I don't know. Something mechanical. Quite beyond me."

"We'd like to have a look at it if we may, sir," said the sergeant.

"I don't think that would be wise. You have my word there is no machine like the one that you have described. Isn't that enough?"

"We'd like to see for ourselves, sir. The tarpaulin, if you please."

"I really don't think I ought."

"That's as may be, sir. But if you'll pardon me . . ." The sergeant quickly undid the tarpaulin and pulled it away.

The machine was stuck in mid-action. On a moonlit street, an enraged husband chased a police officer down the garden path of a house. In an upstairs window, a woman with an unfeasibly large bosom mimed screaming with dismay. The police officer was notable for his uniform trousers being around his ankles. The machine was called "Cuckolded by a Copper." The sergeant blushed. The little policeman looked really rather like him, a resemblance that wasn't lost on his constables. Worse yet, the woman looked a lot like Mrs. Blenheim on Maxtible Street, whose husband worked a lot of night shifts. "Well, that would seem to be that," he said quickly while attempting to put the tarpaulin back. It kept falling off, almost wilfully. "We'll be on our way, sir. Thank you for your cooperation. You've been very patient."

"Not at all, sergeant," Cabal said pleasantly to the officer as he left, shooing his smirking subordinates before him. He watched them go and adjusted his spectacles.

"An interesting place, this carnival of yours, Mr. Cabal," said Barrow from behind him.

"Thank you, Mr. Barrow," he replied, turning.

"It wasn't meant as a compliment. Just a comment: an interesting place. This arcade, for example."

"Oh?" Cabal raised his eyebrows. "How so?"

"These machines." Barrow pointed at the tableaux. "Horror and death the whole length. Then we get to the last one—the machine, incidentally, that the police was told was the one with the recipe for poison—and *that* one is broad comedy. Odd, wouldn't you say? Out of place?"

"People like that sort of thing," repeated Cabal. "So I'm told. It was put in as an afterthought."

"An afterthought." Barrow walked to the door and looked out across the carnival, pondering. "I don't like this carnival of yours, Mr. Cabal. It's distasteful."

"We can't guarantee to cater to everybody."

"That's not what I meant. When I was still in the job, I had hunches the same as everybody else. Sometimes they were right and sometimes they were wrong. But sometimes I would have a feeling that came to me as an actually *bona fide* bad taste in my mouth. Horrible taste, and unmistakeable. I was once sitting in on an interview of a chap who was a possible witness in a murder case. Just a witness, you understand. Respectable man who might, just possibly, have seen something useful."

"And you got this magical bad taste of yours?"

"In spades. And, yes, he was our killer. But at the time he wasn't even a suspect. That's the important thing. I had no reason to suspect him."

"Sure you got the right man? Not just a case forced through because you forgot to brush your teeth that morning?"

"I don't think even the most rabid police-conspiracy theorist would believe that we would frame a man by burying four bodies in his back garden and then building a rockery on top of them."

"A rockery?" Cabal considered. "No, that does stretch credulity a little. You may have a point, in that case. I assume that when you say my carnival's distasteful you are referring to this uncanny forensic palate?"

"When I get home, I'm going to have a very strong cup of tea in the hope it will wash it away."

"You do that. Perhaps, one day, criminological epicurean evidence will be admissible in a court of law. In the meantime, I shall bid you a good day. I should like a few hours' sleep if at all possible."

"Good day, Mr. Cabal," said Barrow, and walked back in the direction of the town.

Cabal walked back towards his office sedately until Barrow was out of sight. Then he ran. He entered the car breathless, unlocked his desk drawer, took the topmost contract from the box, and put it in his inside breast pocket.

"So she did it?" said Horst, and Cabal jumped.

"I didn't see you there," he said, putting away the box and carefully locking the drawer.

"I didn't want you to. She killed her baby, then?"

"Yes. Isn't it marvellous?" He stopped. "Not that she killed her baby, obviously."

"No. It's not obvious. It's not obvious at all. I presume you're going to go and offer her a way out of her dilemma?"

"That *was* the idea," said Cabal. He didn't like his brother's tone at all.

Horst looked at him for a long moment. He checked his watch. "The sun will be up soon. We creatures of the night should be tucked away by then. Leave the day to creatures of the light."

"You're trying to make me feel guilty. It won't work."

"My little brother just engineered the murder of a child. There's nothing I can do to make you feel remorse if that didn't. I offered you the chance of redemption last night. Sorry, my mistake. Father always said I couldn't spot a hopeless case."

"Really?" Cabal pulled on his coat. "How unlike Father to criticise you for anything."

Horst rose from where he was sitting on the blanket box, and Cabal fought to prevent himself shying away. "Don't be specious. You can't keep returning to sibling rivalry as an excuse for everything. 'Oh, don't blame me for my crimes against man, God, and nature. It's my brother's fault for being so perfect.' No jury would convict." He smiled and sat down again. "Would you like to hear something ridiculous? When you came for me a year ago, I was glad to see you. It was my brother who'd come back for me after all. It had taken him a while to get around to it, but better late than never. Yes, you'd sold your soul and I'd become a monster, but, apart from that, it would be just like old times."

"And now you're saying you were wrong?"

"Now I'm saying I was half wrong. I was wrong about which of us had become the monster. This whole year, I've watched who's signed those contracts and I've said nothing, because, as far as I could see, they were going to Hell whether they signed a piece of paper or no. Some might have been a little borderline, but not by enough to make me concerned. That woman last night, though. She would never have done what she did unless you'd suggested it. She'd have worked it out. Now she's damned whether she signs that contract or not. That's your doing. I don't doubt you've got some deal lined up for her if she signs. Do me a favour, would you?"

"A favour?"

"Just do what you're going to do and leave the contract here."

Cabal frowned. "But then it doesn't count against the hundred."

Horst rested his chin in his hand and looked at his brother. He'd never dreamt that his brother could be so obtuse. "That's the point," he explained.

Cabal looked at Horst as if he were mad. "Then there *is* no point." He clapped his hat on and left, slamming the door behind him.

Horst looked at the door for a very long moment, then glanced over at the hourglass. The time was all but gone: a few grains of inestimably fine sand remained in the top bulb. "I'm sorry," he said quietly to himself. "I'm more sorry than you will ever know."

*C*abal arrived at the police station and made enquiries. He was sorely distressed that some poor woman—he managed to avoid saying "soul" at the last moment—had done such a terrible, terrible thing while the balance of her mind was disturbed. It seemed that the visit to the carnival had somehow provided, all unwittingly, the impetus for her psychosis, and—while he naturally couldn't accept any liability—he really wanted to help any way that he could. He had to be quite insistent before he was allowed to see her. He was quite sure that Horst could just have walked straight in and they'd have fallen over themselves to make him a cup of tea. Finally, with heavy hints that he would be paying her legal expenses, he was allowed in alone.

"Well, then," he said finally, sitting down across a plain, square table from her. "This is a sticky mess you've got yourself into." She looked at him miserably, her eyes red from crying.

"I'm afraid the authorities are going to treat you very harshly for this. You probably already realise that." She nodded and looked in her lap, where she pulled and worried a handkerchief endlessly.

"They'll have told you that there is no machine like the one you thought you saw at my carnival, hmmm?" She gave no response. " 'The Mother's Escape,' I think it was."

She stopped fidgeting. She looked sharply at him.

"It was there all right. I got rid of it the moment you walked out of the arcade. I'm sorry to say it was the most ruthless piece of entrapment I have ever been forced to commit. Yes, forced. You see, I really would be very appreciative if you would sign something for me. If you do so, you have my word that I'll reverse what has happened. If you don't, well, you're obviously going to Hell anyway. If you don't sign, the torment will start before death with a life sentence. I understand child-killers have rather a miserable time of it."

While he'd been talking, he'd allowed his gaze to wander around the room: the barred window, the institutional green paint on the walls, some schedule of regulations framed and hung by the door. Then he looked at her and realised that if looks could kill he would assuredly have been dead for some moments. She glared at him, teeth slightly bared, an expression of hot, animal loathing on her face. She spoke so quietly, he almost didn't catch it.

"Necromancer," she said, as if it was the worst word she knew. At that moment, it was.

"An inference is no proof of an implication," he replied, and produced the contract. "Do you want your life back, such as it is? Or shall I leave? I'm a busy man. A rapid decision would be nice."

She looked at the folded paper as if its blank exterior would tell her all that she needed to know. Cabal laid it out flat, turned it so that it faced her, and slid it across to her. She looked at it, obviously not reading. Cabal had an uncomfortable feeling that she was going to start crying again. He drew his pen and offered it to her.

"Sign. Now."

She took the pen and, her hand trembling slightly, she signed.

Cabal walked out into the new day. The last day of the carnival. He needed one last soul and had every chance of succeeding. Why, then, he wondered, did he feel so wretched?

Chapter 12

Cabal patted the pocket containing the contract to reassure himself that it hadn't vanished due to some capricious event at the quantum level. No, it hadn't. He drew a deep breath; some part of him had been rather hoping it might. He was tired, more tired than he could ever remember being, and for a man who regarded sleep as a necessary evil, this was very tired indeed. Despite it, he had no desire to rest his head. No doubt he was well past the point where sleep came easily. Besides, he might dream.

He adjusted his dark-blue spectacles and looked around. It was the first time he'd actually entered Penlow on Thurse, and what he saw depressed him. It looked absolutely idyllic, exactly the sort of place that folk dream of retiring to before they examine their pension fund and end up in a terrace next door to a psychotic with a dog, a baseball bat, and a sousaphone. It raised the question "Where do the citizens of Penlow go to retire?" Cabal didn't care. The place bothered him inexplicably.

A postman shot by on his bicycle, smiling and saying hello as he swept down the road to a junction. Despite there not being another vehicle on the road for as far as the eye could see, the postman slowed, checked both ways, and signalled before joining the main road. A place where bicyclists—postmen to boot—obeyed the laws of the road. Cabal had seen many strange things in his life, of which the walking dead were the least. He'd run for his life from the guardians of Solomon's Key, avoided the attentions of the gargoyle Bok, and studied, although been careful not to blow, a bronze whistle upon which the words "QUIS EST ISTE QUI VENIT" were deeply inscribed. None of these, however, had filled him with such a sense of hidden threat and foreboding as this polite and cheerful postman.

"All I need now is a friendly vicar and I'll know I'm in trouble." He turned and walked into a priest, a man of gentle and genial demeanour in his mid-sixties.

"I *do* beg your pardon, my son. I was just ruminating on my sermon and . . ." He paused and looked at Cabal over the top of his half-moon spectacles. "But you must be one of the people from the travelling carnival, I declare! How do you do! I'm delighted to make your acquaintance. I'm the vicar at Saint Olave's, just over there." He gestured towards a small parish church of heartbreaking architectural excellence in picture-postcard grounds. "Will you still be here on Sunday? Perhaps you would like to attend the service. We've always got space for visitors."

"No, I'm afraid that won't be possible."

"You're moving on, no doubt. In my youth, such a peripatetic life held great appeal. Now, however . . ." He spread his hands and smiled so sweetly Cabal was caught by opposing urges to strike him and adopt him.

"We won't be here," replied Cabal. "That's true, but I wouldn't attend anyway." He smiled. "I'm a Satanist."

The vicar smiled back. Cabal felt a need to check his own smile in a mirror to make sure it was still the thing of fear that he'd carefully cultivated for years.

"Ah, me," said the vicar, infuriatingly unshocked. Cabal might as well have admitted to preferring spring to summer or a fondness for chocolate digestives. "And are you happy?"

Cabal's large quiver of cutting replies proved unexpectedly empty. He had been ready for almost any response but sympathy. "No," he managed to say finally. "No, I'm not. It's not something I chose to be. It's more like work experience. I intend to give it up as soon as possible."

"I shan't argue with your decision. Dear me, no. I cannot argue with your decision. It seems very wise to me. Well, I must be getting on. I'll bid you a good day, sir." Cabal found himself shaking the man's hand, thanking him for his concern, and wishing him a pleasant morning.

Cabal watched the vicar wander off in the direction of his perfect church and bet himself that the sermon would be perspicacious, amusing, and interesting. People would enjoy going to church. He found himself envying them. He stopped and inspected the sensation. What was wrong with him? He sat down on a well-sited and unvandalised bench and set about sorting himself out. He was almost glad when the little girl sat down at the far end of the bench. He loathed children and was glad that here, at least, was a situation he could trust his reactions in.

"Hello," said the little girl, and smiled a gap-toothed smile brightly at him. Cabal suddenly felt broody. An insane urge to find a good woman, settle down, and have a couple of kids—one of each—lit upon him like a thing out of a nightmare.

Staggering to his feet, he managed a disjointed warning against talking to strangers before walking quickly away. He needed somewhere quiet to pull himself together. A short expedition into the churchyard resulted in a hasty retreat, as his feet started to smoke. He'd forgotten about the danger of consecrated ground in his soulless state. That was another inconvenience he'd be rid of once he found somebody. Just one more person. It worried him that he'd forgotten about the danger: combusting footwear was an experience that tended to stay with a person. Yet that was exactly what he'd done—blithely forgotten all about it, seduced by the tranquillity of the place. His sense of foreboding was deepening by the minute.

"Hello, Mr. Cabal," said Barrow, happening upon him at the end of a short parade of shops. "You don't look well, if you don't mind me saying so."

"Yes. Yes, I do," said Cabal, drawing on some inner reservoir of animosity. "I'm always pale. I'm"—inspiration danced lithely out of grasp—"a pale person."

"I had noticed," replied Barrow without reproach. "I didn't mean your colour, though. I was talking about your air. You seem lost."

Cabal looked sharply at him. "And what if I am? What is it to you?"

Barrow smiled. Cabal was getting sick of people smiling at him. He was getting even sicker of the impulse to respond in kind. "It's my town," said Barrow. "We feel responsible for strangers here."

"Do you? Do you indeed?" Cabal thought he was beginning to sound like an old man. Vaguely peevish but without real rancour. His fire seemed to be going out. A desire to escape back to the carnival, where he could be foul-tempered at a moment's notice, was certainly within him, but it was being balanced, no, overbalanced, by an inertia to stay in Penlow.

"I've got some good news," continued Barrow. "I was going to go over to the carnival because I thought you might like to hear it, but here you are, so you've saved me a trip."

"I had business to attend to," said Cabal, while he thought, Why am I explaining myself?

"Offering the girl help with legal expenses. Yes, I know. That was very kind of you." Cabal blanched. Barrow continued, "I've just come away from the police station. I went there after I heard the news from Dr. Greenacre."

"The good news."

"Yes."

Cabal looked expectantly at him, but no elaboration was forthcoming. "Well?"

"I'm sorry," said Barrow, shaking his head and smiling his accursed smile. "I had the oddest feeling that you would already know."

"Know what?" asked Cabal, but he *did* already know.

"The baby. It's recovered."

"It recovered from death? Remarkable. Children are *so* resilient."

"The doctor thinks it wasn't dead to start with, that the poison was really a drug that caused some sort of catatonic coma. Isn't that remarkable?"

"Isn't it? And the girl?"

"I'm not a lawyer, so I don't really know. Perhaps she might have been prosecuted for attempted murder."

"Might have?"

"Yes, there was quite a kerfuffle at the police station when I arrived. They've lost her statement."

"Really?" Cabal shifted his weight carefully from one foot to the other. He didn't want to make the contract rustle against the other piece of paper he'd brought away from there. "This would be the statement in which she admitted her guilt?"

"It would. Odd, that. No statement, no conviction, because she's denying it all now. Still, this little adventure might bring her around. She's not a bad girl, just a little out of her depth. She'd kept how miserable she was to herself. Folk'll rally 'round now they know. Penlow is a very close community like that," he finished significantly.

Close, thought Cabal. *It's positively suffocating.*

He noticed that Barrow was looking past him and followed his gaze. "I like animals as a rule," said Barrow. "But there's something about carrion crows that gives me the willies."

The crow had obviously got bored of hanging around the carnival and come to investigate the town. It sat on a nearby wall that somehow looked a lot less scenic for the addition. It looked at them; first with one eye, then with the other. Then, to show it was a polymath among crows, it went back to the first eye.

"Come here, crow," said Cabal.

With a delighted cry of "Kronk!" the bird flung itself from the wall, and, flapping its wings with more noise than an ornithopter made out of a telescoping umbrella, it landed on his shoulder. It looked around smugly.

Barrow seemed impressed. "I would never have guessed you were good with animals, Mr. Cabal," he said.

"I'm not." He nodded sideways at the crow, which seemed momentarily to consider pecking his ear and then thought much better of it. "There are two ways to get animals to obey you. One way is through kindness, and then there's . . ." He looked sharply at the crow. The near-irresistible desire it had been feeling to take off with his nice, shiny spectacles suddenly evaporated. Instead, it tried to grin in a charming, inoffensive, non-spectacles-thieving fashion. It wasn't a pretty sight. "The other way," finished Cabal, darkly.

"Cruelty?" said Barrow with disapproval.

Cabal was honestly surprised. "No," he said. "Threats."

"I thought threats were for blowhards and cowards?"

"When you're dealing with people, yes. Animals seem to take them in the spirit that they are meant, though." Barrow was looking at him strangely. "Or so I've found," finished Cabal a little weakly.

"Yes. Well." Barrow looked around for something to change the subject. "Do you like the town, Mr. Cabal?"

"Like." Cabal considered. "I'm not sure I'd use the word 'like.' I've been through many little towns and villages with the carnival, and I can honestly say this is a unique place in my experience. It's so *nice*." He said it as an imprecation.

"It *is* nice, isn't it?" replied Barrow, choosing to ignore Cabal's tone. The clock of Saint Olave's struck the hour, startling the crow into the air. "Ten o'clock already?"

"What?" Cabal couldn't believe it was so late so early.

"Time flies when you're having fun, eh?"

Cabal was too taken aback to deliver a hard look. "It can't be. I only just got here."

"It's a while before the pub opens, but we can get a pot of tea and some buns at the teashop," said Barrow. Cabal hadn't been in a teashop in almost longer than he could remember, nor did he have any great desire to break his fast of olde-worlde tweeness. Yet, for reasons he was incapable of remembering later, he allowed himself to be steered into the Church Tea-Rooms by his elbow and never said a peep.

It was left to Barrow to make small talk with the waitress, to order the tea and buns and some other fancies, and, he suspected, to pay. Not that he thought Cabal was tight-fisted by nature. No, you have to know what money means before it has significance one way or the other. Barrow doubted Cabal cared about it in the slightest.

They remained in an unstrained but neutral silence until the waitress came back, deposited the tea things, and bustled back off to the kitchen to tell her mum that Mr. Barrow was talking to one of the funny folk from the carnival.

Cabal took off his blue smoked-glass spectacles, folded them carefully, and placed them in his breast pocket. He looked very tired.

"So—what's life like?" asked Barrow.

"Life?" said Cabal quietly. "It's like a wisp of smoke in a tempest." There was a lengthy pause during which Barrow looked at Cabal and Cabal looked at the little pot of clotted cream as if he expected it to do something.

"I meant," said Barrow, "what's life like running a carnival?"

Cabal started to say something that might have become "How should I know?" but turned into "How shall I begin? Challenging. Very challenging. Fate"—he said the word pointedly, as if he were on poor terms with it—"always has some little surprise or other in store for me. One tries to be prepared." He looked at Barrow, and Barrow was surprised that, just for once, his gaze held no malice at all.

"Expect the unexpected, eh?"

Cabal almost smiled. "A trite saying, and one without even the advantage of being practical. I keep an open mind and try to stay flexible. But the future remains a mystery right to the moment it becomes the present."

"I saw a fortune-telling machine in that arcade of yours. No help?"

"Not much. Recalcitrant, too." He looked up at a print of an eighteenth-century hunting scene and fell silent. Barrow wasn't sure if the comment had been intended as a joke. Somehow he doubted it. Cabal abruptly said, "I disapprove of hunting." Then, without a word, he dropped a slice of lemon into his cup and filled it with Assam. Then, slightly to Barrow's surprise, he did the same for his cup, too. The possibility that this wasn't how Barrow took his tea didn't seem to occur to him. Barrow was struck by the paradox: Cabal was prepared to serve him his tea but not to check whether he liked milk or lemon. As it happened, he didn't mind much either way. Cabal took a sip.

"How do you like your tea?" asked Barrow.

"Very nice, thank you." Cabal watched the few tiny leaf fragments that had got by the strainer settle at the bottom of his cup. "I used to like Lapsang Souchong in my adolescence." He looked Barrow straight in the eye, and Barrow almost expected him to add, "And now you know my secret, you must die." Instead, he finished, "I can't imagine why. Its perfume is too much for me now." He put his cup down and proceeded to smother a scone with cream.

Barrow watched the careful precision of his hands, still in their black kid gloves, and thought Cabal moved like a surgeon. For want of a conversational gambit, he expanded on this. "You don't strike me as the carnival type, Mr. Cabal." The cream knife hesitated for a heartbeat and then continued. "I've met a fair few different types of people in my life, and I think I'm pretty good at summing them up."

"I understood that you'd retired from the police force, Mr. Barrow," said Cabal. He made a curious motion with his wrist as he drew the knife along the side of the pot, and every last vestige of cream was neatly wiped from the blade, as if it had been freshly washed. He drove the tip into the jam, took a blob encasing a strawberry back to the scone, and deposited it neatly in the middle. The result was so precise it looked like the work of a machine. Cabal repeated the action with the knife and laid it, spotless, on his side plate. Cabal raised the scone to his lips. "Old habits die hard, it appears." He took a careful bite.

Barrow persevered. "You're a very serious man, Mr. Cabal. You don't strike me as somebody given to frivolity. If I were playing a game of matching people to their jobs, I wouldn't have got you down a carny-man in a thousand years. Not ten thousand."

"Not a game you should play for money, then. As a matter of interest—"

"A doctor," cut in Barrow, anticipating the question.

"I've impressed you with my flashing bedside manner, then?"

"A pathologist, to be exact."

Cabal studied him seriously. "You see me working with the dead?"

Barrow poured himself some more tea. "It's hardly a great leap in imagination, now, is it? Look at you. You go around with a face like a wet Wednesday, dressed all in black, and, frankly, lacking something in charisma. Even funeral directors have to be able to deal with people." Barrow smiled. Cabal didn't. "The funny thing is that, in my experience, pathologists are often nice, jolly people. They do an ugly job, but that's all it is, a job. They leave it behind when they go home of an evening. You, though. I don't think you've ever left work at work."

"No," said Cabal. "I always take my work home. I've got several clowns under the bed, and a man who can belch the anthems of twelve nations in the wardrobe."

"Ah, but, as I've already said, is that your work?"

"Of course. With the help of my brother, I run a carnival. You can't have failed to notice it. It's that big thing down by the railway station." He finished his tea and put the cup down onto its saucer with a harsh *click*. "Which is where I should be now. Thank you for the tea, Mr. Barrow. It was very pleasant. You must visit the carnival in reciprocation. Perhaps, for a change, when it's open." He produced a card from thin air ("Learn a couple of conjuring tricks," Horst had told him. "People like that sort of thing") and gave it to Barrow. "A complimentary ticket, courtesy of the management."

Barrow accepted the card with a nod. As he read the few words on its face he asked, "May I have another? My daughter, Leonie, loves the fair."

Cabal produced another two tickets. "Come one, come all," he said without inflection. "Bring your wife as well."

Barrow took one ticket from Cabal's hand and put it away with the first one. "I'm a widower, Mr. Cabal."

Cabal put the extra ticket in his pocket (it was intended to vanish, but he'd had so little practice at this trick that, to the untrained eye, it simply looked as if he was putting the ticket away in his pocket). "I'm sorry," he said. He seemed to mean it.

"Thank you," said Barrow.

Cabal spent a long moment refreshing their cups, his intention to leave apparently forgotten. Once more, he didn't ask Barrow how he took his. As he plucked slices of lemon from their little plate with the tongs, he asked quietly, "Do you miss her?" He didn't look at Barrow as he said it.

"Every day," replied Barrow, accepting his cup back. "Every day. Life can be cruel."

"It wasn't life that took her away from you," said Cabal, looking at him directly. There was an even intensity in his eyes, like the gaze of a man who walks into a room where he knows he is going to see something awful and has braced himself for it.

"Fate, then?"

"Death. Death is your enemy. My enemy. Life can be cruel, that's true. Death is *always* cruel."

"Death can be a release," said Barrow. Watching Cabal talk now, he had a sensation reminiscent of watching somebody open a Chinese puzzle box. Part of it was wonder at the complexity. Part of it was curiosity as to what lay inside.

"Release?" said Cabal venomously. "Release be damned. That's just doctors' talk for failure. 'At least they're at peace now,' 'They've gone to a better place,' all those lies. You know what's waiting?"

"I'll know soon enough," said Barrow. "I'll just enjoy life while I can."

Cabal leaned forward. "I know *now*," he said, caution gone. "One place is run by a bored, disappointed sadist. The other . . . Spiritual transfiguration, do you know what that means? It means having everything that you ever were stripped away, bars of light, too intense to look upon." He unconsciously fingered the smoked glasses in his breast pocket. "Homogeneity incarnate. Can you imagine that? That's what the Heavenly Host is, countless thousands of bars of light, souls burning, all the same. Your personality lost forever. *Immortal* souls, hah! It's the final death. Sacrificed to a mania for order." He looked around at the middle distance, his disgust a palpable thing. "Lambs to the slaughter."

Barrow put his cup down. "Why do you hate death so much?"

Cabal seemed to rein himself in. "I don't hate death. It's not a person. There's no grim skeletal figure with a scythe. I try to avoid hating abstracts, it's a waste of effort."

"That's not what it sounded like a moment ago. You sounded like a man who would kill death if he could."

Cabal checked his pocket watch. "I despise waste. That's all."

"That's not all," said Barrow, and instantly knew that he'd overstepped a line.

Cabal got to his feet and straightened his coat. "Good day, Mr. Barrow," he said with stiff formality. "I've enjoyed our little chat, but I have things to attend to back at the carnival. If you will forgive me?" He turned on his heel and went out.

Barrow shook his head. He had the strongest feeling that, whoever Cabal really needed forgiveness from, it wasn't him. He'd met all sorts in his time, but never anybody quite like Johannes Cabal, and he was beginning to think fate had been kind to him up to now. He dropped some money on the table and followed Cabal.

Outside, he saw Cabal walking determinedly in the direction of the station. He was debating whether to follow when he was arrested by a cry of "Dad!" He turned to see his daughter, Leonie, leaving the hardware shop. He instinctively knew that she had been buying the hinge for the shed that he had complained about yesterday with the words "I'll have to get around to that one day." With Leonie, "one day" was "tomorrow," except on those occasions when it was "today."

She came over, smiling with the joys, and Barrow, who had the occasional pang of existential angst, was reassured that his life had been worthwhile. Oddly, though, something lay darkly over the familiar happiness that Leonie inspired in him, like a single small but impenetrably dark cloud on the face of the sun. He turned his head slowly in Cabal's direction.

Cabal was standing stock-still on the far side of the village green, staring at him. The intensity, the unblinking directness of the gaze unnerved Barrow.

He'd once been faced with a rabid dog, an animal that he knew could kill him slowly and agonisingly if it bit him just once. They had stared unblinkingly at each other, not ten feet apart, as Barrow slowly, and by touch alone, broke, reloaded, and closed his shotgun. It had continued to stare at him as he brought the gun to his shoulder and sighted carefully down the double barrels. The sensation that he had felt, a horrible sensation of the dog's burnt and chaotic mind communicating its madness to him through its gaze like a basilisk, still woke him in the early hours in a cold sweat. As Cabal stood motionless, staring, glaring, some of that sensation returned to Barrow, and he shuddered involuntarily.

The realisation that Cabal wasn't looking at him at all released him from his paralysis. The realisation that Cabal was actually looking at Leonie proved unexpectedly confusing. Unable to draw any conclusions, he left his next action to conditioned reflex. Perhaps unfortunately, his inclination was towards politeness.

Taking Leonie's arm, Barrow walked over to where Cabal was apparently rooted to the ground. "Mr. Cabal," he said. Cabal's eyes never deviated from Leonie's face. "Mr. Cabal, I'd like to introduce you to my daughter, Leonie."

"You own the carnival!" said Leonie, recognising the name. "Oh, I love fairs!"

"Mr. Cabal has very kindly given us tickets," said Barrow, patting the pocket that contained them.

"Thank you, Mr. Cabal," said Leonie. "I really do adore carnivals. We only tend to get the little travelling ones around here, though. Nothing you could call a big professional affair. I am *so* looking forward to tonight."

Cabal looked fixedly at her. Smoothly, as if possessed by a will of its own, his hand moved to his breast pocket, withdrew his spectacles, shook them open, and put them on. Seeing the world through smoke-tinted glasses seemed to shake him out of his paralysis of will. "Thank you, Miss Barrow. I'm . . . *we're* very flattered by your interest." He spoke slowly and with curious emphasis, as if his mind were elsewhere. Barrow watched him closely. Leonie was a good-looking girl—even allowing for a father's pride, that was plain to see—but surely Cabal wasn't smitten? The thought of a romantic streak in the sinister Mr. Cabal was disconcerting, even distasteful, especially if his own daughter was the focus of interest.

"How long are you here?" asked Leonie.

"Here," repeated Cabal tonelessly. "This is the last night."

"Then where are you going?"

"Then it is the end of the season," said Cabal. There was a finality in the way he said it that Barrow doubted was deliberate, and that was all the more suggestive for it.

Leonie was talking again. "Well, we mustn't miss our chance. You can be sure we will be there tonight, Mr. Cabal."

Barrow smiled, and it didn't even get within scenting distance of his eyes. He was distracted by the sure knowledge that there was something going on that he didn't like. He could taste one of his famous hunches, and it held the flavour of a beached whale. He sincerely regretted introducing Leonie to this man. He sincerely regretted accepting the tickets. He sincerely regretted that he would have to disappoint Leonie by making her stay at home tonight.

"But why?" It was later, and they'd gone home after saying goodbye to Cabal and Leonie, once again reassuring him that they'd certainly be there tonight. Barrow had just mentioned casually that he would prefer it if she didn't go after all, hoping vainly that she might just accept his wish. No such luck. It was shaping up into one of their rare, and all the more unpleasant for it, arguments.

"Nothing ever happens around here," she said. She seemed hurt, as if he were asking her to stay out of sheer malice.

"There's something wrong about Cabal. About his whole carnival. Things are happening. Unnatural things."

"But you *know* why that is," said Leonie, as if he were being deliberately stupid. "Rufus Maleficarus the necromancer. He's trying to ruin the Cabal carnival. We know that."

"Maleficarus is dead," pointed out Barrow.

"But he's a necromancer. That's the whole point. Life after death after life. They should have burnt him, but they didn't. Now he's come back."

"Do you really believe that?" Life after death after life. Something in the words provoked the glimmer of an idea. In Barrow's mind, cogs of pure thought started to form from the chaos of unordered data.

"We've seen the newspaper. It happened at Murslaugh. The Cabal brothers are heroes there. They're not making it up." She shrugged and shook her head at his stubbornness. It was a gesture she'd learned from her mother. She didn't know it, but it was a knife in his heart every time she did it.

He blinked the pain away and tried to marshal his arguments. They weren't having it and remained an undisciplined mob. "Look, I'm not arguing about this. You are not going."

"What?" She couldn't believe he could be so intransigent. Of course, the crowning point was that she was a grown woman and he really couldn't stop her if she decided to go. That, however, wasn't nearly so important to her that minute as understanding why he was even trying. "What happened to hearing both sides of an argument?"

"All right, let's hear your side."

"My side? My side is that I want to go to the carnival because I want to go to the carnival. It's fun. I would like some fun. It's your side that's lacking."

"I've told you . . ."

"You've told me that you don't like Mr. Cabal. Fine. I think you're being silly, but if you insist, I'll avoid him. I don't want to go for his fascinating conversation." She saw her father fight a smile. Cabal had been all but monosyllabic when she'd spoken to him. "I just want to go on the Ghost Train, throw balls at nailed-down coconuts, and have a bit of fun. What's wrong with that?"

"There's nothing wrong with that, it's just . . ."

"What can possibly happen?" She looked at her father and felt her anger cool a little. When all was said and done, he would die for her, and they both knew it. "What *can* possibly happen?"

Barrow sighed. Here was the crux of it. "I don't know," he admitted, "I really have no idea. Maybe nothing. But, *but*"—he took her hands in his—"maybe something. Try to understand. When I was still with the police . . . No! Hear me out!" Leonie had rolled her eyes at the mention of his old job. When he was satisfied that he had her attention, he continued. "When I was with the police, I came across all sorts. The criminals, nine times out of ten, it was obvious. They forget what morality is—real morality, that is. The stuff that lets us get along with each other. They can mimic it like a chameleon can mimic the colour of leaves, but that's all it is. Mimicry. They've forgotten what it is to think like everybody else, and they get things wrong. Little things, but you get so you can scent them out. Little mistakes. Everything that they do, everything they say is riddled and rotting with mistakes."

Leonie looked at him, worried. He couldn't tell if she was worried by him or worried about him. "Are you suggesting that Johannes Cabal is a criminal?" she said.

"No, not at all, not in the way that you mean. I actually think he's a very moral man. I just don't think that he's using the same morals as everybody else. I think . . ." This was it. He'd painted himself into a corner, and a thousand lazy reporters and ever-so-sincere politicians had rendered the only word that he could use comically melodramatic. "I think . . . Johannes Cabal . . . is *evil*."

Leonie looked at him in disbelief. *Evil*. The word had lost its power through overuse. Now it just meant incomprehensible to the uncomprehending. Barrow wanted to explain the complexities of it, this language of suffering that he had learned at countless crime scenes and in too many interview rooms. The serial killer and the serial burglar shared far more than either would like to admit: the need that has to be fed until next time, the need that results in the suffering of others, the easy justifications. They shouldn't have left it unlocked. They shouldn't have gone down that alley. They shouldn't have been dressed like that. Barrow had heard it all, and he'd always smelled the sour smell of a failed human. Cabal, though, he was of another order altogether. There was almost a nobility in the corruption of the spirit that Barrow was sure was there, was sure that he had detected. There was something different, though. If he could just put a name to it, he was sure that he would understand Cabal all the better. Evil, in as far as he had experienced it so far, was always selfish. It was always just an extension of the most stupid behaviour of the infant playground: "It's mine because I say so. It's mine because I take it." Belongings, sexuality, life. But not in Cabal's case. Barrow played with words mentally as he tried to explain to Leonie what he meant. Cabal's was a (*what?*) evil. Clinical? Displaced? Remote? Deviant? Altruistic?

Altruistic? How can evil ever be altruistic?

"It's against its nature," Barrow said, thinking out loud.

"Evil?" Leonie was still stuck on the word. It wasn't one her father used often. In fact, she couldn't remember him ever using it at all. "Are you serious?"

"I'm serious when I say I don't want you to go to the carnival." He tightened his grasp of her hands. "I'm scared for you. I'm scared for every person who walks through those gates."

"You *are* serious." She nodded slightly, and her trust in him closed the distance. "I won't go."

After she had gone, Barrow reached into his pocket and studied the two tickets. "You," he said to one of them, "are surplus to requirements." He threw the piece of pasteboard onto the fire. "You," he said to the survivor, "are going to get me inside that carnival tonight. Then we shall see." He went to the window to reread the printing on the ticket.

As he turned his back on the fire, he failed to see the ticket that he had thrown there flutter up the flue. It seemed miraculously unburnt. Indeed, as it made its way up the chimney, even the scorch marks faded away. Three-quarters of the way to the chimney stack, it made a difficult turn and headed for one of the upstairs fireplaces. Leonie sat by the window, looking off across the fields in the direction that she knew the carnival to be. Unseen, the ticket fluttered across the room and landed on her desk. It found itself a good, obvious position and practised looking alluring.

Chapter 13

⊸ IN WHICH THE CARNIVAL OF DISCORD OPENS ITS
GATES FOR THE LAST TIME AND THINGS
GO TERRIBLY WRONG

Cabal passed the rest of the day trying to keep his mind off a variety of things. Failure. Damnation.

Leonie Barrow.

First, he worked on his conjuring. The card vanish he'd used to dispose of the extra ticket he'd offered Frank Barrow had been technically correct but an artistic disaster. It would never do. He sat down with a deck of cards in front of a mirror and started vanishing them methodically and steadily until his pockets and sleeves bulged. Then he shook them out and started again. And again. And again. Then, for variety's sake, he started vanishing and immediately reproducing them. The Queen of Spades flickered in and out of existence in his hand. He watched his hands closely in the reflection. He'd made a point of angling the mirror so that he could see only his hands in it. He had no desire to see his face.

When the cards started getting dog-eared and suggestively curved, like Tuscan roof tiles, he turned his attention to other objects on his desk. Pens, pencils, and a ruler mysteriously vanished and then made triumphant returns. He'd been pleased with how well he'd managed to make that woman's confession vanish in the police station.

Thinking of it, he pulled both it and her contract from his pocket and took a moment to examine them. Nea, she was called. He wasn't sure if he'd ever come across a Nea before. It was a pleasant name, and he let it run with abandon around his mind for a moment. Then he drew the little key from his waistcoat pocket, unlocked the desk drawer, and placed her contract beneath the others in the box. At the top, this left a single blank form. By hook or by crook, it had better be signed before midnight. He put the box away and carefully locked the drawer before returning his attention to the confession. He skimmed it and was quietly impressed at how accurate it was, given her disturbed state of mind at the time. He practised making it vanish a few more times before tearing it into ribbons and feeding them to the stove in the corner.

He leaned back in his chair and drummed his fingers on the desk edge. Still a couple of hours before sundown. What to do? Horst had promised to finish his plans for making the carnival more acceptable to the staid people of this town, but, when he looked at them, they didn't seem to have been touched. Cabal thought of the talk he'd had with Horst last night and felt unaccountably worried. There had been something important that obviously mattered to Horst, but Johannes had been distracted and missed it. He hoped it wasn't *too* important.

He looked around the office, seeking distraction. His eye fell upon his large notebook, and he took it up. There was a piece of music that the calliope played, an odd, lurching tune that still sounded faintly familiar. Perhaps if he wrote it out he might remember where he'd heard it before. Not a man usually given to trivial pursuits, he nevertheless felt no qualms as he took up his ruler and pencil, carefully drew out staves, and started writing in notes.

Time passed in quietude broken only by the frequent crunching of the pencil sharpener. Cabal hated working with blunt instruments. Outside, the riggers followed what there were of Horst's plans in total silence; they didn't even need to breathe except for effect. The "House of Medical Monstrosity" had become the "Home for the Genetically

Challenged," and the tone had changed from "be horrified" to "be educated." "The Hall of Pain: Torture Down the Centuries!" had transformed into "Man's Inhumanity: An Exhibit of Conscience," and "Monsters! Monsters! Monsters!" into "Unknown Nature: Cryptozoological Wonders." Cabal himself had started to find his interest piqued by sideshows that he'd spent the last year walking past.

Cabal finished writing and looked at his work. It didn't look familiar. Even tilting his head gently from side to side didn't help. Then, acting on a sudden suspicion, he drew some more staves and wrote the music out again but this time in reverse. It still didn't look familiar, but when he looked at it, it seemed far too cheerful to be a piece he'd naturally associate with this place. He whistled it experimentally. Now he was *certain* he'd heard it before. Outside, the sun hung just over the horizon.

Barrow sat in his garden and watched the day come to a close and wondered idly if he would ever see another. He was going to have to go to the carnival tonight and try to discover what it was that disturbed him so much about it, so wrong and corrupt. He didn't want to. Not at all, not for a second. He just felt he ought. Furthermore, he felt that he really ought to do something about it. He wished there was somebody he could go to for help. However, he had the oddest feeling that if he suggested to anybody that the Cabal brothers—Johannes in particular—were not just proprietors of a carnival but were, in actual fact, founts of evil that must be confronted by glowing crusaders for good such as, for example, himself, then there was a fair chance he'd be relieved of his braces and laces before being brazenly patronised by a psychiatrist long before the night was out.

He thought about what he'd said to Leonie. He *was* scared for her, more so than ever before in his life. He was scared for himself, too. It's only fear, he thought, and that can't hurt me. Some bugger with a hatchet, now, *that's* worth worrying about. He tried to imagine Cabal bearing down on him with an axe, a knife, a crowbar, and he smiled. The ice-cool Mr. Cabal behaving like a thug—now, that was funny. Then he remembered the dead look in Cabal's eyes when he'd seen Leonie, and suddenly it wasn't funny at all. Across the fields, the sound of the carnival's calliope floated to him, the notes ugly and mocking. Barrow realised that the music had started the instant that the sun had gone down. That didn't surprise him at all.

*C*abal ignored the calliope and continued to whistle the reversed music. Damnation, what was it?

"I'm glad you think so," said Horst from behind him.

Cabal turned, the whistle dying on his lips. "What do you mean?"

"You, whistling 'Happy Days Are Here Again.' You have a perverse sense of humour." Horst pulled on his coat and top hat. "If you'll forgive me, I don't like the atmosphere in here very much." The door opened and shut, and Johannes Cabal was alone once more, in all senses of the word.

Cabal looked at the staves with disbelief. He leaned forward over the notebook and rested his fingertip on the first note. "Hap-py days are here a-gain," he sang quietly as his finger tapped from note to note. Yes, Horst was quite right. In abrupt disgust, he tore the pages out and threw them in the wastepaper basket. "Very funny. Most amusing." He pulled on his coat and hat and went to find Horst. Somewhere, somebody laughed.

Horst was walking in long-legged strides between the stands, stalls, and sideshows, pointedly ignoring the riggers that approached him asking for clarifications of his half-written plans. Johannes Cabal had no trouble finding him; he just followed the trail of disgruntled men with wilting bits of paper in their hands. He caught up with Horst by the Mysteries of Egypt, where Cleopatra had managed to buttonhole him. As Cabal approached, he could hear her haranguing Horst.

"Woss all this, then? Eh?" she squalled, waving a sheet of paper under Horst's nose.

"It's your revised script," said Horst with uncharacteristic irritation. "Learn it. Now."

"Woss wrong wiv me ol' script, eh?" She changed gear and her voice became mellifluous, sensuous. "I"—she breathed the word—"am

Cleopatra, Queen of Egypt, mistress"—this with a significant look—"of the Nile. Come with me and discover the pleasures . . . *and* the terrors of the ancient world." She went from smoky seductress to Billingsgate fishwife in much less than a second. "There! W'a were wrong wiv that, eh? I mean, that were the dog's bollocks, that were. Now you've given me this crap!" She waved the sheet in his face. "Woss all this shite 'baht dynasties an' stuff? People dun wonna know 'baht that! They wanna 'ear 'baht shaggin' an' murder an' people 'avin' their brains fished aht their noses an' stuff!"

Horst was never impolite to ladies. Unfortunately for Cleopatra, she wasn't only definitely *not* a lady, she wasn't even technically human.

"Shut up," said Horst in a cold hiss. He sounded a lot like his brother. "Just shut up. Come midnight, you're dust and ashes, just like everybody else in this travelling nightmare, so I really don't care what you think. You learn the script I've given you and you deliver it properly. If I come around this show later and find you delivering the old one, or deliberately making a bad job of the new one, you're not even going to make it to midnight. Do you understand me?"

Cleopatra blinked. "All right," she said in a very small voice.

"Horst," called Cabal as he approached, "Horst, what has got into you?" Cleopatra looked fearfully at the pair of them. "You are dismissed," said Cabal, and she ran off into the sideshow like a frightened kohl-smirched bunny.

"What has got into me?" Horst looked at the dark sky. When he looked back down, his expression was one of purest animosity. "Where *do* I begin?"

Cabal's mind worked quickly to isolate an event that might have caused such a rapid deterioration in relations. "This is about that woman last night, isn't it? The one with the child?"

"Yes, this is about the woman last night. The one with the child. What did you do to her? What dirty little stunt did you pull?"

"I granted her wish. That's all."

"And she signed over her soul for it."

"No. She didn't. She signed over her soul so that I'd take the wish away again. She wanted the child dead, Horst. She's no angel."

Horst waved his finger in Cabal's face. "No, she didn't want her baby dead. For crying out loud, Johannes, she just wanted a little help. Couldn't you see that? Couldn't you see that she just wanted a little help? She needed a babysitter, not a plan for murder."

"I. Don't. Care. What. She. *Needed*," said Cabal, feeling his temper stirring. "She was prepared to sign for what she got. That's all that matters."

" 'That's all that matters'? That is *not* all that matters, by a very long chalk. She's a person, a human being, a living woman. Not just another name on one of your forms. You've ruined her life, you know that? She knows what's waiting for her now, hanging over her."

"I didn't hear you make this kind of fuss over any—"

"Pay attention, Johannes! The difference is that she hadn't done anything wrong until you railroaded her into it. You! You've finally become what you were always meant to be."

Cabal's sixth sense belatedly started tingling. He had the faint impression that somebody was making a fool of him, had been making a fool of him for the last year, somebody who smelled quite strongly of brimstone. "What do you mean?" he asked cautiously.

"You are such a fool," said Horst. "That's what this whole exercise has really been about. I thought you'd have worked it out a long, long time ago. Old Hob down below isn't interested in a pile of souls that he would have got anyway. He wanted to push you into taking one. Corrupting one. That business with Billy Butler was to make you desperate, make you forget that somewhere inside"—Horst's voice cracked slightly—"there's a good man. My little brother, Johannes. That's all gone now. You're not trying to beat the devil anymore. You're doing his work for him. You're not my brother anymore. I can't . . . I *won't* help you anymore." Horst turned and started to walk away.

"Horst?" Cabal's voice was small, disbelieving. Horst braced himself against sentiment, kept walking. "Horst, I need you. I can't do this alone.

I'm so close. Horst!" His brother's stride never faltered. Johannes Cabal's temper was a volatile quantity at the best of times, and he could feel it riding in his gullet now. This time, however, it was different.

There was something else there, a blossoming flower of easy violence that flooded up through his chest and found expression on his tongue, a faint taste of aniseed. "You will help me, Horst," he said, his voice stronger, "or you'll stay the way you are now, forever."

Horst stopped. He stood still a long moment and then turned. "What," he said quietly, "did you just say?"

You have power over him, thought Cabal, although part of him wondered if somebody else was doing his thinking for him. *He can't talk to you like that.* "I said, you'll do what you're told or you can stay a parasite for the rest of time."

Horst took a moment to consider his words. He walked right up to his brother until they were nose to nose and said, "Go fuck yourself, Johannes." There was a sudden breeze as air rushed into the space that used to be full of Horst. Cabal looked around, blinking. He was quite alone.

Who needs him? said a small voice in his heart. *You're the man with the plan. Get to it. One last soul needed. Horst was just holding you back with all his stupid little scruples. Now you don't have to pussyfoot around looking for somebody who wants to give their soul away. Now you can find a likely candidate and take it.*

Frank Barrow moved with surprising stealth through the shadows behind the sideshows. He wasn't sure what he was looking for, but he was damn sure that it wasn't in plain sight. He'd turned up at the turnstiles, handed over his complimentary ticket, noticed that almost everybody else in the queue had one, too, and had then entered the carnival ground with the sullen expression of somebody who expected to be entertained. He'd stood by a ginnel formed between the Parapsychological Perplex Experience (the Ghost Train) and the Sociopathic Mind (a Chamber of Horrors stuffed to the rafters with waxworks of infamous murderers*) and made a great show of winding his watch. The instant he wasn't observed, he'd faded into the background. Now he shook the rust off his old shadowing skills and saw what he might see. He'd stumbled upon the Cabal brothers having some sort of argument but hadn't been able to get close enough to find out what it had been about. An odd thing, though: there had been a point when he'd been sure that Horst was about to punch Johannes, Barrow had blinked, and Johannes had suddenly been alone. He wasn't quite sure where Horst had got to, and, judging by the way he'd been casting about, neither had Johannes. Then Johannes Cabal had paused, and a very unpleasant smile had crept across his face, like a melanoma in time-lapse. It was another odd thing in and of itself, because Cabal had looked very different for some reason, almost like a different person. Then, full of a sense of purpose that Barrow found alarming in its suddenness, Cabal had strode off into the carnival's main thoroughfare.

Now Barrow was moving quietly, unseen, but what he was seeing was worrying. He'd spent a lot of time in his life in places of hard, manual work and was used to their rhythms and nuances. Here there were none. He'd asked at the pub in town: what were the riggers like? The landlord had shrugged; he had no clue. None had been in. Barrow thought this was downright perverse. Unless the Cabals had manned their carnival with Quakers, Moslems, and assorted other teetotallers, then there was no obvious explanation. Unless, bizarre as it sounded, they simply didn't drink. Following a hunch, he'd been to the grocers and asked a few questions there, too. Yes, the carnival had bought supplies, but nowhere near as much as might be expected for such a large operation. "They're on starvation rations," the grocer had said miserably. "They hardly bought enough to feed twenty." Looking at a couple of the

---

* Several of the waxworks, studied closely, could be seen to breathe, blink, and appear rather nervous. This was because they were the real things. A strawberry-picking expedition for the serial-killer wing of Laidstone Prison had proved a sad disappointment for the progressive governor. The carnival just happened to be nearby at the time, and in return for a place to hide, the escaped convicts had naturally been required to fill in a few forms. Fair's fair, after all. Cabal had somehow neglected to mention that their bolthole was going to vanish within the year. Ah well.

strapping men standing by a big wheel, he found the idea of anybody here starving very difficult to believe. He watched them as they smiled and waved at a crowd of teenagers going by. Then another curious thing happened.

The instant the crowd passed out of sight, the two riggers froze solid. Barrow thought that they'd seen something and shielded his eyes against the fierce, clear light of the stringed bulbs, but there was nothing to see, and after a moment he realised that was what they were looking at. There was nothing there, and nobody. Nobody to pretend for, nobody to go through the act of being real people for.

Barrow could have waited for somebody else to come by to test his hypothesis. He could even have walked around and by them to see them go through their paces on his behalf. He could have, but he didn't, and he didn't because he'd as willingly gargle with toilet cleaner. In his extensive experience, out of harm's way was a marvellous and worthwhile place to be, and he wanted to maintain his tenancy there as long as was humanly possible. Dancing up and down in front of a couple of enormous things with arms and legs that did a reasonable impersonation of people might be construed as provocative. "Softly, softly, catchee monkey" had been the unofficial motto of the police when he'd carried a warrant card. When the monkey looked like it would have little difficulty tearing your head off and spitting down your neck, it was particularly good advice.

Instead, he vanished back into the shadows to find more data. He couldn't hypothesise without data. When Frank Barrow built a case, it stayed airtight at two hundred atmospheres.

There was none of the behind-scenes stuff that one might expect, he discovered as he peered through tent flaps and listened at ajar doors. Everything was as dead as dust when the townsfolk weren't there. Nobody spoke, nobody moved (although he was sure he'd heard a mass gasp of exhaled breath when a party had left the hall of murderers in the Sociopathic Mind). Dead as dust. Cold as clay. The cogs of the idea that had started forming earlier were beginning to mesh. He didn't like the look of the machine that they were forming at all. It seemed too fantastic, like a heart pacemaker made from balsa wood and chewing gum. He must have it wrong. He just couldn't quite see how, though. After all, if it's got four legs, yaps, and wants to be best pals with your shin, then it's likely to be a dog. Barrow felt he had enough circumstantial evidence that, if he threw a rubber bone, this particular idea would bring it back for him, plus a large puddle of drool. Barrow had a bad feeling that he knew exactly what was going on.

"I know you," said a voice quietly behind him. Barrow whirled to find Horst standing there. "You're Frank Barrow." Horst raised his hands in supplication. "Really, I mean you no harm."

Barrow belatedly realised that he had settled into a boxer's stance. He grunted with embarrassment and straightened up. Horst looked at him coolly. "I'd got the impression from somewhere that you were Penlow's mayor or some such. Do your duties include skulking around visiting carnivals?"

"How long have you been watching me?" said Barrow, with some bluster thrown in for effect. He needed time to get over his surprise.

"Me? Oh, I get around. I'm here, there . . ." Horst seemed to turn into a long smudge on Barrow's retinas, and then he was standing twenty feet away. "Everywhere," he said, appearing abruptly not two paces away.

Barrow gawped. He'd seen some neat tricks before, but this aced them all. "How do you do that?" he managed to ask.

Horst shrugged dismissively, as if it were on par with ear waggling. "Practice. Natural talent. Supernatural powers. Who knows? Who cares? I don't and you shouldn't. You should be answering my question."

"I wasn't doing anything wrong, what business is it of yours?"

"You might not have been doing anything wrong, but you may have been considering it. Certain authorities hold that the thought is morally equivalent to the expression. That seems like an auto-flagellomaniac's charter to me. Are you a moral man, Mr. Barrow?"

"Eh?" Barrow had been considering escape routes and had just realised what a pointless endeavour it was when up against a man who could break the sound barrier in carpet slippers. "I used to be a police officer."

Horst raised his eyebrows to demonstrate polite interest. "Really? Well, that's nice, of course, but, as I was saying, are you a moral man?"

Barrow let that pass without challenge. "Yes, I think I am. Are you, Mr. Cabal?"

" 'Mr. Cabal' is my brother. Call me Horst. And, yes, I am." He said the words again, as if realising the truth in them for the first time. "I *am* a moral man. There are certain things that have to be done, no matter how difficult they are. Forget about blood and water. I have to forget about blood. And you"—he looked into Barrow's eyes, and Barrow suddenly found he couldn't move, could barely even breathe—"why do you come here when you're so afraid?"

Barrow would like to have said something doughty, but his muscles didn't seem to be returning calls today.

Horst continued speaking. "Don't give me the saloon-bar talk about not having a nerve in your body. I can smell fear, and you're upwind of me. What brings you here when you're so afraid? *Your* morals?" Horst softened his glance, and Barrow could talk again.

"Yes, I suppose so. I've . . ." Now he was here, it sounded foolish. Foolish but no less true for all that. "I've come to stop you."

Horst showed astonishment, going so far as to tap his chest. "Stop me? In that case, I'm afraid you've had a wasted trip. I've already slowed to a dead halt. A very dead halt. You wouldn't believe the half of it."

"Nea Winshaw. Does that name mean anything to you?" said Barrow sharply.

"No. Should it?"

"She claims, *claimed*, that this carnival was instrumental in the apparent death of her child."

"The woman in the penny arcade," said Horst almost to himself.

"That's right. She made a remarkable confession."

Horst didn't seem surprised. Barrow, who had never willingly leapt to a conclusion in his life, carefully put up a stepladder beside one and ascended cautiously. "You mean her story's *true?*"

"I don't know, I haven't heard it. But whatever it is, yes, it's true."

Despite Barrow's hunch, it was still a shock to discover that Nea

Winshaw's extraordinary story was true even in part. And with that discovery, the idea that had been gently assembling itself for the last day finally came together, lit its lights, and puffed into action. "Oh my God. Johannes Cabal is a necromancer," said Barrow slowly, horror-struck. It explained so much, but taking it in was still so difficult. Yes, there was magic in the world, but it was so rare in these modern days. He'd only had to deal with it on a handful of occasions, and even then it had been of the minor hedge-witch sort. Necromancers were at the extreme edge of the world's magic, they were very, very rare, and every time one was detected by justice—state or rough—they became that much rarer.

Horst was moderately impressed. "Not bad. You must have been a good policeman. Any other conclusions, Hercule?"

"I checked the file on Rufus Maleficarus—"

"Oh, that's not fair. If people are going to check the facts every time I open my mouth, where does that leave most of my conversation?"

"He was dangerous all right but not a necromancer, which isn't to say he hadn't tried. Your brother did kill him, though. Quite the local hero in Murslaugh. I sent a telegram to the chief inspector there. There were some other incidents that occurred at about the same time. They've talked themselves into believing that some of Maleficarus' mob was still on the loose and causing mischief. Funny thing was that they never found a single one of the lunatics after Maleficarus caught three bullets. Why do you suppose that was?"

"Well, obviously, they came to work for this carnival."

"Obviously. Your brother has already told me as much, perfectly candidly. It's only obvious to you because you've been sheltering them."

"Me?" Horst laughed. "What makes you think I have any say in anything that matters around here? I didn't shelter them, they just turned up holding Johannes's coattails like a lot of moonstruck sheep. If moonstruck sheep hold coattails. Which seems unlikely, now that I stop to consider it."

Barrow wasn't in the mood for analysing shaky similes. "Why? What does your brother hope to achieve? What is all this in aid of?"

"Now, that I can't possibly tell you. After all, blood's thicker than water. I could never deliberately dish up my little brother."

"Little brother? But he looks older than you."

"You know, I was just considering that very thing the other day. I suppose he must have overtaken me in the ageing stakes at some point."

Barrow's idea machine was whizzing its cogs gamely by now, and every little datum was crunched up, associated like with like, and quickly delivered as gorgeous little conclusions in engaging presentation cases. This latest piece of information was duly processed and popped up moments later, labelled "Horst Cabal has probably been dead at some point."

"You're dead," said Barrow, hoping he was reading Horst's character properly.

"Undead, technically. Not Johannes's doing, I hasten to add. Not directly, at any rate. He *had* promised to find some way of bringing me back to the land of the living. Not that I'm not in the land of the living now, you understand? I'm speaking figuratively. Now I'm not so sure. I need a little time to think."

"I don't understand you."

"Neither do I, I'm afraid. That's why I need to think. It all comes to some sort of conclusion tonight, one way or the other, and Johannes, I don't know what to make of him anymore. I want you to bear one thing in mind." Horst stepped closer and said conspiratorially, "He's a desperate man. More so than you might think. A great deal more than I'd have thought."

"Why don't you stop him?"

"I'm his brother. I can't, I simply can't. I've done all I can, and it's come to nothing. You, though, perhaps you can do something before it's too late. *Before it's too late,*" he said again, as if it were already so. "I've got to go. Good luck, Mr. Barrow."

"Wait! Just a second!" Barrow didn't want Horst pulling his vanishing act just yet. "There's still something I don't understand. What is your brother doing? Why is he here?"

"I suggest that you ask Miss Winshaw."

"She's not saying anything."

"Does she need to?"

Barrow thought back to what he knew about her case. The facts were impenetrable enough. Perhaps he was looking too hard. When she'd been brought in as a murderer, she'd seemed appalled at what she'd done. Her main thought had been horror at the act itself. She'd confessed immediately and comprehensively, obviously seeking some sort of absolution by throwing her own life away. She'd seemed very relieved when she'd put her name on the confession.

Then Johannes Cabal came a-calling. In rapid succession, her baby had turned out to be nowhere near as dead as two experienced doctors had believed, her confession had miraculously disappeared, and she'd started denying everything. Anything else? Why, yes, of course. Her entire attitude had changed. She'd become positively doom-haunted. The only thing that she'd shown any animation about at all was the child's recovery. Not because it meant there was no longer any charge against her, but for the pure fact that her baby lived. For herself, her horizons seemed to have drawn so close she could touch them. What had blighted her expectations? What could Cabal have said? What could a necromancer have said? What do they deal in? Life and death.

"Souls," said Barrow finally.

"Give the man a coconut," said Horst. He paused and looked around. "Start being very careful *now*," he said urgently, and blurred into the night.

Barrow didn't have very long to wonder after Horst's mercurial departure. "Mr. Barrow, what are you doing here?" He turned at the sound of Johannes Cabal's voice.

"I was just having a stroll around, Mr. Cabal. Taking in the sights."

Cabal smiled very slightly and gestured at their surroundings. "There are no sights *here*, Mr. Barrow. You're missing all the fun of the fair." He looked around the clearing. "Where's your daughter, Mr. Barrow? The delightful Leonie?" Barrow didn't like the way he said it at all.

"She's at home. She sends her regrets but is unable to attend."

"Unable to attend. You make it sound very formal, Mr. Barrow. But, of course, you used to be a police officer."

"Retired."

"Yes, retired. Some people have a lot of trouble giving up their old jobs, I believe. Keep finding themselves slipping back into old work habits. Take, for example"—he looked around as if he might find an example floating in mid-air; instead, he found it directly in front of him— "you. Do you ever find yourself looking for crime where there is none? Find it difficult to meet people without assuming they have some sort of dreadful conspiracy up their sleeve? Find yourself sneaking around places like a thief in the night?"

"No," replied Barrow honestly. "Not these days." The two men stood perhaps half a dozen yards apart in the shadows of the sideshows, half a dozen yards of grass between them. To Barrow it seemed like the gulf between galaxies. To Barrow it didn't seem nearly far enough. There was something unaccountably different between the man who stood before him now and the man he'd spoken to that morning. That Cabal had seemed flawed and human. This one, however, was behaving like a stage villain. His arch manner and verbal fencing were beginning to irritate Barrow. He had to be careful—it was far too easy to give away too much. Why didn't he just set up a magic-lantern display for Cabal entitled "Everything I Know About You" while he was about it? "Unless it's for a worthy cause."

"How mysterious. And here I was, sure that we'd come to some sort of understanding. And here we are, with you sneaking around away from the thoroughfare without another soul to be seen."

"Poor pickings for you, then," said Barrow, and cursed the words as soon as they were out of his lips.

If he was expecting a witty riposte from Cabal, he was mistaken. Cabal simply ran at him. Halfway across the distance, Barrow heard a noise he hadn't heard since he'd been on the beat in the thieves' kitchens of the city, the distinctive *click* of a switchblade, and knew that Cabal intended to kill him there and then. As Cabal reached him, his arm extended like a lance tipped with three inches of scalpel-sharp steel, Barrow allowed himself to start falling sideways. He grabbed Cabal's knife hand

and forced him to keep running straight over Barrow's shins. Cabal turned a full cartwheel in mid-air before landing on the tips of his toes and sprawling face-down on the turf. Barrow wasn't too concerned about Cabal's martial artistry on this showing, but he could and would surely call on his small army of thugs. Discretion seemed appropriate, and he ran for the bright lights. Perhaps if he could find an off-duty policeman he might stand a chance.

Almost a minute passed.

Johannes Cabal rolled onto his back and slowly drew the knife from his clothes. He'd been very, very lucky. The blade had scraped obtusely across his side, the waistcoat and shirt having tangled and deflected it. He threw the bloodied knife on the grass in disgust, his gloves quickly joining it. He probed at the wound with his fingertips and winced. *Very* lucky. He stanched the cut with his handkerchief and applied pressure while he tried to reorder his thoughts. He looked at the blood on his free hand. What *had* come over him? Violence was loathsome but occasionally necessary; he had no problems with that. But this? He'd been standing there talking like an idiot, Barrow had rather unwisely given away too much (How *had* he learned the truth of the carnival? No matter, there were more important things to attend to), and, the next thing he knew, he'd had his knife in his hand and was bearing down on Barrow like a member of one of these childish street gangs he'd heard tell of. It was so unlike him. Of course, Barrow would have to go, but it could have been done with a little more forethought. Now he was off and running and spreading fear and apprehension, and it was almost as if Cabal was working against himself.

"Oh," he said sharply. "I see."

A few minutes later, Cabal appeared at the popcorn stand and helped himself to the salt tub with bloodied fingers. Outstanding orders for cartons promptly all changed from salted to sweet. "I abjure thee," he snapped furiously, and threw the salt over his left shoulder. The fascinated onlookers could have sworn they heard a yelp from thin air. Cabal straightened up slightly as if a weight had been lifted from him. The pervasive taste of aniseed left his palate. "Right, where's Bones?" he demanded of the popcorn lady before winding his way off through the crowd.

Down in Hell, Ratuth Slabuth watched with polite interest as Mimble Scummyskirts, an imp of notorious and incandescent fury, washed her smarting eyes with warm saline. "That *is* sterile, isn't it?"

" 'Ow the fenk should I know, eh?" replied Mimble with the easy lack of delicacy that would result in rapid promotion up the non-commissioned ranks. "Wot a sod. Jus' doin' me pisking job, and—bof!—I gets a face full of kelching salt. Exorcised, sweet as kiss-me-skenk! The parbo!"*

"Don't give yourself airs," said Ratuth Slabuth. "You're not actually capable of possession, so it wasn't really an exorcism. You could only colour his actions, not control them." And a fine mess you made of that, he thought. "It was more of an eviction."

Mimble left General Slabuth in no doubt that the difference between eviction and exorcism was a petty one, of concern only to armchair generals who never got off their big fat—

At which point Ratuth Slabuth, who was nowhere near as refined as he pretended, squashed Mimble Scummyskirts into an aniseed-flavoured smear with his thumb and went to report to Satan, leaving the smear to think really bad thoughts for the six hundred and sixty-six years it would take to re-form.

---

* The worrying thing was that every one of Mimble's oaths and curses actually meant something, and every one was far, far worse than anything cleared for release into the world of men. "There *are* limits, you know," Satan had said.

Chapter 14

⚔ IN WHICH NEEDS MUST WHEN THE DEVIL DRIVES

Behind the carnival, the freaks gathered. Cabal had returned to the train for a chance to apply a hasty dressing to his wound and a quick change of clothes. He lifted the lid of the blanket box with the toe of his shoe, but Horst wasn't at home. Typical, never around when he was needed. He dropped the lid with a bang and returned his attention to getting his thin black cravat just so. By the time he'd finished, they were waiting for him outside.

Cabal stood on the topmost step and addressed the search parties. "Good evening. We have two serious problems. Firstly, the carnival will cease to exist in a little over an hour's time, and we are *still* one soul short of the target. Secondly, we have a man on the loose who knows far more about our business than is good for us and, therefore, him. This man will cause trouble if he isn't located and dealt with as soon as possible. Mr. Bones?"

"Yo?" The thin man waved from the back of the group.

"Has Barrow managed to get out of the grounds?"

"No way, sah. We had a couple of peeks of him, but, soon as he sees us comin', he's out of there like a bat out of Hell." He frowned. "Never did understand that expression. They don't have bats in Hell."

"Mr. Bones," said Cabal, "a little focus, please?"

Bones focussed. "I got Joey on the main gate. Barrow ain't going anywhere."

"Good. Have you organised search teams?"

"Sure have, two of 'em. Dolby, Holby, and Colby from the Ferris wheel, because they know what he looks like—"

"Hold on. Who's running the wheel in that case?"

"Oh, a couple of Maleficarus' old crew are handlin' that."

Cabal paused. He didn't like leaving any of the former inmates of Brichester Asylum to their own convoluted devices unless absolutely necessary.

At the Ferris wheel, the two men watched it spin endlessly.

"You see?" said one. "It never ends. Wheels within wheels. Infinite angles."

"Yes! Yes! Ouroboros incarnate! Swallowing his own tail!"

"Swallowtail?" said the first. "Where? Where?"

"Excuse me," called a woman from the wheel. "Could you possibly let us off now? We've been going around for about half an hour and it's getting a bit boring."

The lunatics ignored her. "The circle is complete!"

"Card ten, the wheel of fortune!"

"Ten! Very, very significant!"

"Yes! No! Isn't that twenty-three?"

Cabal shrugged inwardly. They'd be all right. "And the other team?"

"Some of the Things from the Ghost Train—we got Dennis and Denzil fillin' in while they gone," Bones added quickly, anticipating Cabal's question.

"**W**hat we have here," said the skeleton driver of the hastily retitled Parapsychological Perplex Experience, "is some sort of demarcation problem. Now, I wouldn't dream of turning up on the footplate of *your* locomotive. You're supposed to be behaving ghostily, in *there*."

He pointed into the shadowed entrance of the ride. Dennis and Denzil, firmly wedged into the tiny train at the head of the ride, followed the gesture, their necks creaking like new shoes. They turned back to the Ghost Train's driver and shook their heads, *squik, squik, squik*. There was the faintest sound of something rolling around inside of Denzil's skull.

"All right," said the driver, "you don't want to do this in a civilised way, we'll do it yours." Denzil and Dennis looked at each other and nodded triumphantly. *Squik, squik, squik.*

"Konga?" called the driver at the top of the structure. The enormous gorilla automaton who sat on top of the ride and threatened passers-by with a papier-mâché boulder—at least, the passers-by *hoped* it was papier-mâché—leaned over the parapet and looked inquisitively at the driver. Upside down, it looked a lot more threatening for some reason. "I'm having a little trouble with these two," finished the driver, waving a thumb at Dennis and Denzil. The giant gorilla slid a contemptuous glare at them, bared its impressive fangs, and made a *basso profundo* growl that shook their teeth in their dry sockets. What was left of Dennis's and Denzil's eyes widened with much cracking of varnish.

"**T**hose are th' two parties, but we also got all these kine people an' stuff who can jus' stroll round the place, nonchalant like."

Cabal looked at them and sighed. Most of them couldn't stroll if they had a handbook on the subject, never mind doing it nonchalantly. He also noticed that his gaze kept sliding over one part of the group. With a deliberate effort he concentrated on the spot and finally noticed a small man who was so nondescript that even "nondescript" was slightly too exciting an adjective to describe him. "Who are you?" he asked. Everybody around the man tapped their chests in surprise, and it took a few moments of "No, not you, beside you, on the other side, no, *your* other side," before the man realised he was the subject of attention. Interestingly, several others continued to look through the man in puzzlement as if he weren't there.

"Oh," said the man in a soft, unaccented voice, "you mean me."

"Yes," said Cabal, working hard to keep his line of sight locked to the man. "Who are you? I don't remember seeing you before."

"My name is Alfred Simpkins, sir. You were kind enough to take me in when my colleagues and I absconded from Laidstone Prison."

"You're one of the *murderers?*"

"Yes, sir."

"One of the serial killers?"

"Yes, sir."

"So . . ." Cabal looked at the pale little man with his hair combed across his bald patch, his little moustache, his little glasses, his cardigan and cheap suit with the patched elbows. "What's your interest in this?"

"You're looking for Detective Inspector Francis Barrow, retired, are you not? I saw him in the Hall of Murderers earlier this evening, snooping, skulking." Some colour almost came into his cheeks. A couple of his neighbours finally spotted him and yelped with surprise.

Interesting, thought Cabal, he's only easily visible when he shows emotion. Otherwise he's too bland to notice. "He caught you, didn't he?"

"Yes, sir. With your permission, I'd like to kill him." He said it in the same way others might say, "I'd like an extra pint and a carton of yoghurt."

"If you find him, you report it to one of the others. I want him alive." Cabal's thoughts were still on the last unsigned contract. "No personal vendettas—I've got a business to run."

"Very good, sir," said Alfred Simpkins in a tone devoid of anything.

Cabal cast his eye over the rest of the group before nodding with some little satisfaction. "Very good. You know who you're looking for. Find him. Dismissed." As they left, he sought out Bones. "Mr. Bones, have you seen my brother recently? In the last hour or so?"

"Afraid not, boss. I see him round, you want me to tell him you asked?"

"Yes, if you would. Thank you."

𝕭arrow hid behind the Waltzer and considered his next move. He'd already made one terrible tactical error by not getting the heck out of the carnival while he had a chance. He'd managed to convince himself that help could be found here, however, and that had been a big mistake. He hadn't seen a single person whom he felt he could trust to behave sensibly, or who wouldn't simply be put in too much risk. When he belatedly realised this, he'd headed for the exit, only to find an enormous character whose head seemed to be constructed from animated stone standing by the gate, watching those going home with a close attention. Barrow didn't believe that he could hope to go up against the stone-headed man armed with anything less than an anti-tank rifle. A cursory examination of the fencing that surrounded the Cabal Bros. Carnival indicated that he wouldn't be getting out that way, either: twelve feet high and topped with razor wire. He'd assumed that the inward bend at the top was a mistake, that they'd put up the fence the wrong way around. After all, putting it up that way would be far better at keeping people in than out. Now he wasn't so sure it was a mistake at all. He was trapped, then. In that case, he had no choice but to stay hidden until daybreak. From what he'd seen on his previous early visit, most of the carnival's denizens weren't very keen on daylight. He'd watched a group of flickering dark things pass across the roofs and hoardings a few minutes earlier. Only the fact that he was out of the bright lights himself had made them visible; the townsfolk below had remained entirely unaware of the lightly tripping mob of nightmare that had passed only a few feet above their heads, shielded by the brilliant bulbs, neons, and fluorescents that made the darkness beyond so much deeper.

Barrow looked back on the unpleasant feeling of foreboding that had been with him much of the day, the feeling that he had glorified with the word "fear," and smiled. No, that had just been the collywobbles. *Now* he was afraid. They were throwing everything into the search, and that meant things that had only ever been catalogued in chained books in cathedrals. Things that were a long way away from the human monsters he'd spent his working life hunting and bringing to justice. Thinking of that helped him; perhaps he could find some strength there by remembering the predators he'd pulled out of the crowd and thrown into gaol? He tried it.

Smith, the insurance man who collected on a few too many policies for comfort. Yes, he could still remember the look on Smith's face when the verdict came in, like a spoilt child who'd been found out. Jones, the doctor who started to play God with his patients' lives and disposed of the ones he disapproved of. That had been difficult—Jones had been "assisting" the enquiry as an expert witness, and it was the alteration of a piece of evidence that had made Barrow look more closely at his involvement. Ye gods, the trouble he'd had convincing his superiors to probe Jones's background more thoroughly. Brown, the hatter with the very private collection of busts he used to model his wares. If there had ever been a man to revel in his own insanity, it had been Brown. He'd actually become a hatter purely because of the association with madness. When he'd been sentenced, he'd asked to see his captor in private. There, as the Black Maria waited to take him away, he'd leaned close to Barrow and, laughing quietly to himself, whispered, "I'm not really mad. Only pretending, only pretending!" He was led away making shushing noises at Barrow— it was to be their private little joke.

And Simpkins, the man who killed because he could. They'd arrested him on fifteen charges, and he'd quietly suggested in the interview room that there were thirty-two missing persons that they might like to add to the tally. Barrow could still remember Simpkins in the dock while the charges were read, never showing a flicker of emotion but seeming polite, if a little bored. "Do you plead guilty or not guilty?"

Simpkins had pushed his glasses back up his nose, smiled slightly to show that he just wanted to help, and said, "Oh, guilty. Obviously."

In his interviews, he would only talk to Barrow, and ignored questions from anybody else even if Barrow was present. "Why is it so important that you speak only to me?" Barrow had asked finally. "It's very inconvenient."

"Because you can see me, Detective Inspector Barrow. Other people start to lose interest after a while. You, delightfully, always see me."

"I don't understand."

"I've gone through life as a piece of marginalia, faintly written in soft pencil. Passed by, overlooked, ignored. It has been of great personal distress to me, I cannot begin to tell you how painful. Since childhood, I was always the last to be chosen—if, indeed, they remembered to choose me at all. Always considered the wallflower, though I stood full-front and cried, 'Me! Me! Me!' Never loved, never despised, never anything to stir the emotions at all. Alfred Simpkins, the invisible man. After a while, it quite began to aggravate me. That's when I started making people take some notice of me."

"You started killing them."

"Yes, I did. Even that was a disappointment. I'd hoped for some sort of great emotion from those whose lives I took. After all, being murdered for no other reason than because a pallid little man—I am under no illusions as to how you perceive me—wants to prove a point, you would think it would make people angry at the very least. It would seem unfair, would it not? But all I ever got was faint expressions of surprise. You know, I don't believe they noticed I had murdered them. I really don't. They just seemed faintly put out, as if it were a bit of bad luck, an act of God. 'Oh, my carotid artery has been severed with an open razor. I knew I should have cut down on greasy foods.' 'Botheration, I'm being belaboured with a fourteenth-century battleaxe. What are the odds, eh?' I was standing there in front of them with a sub-machine gun or backing over them with a rotary cultivator or whatever and shouting, 'I am Alfred Simpkins! I am killing you! Will you please take a little bit of bloody notice, please?' But they never did. So I kept going. Hope springs eternal, after all."

"You knew you'd be caught, surely?"

"Well, one would think so, wouldn't one? Do you know, I've sat in my living room covered head to toe in blood, cradling the murder weapon in my hands—already labelled 'Exhibit 1'—and been interviewed by your colleagues. Had I seen my next-door neighbour recently? Indeed, I had. A little under three hours previously, when I'd bludgeoned her to death with this very knobkerrie, officer. Well, sir, we have other enquiries to make. Good day. They hadn't noticed. Nobody notices me. Except you, Detective Inspector Barrow. You notice me. The first time you saw me, you knew I'd done it. Do you want to know what I would like to do more than anything, Detective Inspector Barrow?"

"No."

"I'd like to kill you." Barrow had looked at Simpkins hard. "No animosity. Simply because you would notice yourself being murdered. That would be my little bit of affirmation of my existence. Then I would never have to kill again."

Barrow had denied Simpkins's request and not been diplomatic about it. Simpkins was sent down to Laidstone for so many life terms that, even with good behaviour, he was unlikely to be out before the next ice age. Simpkins's attitude towards him had changed then; it *had* become personal.

Barrow paused, curious, and wondered why he was thinking about Simpkins just now, of all times. Perhaps it had been that little man he'd seen walk by in the crowd. He'd been the absolute living spit; the resemblance had just started all these thoughts rolling around his head. All of which was very nostalgic in a forensic sort of way, but it wasn't getting him any closer to finding somewhere safe and stopping Cabal. "Stopping Cabal" seemed very simple when it was only two words. The implications were horrifying in their complexity, however. Stop him how? Stop him from doing what? Stop him when? First things first, he thought, and broke cover.

Walking like a man who has every right to be going into the back of a sideshow, he went into the back of a sideshow. I just need a dark corner, he thought, somewhere I can . . . He paused, inhaled through his nose. What was that smell? An odd, synthetic sour odour. He had a rapacious memory, in that once a sensation had been experienced it was held for good, and so he knew he'd smelled something similar before.

Unfortunately, his rapacious memory hung on to the details, too, refusing to pass them on to the cognitive centres, and so he couldn't quite recall where. He twitched a curtain gently to one side and peered through the gap. What he saw rooted him to the spot. He was on the wrong side of the velvet rope that separated the visitors from an exhibit, if that was the right word. Actually, on this occasion, it was definitely the right word. *Most* definitely. Exhibitionism was the whole point here.

On the far side of the rope, Barrow could make out the shadowy forms of the paying customers. They clung to the area of low light—dim, flickering electrical faux candles showing only form but no detail—loath to be seen and identified. This was a place that many wanted to visit but nobody wanted to be caught in. The reason for the guilty interest lay languorous and lithe upon a chaise-longue, regarding the gawking and sweating mass with an insouciance that slid easily beyond human limits. Since his conversations with the brothers Cabal this evening, it was as if the scales had fallen from Barrow's eyes. For example, he knew without hesitation—as surely as Horst had known about Cleopatra earlier the same evening—that, whatever else Layla the Latex Lady was, she wasn't a lady. She wasn't even human.

There was something in the way that she moved, slowly and deliberately and without apparent recourse to such human fripperies as joints, that was reptilian yet still warmly mammalian enough to provoke a low hum of sighs and wetting of lips from her admiring audience—the white noise of desire. Her skin was dark, dark grey, smooth and gently reflective like that of a young seal fresh from the sea, and as she moved it made a gently organic noise, surface whispering over surface. Barrow inhaled again. That was the sour smell, rubber, and the slightly sweeter smell was talcum powder. She must get through pounds of the stuff every day, he thought. The smooth skin ran over every square inch of her body except her neck and head, which rose from the encompassing sheath like the painted portion of a gunmetal statue. As he watched her, he realised, without any particular sense of surprise, that there was no clear interface between the rubber and flesh: one simply seemed to merge into the other. The only details upon her body were the high heels that seemed to grow organically from her feet, as if part of her biology—as, indeed, they were. No other detail was sharply delineated, not even her fingernails.

Barrow was sorry for that. More detail would have allowed him to close down the whole carnival on public-morality grounds. No such luck; Cabal wouldn't make a mistake like that. Still, he found himself wondering what kind of details they might have been. Her body was like something that Vargas might have dreamt on a particularly humid night. He clenched his eyes shut and told himself that there were people out there, and possibly in here, who would cheerfully see him dead, and a little bit of focus would be gratefully received.

Layla watched the audience with amused arrogance. A typical crowd: mainly men, with a few women, some of the latter asking themselves confused questions. She breathed in and tasted their pheromones, borne by the faint breezes that moved sluggishly through the sideshow. Their scent was fainter than usual, the wind was from the north, but she detected something else, and it was delicious. She found the chemical traces in the air and assiduously picked them out with the tip of her darting tongue, to muttered approval from her admirers, then drew them along the roof of her palate as a connoisseur takes time with a fine wine. Fear. Somebody there was in fear of his or her life, and the taste of it was exquisite. She closed her eyes and allowed the flavour to separate into its components: male; middle-aged; occasional pipe smoker; behind her. She knew all about the search tonight, and now knew exactly where Frank Barrow was. She also knew that she had less than an hour's existence left. Really, she should alert Johannes Cabal; that was the right thing to do. On the other hand, she *had* sprung from Satan's very own personal blood, and this meant that the right thing to do wasn't always the thing that was done. Let Cabal rage. She was going to have some fun.

Barrow watched as Layla gestured to the bodyguard who stood to one side and whispered in his ear. "Right, show's over," he was bellowing at the audience even as he straightened up. "Ain'tcha got homes t' go to?" His manner implied that if anybody didn't, then he knew a nice hospital that they could spend the next few weeks in as an alternative. With a collective sigh and many wistful glances, they filed out, followed by the bodyguard.

The main door closed with a final click. Barrow didn't know whether this was a good thing or not. Layla, on the other hand, seemed to know very well. She rolled onto her back and straightened one leg and ankle, admiring the way the light reflected along her thigh, shin, and foot in a single, unbroken bar. She slowly turned her head until she was looking directly at Barrow.

"Hello, Francis," she said.

Barrow decided it was a bad thing after all. He stepped back from the curtain and opened the rear door of his covert entry. Barely a few inches wide, the door was abruptly slammed shut from the other side, and he heard the lock turn. He rattled the door and heard a laugh. Then he heard the bodyguard say, "Have a nice time, Mr. Barrow," and walk away, laughing the whole while.

Barrow was one of those people blessed with a mind that works faster under stress. It was working very rapidly now, looking for some sort of handle on Layla's likely personality, her possible behaviour. In his uniformed days, he'd been involved in a raid on—delightful old-fashioned phrase—a house of ill-repute. The girls—no matter what their age, they were always "girls"—had shown a certain ennui at the raid and sat around on the stairs smoking and chatting amiably with the young and easily embarrassed coppers. Barrow had been struck by their marked lack of obvious sexuality; despite various stages of undress, leather hip boots, and bullwhips, despite the girls in school uniforms, nurse uniforms, and, confusingly, police uniforms, the house still gave the impression of just being a place of work. They rented out their time and their bodies and their theatrical skills, but that was all. He'd got talking to a tall brunette who wore a long peignoir over some article of clothing that creaked threateningly when she moved. She'd asked him for a light, and while they waited for developments in the raid, which seemed to have stalled for some reason, they talked about this and that. Feeling fired by a faint moral indignation, as he was, after all, a policeman and still believed that his job was to act as society's conscience, he asked her why she did what she did. She had seemed nonplussed. "Why do I do this generally? For the money, of course. Why do I do *this* specifically?" At this point, she'd opened the gown, and before he averted his eyes, he caught a glimpse of something Byzantine wrought in leather. "Because I don't have to touch the gentlemen hardly at all. They do it all themselves, on the other side of the room, while I tell them how bad they've been. The hours are good, the money is excellent, and, apart from the sheer tedium of it, it's the best job I've ever had." At that point the chief constable of the district had turned up in his pyjamas with a raincoat thrown over the top and demanded to know why the raid had been planned without him being told. The operation was stepped down in some haste, and they were all sent home. Interestingly, the tall brunette with the creaking lingerie seemed to know the chief constable by his first name, although she also called him "Patricia" at one point.

Barrow somehow doubted that a filter tip and a friendly chat were going to endear Layla to him. He had to get out of here before she found him. He looked along the narrow corridor formed between the heavy curtains and the walls of the temporary building. Hoping that the front door hadn't been as securely locked as the rear, he set off at a dogtrot. He couldn't hear anything from the main body of the building and imagined her stepping directly into his path. What would he do then? He'd never hit a woman—well, just the once, but she'd been bearing down on him with a chainsaw—and, despite his reservations about Layla's status as a human, didn't want to start now. He made the end of the corridor and broke cover without hesitation, reaching the door in a few steps. He tugged at the safety bar. On the other side, a padlock and chain rattled mockingly. He felt a shadow on his back and spun around.

He was alone. There was no sign of Layla. He didn't delude himself; there was no possiblity that she'd gone, she was probably on the other side of the curtains herself, now looking for him. Fine, that gave him a few moments alone in the main part of the room. Overhead, he noticed something in the gloom that might be a painted-out skylight. It wasn't much, but he was running out of ideas as he stepped over the silk rope and looked a little closer. It *was* a skylight, but he doubted he could reach it even if he stood on the chaise-longue. Still, he wasn't doing anything else. He pulled the low couch a couple of feet to one side, until it was directly below the blacked-out skylight, climbed onto it, and reached up. He was nowhere near. He tried jumping, but that didn't seem to get him any nearer at all. He paused; something had bumped against the curtain. He crouched, concertina-ing himself as small as he could get. He made himself aware of the muscles in his legs, imagined them pulling hard to catapult him up, imagined his hands reaching the catch, knocking it open. Then another jump to get his hands on the ledge, pulling himself up, pushing the skylight open with his shoulders as he climbed. He knew it would have been an impressive feat when he was twenty and wished he could be less rational about the danger he was in. He needed the homicidal strength of a man in mortal fear and fury, the strength of ten he'd seen enough times to know that it existed. He looked up, willed the skylight to be nearer, and jumped.

As his body straightened, the chaise-longue rocked treacherously under the impulse. Barrow forgot all about attaining the skylight and started concentrating on staying upright. The clash in priorities resulted in a low jump that knocked the chaise onto its side. He came down, lost his footing, and fell awkwardly. As he hit the floor parallel to the couch, it added insult to injury by rocking back onto its feet with a solid *thump*.

Barrow lay winded for a moment before pulling himself into a sitting position and leaning against the chaise. This wasn't going well. He looked up and realised it wasn't even going *that* well.

"Why, Francis, you've had a little accident. Let me"—she released the curtain and it fell to behind her as she took a step towards him—"kiss it . . ." Another step. Perhaps it was the angle, a skewed perspective, but she seemed to cover more ground with each step than was humanly possible. ". . . Better." She was standing over him. He looked up at her as she brought the full power of her presence to bear upon him, and strange things started to happen in his brain. Parts of the reptilian brain that encompasses the head of the brain stem began to fire in odd patterns. Barrow almost gagged on a rising tide of thick, cloying lust coloured with the sort of pack behaviour that makes "I was only obeying orders" a favoured defence for war criminals the world over. Unreasoning desire and unquestioning obeisance: a winning combination for the more upper-class predator.

L̲ayla had been born perhaps fifty weeks before and would never see her first birthday. It didn't matter; she'd seen more in those brief months than most saw in a lifetime. Horst Cabal had found the parts that made her up pre-packaged in a catering-size coffee tin labelled *Layla* in one of the cars. He had taken the tin to Johannes and shown it to him.

"Have you seen this?" he'd said, emptying the contents onto Cabal's desktop. Cabal had looked at the mess for some moments before asking, "Well? What is it?"

"*Layla the Latex Lady*, I would guess from the label and contents. Remember that board I showed you? She must have been one of the very few members of this carnival that they sorted out before the plug was pulled."

"So—less work for you. Why should I be concerned?"

"Why? Just look at this stuff, Johannes. I'm having second thoughts about animating her." Cabal had looked quizzically at his brother before taking a pencil and sorting through the mess. There was no rag and no bone. There were several rubber items in place of a rag, most recognisable, some less so. Cabal had located a small sheet of latex, perhaps two dozen erasers, a few objects that he was glad hadn't been used previously, and a couple of others that had made him think some designers must have a difficult time explaining in polite company exactly what it is that they design. For hair, there was a long, loose ponytail gathered into a knot at one end. He'd held it up to the light and marvelled at the multitude of different colours. There didn't seem to be an analogue for bone until Horst had pointed out a large tube of silicone gel. "Oh my," Johannes Cabal had said, otherwise lost for words just for once.

Then there had been the clippings. Held together with a treasury tag was a motley collection of old and yellowing advertisements for corsets, high heels, stockings. Farther in had been pages snipped from the lingerie sections of more modern home-shopping catalogues, photographs of public-toilet walls covered in childish drawings and closely written fantasy, mimeographs of anonymous letters, detailed and disturbing. Cabal had coughed and put the items back in the tin. "People like that sort of thing, you said so yourself."

"That's before I saw all this stuff. I have my doubts."

"We don't have time for doubts," Johannes Cabal had said, cast the tin's contents on the floor, and invoked her then and there.

Cabal had discovered early on that Layla was the carnival's star performer in most senses and deployed her frequently to great effect. He didn't like being anywhere near her, though. She appealed to him in a certain way, and Cabal didn't like being influenced at such a base level.

For Layla was the very epitome, the very physical embodiment, of guilty eroticism: the spirit of the peep show, the sly glance up the library stepladder, the thumbed postcards, the denied impulse, the addictively tawdry, the illicitly thrilling. Fortunes had been built upon it in dilution. Concentrated in one form, lines drawn by a thousand million fevered imaginations and topped with a face that was all things to most men and a fair proportion of women, the effect was nothing short of devastating. Men came to her, and afterwards they found that they had been lessened. Less dignity. Less self-respect. The complex roadmap of the average intelligence was reduced to a one-way highway with no off-ramps and no U-turns in her presence. Everything became dangerously simple.

$\mathcal{T}$hings were getting dangerously simple for Barrow right now. He looked raptly up at her. How had he ever thought that her skin was featureless when, wherever his eyes fell, detail bloomed: anatomical, perfect, titillating, and quite mesmerising? The higher centres of Barrow's mind, his Ego and Super-Ego, were aware that all was not well and were hammering on the bridge door of his mind. Unfortunately, the beastly Mr. Id wasn't receiving visitors today, so Barrow just sat there and trembled and sweated and breathed shallowly. "There, there," said Layla, taking control as always.

She slowly knelt astride him and took his head in her hands. He had the faint sensation of her nails dimpling the skin at the back of his skull. How could she have nails? Her hands were coated in latex, weren't they?

Barrow's Super-Ego was standing on his Ego's shoulders and bellowing through the air vent to the bridge, "We are in big trouble unless you do something, you hairy oaf! Fight or flight! Fight or flight!" Id wasn't listening, naturally. He just sat in the captain's chair with an unseemly tent in his jockey shorts and looked foolishly deep into Layla's eyes, perfect pools of enchanting quicksand from which few escaped.

Barrow didn't, couldn't move as her lips parted and she bent forward to kiss him. Even when her mouth deformed elastically but oh so artistically, he just sat there and waited for whatever she had in mind. Even when her lips settled across the bridge of his nose and the base of his chin, encompassing everything in between, he only distantly wondered where you learn tricks like that. They stayed like that for a few moments as he breathed her breath and remembered having a tooth out under gas when he was seven. Her tongue played across his lips and playfully tickled his nostrils.

Then, with a powerful spasm that ran from her throat to her abdomen, she sucked the air out of his lungs. She was tired of fulfilling human fantasies, she just wanted to kill somebody for a change.

Barrow's brain snapped into working order, albeit a little late in the day to do any good. He grabbed her hair and pulled back frantically, beat at her head with his balled fists, tried to break her grip somehow. All in vain; she was strong as sin, *very* literally. As he struggled and fought, she didn't move a muscle, just looked into his eyes with a cool alien satisfaction as she waited for the life to leave him. He could feel himself growing weaker as his lungs tried to drag some little vitality from the thin dregs of air that were left to them. The room was becoming less distinct as tunnel vision constrained his sight closer and closer to a full blackout, unconsciousness, and death. His fists struck feebly and erratically against her. It felt like punching a tyre and the thought made him want to laugh but he couldn't and he wondered if that was to be his last thought and hoped not because he wanted his last thought to be of Leonie and who was going to look after her when he was gone although obviously she was an adult woman and isn't it dark? an adult woman and could and could and could and cadwallader Memphis divot spigot olly olly oxinfree . . .

Barrow's brain regretfully closed down all verbal functions and awaited the moment when it would have to close down everything else.

. . . and you only appreciate fresh air when you've been cooped up indoors in a tyre factory all day although there's a still a faint smell and what are you staring at?

Barrow's vision blurred and cleared. He was still staring at Layla's face and she was still looking at him, but the orientation had changed, and Layla's eyes looked vaguely disappointed somehow. Suddenly he remembered that she was trying to kill him and he ought to get back to fighting her. He punched out at her body, but his hand met no resistance. He tried slapping at her face and, unexpectedly, she let him go, just like that. His faint but appreciative surprise increased by several magnitudes as he watched her head bounce away from him and come to rest some feet away. He cried out and pushed himself away from it until he came up against the chaise-longue. He looked around frantically, trying to re-orientate himself, panting. He was still in the sideshow, still on the floor. Layla's head lay some feet away, grimacing slowly, while to the other side her decapitated body was still on its knees, writhing. Behind it, a nondescript little man with what looked like a breadknife in one hand scrubbed ineffectually at the great quantity of colourless clear slime that had covered much of the front of his jacket.

"Oh dear," said the man conversationally when he noticed Barrow looking at him. "I don't think this is going to come out."

"Hello, Mr. Simpkins," said Barrow hoarsely.

"Hello, ex–Detective Inspector Barrow," said the man, and continued scrubbing at the stain. "You know, you get used to bloodstains, but this is a new one on me." He indicated Layla's disparate parts. "I didn't actually intend to behead the young lady, incidentally, just cut her throat. But there was nothing to her at all. Once the blade had cut the—well, I hesitate to call it skin—it just kept going. Like slicing German sausage. And—*pop!*—off comes her head. Which would have been gratifying in a professional sense, but then all this dreadful goo came spraying out. Geysers of blood I'm used to—you just brace yourself for it as a necessary unpleasantness, like going to the dentist. But this?" He nodded gravely as if communicating a great discovery. "I doubt it's natural."

"What now, Mr. Simpkins?" asked Barrow. Simpkins cocked his head quizzically. "You said you were going to kill me one day. Is that today?"

"Oh, that old thing," said Simpkins dismissively. "I've saved your life today, ex–Detective Inspector Barrow. In some cultures, that means your life belongs to me. Why should I kill you now? Why take what's already mine?"

"A nice thought, Mr. Simpkins, but relevant only if you subscribe to one of those cultural views. I'm not sure you do."

Simpkins laughed, a suppressed sniffing noise. "You're quite right, of course. Always the detective? No, I was still intending to kill you, but, you know, I don't think I shall now." He held out his hand with two fingers extended in a "V"-for-victory salute. "Two reasons. Firstly, having saved your life for admittedly selfish grounds—I was determined that if anybody was going to kill you, it was going to be me—it seems almost churlish to then go ahead and take it. But secondly, and for me far more pressingly, you remembered me. I don't know if you recall, but as soon as you could talk you said, 'Hello, Mr. Simpkins,' which was touchingly polite in this day and age. Very civil. You remembered me, and I have no doubt you will always remember my little part in your rescue here."

"You can rest assured on that count," said Barrow. Rescued from a synthetic succubus by one of the world's most notorious serial killers— no, he wasn't likely to forget *that* in a hurry.

"You're precisely the sort of person—indeed, the only example to date of the sort of person—that I want to preserve. I would as soon kill myself as kill you. I'm not the suicidal sort, by the by."

"You were hiding in the Hall of Murderers, weren't you?"

"Yes, that was me. With the card pinned to my jacket calling me *Albert Simmonds*, among many other inaccuracies."

"So Cabal's sheltering the Laidstone escapees, is he?"

"Oh gosh, yes. We outnumber the waxworks."

"Why?"

"Why, for the price of our souls. I'm an atheist, so it was no great loss to me." He looked at Layla's corpse, which was slowly deflating and puddling into oddly regular forms. "At least, I *was* an atheist. Besides, we were all Hell-bound long before we signed his forms, so it's still six of one and a half-dozen of the other."

"Forms?" asked Barrow. "He had forms?"

"Oh, yes. I read mine before I signed. The others didn't, a mixture of illiteracy and relief to be out in the open, I think. Rather nicely drafted, although peppered with archaic terms. Still legally binding, though. The bearer has all rights to the signatory's soul on the occasion of his or her death. Probably quite standard if you happen to be working for Satan, I would think."

"Look, Mr. Simpkins . . ."

"You even remember to pronounce the 'p'! Bless you, ex–Detective Inspector Barrow!"

"I need to find those forms and destroy them. Will you help me?"

"Me? Oh, I'm sorry, I'm no action man."

"But, and I hope you'll forgive me for bringing this up, you can go unnoticed where I would be spotted."

Simpkins shook his head with clear regret. "Not here, I'm afraid. That's how I first gathered that there was something amiss in this carnival. Lots of the staff notice me, although, if this young lady is anything to go by, they notice me precisely because they're not people at all. In fact, the less like people they appear, the more likely they are to spot me. No, I'm afraid I can't offer any direct help. If you would value my opinion, though, you might do a lot worse than examine the desk of Mr. Johannes Cabal. It's in the office car of the train." He looked at the knife. "I don't suppose I'll be needing this anymore." He dropped it to the floor and watched it clatter into silence. He smiled. "That was easier than giving up smoking. Good evening, ex–Detective Inspector Barrow."

"Good evening, Mr. Simpkins," said Barrow, and watched him leave via the rear door. He gave him two minutes and then followed, stepping over an odd collection of rubber knick-knacks and yellowed magazine clippings, and picking up the discarded breadknife en route. The rear door had been unlocked with the key. Nearby was a bone wrapped in rag and hair and liberally smeared with fat and beefcake. Barrow guessed that Simpkins had caught the sideshow bodyguard unawares. This was an odd place, but he was finally beginning to understand its rules. He checked his watch. Twenty past eleven. He set off for the train.

Chapter 15

IN WHICH MIDNIGHT STRIKES AND
DAWN BREAKS

Cabal stood at the top of the Helter-Skelter with a pair of opera glasses and directed operations. He was in the way of the late-evening revellers but, characteristically, really couldn't give a tinker's cuss. "Hey, daddio," said a hip young dude, demonstrating that everything old is new again. Cabal slowly lowered the glasses and gave the offending youth a look that would have chilled dry ice. The youth, lacking experience but possessing chutzpah in excess, didn't notice. "You're cramping my style, man. Yo dissin' mah main squeeze."

His main squeeze simpered, curtseyed, and said, "Good evening, sir."

"Let me see if I understand your outlandish mélange of argot, young man," said Cabal, who was fewer than ten years older but who already regarded "young" as a synonym for "stupid." "You're suggesting that by standing at the top of my own Helter-Skelter I am in some way imposing upon your"—he looked at the girl, who simpered some more—"*young* lady."

"Get hip to the jive, mah man," said the youth, jiggling on the spot, crossing and recrossing his arms while making horned hands. Cabal wondered about his sanity. "Ah'm a-saying this, fool, you'd—"

"Hold hard. I think I caught the word 'fool' there. Are you calling me a fool?"

"Sure, yo a fool, fool! Yo a— Oh, I say! Yaroo! Get off, you oik!"

For Cabal had grasped him firmly by the scruff of the neck and thrown him head-first down the chute.

"I trust you can make your own way down?" he said to the girl as he put the glasses back to his eyes.

"Oh, rather. Sorry about Rupert. He's a bit of a nitwit, but *frightfully* good-looking Well, ta-ta." She smiled sweetly and swept down the chute and out of sight.

"Ta-ta, lady," said Mr. Bones, who had just arrived at the top of the stairs. "Mr. Bones reportin' in, general. There ain't a sign of the guy. He's so gone"—Bones paused while a suitable simile came to mind—"that he's comin' back. Kind of." Cabal looked at him oddly. Bones tried again. "What I'm sayin' is, we can't find the man. He's vanished, boss."

"The perimeter is secure?"

"Oh, yeah. Ain't a blue-eyed weasel gonna get out of this place we don't know about. Can't figure it, myself."

A good-natured clattering up the steps presaged the appearance of Bobbins. He seemed upset in a bright way. "Sir! Oh, sir! Look!" He held out a brown paper bag.

Cabal looked into it and then slowly reached in to remove an eraser dripping with goo. He dipped in again to find an old advertisement for ladies' arch supports, also soaked in the stuff. "Layla?"

"Somebody killed her, sir! Who would do such a thing?"

Cabal thought Bobbins was far too nice to be an expression of Satanic influence. "What about her bodyguard?"

"Dead, too! *And* one of the chaps from Laidstone is missing."

Barrow's work, it had to be. Now that he knew he wasn't fighting humans, he clearly didn't feel morally bound to take prisoners. The gloves were really off now. Cabal bit a knuckle and thought hard. It was half past eleven now; he had half an hour left in which to neutralise Barrow and locate one last soul. Time was too pressing to juggle both without Horst's help—*where was Horst, anyway?*—so Barrow would just have to be the lucky donor. Cabal concentrated; if he were Barrow, where would he be heading for? He can't get out of the carnival, he knows and violently disapproves of its function, nowhere is safe, so he's gone on the offensive. What would he target?

"*Scheiße!* The contracts! Barrow's going to destroy the contracts!"

Bones nodded thoughtfully. "That's bad."

"We have to get to the train before he does! Come on!" He made a move towards the steps, decided urgency outweighed dignity, and jumped onto the chute.

*T*he train was unguarded and unoccupied behind the main body of the carnival grounds, although still within the fences that ran across the track fore and aft. After the trouble with Billy Butler, Cabal had become quite paranoid about the train's security. Barrow spent a couple of minutes locating a crowbar from one of the flatcars and made his way to the office. It was locked with a heavy chain and padlock, but the wood beneath the staples gave way first. Barrow was glad of the never-ending din that floated down from the rides and shows: it hid the shrieking as the pins tore out. After looking around to check the coast was still clear, he heaved himself up into the cabin. He pulled the door to behind him and looked around.

In the gloom he could just about make out the desk and a large blanket box, the kind of thing his uncle had always told him contained bodies. He doubted even Cabal kept corpses in his office, though, and turned his attention to the desk. All the drawers were unlocked, and none contained anything of interest. The top drawer on the right-hand side, however, refused to budge. He didn't have time for subtlety; he'd just have to jemmy it open. At least, he would if he had the faintest idea what he'd done with the crowbar. He had the blasted thing a second ago; where might he have—?

The lights came on suddenly, leaving him blinking and shielding his eyes.

Johannes Cabal, who'd taken a moment to put on his blue glass spectacles before turning the light switch, was not at the same disadvantage. "If I were in a better mood, I might make some small joke about asking if you have a search warrant," Cabal said. "As I'm not, we shall get straight onto the business of what I am to do with you."

Barrow blinked the tears from his smarting eyes. Behind Cabal were three huge riggers like the ones from the Ferris wheel and a very thin man. The only other way out of the car was through the windows, and he didn't think they'd stand still while he did that. Even if they did, it was a long way down to the tracks.

Cabal picked up Barrow's crowbar from where he belatedly remembered putting it on an overstuffed armchair. "Very subtle," he commented with light sarcasm. "I would have expected you to have acquired some lock-picking skills from a friendly thief or similar."

"Most thieves couldn't pick a lock to save their lives. If they had enough application to learn a skill like that, then they'd have enough to get a job that would certainly pay more than crime. 'Criminal genius' is an oxymoron. The vast majority of criminals get in by smashing their way in. That's why it's called 'breaking and entering,' " said Barrow, and hoped Cabal wouldn't know playing for time when he saw it.

"Really? How disappointing. Another shattered illusion. Still, that's of little concern at the moment. The thing we should be applying ourselves to is the question of your immediate future."

"What about it?"

"Whether you have one. Would you like to live, Mr. Barrow?"

"We all have to die sometime."

Cabal smiled, although there were elements of sneer about it. "So I'm told. Let me rephrase my question. Would you like to live past midnight, Mr. Barrow?"

"Why? What happens at midnight?"

"Well, if I don't have your signature on a form, I'll have your brains all over that wall as a consolation."

Barrow added this to some of the other facts that had come up during the last thirty hours. It all came together beautifully. "You have a time limit, don't you? Midnight. And you need me to sign because you have a quota to fulfil. Now it all makes some sort of sense," he said.

The smile slid off Cabal's face like a wet fish off an umbrella. "How did you know that? Who's been talking?"

"Nobody told me, per se. I worked it out." Barrow took a leisurely look at his watch. "Less than fifteen minutes left. Sorry, Mr. Cabal, no time-and-motion awards for you. I won't sign."

Cabal took a threatening step forward. "I don't think you understand the gravity of your situation."

"I think I understand it entirely. If I sign, you get some sort of great reward and I spend the rest of my days on this Earth awaiting damnation. Not really a life at all, is it? If I don't sign, you kill me, I go to whatever awaits me, and you take whatever punishment you have coming. I hope it's something very unpleasant, Mr. Cabal, because I really have no intention of helping you. So you'd better get on with it."

Cabal hefted the crowbar. "I've killed before—"

"Good for you," interrupted Barrow. "I hope you enjoy bashing my brains out with that, because, when midnight comes, mine will be the last life you will take. I have to weigh my life against making sure that you lose yours. I think it's worth it. Go ahead, Cabal. Kill me."

Cabal looked at him, appalled. "This is ridiculous. You're behaving as if I'm just some sort of common murderer."

"There's nothing common about you."

"Thank you," snapped Cabal. "I'm serious. I deal in death in the same way a doctor deals in disease and injury. I don't want to spread it, I want to defeat it."

"Necromancer."

"Yes! Yes, I'm a necromancer, technically a necromancer. But I'm not one of those foolish people who take up residence in cemeteries so that they can raise an army of the dead. Have you ever *seen* an army of the dead? They're more expensive than a living one, and far less use. A shambles; they march ten miles and their legs fall off. Napoleon would have approved—that really *is* an army that marches on its stomach. Until it falls out.

"That's not what I'm interested in. I want to deny death. I want to . . . well, for want of a better word, cure it. Is that such a bad thing? Can you look me in the eye and tell me that there was never a moment in your life when, given the power, you wouldn't have brought somebody back from the dead? Not as some sort of ghoul or monster but just as they were? Warm? Living? Breathing? Laughing?" Barrow realised with a shock that Cabal was pleading with him. "Can you tell me that there was never a moment when you would have given anything to have woken up and for them still to be there?"

Barrow thought of a cold October day fifteen years before and said, "We have to accept it."

"No!" roared Cabal in a sudden fury that made Barrow step back. "No, we don't! No, I don't!" He reached into his jacket and produced a piece of paper, some sort of contract. He shook it at Barrow. "Sign this! Sign it, damn you! I am so close to success, so close." He calmed himself to a hoarse whisper, which was more threatening by half. "I need your signature, Barrow. You're standing in the way of science. You don't want to go down in history as a Luddite, do you?"

"What went wrong with you, Cabal? What twisted you up like this? Can't you see that what you're doing is wrong?" He sighed. "No, of course you can't. I admit I've made one mistake about you, Cabal. Up until this moment, I thought you were at the very least a bad, bad man. Perhaps even evil. I was wrong about that."

"Then you'll sign?" asked Cabal, not understanding Barrow's gist, hoping it meant acquiescence.

"You're not bad, you're just mad." Cabal's look of hope turned hard. "When we spoke today, I had the oddest feeling that we had something in common. I think that, somewhere inside you, there's a decent man trying to get out. I even think that all this"—his gesture took in the office, the carnival, the contract in Cabal's hand—"is the result of you just trying to do the right thing the wrong way. If I'm right, then I'm not unsympathetic, but I can't let this go on. No, I won't sign your dirty little contract. Do as you will, but you'll have no co-operation from me."

"Fine," said Cabal, and struck him a glancing blow with the crow-bar. He watched without emotion as Barrow folded and fell at his feet. He sighed and started to accept what he'd known ever since the sun went down and things had gone from bad to worse. That, at the last, he'd failed.

"What do you want us to do with 'im, guv?" asked Holby, pointing at Barrow.

"I don't know," said Cabal. "Does it matter? Just throw him in the fur-nace or something."

He went to the door and climbed down, deep in thought. Perhaps he could collar the first person who passed him, check their ticket number, discover that they'd won the end-of-season big, big prize draw, and award them the entire year's takings. Of course, there was a bit of paperwork they'd have to fill in first. It wasn't a bad scheme, now that he thought of it: desperate but practical, like so much of the rest of his life.

He'd hardly set foot on the ground when somebody was saying, "Excuse me? I wonder if you could help?"

"Certainly, but first may I check your ticket?" he started as he dusted himself off and turned. "You may already have won the end-of-season, big, big . . ." The words died in his throat.

"Have you seen my father?" said Leonie Barrow.

"I'm sure I, uh, I think I saw him back at the carnival. Somewhere. He's round and about." Cabal gently took her arm and started to steer her away from the train. Dolby's bellow made them both turn.

" 'Ere, guvnor." He pointed at Barrow's limp form dangling between Holby and Colby. "I fink 'e's too big to get in the furnace in one piece. Can we chop 'im up a bit first?"

"Oh!" said Leonie Barrow.

"Ah," said Johannes Cabal.

*T*hey sat at Cabal's desk, Cabal behind it, Barrow—wet from the dous-ing he'd taken to bring him around, a thin line of blood running from his head wound and mixing with the water—opposite, and Leonie at Cabal's right. On the desk lay the contract and a pen. Cabal watched but did not interfere as Leonie's hand found her father's.

"Are you all right?" she whispered, as if Cabal and Mr. Bones, who stood behind the little group, wouldn't be able to hear. "What did he do to you?"

"It's only a scratch," said Barrow, gesturing at but being careful not to touch the wound. "I was expecting far worse."

"You're not out of the woods yet, Mr. Barrow," said Cabal, hating the way it made him sound like a music-hall villain. He checked his watch. Less than five minutes. He shot a sideways glance at the hourglass on the shelf. The top globe seemed to be empty, but grains still fell and sparkled. It was now or never, all or nothing. "I still have a contract that needs signing, and I'm under some time pressure here, so if we could cut along, I'd be very grateful."

"What are you doing here?" said Barrow to Leonie, ignoring him entirely.

"Well, what was I supposed to think when you left the ticket in my room? I thought you'd had second thoughts."

"I burnt that ticket. There was absolutely no way that I wanted you here. I'd do anything if you weren't."

"Ah," said Cabal butting in, "I can help you there. Safe passage home for the pair of you." He tapped the parchment. "Just sign."

Barrow looked tiredly at him. "Go to Hell, Cabal."

"That," replied Cabal, with a very tight rein on his temper, "is rather what I'm trying to avoid. But if I go, rest assured that you're going to your just rewards, too."

"And my daughter? What about her?"

Cabal looked at Leonie. She'd been well named: her mane of hair was as yellow and rich as a lioness's, and her face, although pinched with tiredness and worry, showed a certain determination and will that he found affecting. The precious, irreplaceable seconds drew out. Two minutes left. Abruptly, Cabal reached down beside his chair, opened the gladstone bag that lay there, and drew his handgun.

"I'm afraid the time for subtlety has long since gone, Mr. Barrow."

He levelled the revolver at Barrow. "Sign or die." Leonie gasped. Cabal ignored her.

Barrow actually yawned. "We've been though this once already, and my answer hasn't changed. No."

"Very well." Cabal hadn't expected him to crumble suddenly, but it had been worth the attempt. He swung his arm until the gun was bearing on Leonie. "Sign or she dies."

"Dad!" said Leonie, and slapped her hand over her mouth. She frowned at uttering the traitorous word. Cabal realised that she didn't want to upset her father any more than he already was. She was letting him play this game out. Even at this pass, she was still thinking of him. A remarkable woman. Why did he always meet them in such unfortunate circumstances?

"You won't," said Barrow.

"What is this? A dare? Ye gods, man, it's your daughter's life!"

"I know that. I also know you, Cabal. I saw how you reacted when you first saw her in town. It took me a little while to understand what was going on in that mausoleum you call a mind, but I finally got it, distasteful as it seems."

"I don't have time for amateur-psychology demonstrations, Barrow. I'm going to start counting—"

"It was love at first sight."

Despite everything, Cabal actually laughed an honest laugh of disbelief. "Love? *Love*? You are so very, very wrong, Barrow. I'm sure Leonie's a lovely person. In other circumstances, perhaps we could have been friends, and I really would be loath to blow most of her head off, I'm sure. But"—he deliberately thumbed the hammer back—"I'll do it without hesitation."

"You won't do it," Barrow said with finality, crossed his arms, and leaned back in his seat. The tableau was held for a long moment: Barrow certain and determined; Cabal looking at Barrow, and his gun hand levelled unwaveringly at Leonie; Leonie trying not to look frightened, watching Cabal's trigger finger, and noticing it was barely touching the trigger itself.

Suddenly the carnival fell totally silent; the calliope stopped in mid-phrase, the barkers stopped barking. Cabal blinked, raised the gun to a ready position, and checked his watch. "What's this, Bones?" he demanded. "There's still a minute left."

Bones stuck his thumbs in his waistcoat. "That's right, boss. Still a minute for you to get that there contract signed, but as for this here carnival, we're packin' up."

"What?" Cabal rose to his feet. "How dare you? This is my carnival, and I say—"

"You say way, way too much with all them big words of yours. And it ain't your carnival, and it's never *been* your carnival. You just borrowed it for a while, and the loan term's up, *boss*. This last minute, it's ours. And it starts"—he struck a dramatic listening pose by the window; the calliope churned back into life, and Cabal recognised the tune within the first few notes as a deranged, discordant version of "The Minute Waltz"—"now!" Bones danced around like a ferret and clapped his hands. "Time for some *real* fun round here." He stopped by Cabal. "Hey, did I ever mention what a pig's-ass job you did of makin' me in the first place?"

"Frequently."

"I means to say, look at this." Bones's face sloughed off the front of his skull, revealing bare bone and muscle. It hit the floor with a noise like an accident with a rice pudding. Cabal just glared at him. Barrow had attended enough autopsies to have seen worse. Leonie looked away. She had the feeling that the next minute was going to be the worst of her life, one way or another. "That's just shoddy, now, ain't it?" He laughed a high shrieking laugh, rolled the door open, and leapt down to the ground.

The open door let in a tide of sound, including a lot of screams and shouts. "What the Hell is going on?" Cabal said, and stepped forward to the doorway.

Hell was exactly what was going on.

The carnival was falling apart and re-forming into new, horrible shapes before his eyes. He was forcibly reminded of Bosch's *The Garden of Earthly Delights*. It didn't seem like a place to bring the family. The Things from the Ghost Train were flying low and fast between the blossoming flowers of destruction that used to be sideshows, harassing pan-icking townsfolk into headlong stampedes. The giant gorilla had left the Ghost Train, ascended the Helter-Skelter—now a looming tower of spikes and blades—and stood triumphantly atop it, swatting at what used to be the four jockeys from the Day at the Races concession but who now looked like personifications of Death, War, Pestilence, and Hunger, although they still wore their bright racing silks. The gorilla was holding in its spare hand some hapless individual that was fighting feebly to get away. At the base of the tower, Denzil waved up at Dennis, who paused in his struggles to wave back. He didn't feel cut out to play Fay Wray at all.

"Stop that!" bellowed Cabal. Nobody stopped at all. "Joey? Joey! Pull your *verdammt* trousers up this instant! You're frightening people!"

"That's rather the plan, actually, old bean. Sorry and all that," called back Joey, the most well-mannered and polite expression of diabolical will one is ever likely to meet.

Cabal looked around. "Bones, stop them! I'm still in control here!"

"For the next thirty seconds," shouted Bones from a hundred yards away. He became sober. "I'll see what I can do, boss." He turned to the pulsing boil of chaos that used to be a carnival. "Stop that," he said in an effete voice, wagging his finger. He exploded laughing, staggering around with delight at his own wit. Then his head just exploded.

Cabal drew back the hammer on his smoking gun. "I will *not* be mocked," he said to nobody in particular. He turned back to face Barrow. "Sit down," he said to Barrow, who had started to rise. Cabal looked around the office. The panelling was starting to rot, the polish vanishing from the desktop, a smell of damp and abandonment returning to this place, just as he'd found it. He walked back to the Barrows and placed the gun barrel against the side of Leonie's head. "Fifteen seconds. Sign now."

"No," said Barrow, inevitably.

"Then it's all over," Cabal said tonelessly, and aimed at Frank Barrow's head.

Without drama but in swift, certain movements, Leonie snatched the contract and pen from where they lay and signed. She thrust the paper at Cabal. "Leave my father alone," she said simply.

"No!" cried both men, making Leonie jump.

Cabal glared at Barrow. "Now look what you've done with your idiotic intransigence!"

Barrow wasn't so aghast at Leonie's act that he couldn't be taken aback still further. "What *I've* done?"

Distantly, the clock of Saint Olave's struck twelve.

The flow of dust in the hourglass abruptly ran out, settled in the lower bulb, and lay still.

"Time's up!" said Bones's body, appearing at the door carrying a boater full of skull fragments. The voice came directly from the wet stump of his neck and sounded a little muffled. "All aboard the Damnation Express!" He swung out of sight again, and through the open door Cabal could see that the carnival field was empty but for a few people running aimlessly about.

Cabal turned to Barrow and his daughter to speak, but then paused. Barrow was crying freely, Leonie holding him and telling him it was all right. Cabal looked at the contract in his hand and opened his mouth, but suddenly the train heaved forward and he was thrown onto his back. Leonie looked around fearfully. It was odd; the train seemed to be pulling away, but they—she and her father— seemed to be staying still. The walls of the car were becoming translucent, as if they belonged somewhere else or were made of mist. Even Cabal, rolling heels over head in slowed motion, didn't seem very solid anymore.

The train slid away from beneath the Barrows, and they were dumped gently onto the tracks. Except there were no tracks, no sleepers, and no sign that there had been for years. The train, a phantom monster in glowing greens and blues, howled past the station and left it a ruin from an old, old fire, the stationmaster saluting sadly as he was whisked back out of the land of the living and dumped into the place reserved for and deserved by suicides. At least, that was the thinking when the rules were drawn up.

Screaming and ranting, the engine shot away into the night and towards a black horizon. Leonie even had the impression, just before it vanished from sight, that it had lifted from the ground altogether and was travelling into the midnight sky like a great luminous eel from the ocean depths.

"Why did you do it?" asked her father, deep in misery.

"He was going to kill you, Dad. I had to take a risk." She looked at the empty sky. "A calculated risk."

Cabal felt a faint tickling on his lip. He moved his hand to swat it away but had trouble co-ordinating his hand. He tried once, twice, and was just at the point where he decided that it wasn't that unpleasant a sensation, and it was too much bother to deal with it anyway, when somebody else swatted it away for him. Actually, somebody else slapped him hard.

"Uuurgh!" said Johannes Cabal, rolling away from the blow. He climbed onto all fours, his head hurting abominably, feeling disorientated and nauseous.

Horst watched without comment as his brother vomited miserably on the office floor. When he was sure Cabal was just about empty, he reached down, grasped him by the lapels, and threw him across the room. Before he had time to recover, Horst had picked him up again and pinned him against the wall.

"You didn't listen to a word I said, did you?"

Cabal tried to pull himself together. Beside his brother's coldly furious face, he could make out that they were still in the office. It must have carried on rotting while he'd been unconscious—mild concussion, that would explain why he felt so dreadful—for it was now no more than the car full of rubbish it had been when he first found it. The only change was a poster on the wall, decaying and curling already: "The Cabal Bros. Present Their World Famous Carnival of Wonders!" A woodlouse unsuccessfully tried to negotiate it and fell to the floor—Cabal realised what the tickling on his lip had been. Through the windows he could see gnarled trees and a suspicion of low, rolling land. They were back in the Flatlands. The carnival was back in mothballs.

"You took another innocent soul, didn't you?"

"I didn't take anything—"

"Don't lie to me! I was right there in that bloody box, listening to you!"

"Then you know that I didn't take anything!" barked Cabal, wrestling himself free. He glared at Horst as he tried to straighten his jacket. "She gave it to me."

"Gave it to you," said Horst contemptuously.

"Gave it to me! Don't come the moral guardian with me! If you were right there, why didn't you do something?"

"I was ready, believe me. If I'd heard that distinct click your finger makes when squeezing a trigger, it wouldn't have got as far as making the second click it makes when it's finished."

"You didn't stop me shooting Bones."

"You were leaning out of the door and obviously pointing in the wrong direction." He smiled grimly. "You shot Bones, did you? Can't say I'm sorry. I never trusted him. I never trusted any of them. They finally betrayed you, then?"

"Like you were expecting it."

"Damn right I was. Just like you were. You're not stupid, Johannes. Inhuman and morally bankrupt perhaps, but not stupid. Chose their moment, didn't they?"

"Oh, yes, they did that right enough." Cabal brushed some of the debris from the desk corner and sat there. His favoured leather chair seemed to be home to a nest of mice. "Look, I'm not proud of what I've done, but it's done. I've been manipulated from pillar to post, committed acts I'd prefer to forget about, but that's all done with. I'm not pretending that the ends justify the means, but the fact remains, I've won the wager. I get my soul back, and I can get on with my research."

"Whoopee," said Horst.

Cabal stifled his annoyance. Horst *had* put up with a lot. "Now, I'm sorry about last night, the things I said. In my defence, I can honestly say I wasn't quite myself. I'm not insensitive to all the work and effort you put into the carnival, and, well, it would have been a failure without you."

"Rub my nose in it, why don't you?"

"*The point is*," said Cabal, talking through him, "the point is, you kept your side of our deal, so I'll keep my side. I've had a few ideas about how your condition can be treated. If you'll come back to the house with me, I promise you that I won't rest until I've found a cure." There was a long pause. "I've said my piece," finished Cabal.

Horst looked at him for a long moment. "No. No, it won't do. I'm afraid I'll have to turn down your kind offer for several reasons. Firstly . . ." He started to walk to the window but kicked something. He picked up the crowbar, touched the tip, sniffed it. "That's blood. Is this what you hit Frank Barrow with?"

"It is," said Cabal, irritated by the distraction. "He used it to try to get into the locked drawer, to get the contracts. I was expecting something more artistic from him." He stopped, thought. "Just a moment." He walked to the desk and inspected the drawer. There was a scratch on the lockplate, which had previously confirmed to his satisfaction that Barrow *had* tried to force it. He cursed himself for addled thinking.

"Firstly," carried on Horst, regardless, "I really have no interest in being stuck in the same house as you for the years your experiments would inevitably take. Secondly, we both know that your interest would slide back to your main researches and probably leave me high and dry. Thirdly, you're a despicable human being who should have died at birth."

"Sticks and stones," said Cabal, otherwise paying no attention. "The crowbar was on the chair over there. How, then, did Barrow even manage to attempt to jemmy this drawer when the tool was nowhere near to hand?"

"Fourthly, I am never going to be able to live with myself for helping you, not if I live to be a thousand, which, given my condition, is a real possibility."

Cabal was still ignoring him. "And, further, why attack the lock when surely a crowbar would be used against the catch?" He examined the scratch. "This is too fine to have been caused by that bar. This lock's been picked."

"Fifthly, lastly, and I think most tellingly, I'm not going to accept your offer because you've lost your bet."

Cabal looked up at him with dawning horror as Horst reached into his waistcoat pocket and produced a couple of shining lockpicks. He held them up for inspection as, with the other hand, he took a familiar-looking piece of parchment from an inside pocket. He shook it open and turned its face towards Cabal.

It was one of the contracts. It was unsigned.

Cabal felt his legs starting to go and sat heavily on the floor. "Oh, Horst," he said. "Oh, what have you done?"

"I've killed you, brother. Just like you killed me. I would like to think there's some small degree of nobility in *my* actions, though."

Cabal couldn't tear his eyes from the paper. "When did you do it?"

"I picked your desk drawer and stole this about ten months ago."

"Ten months? You've had that for ten months?"

"It took me until then to notice that you never counted the contracts, only ticked them off in that silly book of yours, and a tick is easy enough to forge. You had faith the contracts themselves would stay where you put them. Reasonable faith, as it turned out when I tried to get at them: that lock was incredibly difficult to pick. It took perhaps ten attempts."

"It pays to invest in quality," said Cabal faintly. "Why? Why did you take it?"

"When this all started out, all the people who you got to sign were obviously going to the Bad Place no matter what. I had no problem with that. But sometimes you'd be almost at the point of pulling the cap off your pen for some poor schmo whose only sin was being a bit stupid or gullible. Yes, I know those are cardinal sins as far as you're concerned. Not for me, though. I'd have to jump in and distract you with some more suitable prospect. That's when I decided I needed a bargaining counter."

"So you stole the contract."

"So I stole the contract."

"But how was that supposed to modify my behaviour if I didn't know you had it? What use is a threat if you don't make it?"

"There we have the difference between us. It was never intended as a threat. If we'd arrived here and I'd been convinced that you were doing this the right way, I'd have got this thing signed for you myself. Even somewhere like Penlow, there were still some likely prospects. When you took the soul of that woman in the arcade—"

"Nea Winshaw," said Cabal quietly.

"At least you remember her name. Yes, Nea Winshaw; that was it. I gave up hope. I knew you were beyond redemption."

"Well, I am now," said Cabal with no rancour. "I'm going to have this mortal coil violently stripped from me on Satan's own orders and spend the rest of eternity in boiling sulphur or being impaled by tridents or something equally tedious. Thank you, Horst, ever so."

"I'm sorry, Johannes."

"You should be."

"No, I'm not sorry for what I did. I'm sorry for everything that brought us to here and now, everything that meant I had no choice. I am truly, deeply sorry. If it's any comfort, I still believed you could be saved almost up to the last moment."

"Saved? From what? The only thing I really needed saving from turns out to be my own brother. Redemption? You keep saying that as if it's something I needed. Shouldn't you produce a tambourine from somewhere and start dancing around when you talk like that?"

He rested his crossed arms on his drawn-up knees and rested his forehead on the forearms. His whole life was a waste. His researches hadn't added a pennyweight's value to human knowledge. He was no closer to reaching his goal. Soon he would be dead, and everything that he had done would be forgotten or a cheap joke. If he had applied himself to something useless, like money, he would be a rich man now. Ironically, he *was* a rich man: running a lucrative business that doesn't pay wages can do that. Unfortunately, he was going to be dead long before he'd even get a chance to do something worthwhile with the wealth. "I should never have gone back to the Druin crypt. I should just have put an advertisement in the entertainment press. 'Required: deputy manager for travelling carnival. Talent and greed essential. Moralists need not apply.' "

Horst looked down on Cabal, started to open his mouth to speak, but changed his mind. He had the air of somebody who finally realises that he's been wasting his time. Instead, he walked to the window and looked out at the eastern horizon, tearing up the useless contract as he stood. "The sky's getting light. It's almost dawn. I haven't seen the sun in nine years." He opened the door and climbed down.

Johannes Cabal sat alone with his self-pity and self-loathing for a long minute. Finally, he looked up with an expression of awful realisation. "Dawn?" he said in a horrible whisper. He threw himself to his feet, staggered slightly as the circulation returned to his legs, recovered, and ran to the open door.

Outside, Horst had walked some fifty feet and was taking off his jacket, neatly folding it and putting it on the ground. Cabal paused on the step and shouted desperately, "For pity's sake, Horst! Come in! Come in! Don't do this!"

Across the Flatlands, light from the new dawn swept rapidly towards them. Horst watched it approach with unconcerned equanimity and a gentle smile. Cabal didn't. He jumped down, landing heavily, and started to run towards his brother, pulling his own coat off as he ran, swinging it around to act as a shield against the brightness. "Please, Horst! I'm begging you, don't! You can get back to cover if you run!"

Horst looked at the brightening horizon and felt his skin starting to heat with an odd prickling that was neither pleasant nor unbearable. He could hear his brother, and the naked fear in his voice touched him unexpectedly. He couldn't look at him; he had to stay resolved. He'd lived, one way or another, longer than some, and that was something to be thankful for. Now it was undoubtedly time to go. His eyes didn't waver from the distance.

"Sorry, Johannes. I'm going wherever I should have gone nine years ago."

His last and strongest impulse for self-preservation came and went, and now it was too late. Even he couldn't reach shade in time. He wondered if this was all his fault somehow, whether the sun was going to hurt, hoped that he'd done the right things, knew that these were his last thoughts and that they meant nothing. "Goodbye, brother," he said, and then he thought nothing at all, as then the sun caught them both, momentarily blinding Cabal as it spilt over some distant mountain range. He blinked and cursed and tried to find Horst with his outstretched hands, but there was nobody there anymore. He whirled and clutched, but he knew it was already far too late. When finally he could see, there was nothing *to* see. Just some brown leaves fluttering, and a grey dust flying, and the faint scent of lost chances. Cabal spun around, looking to the far horizons, but he was alone, just as he was always alone.

$\mathcal{T}$he new day found Johannes Cabal the necromancer sitting by a ruined and rotting train on a long-abandoned spur line, his head in his hands, the gravel between his feet splashed wet with drops of saline, his sunglasses tossed carelessly to one side when he couldn't see anymore.

Chapter 16

IN WHICH A SCIENTIST RETURNS TO HELL
AND A DEAL IS BROKEN

"Mad Dan" Clancy carefully considered his next answer. As an outlaw of the Old West, he had never really considered what awaited him after death; he had been far too busy rooting and tooting at the time. Coming off second best in a gunfight, however, he had been flung into the abyss, and confronted with eternity, Limbo, and a fistful of printed foolscap sheets in rapid succession. Of the three, the last terrified him most.

The question (Form UNCH/14/K, Section 45, No. 215) was headed with a warning: "This Form Will Be Invalidated by Any Metachronism Whatsoever." Clancy didn't have the faintest idea in—or just outside—Hell what a metachronism might be, and that frightened him. He'd had seventy-six earlier stabs at filling in UNCH/14/K rejected, but was never told why. Trubshaw, hated Trubshaw, loathed Trubshaw, had said, "We ain't got the hands to mark every one up with all the mistakes. This ain't a schoolhouse, boy! If'n you want to get through this here door, you'd better just get a mite more careful, y'hear?" Then he would cackle and slam the little window in the door shut. Clancy made an almost physical effort to shut Trubshaw out of his mind and concentrated on the question. Halfway through answering it, he distractedly put an extra stroke on an "F"—"All responses must be made in BLOCK CAPITALS except where otherwise noted"—and turned "FOUR FEATHER FALLS" into "FOUR FEATHER EALLS." He stopped and stared at the mistake, trying to erase the errant stroke with sheer willpower. No good. He tried artfully re-forming letters to make it look a little closer to the correct answer but just ended up with "BALLS." It was hopeless. There was nothing for it but to queue for three months *again* to get a requisition form to get a new copy of *this* form.

A shadow fell across him, and before he had a chance to turn, something fell onto the parched ground between his crossed legs. He reached down, and what he found amazed and astonished him. It was the holy of holies, the thing he'd wished for almost as long as he'd been in that godforsaken place. An eraser.

"It's a little greasy, but that should rub off," said the shadow. It had a faint German accent. "Enjoy."

Johannes Cabal approached the Gates of Hell for the second time in his life. Nothing much had changed here except the introduction of a melamine notice over the porter's door reading *Queue Here*. Cabal headed straight for it.

At the door, the procession of transient pre-damnees was in temporary hiatus thanks to a pitched argument that had broken out between Hawley Harvey Crippen and Kunigunde Mackamotzki, aka Belle Elmore, aka Cora Crippen.

"Why am I here?" she wailed theatrically. "*He's* the one who murdered me! *And* cut me up!"

"Cora, please listen," said Crippen for what was clearly not the first time. "I didn't murder you. It was manslaughter. An accident."

"You *accidentally* cut me up and buried me under the cellar floor? In quicklime? That's some accident, you little worm!"

"Damage limitation, ma'am," said a U.S. soldier in the line behind them, better known for his skill with a document shredder than with a rifle.

"But I'm the *victim!*" she screamed. "What am I doing here? Why am I here? Why, why, why?"

Arthur Trubshaw looked up from the Rolodex he was consulting. "Adultery. Multiple counts," he said in a bored voice. He flicked onto the next card. And the one after that. "Lots and lots and *lots* of counts."

Everybody looked at Cora Crippen. She wilted slightly under the attention. "Well," she said quietly, "I was lonely."

"Fascinating," said a new voice. The sight of the fully clothed Cabal parted the head of the queue from the door like a razor shaving a hair. "Hello, Trubshaw. I'm back. Kindly open the door."

Trubshaw squinted at him for a moment. Then a horrid grin settled upon his face. "Oh, so it's you again, is it, Mr. 'Let me in, I ain't got no appointment' Cabal? Well, sure, you can come in." He cackled again, ducked out of sight, and then reappeared with a hefty form that he thrust out of the little window at Cabal. "Soon as ye've done the paperwork!"

Cabal didn't bother taking the wad of sheets but just cocked his head to read the top leaf. " 'Form VSKW/1, Special Circumstances Living Person Admittance Docket Application.' " Cabal straightened up and looked at Trubshaw. "You're not serious, are you?"

"Damn right I'm serious! I wrote this 'n up jus' for you. Gotta admit, it's kinda tricky. You might find yerself havin' to do it a few times afore ye get it right! Say two, three hundred? Heh-heh-heh-heh-he-urrrk!"

It is received wisdom that you can't put a square peg in a round socket. As is common with received wisdom, this isn't entirely true. It is quite possible to put a square peg in a round socket if you are very stupid, are very wilful, or just don't like the square peg very much.

Cabal reached through the window with both hands, grabbed Trubshaw by the ears, and pulled. Shrieking woefully, Trubshaw was dragged through the window until there was enough head showing for Cabal to put him in a neck lock and bring his weight to bear. Trubshaw was not a large man, but his shoulders still wouldn't fit through the window frame at all, until one broke with a crack that made the onlookers wince. Cabal dragged him all the way through and dumped him on the baking ground.

"You sonovabitch!" Trubshaw sobbed. "You goddamn sonovabitch! You jus' wait 'ntil I tells His Worshipfulness what ye've been a-doin' an—"

Cabal wasn't about to listen. He dragged Trubshaw to his feet and snapped fiercely in his face, "I really, *really* don't care. As for you, you've got other things to concern yourself with. Arthur Trubshaw . . ." He whirled Trubshaw to face out onto the plains of Limbo. As far as the eye could see, there were people. People with forms and pencils that they were throwing to the ground as they rose to their feet, a great expanding wave of outraged humanity face-to-face with its tormentor. "Meet your public," finished Cabal, planting his foot in the small of Trubshaw's back and shoving him into the great sea of people, which closed over him in a second.

Cabal had little time for lynch mobs as a rule, but at least if one had ever caught up with him, unconsciousness or death would have made the experience a brief one. No such mercies were available to Trubshaw. As Cabal reached through the little window in the Gates of Hell and undid the porter's door bolt, he smiled. If he was going to have a lousy day, he didn't see why a few other deserving cases couldn't share the fun.

When General Ratuth Slabuth, general of the Infernal Hordes, received word of an invasion of Hell and some sort of riot on the plains of Limbo, he checked his pocket diary against what had happened a year ago, tutted, and said that he'd deal with it. He caught up with Cabal on the Fourth Circle.

"Hello, Cabal," he said, manifesting as discreetly as possible. "Back again, I see."

"You worked that out all by yourself? I can see why you became a general, Slabuth."

"Sarcasm ill behoves you," replied Slabuth archly as he made a mental note to look up "behove" later.

Cabal gave him a look that made him wish he'd looked it up beforehand. "I'm not interested in your ideas for my personal development. I'm here to see Satan, as you well know. Now, step aside"—he looked at

Slabuth's distinct lack of legs—"or do whatever it is that you do to get aside. I have an appointment."

"Very well. But first, purely as a matter of interest, did you get all the souls? All one hundred?"

"Hardly your business."

"So you didn't."

Cabal looked at him evenly, then reached into his ubiquitous gladstone bag and produced the box of contracts. "Every contract in here is signed," he said, carefully sticking to the truth, the partial truth, and some stuff as well as the truth before replacing the box.

"Oh," said Slabuth, the crest of his Grecian helmet falling, "I was sure you were going to fail. Rats."

"Your concern is noted. That Billy Butler stunt was a nuisance, I admit."

"All's fair in love and war, though. No hard feelings, eh?" said Slabuth banteringly, and obviously not caring one way or the other what Cabal's feelings were on the matter.

"I wasn't aware that we were at war, and I'm *sure* there's no love lost. Still, that's very decent of you."

"Is it?" said Slabuth, dismayed.

"Oh, yes. No hard feelings." They looked at each other for a long moment. Finally, Cabal said, "I'll be on my way."

General Ratuth Slabuth watched Johannes Cabal disappear around the corner of the tunnel and stroked his bone chin with one claw thoughtfully. He hadn't got to where he was today without being able at least to detect double-talk, even if he couldn't always read it. Something smelled very fishy here. In fact, something *did* smell very fishy here. He turned to look around and knocked over something that clattered and rolled. He reached down and picked up an almost empty glass jar with a brush running through the lid. A glue jar. What was this doing here?

A mob of imps came barrelling around the corner from the Third Circle, screeching to a halt when they saw him. There was the usual tugging of forelocks, even though none of them had anything faintly similar to locks sticking out of their leathery foreheads, but Slabuth noticed some muffled giggles and an air of mild insubordination about the whole scene. He tapped the peak of his helmet and guardedly said, "Carry on, imps."

They bundled past him in a mad rush to get somewhere quickly. As they disappeared around the corner, he distinctly heard one of them call back, "See you later, Ragtag!" to a sudden explosion of laughter. Ratuth Slabuth glared after them, his ivory brow beetling with suspicion. Whirling about, he flew up towards the Third Circle.

Some minutes later, Cabal barely prevented himself from stepping in some hideous slimy leavings, no doubt the spoor of some bone-chilling, nameless creature of the abyss, like the thingy or the whatnot. For a moment, though, there was an almost psychic flash of recognition, a flash that smelled distinctly of aniseed. Nor was Cabal the only one to feel it as the filthy patch itself shuddered and, unexpectedly, formed an eye that glared at him. It looked a little sore. "Ah," said Cabal, crouching by it, "you must be all that's left of the hapless imp that was sent to suborn me into making a mess of things up top. They obviously have difficulty accepting failure here. As it happens," he said, straightening up, "I was in a hurry when we parted. I think I let you off far too easily." So saying, he stamped on the eye, which made a liquid *pop*. "Good day," he said as he left.

Mimble Scummyskirts lay all-of-a-puddle and thought extra-bad thoughts.

Satan was listening to the prayers of his worshippers on the material plain of Earth and finding it slow going. Voices floated from a glowing point in the sulphurous air while one of the Satanic secretaries fluttered about on leathern wings and made exhaustive notes in shorthand. "O Lord Satan, grant me mine most devoutly desired boons . . . ," ". . . an' I want a car an' I want lotsa chicks an' I want . . . ," ". . . just the Philosopher's Stone, I mean, that's not much to ask . . . ," ". . . to allow me to better do thy bidding . . . ," ". . . all dead! All dead! They'll learn not to laugh at me!"

"Anything at all interesting today, Betty?"

The secretary floated down to his shoulder and checked her notepad. "Not really. Oh, there's somebody beseeching you for aid in their hour of need, et cetera, et cetera, how could you forsake him after he did your bidding, blah, blah, blah, yakkety-smakkety."

Satan scratched the back of his neck. "And did he do my bidding, as a matter of interest?"

"No. He played a record backwards and thought he heard you talking to him."

"Heavy metal?"

" 'Spanish Eyes.' "

Satan nodded thoughtfully. "Now, if it had been 'The Girl from Ipanema,' he might have had a case. This hour of need of his, what is it exactly?"

"Sacrificed a maiden aunt to your greater glory. Now he's going to be executed."

"And so he ought. What do I want a maiden aunt for? I wish people would think these things through."

"No action, then?"

"No action. When he turns up, I want him told that he's been very silly, and stick him in with the faithless priests. That'll take the wind out of his sails."

Betty made a note and checked the list of appointments. "Oh, you're due to meet with a Mr. Johannes Cabal."

"Ah, yes. I've been looking forward to this. When does he arrive?"

"Now," said a familiar voice near his feet. Satan cocked an eyebrow at Betty, who shrugged. He leaned forward to look past his knees. Johannes Cabal stood by the lake of fire, polishing his dark glasses.

"On time, as always," Satan said, and smiled unconvincingly.

Cabal said nothing until he'd finished removing the last streaks from the lenses, checked them by the infernal light, and put them back on. "I suffered interference in the commission of my part of the wager," he said soberly. "Thus, the wager is null and void."

"And it's lovely to see you, too," replied Satan, stifling a stagy yawn.

"As to the wager, it is no such thing. There was nothing in the rules that said I couldn't make things more interesting if I saw fit. I saw fit."

"Don't be fatuous," replied Cabal. "There were no rules per se in the first place."

"Then you have nothing to complain about."

"Fine. Then I claim the period of one year to be a Plutonian year."

"I beg your pardon?"

"A Plutonian year. That's two hundred and forty-nine terrestrial years. Approximately." He crossed his arms. "You don't have a monopoly on facetious interpretations."

"Am I to understand that you're looking for a time extension?" A splendidly smug and supercilious smile slid onto Satan's face. "That you failed to get the hundred souls? I must admit that I'm a little surprised. I was given to understand that you succeeded with fifteen seconds to spare."

"There was a clerical error. I only had ninety-nine."

"Oh, what a shame," said Satan, fluttering his eyelashes. "So I get ninety-nine souls *and* I get to kill you, too? O frabjous day! Callooh! Callay!" he chortled in unctuous joy. "My cup runneth over."

"Your cup does nothing of the sort. It's one or the other." Cabal reached down to open the bag that lay by his feet. He removed the contract box. "Even by the most lax interpretation of the rules, it was a case of either/or. *Either* I get a hundred souls for you, *or* you kill me. There's no mention of any other number. If you want the contents of this box"—he waved it demonstratively—"then we scrap the previous wager and start afresh. Otherwise, their ownership dies with me, and the donors get their souls back."

"But *your* soul would still belong to me, Johannes," said Satan slowly, "and eternity is a long time."

"I respond badly to threats," said Cabal without hesitation, and made to throw the box into the lake of lava.

"Wait!" barked Satan. Cabal paused. "Wait," he repeated in a more even tone. He smiled ingratiatingly, a smile that said, *Let us just skip over this unpleasantness, for we are both reasonable men, at least figuratively.*

His nostrils also flared as he drew in the delicious scent of innocence. Ninety-seven of the souls were worthless, spiritual slag: hopeless cases whose names had never appeared in the celestial ledger more than very lightly pencilled. But those last two, the Winshaw and Barrow women, they were sweet. Nea Winshaw had acted out of character and had required a degree of temptation to sin so grievously. Still, she had willingly damned herself to save her child's life. That was piquant. Now, as for Leonie Barrow, absolutely a good person, and apparently incapable of committing an even slightly naughty act. Well, words failed him (although he could probably have made some grunting noises that put his feelings over adequately). And her soul was all his. At least it would be if he could just get it away from Cabal. Of course, Nea and Leonie would only be his little playmates until Judgement Day, but his mouth watered at the thought of all the fun he could have in the meantime. He suffered from the usual problem of the dissolute epicurean—a jaded palate—and new thrills were rare around here.

Besides, if he played one more hand of cribbage, he'd scream.

The dramatic entrance of General Ratuth Slabuth—he hurtled through the cavern roof and plunged into the lava—shattered Satan's considerations. The molten rock had only a moment to close over his head before it exploded back and Slabuth erupted upwards into a towering column of limbs, angles, and volcanic fury. Lava dripped from his empty eye-sockets, and there was a terrifying scream of primordial rage that battered at the limits of perception. He swept across the surface of the lake and came to a halt standing over Cabal. "You little bastard!" he roared.

Satan settled back in his throne. "You seem distressed, General. Would you like to talk about it?"

Without looking away from Cabal, who seemed only to be concerned by the tiny drops of red-hot rock that rained from Slabuth's body and was otherwise not worried, the furious general growled, "This . . . human has been posting notices in the first three rings of Hell!"

"Oh," said Satan, passingly interested while he thought through the soul situation, "and what did they say?"

"They..." For the first time, Ratuth Slabuth seemed to falter. Indeed, he seemed embarrassed. "They're personal."

Satan looked at Betty, who shot off into the air. Brief moments later, she returned with a small poster. Satan took it and read,

> "BE IT KNOWN IN THESE PRECINCTS OF HELL THAT THE ARCH-DEMON RATUTH SLABUTH, GENERAL OF THE INFERNAL HORDES, WOULD HENCEFORTH LIKE TO BE KNOWN BY HIS PREVIOUSLY PREFERRED NOMENCLATURE, TO WIT RAGTAG SLYBOOTS, DESPOILER OF MILK AND TANGLER OF SHOELACES, INTERFERER OF LIGHT MUSICAL PROGRAMMES UPON THE WIRELESS, AND PROPAGATOR OF UNSOLICITED POST."

Satan frowned. "I was listening to a performance of Paganini—one of my favourites, as it happens—the other day on the Light Programme and there was this dreadful hissing and popping all the way through it. That was your doing, was it?"

"No!" said Slabuth, mortified. "It's a lie! That poster has nothing to do with me! This mortal"—he pointed at Cabal, who tutted infuriatingly at such manners—"made it all up!"

"But you *were* called Ragtag Slyboots, I'm sure?"

"Well, yes, that bit's true, but I left that behind ages ago. Radio hadn't even been invented then! It's all lies!"

"Oh," said Satan, "that's a bit embarrassing. I'm supposed to be the father of lies. Fancy not spotting my own kids. *Tch.*"

Slabuth/Slyboots turned on Cabal. "I'm *really* glad you lost the wager, mortal, because *that* means I get to kill you. Prepare to die!" If he was expecting Cabal to cringe in piteous fear, he was to be disappointed. In fact, if he'd been expecting Cabal to do anything other than shake an admonishing finger and point at Satan, he'd have been disappointed, for that was what Cabal was doing.

"Actually," said Satan in a calm voice that boded bad things, "I think you'll find that the wager was with me, Corporal Slyboots. If anybody has the right to kill him, that right is mine. As it happens, Mr. Cabal and I are renegotiating the terms of that wager. Therefore, I would thank you to return to the barracks and stay out of matters that don't concern you."

"Don't concern me? DON'T CONCERN ME? I'll have you know . . . Hold on. Wait a minute. What was that?" His voice dropped to a disbelieving whisper. *"Corporal Slyboots?"*

"You heard perfectly well, Corporal. I haven't been happy with your performance for some time. In line for gingering up."

"Corporal," echoed Ragtag Slyboots in a ghastly voice.

"I wouldn't look upon this as a demotion if I were you. Although clearly that's what it is. Try to think of it as a challenge. You swept up the ranks in a blink first time around."

"Twelve hundred years," said Slyboots, enunciating each syllable. He slowly took off his helmet, looked at it longingly, placed it at Satan's feet, and slinked slowly away. Satan started laughing long before he was out of sight or earshot.

"You can be terribly small-minded," said Cabal.

Satan wiped a tear from the corner of his eye. *"You* were the one who put up the notices."

"*I* don't have pretensions towards deification."

Satan gave him a wry look. "Do tell. Anyway, to business. You have a commodity that I'd rather like. I'm sure I have a little something that you covet. Shall we deal?"

"There's nothing to bargain about. Will you give me my soul in return for this box? Yes or no?"

"Oh dear," said Satan, "you'll have to do better than that. You forget that, amongst my other creations, I spawned the lawyers. I'm not interested in the box. I want the contents." Satan was delighted to see Cabal's eyes narrow behind his spectacles (looking through smoked glass is a natural ability when one lives in caverns of stinking sulphur fumes). He really had been trying to pull a confidence trick on Satan himself. The past year had obviously changed him. "I'm not one of your rubes, Cabal: don't forget that."

Cabal debated inwardly for a long moment. Satan wondered if he might actually sacrifice himself to save the signatories. Surely he hadn't changed *that* much? "Very well," Cabal said finally, "you get the contents as well. I'll throw in the box for free."

"Deal," Satan said, and laughed thunderously. "Deal!"

Rocks began to fall from the walls. Cabal looked around in sudden fear for his life. Surely Satan couldn't go back on a deal, especially one that he'd made that very minute? Tiers started to thrust out of the walls. Flying things in swarms settled upon them, imps bundled out of small tunnels that opened like geological sphincters in the walls. Several immediately fell in the lava, but that's imps for you.

Satan rose to his feet and stood, massive and malevolent, his head almost lost in the reeking clouds. Behind him, the floor shivered and shattered as his generals, princes, and barons rose behind him: Balberith, Beelzebub, and Carreau; Melmoroth, Shakarl, and Mr. Runcible; Olivier, Leviathan, and Yog-Sothoth, who just happened to be there because he couldn't help it. "Forgive me, Johannes Cabal. Pride drives me, and I want an audience when I really rub your nose in it." He addressed the gathered hordes. "Ladies. Gentlemen. Other things of less certain description. Before us we have a man who attempted to beat me, who attempted to cheat me." Everything booed, hissed, and jeered, stamped hooves, trumpeted. Satan raised his hand for silence, which he got on the moment. "This is a man who was willing to send a hundred of his fellow mortals to never-ending torment"—there were a few ragged cheers—"for the sake of his own immortal soul, for a whiff of spirit that he never valued while he had it but was prepared to whore himself for when it was gone, for *this* . . ." And, like a cheap children's-party conjuror, he produced Cabal's soul.

From the tip of Satan's outstretched index finger, depending from the very tip of his exquisitely manicured fingernails, dangled a sad, dirty white thing, like a bed sheet from a flophouse. It writhed miserably, devoid of intelligence but aware that its true owner was nearby. Cabal had a faintly pleasant feeling, as if he was going home for the first time in years and it would be just like it had always been. He dropped the box onto the floor and stepped back from it. "Very well," he said, "they're yours. Fulfil your part of this." He spoke quietly beneath the renewed shouting and roaring from the deliriously aggressive audience.

But Satan heard him. "Fulfil my part? Let me tell you a joke, Johannes Cabal. I was going to give you your soul back anyway. Kill you? You're far more use to me on Earth than down here."

"I won't work for you. Not anymore," said Cabal evenly, but he coloured slightly all the same.

"You don't have to. Your pathetic schemes do as much damage as a convent-full of possessed nuns. You need your soul to spread chaos in the world of mortals? Fine! Have it!" Satan bared his teeth. *"I wouldn't have anything that tawdry in the house."* So saying, he flung the soul at Cabal.

Cabal never felt it hit him physically, but he suddenly felt he was home, and as he closed his eyes and the derisive screams and jeers grew fainter and fainter, he thought that was where he should really be.

Fortuitously, so did Satan.

He could smell grass and trees, hear birdsong and a nearby river, feel a fresh breeze upon his face that ruffled his hair and took the scent of brimstone from where it lay hidden in his clothes and blew it away and away. He took a long, very deep breath, held it for a long moment, and released it. He opened his eyes. He was on the path in the valley, a stand of trees on the hillside above him, the river running fewer than a hundred paces away to his right. He knew exactly where he was: two miles behind him was the village, a mile ahead was home. He started walking.

It was late afternoon now, and he took the time to enjoy the walk, feeling every stone beneath his shoes, pausing to look up at the clouds, the birds that flew high overhead. He smiled a smile that betokened only a simple pleasure and continued on his way.

He halted abruptly and the smile fell off his face like a badger off a billiard cue. One of the birds was behaving in a very distinctive way: circling around and around something out of sight behind a bend in the path. A black bird that was no blackbird, a great ugly shambles of a creature that went "Kronk!" The day suddenly lost a lot of its appeal.

Cabal rounded the corner to find that the crow was circling over a boulder lying on the hillside near the path. On it sat Denzil and Dennis playing an extemporised version of Rock, Scissors, Paper of Denzil's invention: "Rock, scissors, paper, dynamite, punch Dennis in the face." Judging from the state of Dennis's nose, they'd been playing a while.

Dennis saw Cabal first and turned his ghastly mess of a face towards him. He tried to smile, and the varnish around his mouth cracked and crazed. Denzil took the opportunity to make a cunning winning move in their game and punched Dennis sharply in the side of the head. Dennis made a sound like raffia and fell over sidewise. The crow had come in for a horrible fling of a landing and was hop-skipping hopefully across the grass to Cabal. He looked down at it without fondness.

"Why couldn't you have been something with a bit of style?" he asked it. "A raven. A rook."

"Kronk!"

"A penguin. I really wouldn't have been fussy." He looked at the crow, and the crow looked expectantly at him. "Oh, very well," he said finally, and tapped his shoulder. With the bird ensconced, and in company with the quarrelling dead men, Cabal set off for home with rather less enthusiasm.

Still, even with the unwished-for company, it was still impossible not to feel some small pleasure at seeing his house when finally they approached it. The tall house thrust up out of the hillside as if it had always been there, although its style was only mid-Victorian, the cut stones of its construction somehow appearing soot-stained despite the nearest factory chimney being over thirty miles away. Considering that the nearest neighbour was three miles away, back along the path, it seemed somehow out of place that it should have a garden wall and a front gate. After all, surely the whole hillside was its garden? One might think that, but one would be wrong; there were things in Cabal's garden that he had no desire should get beyond it, which was why every coping stone along the wall top concealed a sigil of warding, magical markings that kept the things inside, inside, and the things without, without.

Cabal paused before the gate. By the post, there were a few bones that certainly hadn't been there a year ago. A couple still had gobbets of fresh meat attached. These he threw down the hillside for the crow, which swept after them making joyous noises, all of which were "Kronk." He shook his head. Circulars, hawkers, and salesmen were welcome here— it was cheaper than having to buy in meat. At least the denizens of the garden would be fed, and he wouldn't have too much trouble with them.

He opened the gate and walked in, followed by Dennis and Denzil. A multitude of tiny chiming voices started whispering from the herbaceous borders. "It's Johannes Cabal! Johannes Cabal! He's back!" Dennis and Denzil, clown faces creaking, looked dubiously at each other. Cabal stopped by the corner of the house and pointed down the path that led around the side. "You two. Nothing personal, but I'm not having a couple of shambling disasters like you shedding pieces all over the Persian rugs. Down there you'll find a hut. That's your new home." As he watched them shuffle slowly out of sight, he ruminated that—not for the first time—he'd have something rather nasty in the woodshed.

The crow clattered down onto the wall and looked at the herbaceous borders with a lively interest. It was in the market for some small snacks, and the whispering things seemed likely contenders. "I wouldn't, if I were you," warned Cabal, as he searched through his key ring. "My garden is a remand home for criminally insane fairies. Where do you think those bones by the gate came from?" The crow looked at him, cocked its head, and demonstrated the intelligence that had its species on vermin lists the world over. It flapped its wings and landed on the small portico over the front door, safely out of the way of fairy darts and slingshots. Discretion wasn't the greater part of valour for crows. It was the only part.

The front door swung open almost soundlessly beneath Cabal's hand. It was dark inside; every curtain was drawn, every shutter closed. On the mat by his feet there was some post, which wasn't unexpected; he'd had a long talk with the garden folk about acceptable visitors and enforced it with flashcards and cold iron. What was surprising was a circular for patios that had somehow got through. Turning it over, Cabal found scribbled frantically on the back, "They've got me cornered for gods sakes get help." He crumpled it up and threw it in the wastepaper basket. What use did he have for a patio?

He dropped his gladstone bag on the hall table and breathed in the air. Musty and a little damp, but not as bad as he'd feared. He would set about airing the place tomorrow, but right now he was expecting a visitor, and it wouldn't do to be unprepared. Where to begin? A fire would be pleasant and serve to start drying the place out. The living-room grate was clean if slightly dusty, just as he'd left it a little over a year ago. In the scuttle he found sufficient coal and some kindling. It all felt cold and a little damp, and Cabal doubted that it would catch without some help. Taking some paper that he had handy, he padded it around the wood and built the coal on top of it, lit a match—a Lucifer, to be exact—and set fire to the paper. He sat cross-legged on the rug and watched the flame drive the moisture from the wood, watched the kindling began to char and, finally, to burn. Some gentle blowing to provide encouragement for the nascent fire, and finally he could lean back, satisfied. He would really have liked to toast some crumpets or pikelets, but there was nothing perishable in the larder; he would have to renew his order at the grocer. He took out his notebook and opened it, touching the tip of the thin pencil with his tongue. Perhaps some tea, then. It would be stale but still drinkable. He started making notes.

Abruptly it became a lot colder in the room, and he realised tea was going to have to wait. His visitor had arrived a little earlier than anticipated. Out of the deep shadows in the corner stepped the Little Old Man. "Ahem," he said, using slightly more phlegm and hacking than was considered polite even amongst camels.

"I was wondering when you'd be making an appearance," said Cabal, without looking up from the notebook in which he was making a list of things to do.

"His Worshipfulness isn't best pleased," said the Little Old Man gravely. "In fact, he's in a regular ranting bate."

"Good. If I can give him so much as a tiny fraction of the pain and disappointment that this year has given me, I shall be a happy man."

"He's saying that you cheated him."

"I did nothing of the sort. Tell him that if he continues to dissemi-nate such slander, then he shall be in receipt of a sharp letter from my so-licitor."

"But he *owns* all the solicitors."

"Then perhaps he should look up 'petard' in a dictionary and take his medicine. Our dealings are at an end, and I did *not* cheat him."

"The deal was the ninety-nine souls you'd managed to get. You've short-changed him. He's not best pleased, I can tell you. You've made an enemy there."

"Surely that's his job."

"You know what I mean. I mean a *special* enemy. Look, Johannes, my boy, you and me, we go right back, maybe we can work something out?"

"The only thing I'd like to 'work out' of you is your liver with a cold chisel."

The Little Old Man took an angry step forward, his pretence at bon-homie vanishing like a snowflake on a griddle. His face worked violently, as if he were having some seizure; then he roared a roar not heard around those parts since the late Mesozoic and started to swell. Growing larger in the flickering firelight, he took a step towards Cabal, who finally deigned to look up at him.

"Ah," said Cabal, "so there you are. Finally taking some notice, are you?" For the Little Old Man was certainly looking rather more Satanic.

The thing that was now not nearly as little or manlike as it had been a moment before clacked its claws on the floor and snarled, "Where are the contracts for the Winshaw and Barrow women? They were part of the deal!"

"No," said Cabal. He got slowly to his feet and looked the thing in the face. "The deal was for the contracts in the box. You've got them."

"Those aren't the ones I wanted! They're garbage!"

"My, don't you sound petulant? I know you were going to get those souls anyway in the course of time, but it's still no reason to be ungrate-ful. I may have removed a couple from the box before I arrived, that's true. But the deal was for the ones left inside it. No less, no more."

"Nea Winshaw! Leonie Barrow! They're the ones I want! Give them to me!" Over the fireplace was a deep shelf upon which sat a wooden box perhaps a foot along each edge. The box had no obvious lid. It giggled unexpectedly. The Little Old Man looked at it sharply. "What was that?"

"Nothing. Somebody once told me that manners maketh the man. Lucky for you, you're not really. A man, that is. Come along, there's no reason for all this animosity. Draw up a chair." He raised an eyebrow and added pointedly, "Enjoy the fire."

"Enjoy the fire? Have you any idea how much fire I've already got? I can't imagine why . . ." The Big Old Thing paused and looked at the fire. "You didn't?"

"I've been away a year. The kindling was a little damp. Fortunately, I had some wastepaper that started the fire splendidly. Actually, it wasn't paper so much as parch—"

"You . . . ! You . . . !" The thing that wasn't quite the Little Old Man seemed stuck for imprecations. "You didn't?"

"I did," said Cabal. "And I had every right to do so. You only had yourself to blame; you should have had Trubshaw oversee the exchange. His pathetic little penny-ante, nit-picking, anal-retentive mind would have insisted on every contract being counted out. Speaking of whom, how *is* dear Arthur?"

"We can't find him," seethed the Thing. "The damned out on the plain won't hand him over! Your doing again!"

"Oh, yes," said Cabal, matter-of-factly. "My doing again."

"You haven't heard the last of this!" the Thing roared, and vanished, leaving a stinking fog of sulphur fumes.

Cabal wafted at the smoke with his hand. "I rather think I have," he said to himself. He put his hands on his hips and looked around the room, turning on the spot. "Now, what was I doing?" He consulted his notebook. "Ah, yes. Tea."

*T*he day died slowly, and the night came to the valley. Cabal didn't notice; he had drawn up many observations and plans over the last year and would soon start the great task of cataloguing them properly in his exten-sive coded records. The preliminary work took him several hours, two pots of tea, and a tin of luncheon meat that he ate from the can. The As-sam tasted like boiled wood shavings; he would certainly have to go to the village and lay in new supplies the next day. He also drafted a couple of let-ters to addresses in Penlow on Thurse, explaining that their contribu-tions, although appreciated, had proved surplus to requirements. Finally, as the evening wore on, he saw that he had written the same line twice and realised that his attention was wandering. It was time to rest.

He snuffed the candles out, poked the glowing coals a little, placed the fireguard carefully, and left the room. Out into the hallway and back towards the kitchen. He stopped by the door under the stairs, opened it, took down the oil lantern, and lit it. Then he descended into the cool air of the cellar.

In the corner was the generator, and this received his immediate at-tention; he'd been quite happy to work by candlelight earlier, but now he needed electricity. He tapped the fuel gauge, found it satisfactory, and turned over the motor. After a couple of dry attempts, it caught, and the maintenance lights on the wall started to gently glow.

He looked around. The cellar looked innocent enough: a few shelves with empty paint cans upon them, some old tools, bundles of ancient newspaper, a couple of mousetraps here and there. Cabal had made a study of cellars to make sure that his looked utterly average. He had done a good job. He stepped into the small, empty fruit cellar, ran his hand over the nitrous stonework, and worked a hidden catch. Placing both hands against the wall at shoulder height, he pushed hard, and it swung in and away. He fumbled in the darkness for a moment before finding a switch.

Beyond lay a large room, some forty feet along an edge and ten feet high. Along the walls were workbenches, shelves lined with specimens hanging in formaldehyde, instruments, and bookshelves loaded with dark tomes stolen from restricted collections. In the centre of the floor, beneath a surgical light, was an operating table that doubled as a post-mortem slab. Cabal looked around for a moment as the last of the bluish fluorescent lights finished flickering into life. Everything was as it should be, everything in its place, that which he had left dead was still dead. That always simplified things.

He shrugged his jacket off, slung it onto the table, braced himself, and shoved the heavy piece of surgical engineering out of position. Moving the light to one side revealed the end of a block-and-tackle run that extended over to the far wall. He shifted the block from its storage place until it was over the slabbed floor exposed by the table. The slabs were massive—some four feet wide by eight long—but the one that usually lay directly beneath the table was special in two respects. First, it was only faced pumice, and so nowhere near as heavy as its neighbours. Second, there was a recessed ring in its exact centre. Cabal drew the hook down from the block and tackle and latched it onto the ring. He took the rope and pulled. He often thought he should replace this manual system with an electrical one, but he had put it off so often he had finally realised that he liked to use his own strength here. It was important to him that lifting the stone was an act of personal effort.

The gear clicked and ratcheted as he slowly raised the great slab. When it was safely clear of the floor, he gently pulled it away to one side on the rail, careful not to let it build up any difficult momentum. Once he had it clear, he walked back and stood, with his hands on his hips, over what lay revealed. The pit exposed was topped by a great pane of thick glass, and Cabal looked at the dark, reflective surface for a long moment. He thought of the last year and all that had happened to him and been done by him. He thought of all the towns and all the people, the tears and the misery. He thought of the carnival now rotting on the lost spur line, and all the undeniable evil it had wrought. He thought of Nea Winshaw in the interview room, and Leonie Barrow's defiance right to the last. He thought of his brother, Horst. Then he looked at the glass and said to himself, "It was all worthwhile."

He knelt by the pit and felt for a concealed switch beneath the lip. In a moment, bright neon tubes were flickering into life a yard below—beneath the great glass tank a yard square by two long that lay there.

Cabal looked down at the young woman lying suspended in its heart like a beautiful insect in amber, her hair—as rich and as yellow as a lioness's—floating in a halo about her head. He touched the glass with his fingertips. This was all he had. All he had ever had since a day ten years ago. His glance darted around to ensure that seals were secure and none of the strange, perfect preservative had leaked. This was as close as he could get for now; he dare not break the seals and open the glass coffin until he was sure of success. Now, at least and at last, he could finally hope.

He lay down on the floor with his face on the cool glass and felt comforted. His eyes flickered and closed. He spoke a word, a name, quietly, his breath clouding the glass. Then Johannes Cabal slept.

⚗ ACKNOWLEDGMENTS

Ray Bradbury, for being a personal hero, and inspiration for this novel. It was *Something Wicked This Way Comes* that put in my mind the question "Where would an evil carnival come from, anyway?"

Marsha A. Davis, for encouragement, advice, and breaking the news about my punctuation as gently as possible.

Michael Davis, for putting up with Marsha saying, "Jonathan says . . ." on a regular basis.

Jane E. Eddlestone, for research, enthusiasm, and "enigmatic sauciness."

Katharine Long, for her valued friendship and remarkable patience.

Linda "Snugbat" Smith, for her splendid illustrations.

Emma L.B.K. Smith, for her photographic prowess.

The Mediæval Bæbes for *Salva Nos*. I normally disapprove of authors who give sound track listings for their work, but I am always prepared to make an exception for myself. This album was played throughout the writing of the book and had, I am sure, an effect on my imagination. Whether you consider this an advertisement or a dire warning is entirely up to you.

And

Louise and Madeleine, for reasons too numerous to mention.